HOPE

CATWALK SERIES - BOOK TWO

S.Q. ORPIN

Published by Wild Hibiscus Press

PO Box 1761 Lafayette CA 94549

Cover created by Fresh Design

Hope is dedicated to my sisters, Judy and Deborah.
Thank you for your friendship, love, and support.

THE CATWALK SERIES

The Catwalk series was inspired by the exciting but perilous world of modeling in Los Angeles. Dream was motivated by an accident that redefined the life of the author's model-niece, Sterling. Wanting to give a voice to additional characters and in response to a 'What next?' storyline, Catwalk expanded to a five-part series. The stories encompass a deep examination of characters struggling to find meaning in life and love.

The books are written from multiple viewpoints allowing the reader to explore the diverse characters, while delving into the deep, and sometimes dark, human existence and tumultuous relationships. The series contains adult situations and language, including sex, trauma, and violence.

Dream introduces the cast of characters and the relationship developing between Casi and Kyle. It layers the superficial world of modeling with the lifestyle of a small-town man, creating challenges and pitfalls. **Hope** continues as reality and conflict consume the couple and supporting character storylines develop. **Trust** explores the emotional rollercoaster of love, career, loss, and coming to terms with the past. **Seek** reveals secrets and back story, helping the characters move forward as emotional scars are healed. **Love** is the final book in the series, which spans five years, achieving triumph and finding meaning in life and love. The series primarily focuses on the main characters of Casi and Kyle, but supporting characters are intricately woven throughout the five books.

CAST OF CHARACTERS

Casi (Roberts): A former swimsuit model in LA. Born in Burnaby, Canada, and now living in Blackberry Falls, WA, with her husband, Kyle.

Kyle Jensen: A master woodworker with his own business in Washington State. Married to Casi.

Jake: Kyle's older brother and business partner.

Gail: Jake's ex-wife and mother of his two children.

Olivia: Jake's daughter.

Reid: Jake's son.

Mary Ann: Gail's best friend. Briefly dated Kyle.

Lia: Lauren's older sister. Dating Jake.

Lauren: Lia's sister. Dated Kyle for three years. A chef in Seattle.

Fran: The mother of Lia and Lauren.

Anna: A lumber rep in Seattle. Briefly dated Kyle.

Georgia Jensen: Kyle's and Jake's adoptive mother.

Peter Jensen: Married to Georgia, and the adoptive father of Kyle and Jake.

Tara: Biological mother of Kyle and Jake. After their musician father, Tommy, died, she turned to drugs and lives on the streets. The brothers were put in foster care when they were one and four years old.

Jack Roberts: Casi's father. He owns a restaurant and brewery in Bellingham, WA. Divorced from Casi's mother, Sonya. Married to Ava.

Ava: Jack's wife and Casi's stepmother.

Sonya: Casi's troubled mother.

Mary: Casi's mentor and Ava's close friend.

Alix: Casi's ex-boyfriend. Celebrity, graphic artist.

Dylan: Casi's best friend from LA. Also, her hairdresser.

Earl: Peter's best friend and former partner in a plumbing business.

Grady: Kyle's best friend from high school who was killed in a boating accident.

Brian: The Jensen brother's accountant.

Amber: Kyle's high school girlfriend.

Nicole: Kyle's high school girlfriend, after Amber.

Amy: The receptionist at the wood shop. Dating Riley.

Riley: The apprentice at the wood shop.

Ray Dawson: Casi's former doorman in LA. He is an avid cook.

Dawn: Casi's best friend from high school. Married to Joey.

Joey: Casi's high school boyfriend.

Dingo: Kyle's German short-haired dog.

Jezebel: Casi's calico cat.

CAST OF CHARACTERS

Casi (Roberts): A former swimsuit model in LA. Born in Burnaby, Canada, and now living in Blackberry Falls, WA, with her husband, Kyle.

Kyle Jensen: A master woodworker with his own business in Washington State. Married to Casi.

Jake: Kyle's older brother and business partner.

Gail: Jake's ex-wife and mother of his two children.

Olivia: Jake's daughter.

Reid: Jake's son.

Mary Ann: Gail's best friend. Briefly dated Kyle.

Lia: Lauren's older sister. Dating Jake.

Lauren: Lia's sister. Dated Kyle for three years. A chef in Seattle.

Fran: The mother of Lia and Lauren.

Anna: A lumber rep in Seattle. Briefly dated Kyle.

Georgia Jensen: Kyle's and Jake's adoptive mother.

Peter Jensen: Married to Georgia, and the adoptive father of Kyle and Jake.

Tara: Biological mother of Kyle and Jake. After their musician father, Tommy, died, she turned to drugs and lives on the streets. The brothers were put in foster care when they were one and four years old.

Jack Roberts: Casi's father. He owns a restaurant and brewery in Bellingham, WA. Divorced from Casi's mother, Sonya. Married to Ava.

Ava: Jack's wife and Casi's stepmother.

Sonya: Casi's troubled mother.

Mary: Casi's mentor and Ava's close friend.

Alix: Casi's ex-boyfriend. Celebrity, graphic artist.

Dylan: Casi's best friend from LA. Also, her hairdresser.

Earl: Peter's best friend and former partner in a plumbing business.

Grady: Kyle's best friend from high school who was killed in a boating accident.

Brian: The Jensen brother's accountant.

Amber: Kyle's high school girlfriend.

Nicole: Kyle's high school girlfriend, after Amber.

Amy: The receptionist at the wood shop. Dating Riley.

Riley: The apprentice at the wood shop.

Ray Dawson: Casi's former doorman in LA. He is an avid cook.

Dawn: Casi's best friend from high school. Married to Joey.

Joey: Casi's high school boyfriend.

Dingo: Kyle's German short-haired dog.

Jezebel: Casi's calico cat.

Dare to Dream, Hope, Trust, Seek, and most of all, Love.

PROLOGUE - DREAM

Cassidy Roberts had stars in her eyes when she was scouted for modeling at seventeen, on the beach in Burnaby, Canada. She moved to Los Angeles with her mother, Sonya, and changed her name to Casi. She distanced herself from her father, Jack, and stepmother, Ava, determined to reinvent her image and leave her old life behind. Sonya micromanaged Casi's career and immersed herself in the chaos of Hollywood life until Mary stepped in as Casi's mentor and redirected her to a better path. Her career blossomed in the world of lingerie and swimsuit modeling, accenting her curvaceous figure.

A dozen years later, as an experienced and in-demand model, Casi lived with her celebrity artist boyfriend of four years, Alix Grey. She created a life of excess, parties, and glamour, but was unfulfilled and petrified about turning thirty. When she met Kyle Jensen, a craftsman from Blackberry Falls, WA, she became instantly smitten. After she broke her pelvis in a car accident, her career was jeopardized and Casi spiraled down, becoming lost and confused about which direction to take. She bought a loft in Hollywood, and focused on her career, capitalizing on her success, while also finishing her business degree. She followed her heart and pursued a relationship with Kyle, ignoring the issues involved with moving to a small town, and dealing with Kyle's untrusting brother, Jake.

An opportunity to be part owner in a surfing line, Sand and Surf, with ex-boyfriend Alix, promised to be lucrative and provide extra income. Casi naively accepted the deal, assuming everything would fall in place. Passionately in love, Kyle and Casi married in Hawaii, determined to prove everyone wrong and live a happy life, with their cat Jezebel and dog Dingo, in their house on the lake in Blackberry Falls.

1

———

WILLING PARTNERS

*J*ake watched his brother, Kyle, and new wife, Casi, walk back to their room, holding hands, and radiating love. When he returned to his own room, he slid in bed beside his girlfriend, Lia, and pulled her toward him, hoping she was in the mood. She pushed him back and rolled away, pulling the blankets tighter. He got up and dressed, glancing back at her softly sleeping form. He quietly extracted a condom from his suitcase and decided to return to the beach party, unable to stay in bed resenting the woman beside him. He walked along the beach and noticed several people huddled together on a log. He glanced over and recognized Casi's mother, Sonya, praying she hadn't seen him.

Her tinny cackle penetrated the night air. "Come join us, Jake? I bet you like to have fun." She held her palm out to reveal a kaleidoscope of pills.

"Not the kind of thrill I'm searching for tonight," he said.

He wouldn't tell anyone what he witnessed, just like he wouldn't reveal he went to the beach in hopes of finding a willing partner. He smiled at a group of women who appeared to be in their early thirties, celebrating a recent divorce. He grinned as he told them he was also newly single, in Hawaii for his brother's wedding. He didn't

I

mention Lia. Several drinks later, he walked hand in hand with the divorcee to find a quiet spot on the beach. He had been nervous at first, only having been with Lia since his divorce. Even though he informed her he wanted to date other women, he hadn't acted on the desire. The woman was eager to please him, wanting to make her last night in Hawaii memorable. She also produced a condom, and they laughed at their shared quest for meaningless sex. When they finished, she kissed him and said, "Thanks for giving me a fling on the beach to tell my friends about my handsome, blue-eyed stranger."

"My pleasure," Jake replied, not asking her name.

He relaxed in the sand and gazed at the stars, almost falling asleep. A light rain started, and he sat up, brushing the sand off. He hoped Lia hadn't discovered he left as he walked up the beach. A motionless form crumpled in the sand caught his eye. "Damn it," he swore, instantly recognizing Sonya.

He touched her shoulder, trying to rouse her. "Leave me alone." She shoved his hand away.

"It's Jake. You can't stay out here in the rain."

"Jake." She touched his face and started to cry.

He helped her stand, keeping an arm around her as she stumbled up the walkway. Unclear where her bungalow was, and unable to rely on her directions, he considered his options. He propped her against a planter and knocked at Casi's father's door.

"Jake? What's going on?" Jack inhaled sharply.

"I need your help," Jake sighed.

"Is something wrong with Casi?"

"Not your daughter." Jake indicated Sonya slumped against the planter. "Your ex. I found her on the beach and couldn't leave her there in the rain."

"At this hour?" Jack eyed his shifty demeanor.

"I'd rather not explain," Jake said with a wink.

Jack grinned. "Thank you for rescuing her. Bring her in." He turned to his wife, Ava. "I'm sorry, Sweetheart." She exhaled, familiar with the drill.

"Where do I put her?" Jake asked.

"What did she take?" Ava sauntered over and felt Sonya's wrist to assess her pulse as she peered in her blood-shot eyes.

"I'm guessing maybe Ecstasy?" Jake shrugged.

"Bathtub," they both said, considering the safest place.

"Do you know how long it's been since she took it?" Ava asked.

"I walked by her a few hours ago," Jake said.

She raised an eyebrow. "Just out for a walk, were you?"

He rolled his eyes and Jack laughed, "You're single now, don't worry about an explanation."

"What about your girlfriend?" Ava raised an eyebrow.

Jake sighed, "It's complicated. After being married for sixteen years, I'm not quite ready to commit."

They pulled blankets from the bed and settled Sonya in the bathtub, making sure to wedge her on her side.

"Please don't tell Casi about this," Jack pleaded.

Jake smiled. "Can we pretend we never saw each other?"

"I will gladly say I went to the bar with you if you need an alibi for your whereabouts," Jack offered.

Jake strolled back to his room and rejoined Lia. "Where were you?" she asked, turning toward him.

"At the bar with Jack." He elaborated when he saw the blank expression on her face. "Casi's dad."

"Are you sure you weren't with her stepmother? I noticed you checking her out at the pool," Lia snipped.

"She is super-hot, but it was only Jack," he insisted. Lia slid her hand to grasp him and waited for him to respond. "Let me get a condom." He searched through his suitcase to buy time to fantasize himself into the mood.

"I told you I'm on the pill."

"Is that what you tell your other boyfriends?"

"I've made it clear I want to be exclusive."

He sighed, not wanting to discuss exclusivity. He rejoined her and kissed her neck, trailing to her large breasts. It only took him a few minutes to get aroused and figured it was just his luck Lia suddenly wanted to have sex after his urge had been satisfied.

2

WEB OF DECEIT

The wedding had been amazing, exactly as Casi had hoped for, even though she didn't have a clue what she wanted in the first place. Waking up in Kyle's arms as his wife was ethereal and scary as hell. Married sex proved to be as amazing as single sex, so that wouldn't be a problem. "Good morning, Mrs. Jensen," Kyle teased.

She giggled. "That sounds weird."

"How does it feel to be a wife?"

"It hasn't sunk in yet." She stroked his cheek.

He smiled and bit the tip of her finger playfully. "I don't want to push you because you're busy with the campaign…"

"I know," she interrupted. "You need to add me to your health and car insurance."

He nodded. "As soon as possible. I also think we should have a joint bank account to make things easier."

Casi sighed. "Can it wait until I get back from LA?"

"I don't want you to forget." He inhaled and wished she had already taken care of it as he suggested over a month ago.

"I'm not sure about changing my name." She winced.

"You don't have to take my last name. I can still add you to the policies. All I need is your social security number and copies of your ID. You can fax it to me when you get back to LA."

"Let's go eat breakfast, Husband." She kissed him to end the conversation.

&

Sonya woke up angry, insisting Jack tried to imprison her. She left, slamming the door, refusing to look at Ava.

"I thought we were done with your ex-wife and her drug problems." Ava yawned, exhausted from a sleepless night.

"I hoped we were." Jack squeezed her hand as they entered the restaurant to join the group for breakfast.

Lia regarded Jack across the table and noted his bleary eyes and tired expression. "What did you do last night?"

"I went to the bar with Jake, sorry I kept him out late. It turns out we have a lot of common interests," he stated. She nodded; glad Jake had been truthful. Sonya winked at Jake, remembering where he had been and plotting when she would use it against him.

Everyone spent the day enjoying the island. Casi encouraged Kyle to rent dirt bikes with Jake, wanting him to enjoy the trip as much as possible. She sat on the bluffs with Lia, watching them ride up and down the dunes. "They're acting like teenagers." Lia rolled her eyes.

"Isn't it great?" Casi giggled.

Lia sighed and regarded her hands as she twisted her fingers together. "Will you guys start a family right away?"

Casi shuddered. "Neither of us want children. We have Dingo and Jezebel to fulfill any parenting desire."

"Of course, you want kids. Isn't that the point of marriage?" Lia spun around with her mouth agape.

"Honestly, I'm not sure what the point is. I don't need a piece of paper to tell me how much I love Kyle. I doubt much will change between us."

"Everyone wants to get married and have kids. I've always dreamed of being a wife. It seems important," Lia lamented.

"I'm unsure about changing my last name. I married Kyle to show commitment, not to become his property." Casi turned to Lia. "Don't rush Jake. He needs time to be single."

"Don't forget, I've known him for over a dozen years." Lia set her jaw.

"He was married with kids for all those years," Casi challenged, noting the determination in Lia's face.

In the evening, as they walked to one of the neighboring hotels for dinner, Kyle asked Jake, "What does Jack drink?"

Jake smiled at the insinuation. "Scotch?"

"Good guess. Please be careful."

"I brought your Costco condoms," Jake joked, referring to the giant box Kyle added to their cart after his divorce.

After dinner, they found an outdoor lounge and had drinks. Jack led Casi to the dance floor and Ava smiled, knowing it had been tough on him to be away from her for so long. "I'm not as smooth of a dancer as your husband, but would you like to dance with me?" Kyle asked.

"I would love to." Ava smiled and took his hand.

"Your girlfriend doesn't seem interested in you," Sonya breathed in Jake's ear, watching Lia leave. "Maybe I could be your lover tonight?"

He moved away. "Stop playing around."

She kissed his neck and ran a hand over his chest. "I can give you all sorts of thrills."

"I'm sure you could." He attempted to untangle her.

"Shall I tell your girlfriend where you were last night?" She boldly slid a hand over the front of his pants, making her intentions clear.

"I can inform your daughter what you were up to."

"Oh touché." Sonya undid the wrap of her dress to expose her breasts as she turned her back to the lounge. "I think I'll go for a walk on the beach. Maybe you would like to join me?" He tried to avert his eyes, but her toned figure mesmerized him. He also noticed Casi inherited her mother's breasts. He glanced at the dance floor, and then at Sonya, seeing she had completely removed her clothing. He knew he shouldn't follow her but felt the condom in his pocket. Sonya turned and smiled. "I knew you would come." He ensured they were far from the lounge and out of sight. She kissed him playfully, biting his bottom lip before she pulled him down in the sand. She lifted a small plastic bag from her purse, perusing the colorful contents.

"I'm not doing that."

"Suit yourself, but I like sex better with a little kick." She decided on a yellow tablet, placing it on her tongue and closing her eyes. Without warning, she leaned forward and kissed him deeply, not letting him pull away as the pill dissolved between them. He glared at her, shoving her away as she laughed, and he spit the bitter aftertaste in the sand. He felt the effects within minutes and gave into the euphoria as she kissed him. She tugged off his t-shirt, driving him crazy with her tongue as she worked her way down and unzipped his jeans. "I love the tattoos. Sexy," she purred. He located the condom, struggling to get it on in his daze. Sonya facilitated before easing herself on him and bringing his hands to her. "Have you seen how beautiful Casi's breasts are? You can tell where she got those."

"Please don't talk about her," he mumbled, not wanting the high to end or to be accountable for his actions. He lost himself in the sensation of their bodies as she writhed on top of him.

"Yes, Jake!" She threw her head back and ground her hips against him. "Harder," she breathed, skilled at bringing herself to orgasm and sensing an inexperience on his part. She gasped, letting him finish before she rolled off. "What do you think my daughter would say?"

"I don't know, and neither will you. Otherwise, I'll tell her you're a drug addict." He zipped his pants. "You won't shock anyone in my family, they are aware I'm a loser."

Sonya winked. "Thanks for a good time. Call me if you are ever in LA. I would be happy to give you lessons and improve your performance."

"Don't wait by the phone." He offered her a hand to stand.

"No thanks. I think I'll hang out here for a while."

"You need to put your clothes on." He knelt to help her. "It's not safe for you to be out here like this."

"Aren't you a gentleman?"

"Yes, us small-town men are always chivalrous." He walked her back up the beach, intending to part ways when they reached the hotel.

He cringed when Jack came down the stairs, witnessing Sonya trying to kiss him goodnight. Ava rolled her eyes, whispering to Jack as Sonya laughed and scampered away. "Got caught in her web, did you?" Jack asked. Jake shrugged, directing his gaze to his feet. "I hope you used a condom. That woman has been around the block a few times." He narrowed his eyes and grasped Jake's arm. "I don't care about Sonya, but if you bring that shit around my daughter, we'll have a problem."

Jake's nostrils flared. "I'm not a drug addict."

"You're high now," he challenged.

"I willingly took her up on her offer of sex, but drugs weren't part of the deal. I don't even know what the hell she gave me." Jake clenched his jaw.

3

EXCUSES

Casi savored her last days with Kyle in Hawaii, walking on the beach, swimming, and making love in the moonlight. They kissed goodbye at the airport, each headed to a different gate. Kyle sighed as he hugged her. "Our plan is to live between the two states, but I hate to be separated from you."

"I hate it too." Casi wiped a tear and pressed her cheek to his chest.

On the flight, she told herself everything would be fine, aware the next few years would be difficult. Dread engulfed her considering there might also be some unexpected challenges, and she hoped it wouldn't break them.

Her ex-boyfriend, Alix, met her at the airport with a tight expression. "We need to talk." Casi cringed at her four least favorite words in the universe; nothing good ever followed them. "Johan wants to roll profits back into the Sand and Surf line for the next year to help it grow more rapidly. Business is slower than he anticipated, and the investors are nervous."

"Are you saying I won't be getting my ten percent from the sales?" Casi bit her lip to slow the panic rising in her chest.

He winced. "After expenses, there haven't been enough profits.

We're at the bottom of the list when it comes to getting paid. At least you got the money for doing the shoots for the campaign."

"That money is practically gone! I have a mortgage on a loft I barely live in, and I wiped out my savings to buy the damn thing. I have credit card payments and expenses." She squeezed her eyes shut at the realization she had been reckless with her expenditures.

"I haven't had an art installation in months and I'm living on the edge." Alix furrowed his brow.

"Why am I even in LA then?" Casi yelled.

"You'll get more work. You can make good money here, Babe."

"I'll contact my agency and inform them I'm back in town." Casi shivered at the prospect of doing more lingerie shoots. Since being with Kyle, her body became private between them and she wasn't anxious to strip down for commercial profit anymore.

The week of Thanksgiving, Casi realized she hadn't booked her flight for Seattle, distracted by scrambling to find work and being creative with her finances. She discovered even standby flights were sold out, and she prepared to call Kyle, disappointing him one more time. He answered on the first ring, anticipating her call, already prepared for her excuse.

"Hey, it's me," she said.

"I have caller ID," he said dryly.

"I can't get a flight. Do you think I should drive?"

"It's not safe in your car. There could be snow on the pass and you're not an experienced winter driver."

They both paused. He didn't want to get mad she had waited so long to get a flight, and she was tired of explaining how busy her schedule was. "I'll try to come after Thanksgiving. At least we could spend some time together for a few days." She asked about Dingo and Jezebel. He said he had to take care of some business and she interpreted it as an excuse to hang out at the bar with Jake.

❧

By early December, it had been six weeks since Casi had seen Kyle and she missed making love and sleeping beside him. She was nervous about going to Blackberry Falls because she had an increasing uneasiness about her life in LA and feared the comfort of being drawn back into the simple small-town charm. Part of her wanted to chuck her life in LA. She grew tired of the clubs, the traffic, and the unending problems in her business venture. The only thing going well was her marketing class, which would be done by January. After running into Alejandro at Coffee Bean, she understood the time had come to head to Blackberry Falls and remember her marriage vows.

Casi hadn't told Kyle she was coming. She canceled too many times and figured she needed to be physically there for him to believe it this time. Luckily the snow had not started, so the drive from Seattle in the rental car proved easy. She drove around the bend on the lane and could see him on the dock, preparing to go fishing. She smiled, glad he kept himself busy. Dingo chased after the lures Kyle attempted to sort in his tackle box. She parked and strolled through the house, grabbing a beer, and petting Jezebel on the head as she walked in the bedroom to get changed. She hadn't anticipated seeing a naked woman sleeping in her bed, making her choke on the beer. She bolted out the back door and chucked the beer bottle at Kyle, missing his head, but causing him to knock over his fishing gear. "You son of a bitch!"

"What the hell, Casi?" Kyle took a step back at the volatile greeting.

"You're a liar!" She lunged at him, tripping on the fishing pole and ending up on all fours. He tried to help her up, but she threw his gear in the lake in anger. He grabbed the tackle box away from her, and she clawed at him, making him lose his footing on the edge of the dock, bringing them, Dingo, and the tackle box into the chilly water. Dingo pulled himself out, shaking his fur, and wildly barking at them. Kyle unceremoniously shoved her up on the dock, then climbed the ladder, cursing at the loss of his gear.

"Kyle?" A woman stood on the back porch, now partially clothed in one of his t-shirts.

"Go home, Chelsea," he instructed. "Leave my t-shirt." He touched Casi's shoulder. "It's freezing, let's take off these wet clothes and you can hear me out." As they stripped down in the mudroom, Kyle explained, "Jake and I had a few people over last night and she had too much to drink."

"You forgot about her when you got out of bed this morning to go fishing?" Her lip trembled as a fat tear slid down her cheek.

"I am not the one sleeping with her, so yes, I didn't consider her." He grasped her shoulders and looked her square in the eyes.

"Jake?" she gasped. He nodded and walked toward the bathroom. She noticed the condom wrapper on the nightstand and his discarded t-shirt on the bed. She wrinkled her nose and scrambled in the shower after Kyle. "That's so gross. Why did he use our bed?"

"It's not like you're ever in there." Kyle exhaled. "I guess I fell asleep on the sofa." He hugged her tightly. "I wouldn't cheat on you."

"I'm sorry about your fishing stuff. If you want to have sex, it's happening in here because I'm burning those sheets." Casi shivered.

"I always want to have sex with you." He grinned and leaned in to kiss her as he ran his hands over her soapy body. She wrapped her arms around his neck, kissing him with longing, realizing how much she missed him. He lifted her up and pressed her against the wall, and she swung her legs around his waist. "Good thing you're so skinny." She frowned, and he chuckled. "I meant it as a compliment." She switched the water to the pulse setting and reclined as the vibration stroked between their intertwined bodies. Kyle moaned, clutching her hips as he thrust, enjoying the sensuous stimulation of the warm water. Casi grasped the base of the shower head, arching her back as the orgasm started. She reveled in the feeling of the liquid pellets on her body. They made love until the water turned cool, then wrapped themselves in towels. "You cut your hair," he noted.

"Yup, time for another change." She fluffed the shoulder-length bob, not sure if she liked it. She had felt restless, and this time checked with her agency before cutting it. They approved, and Dylan made it even blonder. She smiled at him as he watched her dry her hair. "You don't like it?"

"No, I mean yes. You look different every time I see you." He surveyed her body with concern. She assumed he noticed her bones protruding and quickly dressed in leggings and a t-shirt when he went to the laundry room.

She heard the fridge opening and frowned at Jake in the kitchen getting a beer. "Asshole!" She punched him on the arm, which made him chuckle. She grabbed a spatula from the crock by the stove, and took another swing, creating a satisfying thwack. "I can't believe you had sex in my bed, or that you're cheating on Lia!"

He swiftly grabbed the spatula and smacked her hard on the bottom, making her yelp. "I'm not committing to anyone for a while. Kyle's bed was convenient, and it's not like you're ever here."

Kyle prevented Jake from taking another swing. "Don't hit my wife."

"She hit me first. Why is she so skinny?" Jake curled his lip as he scanned her. Kyle shrugged, wondering the same thing. He wasn't thrilled she had been away so long, and worried things weren't going well in LA.

Casi shoved Jake from her path. Her back hurt and she didn't feel like getting in an argument about her stress level or being quizzed to death about Alix. She loved seeing Kyle and the sex in the shower invigorated her, but life seemed easier in LA. "Do you want to go for a walk with me and Dingo?" She laced up her sneakers.

Kyle smiled in reply and put on Dingo's leash, taking her hand. "I would love to walk with you. Jake, wash our sheets and make the bed while we're gone," he called over his shoulder as they left.

They hiked the trail around the lake, both contemplating what to say that wouldn't ignite an argument. When they stopped at the ridge, Casi sighed and surveyed the water. "It's beautiful here."

"It would be nice if you were here all the time." He slid his arm around her, and Dingo wagged his tail.

"We just have to make it through this year, ok?"

"Although we agreed on that before we were married..." he hesitated and lifted her chin to look her in the eyes. "What's going on in LA? I feel like you're not telling me everything."

"The Sand and Surf deal is problematic. I'm committed to our marriage, Kyle. Don't worry about us."

He nodded. "I miss you. I want you here with me in the morning to enjoy coffee by the lake, to go on walks, or even watch TV together. I'm being selfish, but I need you with me. I thought this would be easier. A hundred times a day I think about you and want to share something, but it's not important enough to call or even text."

"I need you too. I hate being in LA." She fell into his arms. "I'll expedite things there, although I don't know what I would do for work here."

"I'll enjoy every minute of your visit. I don't want to waste time making you anxious. I can take care of us financially, so don't stay in LA if it's only to make a little money."

Exhaustion overcame her when they arrived home. She curled up on the sofa with Jezebel as Dingo nestled below her on the floor. She realized how much she missed her pets, the warmth and softness of their bodies, and the way they followed her around adoringly. Kyle sat beside her and gently moved her head to his lap. "Want pizza for dinner? I don't feel like cooking and you seem worn out," he said.

"Perfect." She held a thumb up.

"Sounds good to me." Jake settled beside them on the sofa.

She snuggled against Kyle and enjoyed the sensation of him rubbing her back. She wanted to tell him the truth about LA and let him fix the mess she had made, knowing he would in an instant. She woke to the smell of pepperoni, giggling as a piece of sausage rolled down her shoulder. "Sorry," Kyle said, reclaiming the lost meat.

"I didn't realize I drifted off. I am so comfortable." She yawned and reached for a piece of pizza. Jake handed her a beer, and they found a movie on TV. She reveled in the happiness of the moment. She guessed they did this often, easy in their routine together, pleased her presence seemed to add to the contentment. She wondered why she wanted more. What did LA have that she couldn't find right here? Sure, Dylan lived there, but they could figure out a way to be together, she reasoned.

"I'm not a fan of the hair. I like it longer." Jake poked at a strand.

"I don't care what you think." She stuck her tongue out but secretly regretted the cut and letting Dylan make is so blonde.

"What about Christmas?" Kyle asked out of the blue, making them both look at him. He realized the randomness of his question and laughed. "This is ideal, sitting here together. You probably have to go back to LA... soon."

"I do," she lamented. "What's the plan for the Holidays?"

"I usually go to my parents for a few days. It makes them happy, and it's nice to take a break from work. My mom does an amazing job of decorating the house and bakes for days." Kyle's face lit up with contentment.

"This will be my first Christmas as a single man." Jake furrowed his brow. "I'll probably go home. It'd be weird to be alone."

Casi knew she needed to make a point to be there. "I think that sounds wonderful. If I'm invited, then I'll definitely come."

"Of course, you're invited. We'll take Dingo and Jezebel and maybe have a beautiful white Christmas if we're lucky." Kyle stroked Dingo's ears as the dog wagged his tail.

"Will I get to sleep in your room now we're married?"

Kyle grinned. "I already bought a bigger bed."

4

——————

THE GIRL FROM SEATTLE

Jake pulled in the parking structure of the hotel, nervous about meeting the representative from the lumber company. Since his divorce, he had kept himself busy with work, the bar, and the idea of a newfound freedom sleeping with women other than his wife. He suspected Lia wanted more but could barely breathe these days with her around. She continually showed up at his apartment or texted him, not understanding sometimes he wanted to hang out with his brother. He enjoyed having sex with her, certainly better and more frequent than when he had been married to Gail, but not spectacular. Kyle didn't tell him much about his sex life, but the few details he did share, Jake figured he missed out in his own endeavors. Sonya's comment about his lack of experience remained in the back of his mind, making him question his abilities to perform.

He was unsure about meeting Anna, the district representative for the company. She suggested they go for drinks and discuss the orders to be placed. Kyle dated her briefly over a year ago; more like hooking up, he said. He laughed when Jake showed him the email from Anna and told him to go for it, saying he would have a good time. Jake preferred not to be compared to his brother, especially since Kyle had a lot more experience. He also had Casi, and he figured that was like having twelve women rolled into one. He checked his hair in the lobby mirror and walked in the bar, trying to appear confident.

"You sure look a lot like your brother," Anna mused, planting a kiss on him unexpectedly, as he took a seat beside her.

"He favors me, I'm older." Jake focused on the purchase orders and inhaled sharply when she slid a hand over his thigh with a suggestive smile.

Kyle warned him she was fast, but he had just walked in the room. He ordered a drink, and they got the business discussion out of the way, placing the order for the pre-season work. He started to relax with his second drink and responded to her flirting. He found her attractive; shapely, with dark red hair and creamy skin. He liked her sherry colored eyes, with a devilish glimmer. Her low-cut blouse caught his attention as he glimpsed her lace bra when she leaned toward him. She suggested they have another drink in her room and he smiled his reply. She kissed him again in the elevator, leaning against him, and making her intentions clear. She told him to make himself comfortable as she flipped on a music channel and went to change, and he fixed two drinks from the bar. She came back wearing a lace thong and bra ensemble, making him swallow his drink too fast, choking on the liquid.

She giggled and sat on his lap. "Do I make you nervous?"

"Extremely," he answered honestly.

"How is your brother, anyway? I haven't seen him in a year," she purred, unbuttoning his shirt.

He wished they weren't talking about Kyle as she stroked his chest. His confidence had increased since becoming more fit, and he let her take the lead. "He's good, he got married." He stroked the silky smoothness of her inner thigh.

"Married! Wow, he didn't seem like the type. Who's the girl, someone from your little town?"

"No, she's from LA. He met her there when he was on a job about a year and a half ago." He nuzzled her neck, not realizing the implied overlap.

"I guess I wasn't the only one getting his attention." She licked his earlobe as he moaned with pleasure.

"Oh no, they weren't together at the time he was seeing you." He fumbled to fix his oversight.

"Seeing me? What did he tell you about me?" Anna laughed and reclined on the bed.

"Only how beautiful you are." Jake stood by the edge of the bed and smiled as she unzipped his pants while he removed his shirt.

"Liar." She eyed his erection, grasping him while she ran her tongue over him, making him groan. She pulled him toward her on the bed and rolled on top of him. He felt like he lagged from the speed this woman moved and tried to interpret what she directed him to do. "Hmm, you don't seem as experienced as your brother."

"I'm newly divorced after sixteen years of marriage," he admitted.

"Oh well, I guess I'll have to teach you a few things."

"I'm a very willing student." His deep blue eyes twinkled. He held on as long as he could, wanting to climax the moment he entered her. She drove him crazy with her kissing and licking, and hands everywhere. He cursed his brother for not preparing him for her superior skills and what to expect. When he climaxed, Anna giggled and grasped his hand to her while she twisted on top of him, bringing herself to orgasm. He went to the bathroom to discard the condom and admired her slender, nude body as he walked back toward her. He hoped she understood recovery time and was convinced not even his brother could have back-to-back orgasms.

Anna reached out, and he rejoined her as she ran her hands over his chest. She traced his tattoos with a finger, and he enjoyed the sensation. "What's the story behind your tattoos?"

"I thought they were cool," he said without conviction.

"Your brother said the same thing," Anna laughed. He smiled at her, drawn to her husky laugh and confidence. "Tell me more about his wife. What does she do for a living?"

He chuckled. "She's a swimsuit model." He reached for her laptop, figuring that would be the next question. He located Casi's modeling pictures and turned the screen to her.

"Holy shit, she's gorgeous! Is she a bitch?"

Jake smiled, thinking how far his relationship with Casi had come. "No, she's sweet and totally in love with Kyle." He opened Facebook, pulling up Casi's profile featuring the picture at the club, noting her status hadn't been changed to married.

"Damn, she does look like she's in love with him and he's crazy for her. I'll have to whip you into shape to be my new lover," she determined, trailing down his stomach to explore him further.

This woman is insatiable! Jake thought as he stroked her hair.

Jake ambled into the coffee shop the next morning. Kyle waited for him, with a grin on his face, two coffees already in hand. Lia stood at the register and Jake greeted her casually before whispering to his brother, "You could have warned me, asshole!" He punched him in the arm before taking a cup.

"I said she was fast." Kyle avoided Lia's questioning glare as she watched them laughing.

"Fast? Lightning speed. The hands and mouth everywhere. Jesus, I could barely keep up!" Jake shook his head.

"Did she ask about me?"

"Many times, especially when I finished so quickly." Jake rolled his eyes. "I told her you were married and showed her Casi's picture."

"Was she impressed?"

"Very. I didn't tell her how messed-up in the head she is."

"Thanks," Kyle answered, not contradicting the statement.

"I have homework," Jake reported. "Can I borrow Casi?"

Kyle flipped him off. "Not in your wildest dreams." He understood he had been sending his brother into the lion's den when he suggested he make the trip to Seattle to meet the lumber rep. The prior year he had been on his way to see his ex-girlfriend, Lauren, figuring it would be good to catch up and maybe start dating again, giving into her relentless pursuit to rekindle their relationship. He had been perusing the last aisle of the craftsmen show when he met

Anna. Her booth featured high-end finishing woods, and his interest grew beyond what he required for the business. He had been feeling lost after breaking up with Casi in the summer, and he found Anna's copper hair and a pretty smile alluring, and he asked her out for a drink. She readily accepted and kissed him that evening at the bar, then invited him to her room. She reminded him of Casi in her confidence and ability to express herself sexually. All thoughts of Lauren had disappeared as he took the elevator up to her room. He enjoyed having sex with her and exploring her body without the pressures of a relationship. She had been good for him, allowing him to fulfill his desires without any emotions involved. She was open sexually, and he liked how she was unapologetic about her needs and he had been happy to satisfy her. It fizzled by Christmas when he became depressed about the loss of his dog, Colt, and then Casi returned and he never thought about Anna again. He wondered what might have happened if he had seen Lauren that day after all. Would he have been tempted by Casi when she returned to Blackberry Falls? He knew in his heart, no matter what his relationship status, Casi would have won him over with her dazzling smile and the promise of a kiss.

5

WRECKAGE

"Casi, listen!" Sonya pleaded.

"No, Mom." Casi crossed her arms over her chest. "I don't want you involved in my career. Mary would never approve."

"You've barely been working." Sonya wagged a finger.

"It's not my fault the stupid company is struggling. I'm sorry I can't help you, but I'm scrambling to pay my own bills."

Sonya grasped her elbow. "Meet with the photographers and find out more about the shoot. This has nothing to do with Mary, it's an editorial, not a stupid fashion show."

Casi shook her head. "I'm going home to Blackberry Falls tomorrow. I'm spending Christmas with Kyle's family."

"That is not your home, Casi!"

"My home is with my husband. Where's yours?"

"He found a younger woman, just like yours will."

"You're right. If I don't start making him a priority, he probably will find someone else. Won't that be great? We can get drunk together and talk about how our husbands abandoned us."

Sonya responded with a slap across her face. "You are an ungrateful little bitch! Don't come crying to me when your marriage fails. Maybe then you'll appreciate all the shit I've had to deal with. Do yourself a favor though, don't make the mistake of having a kid."

"I want to live my own life. Why won't you let me?"

&

Casi checked the weather report and decided to drive, not wanting to deal with holiday travel and checked bags. She needed time to think about where her career might be headed and figured the drive would be a good time to mull over her options. She made it to Ashland, Oregon, and spent the night at a nice hotel, watching pay-per-view movies. She realized the extravagance of the expenses, but penny-pinching seemed useless with her dire financial situation, anyway. She called Kyle, not previously informing him about the road trip because she knew he would fret about her capabilities to handle the weather. Her little Volkswagen didn't perform well on long distances; it chugged on the hills and the convertible top made for a chilly ride. Paid in full and in her name, were the only things which were important to her.

"Driving? Are you crazy? If something happens, you'll be out there all alone." Kyle's voice cracked with concern.

"I'm sure a trucker would stop and pick me up," Casi teased.

"That worries me even more. Don't stop at rest stops, only well-lit restaurants that have a lot of people," he warned.

"I'll only stop at Starbucks."

"And gas stations." He rubbed his temple. "Make sure you don't get low on fuel, there are a few long stretches without stations."

"Kyle, I've driven it before." She tried to sound confident, although she was secretly nervous about Grants Pass if it snowed.

"Jesus, Casi, I wish you weren't driving. I won't sleep until you get here."

&

Casi got an early start the next morning and approached the exit for

Blackberry Falls by afternoon. The snow began to fall, but the sun shone brightly, and the drive was pleasant. She cranked the heat and the stereo, almost missing her exit. She over-corrected too fast and spun out on a patch of ice. The car hopped over the medium, striking a tree. "No!" She pounded the steering wheel. She wasn't hurt, only shaken. One more item to add to her list of crap costing her money and another thing proving Kyle right. She still had her basic insurance, which probably wouldn't cover the repairs, plus a huge deductible. The hood was severely twisted, and a tree limb sliced through the roof. She climbed out and assessed the damage. A truck carrying logs pulled over, and the driver asked if she needed help. She grabbed her bags and her bobble-head dog from the dashboard and climbed in the cab. Still early enough in the day that Kyle would be at work, it seemed like the safest address to give the trucker.

"Jensen? I know them, I do business with those brothers."

"I'm married to Kyle." Casi blinked at the word 'married' sounding foreign on her tongue.

"Wow, small world." He whistled.

He parked at the wood shop and any hope she had of not being noticed vanished as Kyle and Jake returned from a late lunch. Kyle recognized the driver and came to shake his hand. "Are you delivering in the area?"

"Well, a delivery of sorts. I found your wife out on I-5, got in a little wreck." He grinned and tipped his hat as she gathered her bags.

"Casi, are you ok?" Kyle asked tenderly, giving her a hug as Jake poked her and called her a bad driver.

The trucker told them the location of the car. "That little rag-top isn't going to make it through a snowstorm."

Kyle put her bags in his truck and called the towing company, witnessing her devastation about the car and understanding she didn't need to hear about winter driving conditions or the fact she should have been on their insurance. "I guess you're stuck here with us until it's time to go home because it's the last day before we close for the holidays and we have a lot of work to finish."

Casi went to the office and called Lia to see if she wanted to hang out, telling her about the wreck between sobs. She glanced at the brothers on the work floor before phoning Alix with a heavy heart. "Book the editorial my mom has been pushing for. I need the money." Lia arrived, walking past Jake without a word.

"What's she doing here?" Jake whispered.

"Shit, Casi must have called her." Kyle eyed the women hugging.

"I'm going to get coffee," Casi called out as they left.

Lia took Casi to the bar instead of the coffee shop, and they ordered appetizers and cocktails. "What did I miss? Why is everyone acting strange?" Casi raised an eyebrow.

"No surprise, Jake's being an asshole." Lia stirred her drink without taking a sip. "I thought we were good. He finally got rid of Gail and had his own place. Then he started acting strange, reminding me he's single and can do what he wants. At first, he came over all the time and we seemed to be headed somewhere, but I found out he was also sleeping with the checker at the grocery store."

"Jeannie?" Casi gasped.

"No, Chelsea."

"How did you find out?" Casi recalled the woman sleeping in her bed.

"She bragged about it on Facebook!" Lia almost yelled. "Like he's anything to brag about."

"Why not?" Casi cocked her head in confusion.

"I mean in bed. He does his thing to get what he needs but then rolls off and you're waiting for him to go home so you can use a vibrator." Lia shrugged. "It was exciting in the beginning, but now it's not worth the effort of shaving my legs."

Casi almost choked on her drink. "Damn, I would've thought he'd be eager after all that wasted time with Gail."

"You know what's even worse?" Lia lowered her voice. "I heard he's been seeing, and I use that term lightly, the woman from Seattle, who Kyle dated last fall. Imagine her disappointment!"

"What? That's crazy! Wait, what's her name?" Casi grabbed her phone.

"Anna, something. I saw her on Facebook. Jake's new friend," she said with disgust.

"Oh my God, she sent me a friend request!" Casi noted the location and the mutual friend.

"Accept it!" Lia clapped. "We can stalk her."

Casi smiled. "Think of it this way, if the woman has been with Kyle, she won't be satisfied with a mediocre lover. Maybe she can educate Jake, and when he smartens up and comes back, he'll be way better in bed."

"You have such a great way of looking at things."

"Honestly, I think it would be good for him to get out there and sow his wild oats before he settles down again." She winced from her back pain.

"Did you hurt your back in the car wreck?"

"It's been hurting for a while. It's stress. I've been nauseous too, which sucks because we're going to Kyle's parents for Christmas and I don't want to be coming down with something." She downed her drink.

"Maybe you're pregnant?"

"That's the last thing I want, ever! I'm on the pill, so...fuck!" Casi rubbed her temple. "I forgot to fill my prescription when I got back from Hawaii. My sucky insurance only allows a three-month supply at a time." She crinkled her nose as she attempted to remember when the prescription ran out.

"Well, a surprise baby could be fun." Lia wrung her hands.

"Kyle would be pissed, and I don't want kids, especially with everything going on in my life."

"He would come around. It might bring you guys closer."

"It would definitely tear us apart. We were both clear from the beginning about our choice. Can you take me by the store on the way home to buy a pregnancy test?"

"I think we should buy two," Lia said with a meek smile.

They went out of town for the purchase, not wanting anyone they knew to see them. They drove to Lia's apartment, armed with potato chips and dip to eat while they waited for results. Casi went first, then ate half the bag of chips while she waited for Lia.

"On three, we turn them over," Casi directed.

"Ok, one, two, three." Lia peered at the stick in her hand.

"Thank God!" Casi screamed, seeing the negative sign.

"It's positive..." Lia held up the undeniable plus sign. "I'm happy. I'm thirty-six, and I don't have time to wait for the perfect scenario to bring a child into this world."

"Are you going to tell Jake? I mean, he's the dad, right?" Casi asked, instantly sorry for him and yet another surprise baby.

"He's the father. I'll tell him soon. Don't say anything, ok?"

"How long have you suspected you were pregnant?"

"Since Hawaii. This is the third time I've been pregnant." She wiped a tear. "I'm keeping this one."

"I'll be there for you." Casi grasped her hand. She called the pharmacy to renew her pills before they went on Facebook to check out Anna's profile, snooping through her pictures, trying to find one of her not looking perfect.

"She's pretty," Lia sighed.

"She's very professional." Casi felt a pang of jealousy in response to the perfectly coiffed woman.

Kyle had her car towed to the local shop but guessed they wouldn't get an answer on a possible repair until after the holidays. They picked up Jake on the way to the coffee shop and Casi hoped it wouldn't be difficult being around him, hearing way too much information about his sex life and impending fatherhood.

"Why are you looking at me weird?" Jake scanned her expression.

"This is just my face," Casi claimed.

"What did Lia say about me?" Jake narrowed his eyes.

"Nothing, she's pissed you have been whoring around town," she answered honestly.

"And your advice to her?" He slid closer.

"I said it might be good for you to get out there..." She tried to bite her lip, but it came out anyway, "and get some more experience," she blurted, spilling her coffee in a fit of laughter.

"Fuck you." He glared at her and Kyle elbowed her while concealing a smile.

6

———

WHISKEY KISSES

asi wished the pain in her back, radiating to her side, would vanish. She assumed it stemmed from her period, screwed up from missing her pills. She hoped it wouldn't come while she visited, always awkward in a house dominated by men. Georgia had the farmhouse decorated beautifully and Casi relaxed and participated in the holiday festivities, something she had never experienced. She looked forward to helping Georgia prepare for the big Christmas dinner, enthralled by the menu. They baked pies, breads, cookies, and a huge fruit cake which appeared lovely, but she gagged when she tasted the candied fruit, faking a smile as she forced the desiccated bits down her throat.

On the morning of Christmas Eve, Casi snuggled into Kyle's arms, enjoying the queen-sized bed. She awakened to Jake's voice in her ear and his body pressed against her. "Are you ready for our brother's tradition?" Startled, she scampered over Kyle, hitting the floor with a thud as he awoke, rubbing his eyes. "You might have to hold her down for me, she's a wild one," Jake chuckled, sprawling on the bed, fully clothed.

"I swear you wake me up earlier every year." Kyle yawned.

"Get dressed Casi, it's time to cut down the tree," Jake said with the excitement of a little boy leaping from the bed.

"Meet us downstairs. Grab her a jacket and gloves," Kyle instructed, directing Casi into clothing.

They climbed in the truck and Jake handed out steamy cups of cocoa with fluffy marshmallows. The snow began to fall, and the crimson sun peeked through the trees. They drove to the forest and Kyle told her about the tradition of cutting down the tree on Christmas Eve. After they returned from college, Peter opted out, saying they were old enough to do it on their own. They honored the tradition, making Christmas feel special. She helped them choose the perfect tree and while they cut it down, she made a stockpile of snowballs to bombard them. They laughed it off, and tied the tree in the truck, then raced after her, shoving snow down the back of her jacket until she screamed for mercy. They returned with rosy cheeks to a house that smelled of pancakes and bacon.

After breakfast, Casi helped decorate the tree and Georgia handed her a prettily wrapped box. She opened it to find a beautiful red blown-glass heart ornament. "Now that you're a Jensen, you should have your own special ornament," Georgia noted with pride. Casi didn't mention she hadn't legally changed her name as she hugged her.

They spent the day playing games and watching Christmas movies, ending with fondue for dinner as they chatted about what still needed to be done for the next day.

"We're going to the bar later," Kyle announced casually.

"Maybe Casi wants to stay here with us," Peter suggested.

"Thanks, but I'd prefer to go with them," she said eagerly. They exchanged looks and tried to explain it wasn't the kind of bar she was used to. She insisted she would be going.

"Casi, what do you normally do for the holidays?" Georgia asked. "Do you spend it with your mother or father?"

"Neither. Last year, I made a disaster of a dinner with Dylan and then we went to a movie. I spent New Year's Eve in Vegas with Alejandro," she quipped, as Peter choked on his fondue, trying to wash it down with wine.

"You never disappoint us with your honesty." Jake smirked. "Is Alejandro even old enough to enter a bar?"

"He's twenty-four, I think." She smiled at Georgia. "He's a super-hot, Argentinian soccer player."

Kyle rolled his eyes. "I hope you don't find it boring being in this little town for the Holidays."

"I'm having a great time." Casi twisted to face him. "Did you spend last Christmas with the girl from Seattle?"

Kyle furrowed his brow, unclear why she would bring up Anna. "No, we weren't together then."

"Who's the girl from Seattle?" Peter asked, thinking it would be strange to refer to Lauren that way.

"Anna. I've heard Jake knows her too." Casi's face contorted with laughter.

"Did you hear about her from Lia?" Kyle asked slowly.

"At first, but then the weirdest thing happened...Anna sent me a friend request on Facebook. We're best friends now." Casi winked at Jake.

Jake's cheeks flushed. "I hate you!"

"Jake!" Georgia and Peter said at the same time, wondering what the uproar was about.

Kyle went to warm up the truck and Jake followed him while Casi got ready. She came down the stairs in tights with a mini-skirt and a cleavage-enhancing sweater. "Bye. See you guys later."

"Stop right there, young lady." Peter stepped in front of her and blocked the door. "You're not wearing that to the bar." Casi stared at him in disbelief as he demanded she put on something more appropriate. She felt like a scolded teenager as she slunk back upstairs and changed to jeans. Peter made her switch her top three more times and then insisted she wear a jacket. They heard a horn as he gave her final approval. Peter walked her out to the truck and opened the door. "Since when do you honk for a lady to come outside?"

"That was Jake!" Kyle punched his brother's arm to defend his lack of chivalry as Casi climbed in over Jake, and Peter shook his head.

"Your dad made me change my clothes three times!" Casi explained as they drove.

"Great, now he's going to think I let you go around looking like..." Kyle stopped, seeing her wide-eyed reaction.

"Let me? What were you about to say? A tramp?" Casi glared at Kyle.

"I love you. You look gorgeous in everything you wear." Kyle grasped her hand and kissed her knuckles.

When they walked in the bar, it became clear why Peter made her change because it had more of a biker vibe than a social atmosphere. The booths had high wooden sides, and she slid in quickly, feeling conspicuous. After a few rounds of drinks, she relaxed and joked with Jake about the messages from Anna. "Tell me what she said," he demanded.

"She thinks I'm beautiful." Casi flipped her hair back in mock vanity.

"Whatever. What did she say about me? What did Lia say?" He furrowed his brow with deep concern.

"Wait, first I want to tell you about the part where Anna asked if I wanted to have a three-way with her and Kyle." She giggled when Kyle spat out his whiskey in disbelief. "She's a wild one, huh?"

"Did you answer her?" Kyle's eyes widened.

"I told her I would get back to her." She gave him a wink. "Then she asked if I could give Jake some pointers in bed."

"What's wrong with you people? I can't be that bad, I always get where I need to go." Jake crossed his arms over his chest and stared at his glass.

"That could be part of the problem. The consensus isn't that you're horrible, you're definitely average. You lack experience in fulfilling a woman's needs." Casi sipped her whiskey with a nod.

"Consensus? Are you taking a damn poll?" Jake gasped.

"I can't believe you girls talk about that stuff." Kyle hesitated. "What did she say about me?"

"She is impressed with your skills. But, don't forget, you had already been with me by that time," Casi noted.

Kyle rolled his eyes. "I already had a lot of experience before you."

"True." Casi patted his hand.

"Sex is natural. I've been doing it since I turned fifteen, it's not rocket science." Jake regarded Casi. "I believe your kind over thinks it."

"My kind?" Casi narrowed her eyes.

"You fancy types, like Anna. Lia was fine before she began jabbering to you and comparing notes." Jake smoothed his hands across the table.

Casi finished her drink. "Kyle go get another round; I need five minutes with your brother." She slid beside Jake and took a sip from his glass.

"Oh, hell no." Kyle grasped her arm.

"It'll only be a kiss, nothing more," she chastised and put her hand on the side of Jake's face.

Jake smiled and winked at Kyle. "Let her show me what I'm lacking." She took another sip of his drink, and brought his face toward her, kissing him softly at first, before parting his lips with her tongue, letting him taste the whiskey. Kyle jumped up and ordered cocktails, plus a shot while he waited at the bar.

"Your wife is kissing your brother," the bartender noted.

"She's very friendly." Kyle downed the shot and stared at his watch. "Time's up, I want my wife back." He escorted her to the opposite side of the booth with a shiver.

"I realize the error of my ways. I've been missing out." Jake grinned.

"You're welcome." Casi smiled.

"When do I get another lesson?" Jake cocked his head.

"Never!" Kyle grabbed his brother's drink. "And you are driving home."

"Training wheels are off, and you can apply the knowledge to other parts of the body, but you'll need to use your imagination." Casi pulled Kyle toward her for a passionate kiss.

"Not enough of a time-lapse!" Kyle wiped his mouth. "You probably still have Jake's spit on you."

"You need to practice for the threesome." She pretended to pout.

"Would it involve Jake?" Kyle winced.

"That would make it a foursome." She raised an eyebrow.

"Forget Kyle, take me and Anna." Jake leaned in eagerly.

"Anna is willing to have both brothers," she countered.

"No!" they both said in disgust, as she laughed hysterically.

7

ZONED

asi awoke the next morning to Kyle's penetrating sapphire gaze. "That's creepy." She placed her palm over his face to block his view.

He smiled. "Did you enjoy kissing Jake last night?"

She shrugged. "Actually yes, but not for the reason you think."

"Not because you've always had a brother fantasy, and this is the first step?" He gave her a mischievous grin.

"Not like Anna." She laughed. "The three-way is never happening. I'm not into women and I'm not sharing you."

"It's not a desire for me either. I can barely keep up with you. We don't need Anna in the mix."

"So, she's pretty hot in bed?"

"She's very experienced. I never had feelings for her though."

"Is that why you sent Jake to her, so he could gain some skills?"

"He went for business; she seduced him on her own."

"You arranged for him to meet her."

"To place our order for high-end finishing woods," he insisted.

"Can't you order products online?"

He sighed. "I thought it would be good for him to see another side of the business and be involved with ordering. He needs to get out there and not always be at the wood shop. I figured if Anna found him attractive, she would make a move on him."

"That's why I kissed him. I didn't like the way Lia talked about him, it made me feel..." Casi bit her lip.

"Protective?" Kyle finished, aware of her motivation.

"I felt terrible when he was hurt. He has deeper emotions than I originally thought. I wanted to boost his confidence."

"Look who is acting like a sister."

"I care about him," she paused, considering his devastation to learn about Lia's pregnancy.

Kyle peered at her with interest. "And?"

"It's a new feeling to care about anyone other than Dylan."

"And me?"

"I love you, that's automatic. Tell me more about Anna. I know you met at the convention last year and you asked her out for a drink." She glanced away when she felt tears spring to her eyes.

"Why does that bother you? We weren't together. What did you think I was doing when you were away with Alejandro?" He took her chin in his hand to read her expression.

"Masturbating to my pictures?" She giggled.

"Maybe," he confessed.

"Honestly, I'm a little jealous."

"Why?"

"Anna seems professional and confident. Every woman notices you and your gorgeous blue eyes. I'm sure she was flattered by the attention of such an attractive man."

"I picked you. Not to be my girlfriend, but my wife."

"Did it bother you when I kissed Jake?"

"Honestly, I'm glad you did, which makes me as twisted as you. If he's going to learn, he should have the best teacher. It stops there. He can figure out the rest on his own." He gave a slight smile. "Growing up, Jake was my idol. He kissed a girl first, and all the other good stuff. He would come home and give me details, and I was eager to be old enough to find out what it was all about. He showed me the ropes at parties in college, and I admired him. After he started a family, things shifted, and I became the cool one who had all the dating experience."

"I bet you were popular in college."

He smiled and then his eyes clouded. "When Jake struggled with home life, he found comfort in food and rarely exercised. After he gained weight, his confidence plummeted, and Gail made it worse by constantly criticizing him. He changed so much from his teen years and lost himself in the agony of his life."

"He seems happier now that he's in better shape."

He kissed the tip of her nose. "You've helped him change. You're a good friend and encourage him to do things. Thank you." He rolled on top, entering her slowly. "What's wrong?" He paused mid-thrust when he saw her wince.

"I have cramps, sorry. I'm not enjoying this."

"I'll wait until you're in the mood." He slid beside her and rubbed her back. "Does that help?" He frowned when her phone rang, and he noted Alix's name.

"Hello? Oh, hey. No. No." She pulled away, keeping her voice low as she answered. "I haven't had time yet. I don't know when I'll be back. Alix, please stop!" Tears streamed down her face.

Kyle removed the phone from her hand. "It's Christmas. Casi's with her family today. She'll call you later." He hung up and hugged her tightly. "What's going on?"

She sobbed against his chest. "Everything is a mess. The business is screwed up and I hate being away from you. I want to move to Washington."

"Business is tough, there will always be rough patches." He surveyed her broken demeanor. "We'll figure it out and get you to Washington as soon as you wrap things up in LA." He kissed the tip of her nose.

৯

"What time zone are we in?" Casi regarded the TV listings.

"Twilight." Jake's eyes crinkled as he nodded to Kyle and Peter.

Casi's eyes widened. "Is that why they named the vampire movies after this area?"

"It was filmed close to here, so most likely." Jake twisted his mouth to avoid laughing. "You should post that on Facebook, so everyone will know how smart you are."

Georgia hid a smile as the men broke into laughter and Casi eyed them suspiciously before retrieving her laptop. "You liar, Jake!" She rolled her eyes. "So, what is the real answer?"

Kyle wiped tears from his eyes. "Casi, you drove in basically a straight line from LA. It's the same time zone. Pacific,"

"Even though we're farther north?" she asked.

"Dear God, Casi, check a map." Peter jumped up and grabbed an atlas. "You do realize we're on the Pacific Ocean, right?" She narrowed her eyes, unsure about the validity of the information. Peter shook his head and showed her they were north of LA and on the same coast. "It's called the Pacific Northwest. I thought you grew up in British Columbia?"

"Yes, how is that relevant?" Casi blinked.

Kyle chuckled. "She's amazing with technology. Maps are too linear, I suspect." He drew Casi to his lap. "BC is directly above us. Remember when you drove there?"

"So, the timelines go up and down?" Casi bit her cheek.

"Pretty much." Kyle scanned her furrowed brow. "Mountains and borders don't interfere with them.

"Huh, who knew?" Casi's jaw dropped.

"Everyone over first grade," Jake reported.

Georgia smiled, enjoying the banter as she handed a present to Jake. "It may be too big, you're so much trimmer now!"

He smiled at the billowing sweater. "I suspect I'm down a size or two."

Kyle placed a wrapped box on Casi's lap. "My constellation!" She held up a diamond-studded, platinum necklace in the shape of the constellation Cassiopeia.

"Only the good parts of the legend. As beautiful as the queen, but without the vanity that had her banished." Kyle secured the clasp and whispered, "You shine brighter than any star."

Casi opened a gift from Georgia, revealing a handmade scarf and hat in a soft pink wool. "Is this alpaca?" She paled, and tears sprung to her eyes.

Peter chuckled when Georgia seemed confused. "Casi, we didn't kill the alpaca. We only shaved her for the wool. It grows back."

"Thank you, it's beautiful." Casi exhaled with relief.

"One more gift." Jake tossed a box to Casi.

"You got me a present?"

"It's not a big deal. I was with Olivia at the mall. She wrapped it." Jake fidgeted with his sleeve while Georgia and Peter exchanged glances.

Casi laughed when she discovered flannel pajamas with a monkey pattern. "That's awesome, Jake! He calls me Monkey all the time."

"She's like a crazy monkey, climbing around and yammering, trying to annoy me. She also needs to wear more clothing," Jake stated.

"Why are you crying?" Kyle wiped a tear from Casi's cheek.

"This is the first time it's felt like Christmas since my dad left," she said quietly. "My mom was always high and in bed for days around any holiday, but she would never let me go to my dad's. Dylan's Jewish, so we get Chinese food and watch movies. When I was with Alix, it was about attending the perfect party with celebrities."

Kyle hugged her. "This is how we do it here and now you're a part of our family and all the traditions."

Casi helped Georgia in the kitchen while the men built a fire and organized the bar for the guests. The table was exquisite, with candles and decorations cascading from every surface. She lost count of the friends and family who visited. Some came for drinks, while some stayed for dinner, and others dropped in for the array of desserts. She had taken care to choose an outfit she thought would be appropriate; a cocktail length, plum knit dress. She curled her hair and pulled it partially back, trying to appear more classic than edgy. Peter smiled and gave her a hug, whispering how beautiful she looked. Kyle beamed with approval while Jake nodded. She loved how expressive Georgia and Peter were, hugging and kissing her, and calling her Honey. The plethora of cousins and family became confusing, and she lost track of which side they originated from, forgetting names within minutes. She was shocked to discover the brother's biological cousins, not aware they kept in touch. She saw the similarity in the blue eyes and thought how generous the Jensen's were to open their home to everyone. The cousins were rougher, having grown up in a life far removed from the childhood provided for the brothers.

Peter introduced her to his friend Earl, who smiled and hugged her tenderly. He asked about Jake's family, wondering where Gail and the kids were. "Jake's divorced now, Earl," Peter reminded him.

"That's right. You told me, didn't you?"

Peter nodded, and Casi observed there seemed to be a lot of things Earl forgot throughout the dinner. When he came to say good-night, he asked again, "Who are you married to?"

"I'm married to Kyle, Jake's brother," she said.

"Peter's boys," he reiterated.

"Yes."

While they relaxed in the living room after everyone left, Jake poked at a log in the fireplace. "When were you going to tell us, Earl has dementia?"

Peter's shoulders slumped. "The episodes come and go. There were a lot of people here, and it's harder for him to keep track."

"What's the plan for him long term? With Ingrid gone, will he go live with his sons?" Kyle asked.

Peter set his jaw. "They don't get around much to see him. They're busy with their own families."

"He's their family!" Jake clenched his fists.

"He's my best friend. We grew up together and I'll take care of him. He'll move to the cottage by the river when he needs to." Peter's nostrils flared and Georgia wiped a tear as she nodded in agreement.

"How will you know when it's the right time to transition him?

Are you sure he's safe at home alone?" Jake set up a chessboard on the table.

"I've slowly been moving his things to make it easier. He's aware of what's going on and wants to have a say in it. His sons took a mortgage out on the house, so a retirement home is not an option, but he's not quite ready to walk away and let them have it," Peter said bitterly.

Kyle cleared his throat. "Dad, ten years ago, Earl insisted on lending me money to buy the building for the business. I didn't want it, but Libby convinced me it would keep his investment safe."

"Why was my sister involved?" Peter exclaimed.

Georgia smiled. "Libby has always looked out for Earl and I'm sure she understood Kyle would be the best person to protect his future. His children have never been concerned with his welfare."

"I paid the money back into an investment account and it's been earning interest all these years. Let me know if he needs access to it." Kyle put his hand out as Jake stormed toward him. "Libby asked me not to say anything until the time came to withdraw the funds."

"Did you know about Earl's condition?" Jake glared at him.

Kyle shrugged. "I suspected Earl might be faltering when I went by his house last year to borrow some tools. He had misplaced paperwork and Frankie was upset because he needed it to get the mortgage. Earl didn't understand what his son was doing, so I contacted Libby. She said Dad was already taking care of him."

Jake narrowed his eyes. "Why do you exclude me from these decisions? Do I not have a say in the business? Or this family?"

"We are equal partners. I don't oversee how you manage the building tasks and you have trusted me to handle the business end." Kyle grasped Jake's hand. "The money allowed us to buy the building rather than rent. Everyone profited from the deal. It wasn't a windfall, just an investment."

Peter nodded. "You did the right thing, Kyle. My sister respects your business knowledge, and she helped you both get started while she protected Earl." He moved a piece on the chessboard. "Jake, I knew I could lean on you when the time was right. Earl has always had a special bond with you, and I'll need you to help me get him settled in the cottage when his dementia progresses. I guess the best thing is to let the house go to his sons and let them deal with it?"

"They chose to get their inheritance early without regard for their father's welfare. No one knows about the investment and Earl will be well taken care of." Kyle nodded.

Casi tried to get comfortable on the couch but couldn't ease her back pain. She felt her mood keeping pace, becoming irritable when Jake shoved her over and stole her blanket. She jumped up and abruptly announced she needed to take a shower.

Jake sneered, "What's got her panties in a twist?"

"PMS," Kyle whispered. Jake shivered, and they both laughed, getting a stern look from Georgia.

Casi hoped a shower would help. Nausea gnawed at her, making her dizzy. She wondered if the car accident had reactivated damage from her broken pelvis, feeling a fire radiating through her groin. She told Kyle she wasn't in the mood for sex, but the internal pain and pressure were the real cause for her lack of desire. She grew concerned it might be more than period cramps and hoped her mistake with the pills hadn't caused an issue. The pregnancy test had been negative, and she prayed it hadn't been inaccurate. She undressed and the pain rapidly intensified, causing her to throw up. She held a cold, wet cloth to her face and tried to will it away, but it increased until it flared through her pelvis. A sudden sharp jab brought her to her knees with its intensity. She felt the dampness between her legs and reeled from the amount of blood gushing out. An immense fire seared through her body and she screamed for Kyle as she writhed on the floor.

Jake chuckled. "She probably found another spider."

When the second blood-curdling shriek came, Kyle jumped up, taking the stairs two at a time. "That's not a spider scream." He stopped in his tracks when he saw Casi on the floor, clutching her stomach and covered in blood from the waist down. He hollered for help, cradling her in his arms. Her skin was ablaze, and she cried in agony.

"Holy shit!" Jake surveyed the blood.

"Call an ambulance," Kyle ordered. Georgia ran in the bathroom and swaddled Casi in towels. "What's wrong with her?" he pleaded, guessing it was a mysterious female ailment.

"The ambulance is on its way." Jake knelt and brushed the hair from Casi's cheek. "You'll be ok."

Kyle carried Casi downstairs to wait, and they tucked a blanket over her. When he heard the siren, he rushed out the door to greet them, placing her on the gurney before they brought it out of the back. He climbed in and held her hand, asking the medic to give her something for the obvious pain.

Georgia surveyed the trail of blood in the snow with tears in her eyes. "Drive to the hospital and be with your brother."

When Jake arrived, he found Kyle sitting in the waiting area, wearing a blood-soaked t-shirt and wringing his hands. He pulled off his jacket and placed it tenderly around his brother's shoulders. "Have you heard anything?" Kyle shook his head, unable to speak.

Jake's phone rang, and he noted it was Lia. He wanted to ignore the call, but Kyle told him to answer. Kyle watched as he walked to an alcove and guessed he filled her in on Casi being in the hospital. Jake listened for a while, taking in whatever information Lia gave him. He suddenly became enraged. "Are you fucking kidding me?" He threw the phone and kicked the wall a few times for good measure before bending down and retrieving his cell. He stomped back and slumped in a chair beside Kyle.

"I take it that didn't go well?" Kyle assumed Lia had gone off on him for seeing other women, under the pretense of calling to say Merry Christmas.

"Lia thinks Casi is having a miscarriage because she apparently forgot to take her birth control pills since Hawaii." Jake's nostrils flared.

Kyle wrung his hands. "That is a possibility. I researched her symptoms because she has been experiencing a lot of back pain.

I'm not sure if I would prefer that or an STD, which is also an option."

"She's pregnant." Jake put his face in his hands.

"We don't know that." Kyle frowned.

"Not Casi, Lia." Jake's voice broke.

Kyle rubbed his back and exhaled. "Christ, not again!"

The doctor asked Kyle to speak with him in the hallway. He listened intently as the test results ruled out pregnancy and STD's, concluding she had an ovarian cyst which ruptured. "There will be severe scarring of her fallopian tube and since she already has a weakened pelvis from the car accident two years ago, pregnancy is not advised because it presents a significant risk."

"Neither of us want children. What's in her best interest? I need her to be healthy." Kyle evaluated the information.

The doctor nodded. "I recommend we perform a tubal ligation to prevent an accidental pregnancy in that case. It would eliminate birth control and there are no side-effects other than cramping and pelvic pain for a few days. We could harvest eggs in the future, although it will be difficult and risky for her to carry a child, so you should consider a surrogate. The cost is exorbitant, but it's not a decision you need to make now."

"Is the tubal ligation safe?" Kyle scanned the paperwork.

"We must perform a laparoscopic surgery for removing the cyst, and the procedure can be done at the same time."

Kyle's eyes welled as he signed the papers. "Protect her at all costs. She is everything to me."

The doctor squeezed his shoulder. "She will be fine."

Kyle returned to Jake and leaned against him while he shared the results. "I realize you're freaked out about Lia, but I can only focus on Casi."

"I'll have nine months to panic." Jake scratched his head in recollection of her insistence on being on the pill and realized she lied. "Or less."

Casi's eyes were glazed from the morphine when Kyle came in. He hated seeing her spaced out, reminding him of the last time she had been in the hospital, but thankful the pain had stopped. The doctor explained the issue and the procedure which had been performed after discussing it with her husband. Her eyes went wide as she tried to focus on Kyle. "How could you sterilize me without my permission?" She continued to cry, not letting him comfort her, and the doctor suggested he may want to wait in the hall while he gave her more information.

Jake heard the screaming and met him outside the room, witnessing his devastation. "I can't do anything right for her." Kyle clung to Jake.

They decided they should call Ava and ask if she could comfort Casi. Kyle hoped it wouldn't further piss her off since she refused to let him back in. Ava and Jack arrived a half hour later, and she slipped in the room while Jack escorted the brothers to the cafeteria. He put an arm around Kyle's shoulder as he stared at his coffee. "I don't understand her. I'm failing miserably at this marriage."

Jack patted him on the back. "Casi is a handful. Why do you think I only had one child? I knew from the minute she was born she would run circles around me." He smiled at Kyle. "You're doing fine. When she was about sixteen, there was a medical issue that no one wanted to share with me." He rolled his eyes. "She had cysts on her ovaries. Sonya couldn't be bothered to care, and Ava stepped in to help. She made the decision to allow Casi to go on the pill and I had a fit. I didn't feel it was her place, and we had a blowout fight about parenting. In the end I had to admit Ava was the only one focused on what was best for Casi while Sonya and I were self-involved." He sighed. "You made a choice based on her welfare. Thank you for putting her first." His eyes filled with tears. "I don't want a grandchild, only a healthy daughter."

"I have another child on the way if you change your mind." Jake sulked.

Jack cocked his head and listened to the details. "Women can be overwhelming at times."

8

PORNOGRAPHY

Kyle picked Casi up the next morning. She remained quiet and shivering with pain. He filled the prescription while she waited in the truck, head pressed against the side window. He yearned to take her hand and soothe her as they drove home in silence, and he was thankful he wouldn't be alone with her for long, overwhelmed by her emotions. Georgia waited on the steps, having been fully briefed by a tearful Kyle on her condition. She led Casi up the stairs and settled her in bed. Casi refused to eat and threw up twice. Kyle hovered in the background, waiting to be told what to do. Jake stayed out of the way, sharing secret looks with him as they helped Georgia prepare the evening meal.

"Maybe I should sleep in the guest room?" Kyle hesitated in the hall.

"She's your wife, you must try to console her." Georgia directed him in the room. Casi curled up in a tight ball, still sobbing pitifully. Georgia knelt beside her, easing back the covers as she placed a heating pad on her stomach. "Would you prefer for Kyle to sleep in the other room?"

"I want him here with me." Casi's voice quivered. Georgia gestured to the bed, indicating he should get in quickly. He stripped down to his underwear and carefully slid in beside her, holding the heating pad in place, which seemed to comfort her, somewhat. "Don't talk, ok?" she said weakly, making Georgia smile as she left the room. That was an easy promise for him to keep because he didn't know what to say. He held her throughout the night, glad when he felt her relax against him and fall asleep.

The next morning, Kyle got out of bed quietly, not wanting to wake her. Casi slept peacefully, and he prayed she felt better. Georgia made breakfast, and they sat at the kitchen table. "Thanks for taking care of Casi. I have no idea what I'm doing." Kyle stabbed at his eggs.

"It is a difficult time, especially so early in your marriage." Georgia put her hand on his. "She's in a lot of pain, but it's hard on her emotionally too."

"I tried to do the right thing." Kyle squeezed her hand.

"You did what you thought the situation warranted in her best interest because you think logically. Although she said she didn't want children, you took her choice away permanently."

Kyle put his head in his hands. "The doctor said it would be serious if she got pregnant. I was concerned she might screw up her pills again. I should've gotten a vasectomy. I reacted in the moment." He lifted his eyes to meet hers. "I was terrified she might die."

"Give her time to adjust. Marriage is a big step, and now one more thing has changed in her life."

He nodded, wishing he could go back in time and discuss it with her before he signed the papers. He knew he couldn't ask about the health or car insurance and needed to be patient. He paid the bill at the hospital, cringing at the cost with her poor coverage.

"Jake, you don't look well. Are you coming down with something?" Georgia noted as they moved to the living room.

Jake shrugged. "Yup, fatherhood."

Georgia sighed. "Is Olivia giving you trouble again?"

He rolled his eyes. "When isn't she? But she's not the problem this time. Lia is pregnant."

Peter squinted his eyes. "The girl from Seattle?"

"No, Peter, the woman he brought to Hawaii," Georgia seethed, angry at the news. "Lauren's sister."

Peter's jaw tightened. "I didn't realize you were serious with her. Is your divorce even final?"

"We're not serious. The divorce just became final last month, and I didn't want to get fucking tied down again!" Jake's voice boomed through the room and Casi came in quietly and slithered on Kyle's lap, wrapping her arms around him as he held her tenderly. "You kept Lia's pregnancy a secret and didn't tell me!" Jake wagged a finger at her.

"It wasn't my place to do it," Casi replied.

"Is there anything else I don't know?" Jake narrowed his eyes.

"Apparently, you don't know how to use a condom!" Casi pressed her cheek to Kyle's with a slight giggle. Peter slapped his knee and laughed as Georgia handed her a cup of coffee with a smile.

Peter regarded Jake, picking at his hands. "I'm unhappy with this news. I don't see how this improves your situation when you're already faltering."

"I'm a loser and a constant disappointment to you!" Jake squirmed in the recliner. Georgia tried to console him, but he pulled away. "Give up, Mom. All the love in the world is obviously not going to fix me. You made a mistake when you picked me. Be glad you got Kyle in the deal." She covered her face with her hands and burst into tears, rushing to the kitchen. Kyle threw a magazine at Jake and gestured for him to go apologize. Peter glared at him, indicating it wasn't a suggestion. Jake went to the kitchen and wrapped his arms around his mother. "I'm sorry I lashed out at you. I'm overwhelmed, and I'm freaking out. I didn't handle it well the first time around, and it might break me this time."

She nodded. "Jake, we love you and you've never been a disappointment. We'll help you do whatever you need to."

❧

Over the next few days, Casi barely ate, picking at her food and being unusually quiet. The pain and nausea were gone, and she pushed the procedure from her mind, refusing to talk about it. At breakfast on New Year's Eve, her phone rang constantly as it charged on the counter. She pushed her eggs around the plate, oblivious. Jake finally jumped up after the eighth time and answered, then handed it to her saying it was Alix. She glanced up with a blank stare and took the phone, moving to the hall. She informed Alix she had been in the hospital, not elaborating. The conversation escalated. "I don't know when I'm coming back! I said I'll be there, and they can fucking wait!"

Gazes were redirected to the unfinished meals on their plates as she returned to the table, slamming her phone on the counter. Kyle spoke first, "Why does Alix care when you return to LA?"

"I'm supposed to do an editorial he set up, and they want to shoot it as soon as possible." She sipped her coffee.

"An editorial? What magazine?" Georgia asked.

"I've never heard of it. It's for motorcycles or something." Casi shrugged. "I think it's called Edge?"

Kyle spit out his coffee. "You are absolutely not posing for that magazine!"

"I'll do what I want, stop trying to control me!" She bristled with anger.

"What the hell is Alix thinking trying to get you involved with that?" Kyle grabbed his laptop from the desk.

"Casi, it's a sleazy magazine," Jake insisted.

Kyle brought the computer to the table, displaying scantily clad women, suggestively posing on vehicles. "Why are you showing us pornography?" Georgia put a hand over the screen.

"Those are the kinds of pictures they put up in mechanic's shops. I agree with Kyle; this isn't a good fit for you." Peter cringed.

"I signed a contract. I'm committed," she lied, figuring her word to Alix was as solid as a contract. "I'll be fortunate to get any work with scars across my stomach." Her nostrils flared.

Kyle spun around to face her. "You have two minuscule incisions that were necessary for the removal of the cyst. The procedure was performed during the required surgery." He surveyed her rubbing her abdomen in defiance. "There's no way Mary will approve. This is the end of your career once you pose for this crap." Kyle raised an eyebrow, recalling her odd behavior. "How much trouble are you in?"

"Stop yelling at me! How dare you bring up Mary! You don't know anything." Casi dissolved into tears. "I hate being married and I hate you!" She bolted for the stairs. Kyle snapped the computer closed and grabbed his keys. Jake fell into step behind him as they stomped out to the truck while Georgia and Peter looked at each other wide-eyed.

Peter pushed himself back from the table and walked up the stairs. He knocked at the door and didn't wait for an answer. He sat on the edge of the bed and stroked Casi's back. "I love you like my own daughter. Consider how your father would feel about you posing for those pictures."

She looked at him with tear-filled eyes. "I'm overwhelmed by Kyle taking control of my life, it's too much. I can't breathe."

"He loves you and he's trying to be a good husband. He's used to overseeing his life, and Jake's. Stop pushing him away, you are breaking a good man. Remember our talk in the garden about commitment? You are not alone anymore, and your choices impact him." He touched his finger to her lips when she began to speak in anticipation of her words. "He chose the operation to save you, not to dominate you. It is tearing him up inside that he didn't consider other options."

"I understand that. Jake's not the only screw up; I'm in a big mess and I'm spinning out of control. I can't bring myself to tell Kyle."

"It's time to grow up and face your problems. Jake hasn't lost him yet. Be honest with him," Peter advised.

Georgia prepared dinner as Kyle entered the kitchen and helped himself to a beer, handing one to Jake. "Where's Casi?" He leaned against the counter with a sigh.

"In the living room with Dad, they've been in there all afternoon."

He could hear laughter and noted Peter on the sofa with his arm around Casi, curled up with a blanket. They had a bowl of popcorn and were laughing as they watched a ridiculous horror movie. Jake and Kyle locked eyes at the scene. Jake joined them on the sofa, pulling her blanket on his lap, as he grabbed a handful of popcorn. Kyle sat in the recliner, watching them. Casi smiled at him. "I'm not going to do the editorial."

9

———

LA LA LAND

They returned to Blackberry Falls in a contemplative silence, each considering what the year held for them. Jake turned to Casi as they approached the exit. "Did you kiss me at the bar out of pity because you knew about Lia?"

"You didn't think the kiss was romantic, did you?" Casi's eyes widened.

"I thought we were friends. I realize now it's a game to you."

"It is not a game, Jake. It killed me not to tell you about the pregnancy. I kissed you as a friend because I care about you." She slipped her hand in his. He nodded, the devastation radiating from him.

"We'll figure it out together." Kyle checked his watch and turned toward the wood shop. "We have more at risk now, but we have to consider what is best long term." He turned to Casi. "Has Lia indicated what she expects?"

"I don't know what she wants. She hasn't returned any of my texts or messages." Casi frowned with confusion about Lia's silence.

Kyle parked in front of the building and smiled at the tow truck driver from the dealership. Casi hoped it meant her car was fixed, feeling dependent without it. Kyle signed paperwork, then turned to Casi as she got out of the truck. "Here you go." He handed her a set of

57

keys and pointed to a sparkling ruby red compact SUV, with chrome trim.

She glanced at the beautiful car and started to cry. "No, Kyle. I don't want it." She pressed the keys back in his palm.

Jake scoffed, "You're a spoiled brat. What would you prefer? A Lexus?"

Kyle stormed in the building. "I give up!" He tossed the keys on Amy's desk without a greeting.

Casi stood outside looking at the car while she hugged herself against the cold. She peered in the window and noted the charcoal leather interior and panoramic sunroof, noticing her little bobble-head dog perched on the dashboard. She walked inside and smiled meekly at Amy before waiting at the painted yellow line. Heavy metal music blasted, and they did their best to ignore her. She waited patiently until Kyle finally switched off his saw and came over to her, turning down the music.

"I'm sorry. I expected my car, and I wasn't prepared." She put a hand on his chest.

"Whatever." He turned back to his project.

"Wait, Kyle!" She inhaled sharply, realizing she owed him a better explanation. "I can't afford it! I'm barely getting by as it is, and I can't take on a car payment." An understatement at best.

His eyes softened. "I can afford it. It's paid for and insured." He gave her a kiss on the forehead. "They couldn't salvage your car. I realize now I should have spoken to you about options, but I was excited to surprise you." He looked away. "I made the decision before everything happened."

"It's a wonderful surprise. I love the color and I appreciate you saving my little dog." She kissed him tenderly. "Thank you for taking care of me. Is it alright if I take it for a test drive? I want to talk to Lia."

He squeezed her hand. "It's your car. You don't need to ask permission. Enjoy it." He grinned. "It has heated seats."

She took the keys from Amy's desk with a smile and walked outside. The leather smelled amazing, and her bobble-head seemed at home in the luxurious interior. She flicked on the heated seat and settled back in the warmth as she drove to Coffee Junction. She was glad to see the rush had passed and hoped to get a chance to talk with Lia.

"Can you believe the asshole hung up on me when I told him?" Lia rolled her eyes as she poured an espresso drink.

"Actually, I can. That was a terrible way to tell him."

"Why are you defending him?" Lia narrowed her eyes.

"I was in the hospital, fearing I might die. The timing was bad for your announcement. Why did you tell him about my pills? You knew I wasn't pregnant. Kyle was distraught, and I don't think you understand everything we went through," Casi explained.

"Kyle is always devastated about you. It must be nice to have someone care so much. It's too bad that's not enough and you need Jake as well. Tell me, was it difficult to screw them both at their parents' house? Or were you going to include Jake in your disgusting threesome?" Lia slammed the milk jug on the counter.

"Lia! Why are you being so cruel?" Casi blushed from the accusation.

"You forgot to log out of Facebook at my house. I read your messages to your best friend Anna about kissing Jake at the bar and getting him ready for her." Lia threw Casi's coffee in her face. "Go back to LA. Kyle was better off before he met you and he deserves more than a conniving slut as his wife. I'm sure it won't last, so save him the pain of another heartbreak."

Casi ran out of the coffee shop and jumped in her car, shaking. She peeled out of the driveway, almost hitting another vehicle, getting flipped off by the driver. She skidded to the side of the road and logged into Facebook and changed her password. She contemplated her options as her phone rang. "Darling, I heard you were in the hospital," Sonya said.

"An ovarian cyst ruptured, and I had a tubal ligation!" Casi dissolved into tears for the millionth time.

"Well, that's drastic. I'm aware you don't want children, but you should have waited to make such a permanent decision."

"Kyle signed the papers while I was sedated. The doctor told him it was the best choice."

"I warned you he would attempt to control you!" Sonya said triumphantly. "He took away your reproductive rights because it suited his agenda. When are you coming back to LA?" Casi told her about the car. "It's a lovely gesture to get you a car in exchange for your womanhood, but when will you realize he's trying to own you? The only thing that's yours is the loft, and you'll lose it if you can't pay the mortgage. I'm sure that would make him happy to have complete control over you."

"Mom, I promised Kyle I wouldn't do the editorial. He says it's a sleazy magazine." Casi blotted the coffee from her shirt.

"Now he's making decisions on your career? You don't have any other offers on the table. Grow up and realize what your options are."

Casi drove straight through to LA, stopping for coffee six times, and to use the bathroom several more. After almost seventeen hours, she was wired. She sent a text to Kyle when she stopped in Portland, simply stating, "Gone to LA, not sure when I'll be back." She knew she should have told him in person, but her emotions spun out of control. She realized he probably thought she was mad about the car, although it had not stopped her from taking it. It was beautiful, roomy, and had great traction on the road. She just didn't feel she deserved it.

She arrived at the loft and sent Alix a text to meet her, then grabbed a beer and headed for the shower. When she came out of the bathroom, Alix was there and acting strangely. He told her to dress in leggings and a t-shirt and reminded her to take off her rings. She put them in the small carved box Kyle had made for her, feeling like she was cheating on him.

The shoot was in a basement down a side alley. She had a bad feeling from the time she arrived. Girls lounged on makeshift sofas, texting and smoking joints, shadowed by the dim, unprofessional lighting. "Where did you bring me?" Casi's eyes widened with alarm.

"It's cool, it only appears sketchy." Alix fidgeted with the zipper on his leather jacket, belying his claim.

"Damn, you're hot," the photographer admired.

"Darling." Sonya gave her an air-kiss. "You made the right choice."

"I don't want to be here, Mom," she whispered.

"You'll be fine. It's a lot of money," Sonya reminded her. "You need this to pay your mortgage."

"Sonya, I'm unsure about this." Alix blanched.

Sonya shushed him. "You'll get your cut, now back off." She yanked the waistband of Casi's leggings and clucked her tongue. "I hope you brought concealer. We wouldn't want those disgusting scars to distract people from your glorious breasts."

They led Casi to a desk and put paperwork in front of her to sign. She cringed as she wrote her name on the line, sickened by her actions. They handed her a check, and she shoved it in her purse without looking at it. Sonya smiled at her own check; an incentive paid for booking Casi.

Alix kept his hand on the small of her back protectively, leading her to the changing area behind a torn curtain.

"I can't do this," she pleaded when he handed her a swimsuit and pulled the curtain closed.

"It's no different from any other shoot. You won't be fully nude, I promise," he assured her.

"It's a low-class magazine. I don't want to be in it." She hyperventilated, considering Mary's reaction. She realized her marriage would end and Kyle's family would hate her. Lia's words had sealed this fate. She did cause misery and ruin lives, and Kyle had been better off. She would take nothing from him and return the car. She would leave Jezebel because she couldn't even take care of a cat properly. "Who's going to hire me now?"

"Take the money and get the hell out of LA. Face it, this is where

your career ends. You wouldn't be here if you didn't know it already."
Alix kissed her on the forehead.

She had to say she had given it her all; shown up to castings and taken every opportunity to get ahead. She had reached the end of the road. He was right, she needed to take the money and get the hell out; sell the loft and maybe move to Bellingham or perhaps go back to Burnaby. She could start over with a little money left. She tried to focus on that as she slipped on the tiny red bikini. Poorly designed and obviously meant for what it revealed rather than as a functional suit. She dabbed concealer over her scars and Alix nodded with approval. He guided her to a motorcycle while an assistant directed her to lean against it. She felt like a beginner model as she posed stiffly, unsure what to do with her hands. They took several photos, adjusting the bikini to reveal as much as possible. She changed to another bathing suit; a one-piece, pretty much held together with string. They asked her to sit on the motorcycle, knees out, and chest forward. She was concerned the suit rode so far up; it exposed her entire backside. They liked the look. After a few more shots, Sonya sauntered over and brushed the hair from Casi's face. "Darling, you need to relax." She forced a small pill on Casi's tongue and held her mouth closed with her thumb, grasping her chin. Casi shook her head but Sonya refused to release her until she swallowed.

She changed for a third time to a black lace-up swimsuit, plunging to her bikini line. As she came out of the changing area, she noticed Alix walking up the stairs. She screamed for him, but the large, muscular man beside him prevented him from returning. The photographer told her not to worry, he had a phone call. He handed her a cocktail and told her to relax.

She began to feel light-headed, slightly nauseous, and hot. Her skin prickled with sensitivity, making the material burn her skin. The assistant led her to a new motorcycle and helped position her on top, fixing her hair around her face and opening the swimsuit to reveal most of her breasts. She felt euphoric as she reclined, and the room started to spin. The rest of the shoot was blurry as she faded in and out of reality. When she left, she glimpsed Alix smoking by the door, waiting for her outside. He came toward her, but the photographer grabbed her by the elbow and one of the stocky assistants intervened, telling Alix the photographer would take Casi home. She heard Alix say, "Sonya, don't do this!" followed by her mother's laugh. Then everything went black.

Kyle's cell rang, and he noticed Casi's number and felt like throwing it. He hadn't heard from her all day and didn't even know if she had made it to LA safely. "You made it ok? Why did you leave in such a hurry?" He monitored his speech to subdue an argument.

"It's Alix. I have Casi's phone."

"Why are you calling me?" Kyle grabbed for the workbench as his stomach lurched and he waited for the tragic news.

"I messed up. Bad. I need you to come to LA and get Casi." Alix broke down.

"What did you do? Where is she?"

"Please get here soon, she needs you. She's at the loft. I gotta get out of here. I'm leaving for South Africa tonight."

"You son of a bitch, what happened?"

"I'm sorry." Alix hung up.

Kyle called the phone several more times, but it went to voicemail. He yelled to Jake and told Amy they would be away for a few days, asking her to feed the animals, as he gave her the keys and money from his wallet. Jake shut down the equipment and waited by the truck, hearing Kyle's voice fracture. He didn't know who had been on the phone, but prayed they weren't on their way to the morgue. They had been on the road for several hours before Kyle could tell him about the phone call. They drove straight through, not stopping to sleep or eat, grabbing coffee in each state.

They arrived late in the afternoon the next day and double-parked in front of her building. Kyle raced up the stairs to Casi's loft and pounded on the door. He could hear music, but no other sound. He banged one more time, calling her name. When she didn't respond, he backed up and kicked the lock with the heel of his boot until it broke loose, and the door flung open. A sob caught in his throat when he saw Casi in a discarded heap on the bed. He rushed to her side and brushed the hair from her face, begging her to wake up. Her eyelids twitched, and he exhaled, placing his forehead to hers and letting his tears fall on her mottled skin. He noticed she wasn't wearing her wedding ring and his heart broke.

"Not dead?" Jake asked with relief.

"Probably drunk or high." Kyle surveyed the scene; a condom wrapper tangled in the sheets, two glasses of whiskey and a joint on the nightstand. The bedding was in disarray and crushed beer cans littered the room while lines of white powder were accented with an open bottle of Jack Daniels. "Fuck!" Kyle launched the bottle at the cabinets, immediately sorry when he saw the mark it left.

Jake strolled to Casi and tried to rouse her. She cried out and pushed his hand away, shivering in the remnants of a torn pink negligee. He eased her upright, and sat beside her, adjusting the material to provide more coverage. She peered at him through slits in her eyelids, unsure of her surroundings.

Kyle regarded her sadly, kicking a beer can with the toe of his boot. "Jake, I can't handle this. Please take care of her." He flew out the door without another word.

Jake embraced her tightly, smoothing his hand over her frail frame. "Monkey, what did you do?" Casi's head fell back, and she stared at him with glazed eyes, unable to form a sentence. "Let's get you cleaned up. You smell like cigarettes and something foul." He carried her to the bathroom and adjusted the water temperature. "I'm not getting frisky." Jake eased her negligee off and coaxed her in the shower, propping her against the wall for support. He noticed her scars were inflamed and bruises decorated her arms and throat, with a burgeoning black eye. "Clean everywhere," he instructed. A wave of nausea enveloped him, and his anger swelled. He took a deep breath and stormed to the kitchen and swept up the glass. He tore the sheets from the bed and threw them in a pile, then pulled clothes from the closet and folded them on the bed. He texted Kyle, "Bring boxes and tape, a new lock, and wood filler." He checked on Casi and cringed as she held her mouth open under the stream of water. He watched her struggle with the shampoo bottle and wondered what the hell she had taken. He reached in and assisted her to lather her hair, getting wet in the process. "Scrub your private parts." He averted his eyes but witnessed blood circling the drain. "Oh, God, Casi. What the hell happened to you?" His anger dispelled as he watched her quiver, disoriented in the cubicle of the shower. He helped her condition her hair, and she adhered herself to the wall, finding comfort in the glossy tile. He warmed the water and directed the spray across her back, watching her relax.

Kyle came back carrying tools and supplies. "Where's Casi?" His eyes were red with sorrow.

"Shower." Jake began taping boxes.

"How long has she been in there?"

"About an hour. I wanted to make sure she came out clean."

Kyle smiled meekly, thankful for his brother's assistance. "You're wearing my t-shirt."

"Mine got wet when I washed her hair. She is pretty much useless. Did you know how many of your t-shirts there were here?"

"She steals them." Kyle took a deep breath and entered the bathroom. He grabbed a towel from the rack and braced himself to face her. He glanced over the bruises and inflamed scar as he turned the water off.

Casi gravitated to the towel he held, pupils dilated and a blank expression. "Kyle?" she asked with confusion. "Where's Alix?"

"Was Alix here?"

"He left me there." Casi collapsed in his arms.

"Where did he leave you?" She stared off into space again and he gave up trying to ask her.

"I found this in her purse." Jake handed him a check for twenty thousand dollars from Edge magazine.

"She did the shoot! That's what Alix is sorry for; he set up the damned thing and left her for those bastards." Kyle fumed.

"Why would he do that? I thought they were friends."

"He probably got paid for it. I think their business deal went sour, and he panicked because his source of income dried up." Kyle surveyed Casi standing at the window, wrapped in a towel, mesmerized by the building across the street. "Come away from there." He directed her to the chair. He noticed backward writing on the window and read it aloud, "Thank you." with a heart drawn in lipstick. *Did her lover write that? No, he would have left it on the nightstand,* he thought with disgust. He regarded the building across from them, remembering the telescope.

"Do you think we should call the police?" Jake asked.

Kyle shook his head. "I'm worried she may be involved in things we wouldn't want the authorities alerted to."

"I think we should take her for an exam to make sure everything is ok." Jake grasped Kyle's arm.

Kyle noted Casi blinking at the ceiling. "Do you think she has brain damage?" he asked with genuine concern.

Jake chuckled. "No. The other kind of exam. There was blood in the shower. She may have been assaulted."

Kyle wiped his eyes with the back of his hand. "We need to take her home." He shifted his gaze to the nightstand. "Alix was here." He grabbed her phone and punched in a code.

"You figured out the password?" Jake asked.

"I've always known it. I've respected her privacy until now." He glared at her as she tried to focus on the flowers of the chair. He read the texts to and from Alix; Casi insisting she wouldn't do the shoot. Alix kept referring to the money and how she needed it to get out of her financial mess. He saw a call from Sonya, roughly at the time she would have left for LA. "What do you want to bet her mother is involved?"

Jake nodded. "Maybe that's who gave her the drugs?"

He noted the last text, "The shoot is on East Street at the corner of Rochester. I'll pick you up, so you don't get lost."

Casi's reply, "I'm at the loft, come meet me."

He found nothing else of interest. "Can you distract the zombie? I want to search through her computer." Jake moved Casi to the bar and dumped silverware on the counter. She reached for the shiny objects and started stacking them. Kyle tried not to smile, thinking what a good father Jake was.

"Lets Google her symptoms and figure out what drugs she's on," Jake suggested. They determined from the clenching of her jaw, disorientation, and heightened senses, she may have taken Ecstasy or a blend of MDMA. They prepared themselves for the effects of her coming down.

"Here comes the nausea." Kyle winced as Casi staggered toward the bathroom. Jake reoriented her, almost reaching the toilet before she threw up. "Did she make it?"

"Not quite." Jake sighed and wiped his boot.

Kyle sorted through her desk, deciding he had been respectful of her privacy long enough. Her recent behavior indicated something was very wrong. He found a small fire-safe and popped it open with his pocketknife. It contained her passport, social security card, citizenship papers, Canadian paperwork, about two hundred dollars in cash, and a notebook with passcodes for her accounts. He wondered where her rings were, hoping she hadn't left them at the shoot. He pulled up the accounts listed in the book. After the sixth credit card, he could see the seriousness of her debt. She barely had a hundred dollars in her savings account and her checking account would be overdrawn after the mortgage came out. It made sense why she panicked. She wasn't behind on payments, but a review of deposits showed she hadn't gotten income for the last three months. He understood her motivation for doing the shoot; the money would go a long way to paying down her bills and keeping her afloat.

He created a spreadsheet and detailed her accounts in the columns, putting together an estimate of what she owed and when the payments were due. He entered her banking information in his personal account and transferred enough money to cover the mortgage and any pending bills. He used her social security to access her credit record, figuring he might as well have the full picture. Her credit could be fixed, too much debt, but she made her payments on time. He contemplated her reaction to the new car and her resistance to be added to his accounts. He searched through the drawers, locating files on the loft and called a real estate company to list it for sale. He watched her resisting Jake's attempts to put on clothes and hoped she had finally hit rock bottom.

"Why is everything on the bed?" She poked at a pile of socks.

"We're taking you home," Jake said tenderly. She pushed away the shirts he offered. "Where did you move your t-shirts?"

"Put on something of hers." Kyle clenched his jaw.

Jake took off the shirt he wore and slipped it on her. She smoothed it over her chest, wrapping her arms tightly around herself. "I guess I'll have to wear my wet one since you want to play games." Jake raised an eyebrow.

Kyle exhaled and threw him a t-shirt from a bag at his feet. "I want to make the repairs tonight and get this place on the market tomorrow." Jake nodded, and he ran a hand over the door jamb. "Thanks for being here with me. I couldn't have handled it on my own."

"That's what brothers are for," Jake chuckled, knowing he usually needed Kyle's help. "Let's order a pizza and get to work."

Kyle stood at the doorway, watching Casi tremble at her reflection in the mirror with tears streaming down her face. "Where are my rings?" She twisted her bare finger.

He wanted to wrap his arms around her, but her betrayal cut too deep. "We want to get packed up tonight so we can leave in the morning."

She directed her eyes to his image in the mirror. "Ok."

10

OUR GIRL

They worked late into the night, packing the loft and filling the vehicles with her belongings. Kyle sidestepped the offending bed and slumped in a chair for a few hours of tormented sleep, overwhelmed by exhaustion and emotions. He stumbled to the shower and changed to clothing he had left at the loft, handing Jake clean items. They walked to the truck and Kyle grasped Casi's arm, turning her to face him. "I'm aware of everything. I've gone through your files and accounts." She nodded, too mortified to speak, and slid on to the bench seat, twisting her hands as they drove. Kyle pulled the truck over suddenly. "Get out."

Casi looked up and down the street, confused why they were stopping, then started to cry when she saw the sign for the clinic. Kyle filled out the paperwork and requested they both be tested for all STD's, plus a drug screen on Casi.

"How do you get one of these things?" Jake peered over his shoulder.

"You've never had an STD test?" Kyle realized he had been married since twenty-two and handed him a form. "It probably would be a good idea, especially after you had sex with a random woman in Hawaii."

Jake nodded, thinking it would be prudent after having sex with Sonya. "Ask about the exam for Casi," he whispered.

When they were called, they each sat down at the long counter, divided by privacy screens, and held out their right arms. Kyle glared at Casi while he had his blood drawn, disgusted she had put him in this position. "Oh Honey, you're dehydrated; I'm having trouble finding a vein," Casi's nurse said, poking her several times. Kyle walked to the vending machine and came back with a bottle of water, handing it to her without a word. The nurse rubbed Casi's arm with sympathy, picking up on Kyle's reaction to a cheating wife. She did a swab of Casi's cheek, watching the tears roll down her face. She frowned at the bruising, glancing at Kyle, who turned away. She drew the blood in silence and informed them they would have results in about a week and could check them online. She opened a door to the back hallway and indicated Casi should come for an exam.

"No." Casi clasped her knees to her chest.

"My brother will go with her." Kyle shoved Jake forward.

Jake glared at Kyle. "This is completely out of my comfort zone!"

"I can't hear it firsthand," Kyle hissed in his brother's ear.

Jake stood to the side of the examination table as Casi removed her leggings and underwear. He helped her on the table and covered her with a paper sheet and held her hand while they waited for the doctor. "My sister-in-law was at a party and we're unsure if she was sexually assaulted."

The doctor nodded, briefly inspecting the bruises and the traumatized appearance. Jake held her in his arms as the internal exam began. She winced, then cried out. "She has bruising on her pubic bone." The doctor relayed. "She's very thin."

"She is." Jake felt her ribs beneath his fingers. He told the doctor about the blood in the shower, adding she had a tubal ligation recently.

"To be blunt, someone got rough with her, but there is no sign of intercourse. The blood may have been from the procedure, or external trauma from the attempted assault, which would explain the bruising as well. Take her home and feed her."

Jake thanked the doctor as he held Casi against his chest, letting her cry. He helped her get dressed and led her outside.

Kyle leaned against the wall and scowled at them as they came out. "Well?" Jake explained what the doctor said, and Kyle grabbed Casi by the shoulders, speaking harshly. "Do you realize this is my worst fear for you? Everyone worried about you cheating, but my concern was that you would get raped by some asshole who took your flirting too far. At least if you had cheated, it would have been your choice!" He shook her, trying to get a reaction.

"Kyle, that's enough!" Jake pushed him back.

"She can't even grasp why I'm upset." Kyle stormed to the truck.

They drove to a diner and Jake scooted in the booth. Kyle sat beside him and focused on the menu. Casi picked at the bandage on her arm, distracted by the sensation on her skin. "Stop! You look like a junkie," Kyle said flatly. She stabbed at her food, only taking a small bite and barely touching her coke. "Casi, eat!"

Jake shoved him out of the way to access Casi. "Take a couple of bites." She took a mouthful, unable to swallow. The waitress came back, eyeing Casi and the tears on her face. "Can we have a chocolate milkshake, please?" Jake requested.

"It's all in her head," Kyle hissed.

"Maybe. But it could be from the drugs. You have no idea how much they gave her and how that shit messes you up."

The waitress brought the shake, and Jake held the glass as Casi took a sip. "Better?"

"A little." She shivered.

Jake drank from the glass and held it out to Kyle. "Want some?" Kyle glared at Casi and she leaned into Jake, feeling his wrath. "Stop eyeballing her!" Jake threw a spoon at him.

"How's the shake, Honey?" The waitress asked.

"Good, thanks," Jake answered for her.

"Maybe give her some water?" The waitress suggested. He nodded, but Casi refused to take a sip.

The waitress leaned in, touching her hand lightly, asking if she was ok. "She's fine," Kyle snapped, then realized he was being a jerk to a woman showing concern to someone crying at breakfast. "She's selling her loft and leaving LA, and that's hard for her. We have had a tough morning."

The waitress nodded. "Honey, you're young and gorgeous; get out of this town before it eats you alive, or ten years from now you'll find yourself working here." Kyle paid the bill, leaving a hundred-dollar tip for the sound advice.

"I'm going to throw up," Casi blurted. Jake grabbed napkins and rushed her outside, making it to a bush just in time.

He held her hair back and kept one arm around her waist to prevent her from falling. He wiped her face and kissed her cheek. "Bet you'll never do those drugs again, huh?" She leaned her head against his chest, shaking and convulsing.

They went to the real estate office to list the loft and Kyle left them the keys. He explained they were returning to Washington and would like to handle everything by phone. The realtor informed him the market was slow for condos, but things could turn around. He drove down East Street and turned to Casi as they neared the corner of Rochester. "Does any of this look familiar?"

She glanced up from her hand, still troubled by her missing rings, and gasped when she saw the red awning above the entrance to the basement. Kyle pulled over and parked the truck in front of a fire hydrant. "Why are we here?" She adhered herself to the seat.

"We're returning the check in exchange for the photos. I don't care if you signed a contract, I'm not letting you get treated this way. You think I'm controlling, but at least I care about your best interest." He pulled her out of the truck behind him.

She directed him to the basement door, shivering at the memory of the day before. "This place is sketchy as hell." Jake surveyed the room.

A weathered, gray-haired man greeted them rudely, asking what they wanted. He recognized Casi and narrowed his eyes, informing them the photographer had not shown up again after leaving with her. Kyle handed him the check and asked for the photos. The man scoffed and threw the check back, refusing the deal. Kyle tore it up and grabbed the man by the collar. With a sharp blow, Jake knocked out a stocky assistant who tried to intervene.

As the fight ensued, a small hand touched Casi on the sleeve. The photographer's assistant, who had kindly helped her when she staggered around the set the day before, handed her an envelope containing the contract, a flash drive, and proofs. "Get out of here now and never come back." Casi bolted up the stairs, yelling for the brothers.

They burst into the sunlight, followed by shouting and an explosive vibration. Jake yanked open the door of the truck and pushed Casi inside, before turning to see Kyle collapse to the ground, blood gushing from below his right rib. Time stopped as Jake ran back and fell to his knees, pressing his palm to the gunshot wound. Casi called 911, dissolving into tears as her legs buckled and she crawled over to Kyle.

"Don't you dare leave me," Jake demanded.

"We got the pictures. Take care of our girl," Kyle breathed as his eyes fluttered closed and he went limp in Jake's arms.

11

PARALYZED

They waited for an update while Kyle was taken to surgery. Casi balled up her blood-soaked sweatshirt, clinging to the hope he would pull through. "Jake." She touched his arm as he struggled to control his breathing.

He pulled away. "Don't, Casi! If he dies, you'll have killed both of us."

"I'm sorry!" She crumpled in the corner of the room.

The minutes ticked by, stretching to hours. Jake brought her water and gently rubbed her back, letting his anger subside as he felt her delicate frame shake with sobs.

"Mrs. Jensen?" The doctor repeated as Casi stared at the wall until Jake squeezed her arm.

"They are talking to you." Jake guided her to a chair.

"The bullet struck several inches below your husband's right rib. It tore the muscle significantly but didn't hit any organs. He'll need to be in the hospital for a week or more, so we can ensure he doesn't tear the stitches. Infection is our biggest concern." He explained Kyle wouldn't be able to use his right arm for at least a month and would be sore for a while. Casi stopped listening and pushed past the doctor to the room, throwing herself at the bed. "Mrs. Jensen! He just came out of surgery!" Jake chuckled as she scampered in bed beside Kyle. He touched his brother's face tenderly and fought back tears. "He's sedated from the surgery. He'll wake up soon," the doctor informed them, giving up on moving Casi.

❧

Jake woke to pressure on his hand. He smiled and squeezed Kyle's hand back. "I guess I fell asleep waiting for you to wake up. Thanks for not dying."

"You're welcome. I knew you couldn't live without me."

"That's twice now. You're taking years off my life."

"Ugh, I'm not paralyzed, am I?" Kyle strained to move.

Jake chuckled. "Nope, only a sleeping monkey cutting off your circulation. Do you want me to wake her up?"

Kyle sighed. "It's easier when she's asleep."

"It will get better. This is the 'for worse' part of your vows." He held his palm out with Casi's rings. "Ready to put them back on? I saw you put them in your pocket at the loft."

"It would be less painful to not love her."

"I would rather have a drugged-out wife who royally screwed up, than another baby on the way with a woman who despises me." Jake carefully slid the rings back on Casi's finger.

Her eyes fluttered open and tears escaped when she noticed them. "We've had enough tears for a while." Kyle kissed her cheek and gazed at her, finally able to make eye contact.

"I'm sorry," she whispered.

He exhaled. "Let's go home and figure it out from there, ok?"

"Home sounds good." She threw her arms around his neck.

"I need you to move now," he directed.

Jake lifted her off the bed. "Why don't we have something to eat while Kyle gets the feeling back in his arm?"

Kyle grabbed her hand. "Eat a proper meal. I want to go home, and you need to drive your car. Please cooperate with us. I'm tired of arguing."

76

"I will," Casi promised.

Jake placed a sandwich and banana in front of her and twisted the lid off her water. "Eat all of this and we'll head back."

She took a bite of the sandwich. The bread was dry and tasteless, but she forced it down her throat to prove her commitment. She smiled at him sheepishly. "Thanks for taking care of me. You're an amazing friend."

"I told you in Hawaii you would get me in the deal. I keep my promises."

"Do you think Kyle will leave me?"

"No, but give him time to take it all in. You've pushed him beyond his limits, and it crushed him to find you at the loft."

She shivered. "I'm ready to make Washington my home."

"You'll be happy there." Jake took her hand. "Let Kyle fix things. It's what he does best. Resistance is futile."

"I hoped I could figure it out on my own..."

"The plus side of marriage is you are no longer alone. You have a partner now." He walked with her back to the room. "She consumed a terrible sandwich, banana, and a bottle of water without chucking."

Kyle grinned. "Good job."

The nurse came in and he insisted she remove the catheter. He instructed Jake to help him dress while the nurse ran to get the doctor. "Mr. Jensen, we do not advise you to be out of bed. You have stitches and are extremely bruised. You need at least a week to heal enough before you should be moved," the doctor pleaded.

"I can lounge around at home. I'm sick of this town," Kyle said firmly, not mentioning they had a seventeen-hour drive. The doctor realized he wouldn't take his advice and gave Casi a list of care instructions and a prescription for painkillers and antibiotics.

They propped him up on the passenger side of her car with pillows, making sure the seatbelt didn't press against the wound. "We'll follow you. Take it slow in case of ice." Kyle rolled his eyes. "We need to stop for gas, she's on empty."

Jake knocked on her window before she could get out of the car at the gas station. "Wrong side. Pull over to that one." He pointed to another pump.

Kyle shook his head. "How did you drive all the way to LA without noticing that?" She fought back tears, understanding it would irritate him further if she cried. He took her hand. "See the arrow beside the tank on your dash? That indicates which side to fill up on."

"Do you want to stop for the night in Ashland? It's about ten hours." Jake cleaned her windshield and checked the fluids.

"I would prefer to drive straight through if we can. I'm desperate to get home." Kyle popped a pain pill and took a sip of water. "Wake me if you need anything." As they left California, she shivered, hoping the worst was behind her. She watched Jake's indicator light to see when they would pull over for coffee or gas, glad he kept a good pace.

"Can you make it another seven or so hours?" Jake asked when they reached Ashland.

"I just need coffee." She suppressed a yawn. They headed through the pass slowly, carefully maneuvering the steep grade in the dark. As they descended, the car skidded on a patch of ice. "Kyle!" she gasped, unsure how to correct the inevitable spin out, as the fear paralyzed her.

Kyle snapped to attention and assessed what to do. "You're ok. Take your foot off the accelerator and don't use the brake, yet." He put one hand on the steering wheel after he switched the car to low gear. "Good, now lightly pump the brake and we'll turn out of the spin as we continue down the hill."

"It's too fast. I'm going to hit Jake." She braced herself.

"Jake slowed down on purpose to help you maintain your speed. It's only paint," he said as the bumpers collided. "My truck is a lot heavier and it will keep you safe." As the grade leveled out, she got the car back under control. "Take the next exit for the rest stop." Kyle texted Jake. She found a spot and put the car in park, still shaking. "You did great," he praised.

Jake came over and opened her door. "Are you ok?" She burst into tears as he hugged her. "I bet that scared the shit out of Kyle."

"A little. I'm glad we were in this car instead of that bug. We would have been over the side of the mountain for sure."

Casi wiped her eyes. "This is a fabulous car, Kyle. I'm sorry I was ungrateful." He took her hand and gave it a squeeze. He realized they had a long road ahead of them to fix their marriage, but he knew without a doubt how much he loved her.

Amy jumped up from the sofa when they traipsed in, disheveled, with Kyle obviously wounded. They told her they would explain it later and she should take the next day off and return to work on Monday. Kyle called his parents, giving them a brief recap of the shooting incident, explaining they had been packing Casi's belongings to move her to Washington when it happened.

Jake suggested they unload the truck, insisting they could handle it while Kyle rested. He observed the boxes of clothes coming in the bedroom and tried not to appear alarmed. "I'll sort through it this week, I promise." Casi bit her bottom lip.

"It's fine. There's only one thing I can't have in here right now." Kyle surveyed the pile.

"Alix's painting," she surmised.

"Jake can take it to the shop tomorrow and store it."

"My pine hutch is the only thing I want and maybe some pillows in the living room? Can we store the other furniture for now?" She shifted her weight as she stood before him.

"Put things how you want them and take the rest to the shop. Casi, this is your home and I want you to feel comfortable."

Jake shrugged as Casi arranged the large colorful pillows around the living room. "Looks girly. I guess that's good." He walked in the bedroom. "I'm going to stay over in case you need anything."

Kyle smiled, realizing his injury had been traumatic for Jake. "Thanks. I'll feel better with you here."

"I'll take a shower. Do you want your wife to give you a sponge bath?"

"Casi, how long until I can take a shower?" Kyle turned to her with alarm.

"One week." She rifled through her notes.

"You're going to stink in a week." Jake shuddered.

"Can't I put duct tape on the stitches?" Kyle raised an eyebrow.

"Pretend you're camping." When Jake went in the bathroom, she came over and sat on the edge of the bed. "Can I sleep in here with you?"

"We have hit a rough patch, but we'll fix it and our marriage will become stronger. You belong beside me, always."

A tear slid down her cheek. "I'm sorry. It got out of hand."

"Please stop lying to me and come clean about the business and your debts. You're fighting me for control, but you're running around in circles and creating more issues," he warned.

"I'm completely defeated and have no idea what to do next."

"Take some time off and breathe. I can cover all the expenses. We'll figure out where to go from there. You are safe here."

"I've modeled since I turned seventeen. I don't know what else to do. I thought the Sand and Surf deal would be a good business opportunity."

"So, it went under?"

"Pretty much. Johan never told us he had other investors, and they were in receivership." She stared at her hands.

"Do you understand what that is?"

She shook her head. "Only that I haven't gotten money in months. Alix doesn't think we'll ever get any."

"It's problematic. We can have the attorney read through your contract and see what can be done to protect your interest in the company. Relax for now and let me handle it."

"I really screwed things up."

"There's only one direction to go, up." Kyle squeezed her hand.

They all slept through the arrival of Georgia and Peter, but happily awoke to the aroma of coffee. Jake stretched on the sofa and smiled at his mother before going to check on Kyle. "The parents are here," he said.

"Help me to the sofa. I don't want them to think I'm an invalid." Kyle reached out for his assistance. Casi brought Kyle coffee and set it on the side table, handing him his pills with a glass of water.

"How did this happen?" Georgia fretted. "First, Jake is attacked, and now Kyle is shot?"

Casi felt the anger emanating from Peter, accusing her with an icy glare. She swallowed hard and confessed. "It's my fault. I did that photo shoot, and it all went to hell. They had to come get me and things got rough."

"Casi!" Peter yelled. "You promised not to do it!"

"I couldn't get out of it!"

"You betrayed Kyle!" Peter fumed.

"Dad!" Kyle fumed. "That's between us."

"She may be your wife, but she's part of this family, and she needs to be accountable for her actions."

Jake rushed to Casi and pulled her close. "She went through hell over there. Stop making her feel worse." She clung to him as he whispered in her ear and rubbed her back.

Kyle whispered, "They bonded in LA."

"Kindred spirits," Peter scoffed. "What needs to be done to fix this disaster?"

Jake sat down with Casi beside him and handed her a cup of coffee. "We've already taken care of it. That's when Kyle got shot. We have the pictures and we returned the check."

Peter nodded, figuring details were missing as he observed Casi's bruises and demeanor. "Are you staying in Washington now?"

She nodded. "I'm done with LA."

"You'll have a better life here." Peter ran a hand through his hair. "Georgia, take her to the store and get groceries for the week. We will help get them settled."

"Jake, get my wallet and give her money," Kyle said.

"Kyle has taken over our finances." Casi blushed.

Peter smiled. "I think that's probably a good idea."

"Let me help you get ready." Georgia smoothed a hand over Casi's bruised neck. "It's chilly out." She went with Casi to the bedroom and cringed as she watched her remove her t-shirt. "Sweetheart, you are too thin. This can't be healthy."

"I know." Casi cried into her balled up shirt. "You must hate me."

"No, I don't," Georgia said tenderly. "You're part of our family. We'll always take care of you. Are you sure you're ok?"

"I've destroyed our marriage."

"Marriage is hard at the best of times. Kyle will stand by you and help you through this. You'll come out of it stronger together."

"Jake was wonderful to me."

"I noticed how protective he is." Georgia watched Casi skillfully applying makeup to cover the bruises on her face, and her heart ached for what else she might be hiding from her past.

12

INDEBTED

Georgia guided Casi throughout the first week, showing her how to do laundry, shop for groceries, and clean. They put together a schedule of daily tasks, which gave her a sense of accomplishment. A cloud of melancholy would surround her each evening as she watched Georgia leave, feeling unbelievably alone; unsure how to deal with a difficult patient, and unable to talk about what she needed to do to fix their marriage. What she enjoyed the most were the long talks with her mother-in-law as they worked. Georgia smiled as Casi scrubbed the bathroom, seeing it was an unfamiliar experience. "Housework seems trivial compared to having a career, but when we first adopted the boys, I relished the mundane chores to take my mind off the colossal responsibilities of being a mother. I found it peaceful and relaxing to start each day with a list of tasks, crossing off each one as I went along."

"I'm actually enjoying it." Casi lowered her voice. "I'm not sure how to deal with Kyle. He's moody and sighs a lot."

"He's not used to inactivity." Georgia clucked her tongue. "He's being a pain because he wants to be at the shop, and Jake won't let him. They took on an apprentice to help with the workload. You might know him, Riley, from your dad's brewery."

"Riley? That cute brother? Does that mean my dad heard about what happened in LA?" Casi sat back on her heels.

"He called us to ask about Kyle, but we didn't say anything about your ordeal; only how you're in Washington now."

Casi had seen a Facebook message from Ava but hadn't opened it. She felt Kyle constantly watched her and tried to stay busy, to look like she earned her keep. She was glad Georgia came daily and Jake slept over at night, which meant she wasn't alone with Kyle and his questioning glare.

A month after the shooting, Kyle went back to work full-time, cautious with his rib, but able to get around well. He took on the lighter work and spent time in his office doing paperwork when his side started to hurt. Casi breathed a sigh of relief, feeling claustrophobic with him around. The doctor cautioned them not to engage in sex until at least a few more weeks, and she was secretly thankful. Although she gained a few pounds under Georgia's watchful eye, she was still underweight. Coupled with his constant bad mood, and the faint memories of her experiences in LA, she preferred to remain distant from him and engrossed herself in taking care of their home. She looked forward to seeing Jake each evening, the polar opposite of his brother, pleasant and complimentary. She taught him how to play Candy Crush, and his incompetence amused her.

"Casi, we need to sit down and go over your bills. I'm sure payments are due," Kyle sighed. She nodded and cringed when she retrieved her list of accounts, embarrassed to show him. She handed him the book and walked back to the kitchen. "You need to do this with me." He placed another chair by the computer. "You can't keep ignoring it."

"I don't have any money and the loft hasn't sold. Do you want to punish me by making me see my debt?"

"No more tears. The waterworks are irritating." He swallowed and exhaled. "Let's look at the big picture and come up with a strategy."

He put his arm around her when she sat. "I will pay off all your credit cards and I've paid the mortgage on the loft."

She frowned. "What about my phone?"

"Unfortunately, that's a luxury you won't be able to keep. We're better off buying out the contract and adding you to our plan when the time is right."

"When you feel I deserve it."

"I'm not trying to monitor you, but you can make better use of your time instead of texting and being on Facebook." She fought back the tears, feeling like he had dealt her a deadly blow. He went through each account and instead of being relieved as balances were erased, she had a stabbing pain in her heart at the loss of control in her life. "Zero debt," he announced when they completed the last account. "Happy?"

"Thanks." She wanted to throw up.

Casi laughed hysterically as she leaned into Jake, watching him trying to figure out how to make a striped candy in Candy Crush. "The dumb things explode every time I get close!" he complained.

"Yes, as soon as you get three. You have to plan ahead."

"This game sucks." He restarted the game.

Kyle came in and watched as Casi sipped her wine. "Is dinner ready?"

She cringed at his tone. "It's in the oven. It has another twenty minutes."

"I'm going to take a shower." He hesitated at the doorway. "I'm guessing you don't want to join me?"

"I need to make the salad." She strolled to the kitchen, refilling her wine on the way.

"I see cocktail hour starts early around here." He stormed to the bedroom.

Jake put an arm around her shoulders and gave her a squeeze. "You're making him grumpier by withholding sex."

"I don't feel like being with him when all he does is bitch at me."

"I understand, he's been a jerk to me too, but we have to fix him. Let's go to the bar tonight and maybe we can loosen him up, and then you can alleviate his mood in bed."

"Are you pimping me out?" She shoved him.

"He's your husband, it's your duty."

Kyle finished showering and came back to the kitchen, surveying her serve the dinner. "Great, chicken again."

"It's all I know how to make." Casi frowned at the bland plate.

"There's a freezer full of fish and game. Try a new recipe. The internet is full of useful information other than social media and discount shoes."

Jake silenced her with a look. "Let's go to the bar tonight. Do something different for a change."

"Different how? You are there almost every night." Kyle grabbed a beer.

Jake narrowed his eyes, "It would be different if you guys came. We could play pool and you could show everyone you are not dead. We haven't been to the coffee shop in months and people are beginning to wonder."

"We haven't gone because you impregnated the barista." Kyle chuckled at his joke. "Fine, it would be nice to get out of the house."

Jake left ahead of them, not wanting to wait for Casi to get ready. Kyle changed his shirt and waited for her to get dressed while he responded to Lauren's text. She called him frantically a few weeks prior, upset by the news of his gunshot. It had been good to hear her voice, in the midst of the turmoil in his relationship. He realized the constant texting and phone calls made him short tempered with Casi, but was eager to renew his friendship with Lauren. He put away his phone, glancing up as Casi came out. "Pretty." He frowned at her wayward hair.

She caught the look. "I cut my own bangs. I don't have money for a hairdresser. Dylan would be pissed if he saw what I did."

"It's fine, but maybe try tucking it behind your ear or something?"

He considered if that might help the rogue piece sticking up on the side.

They arrived at the bar about an hour after Jake. She had managed to fix her hair with gel to be more styled than hobo. They saw Jake doing tequila shots and drinking a beer. He chatted with a rough-hewn woman, who may have been more comfortable in a biker bar. She had on a tiny denim skirt with a see-through black shirt, covering large breasts. Her overly dyed hair and harsh makeup made her appear a lot older than she probably was. Casi didn't like the way she hung on Jake as he bought her drinks. Kyle gave her the once over as he sat beside his brother. The bartender put down another shot for the pair, and Casi grabbed it and then stole Jake's beer. The bartender smiled and poured another round of shots at Jake's request, after giving her a shove. Kyle ordered a scotch and sipped it, watching Casi throw back two more shots and drink most of Jake's beer. "There's an open table, let's go play pool." Kyle grabbed his brother's arm.

"I'm good right here." Jake eyed the woman.

"I came here to hang out with you, not watch you drink."

Jake ordered a whiskey and walked to the pool table, and the woman found interest in someone else. Casi had a few more drinks, and the room began to spin, making her wonder how Jake could consume so much alcohol on what seemed to be a daily basis. Kyle went to the bathroom as Jake reset the table for a new game. Casi queued up a song and danced against Jake, giggling and running her hand up his chest playfully. He turned and kissed her, parting her lips with his tongue, showing her how much he learned since their kiss at Christmas. He bit her lip and resisted her attempt to push him away. He suddenly found himself on the ground, with Kyle standing above him, fists clenched. He rubbed his jaw and downed the rest of his drink in one sip as he strolled over to the woman in the denim skirt and left with her in tow.

"He shouldn't drive!" Casi exclaimed.

"He won't." Kyle assumed Jake would only have sex with the woman in the parking lot. "And I think you've had enough to drink."

He noted her cheeks redden with embarrassment. He smiled and reached out a hand, leading her back to the bar.

She wrapped herself in his arms. "I'm sorry."

"I've been an asshole to you lately and we still haven't talked about what happened in LA. Let's not add more problems to our marriage though, ok?"

"I got overly excited about going out and the shots hit me harder than I expected." She snuggled against him and ordered a coke. The bartender smiled as he slid it in front of her.

"Kyle, a crazy bitch is going psycho on Jake's truck!" A man yelled as he ran in the bar.

They rushed outside to witness Lia swinging a bat through the side window of the truck, already having taken out the windshield and side mirror. Kyle grabbed the bat mid-swing. "What the fuck are you doing, Lia? Do you realize how much this will cost to repair? What point are you possibly trying to prove?"

Two police cars drove in, lights flashing. The officer directed Kyle to drop the bat and put his hands behind his head while he knelt, and they checked his pockets. Jake was ordered out of the truck, shirtless, the top of his jeans undone. The woman was escorted out once she put her clothing back on. Casi tried to explain what happened, and they demanded her to step back as they handcuffed Jake when he became belligerent. The officer shoved him to the ground, charging him with drunk driving since the keys were in the ignition. Lia quietly got in her car and drove away, unnoticed.

"Please don't arrest him. We were planning to take him home when he was done with her." Casi pointed to the woman.

"You don't seem to be in any condition to drive either," the officer said, smelling the alcohol on her breath and watching her sway.

"That's my husband's truck. They have a business... Jake can't lose his license!" She started crying. "We've had a hard year already."

"You're not from around here, are you?" the officer asked, taking in her edgy appearance in leather pants, with a well-toned body.

"I just moved here from LA. My husband and his brother have lived here a long time though." Her lip quivered.

The officer took the handcuffs off Jake and let Kyle stand. "Ok, Jensen Brothers, we know who you are. We'll cut you a break this time." He took the keys from the ignition and handed them to Kyle as they left.

Kyle walked to his truck and grabbed plastic and duct tape from behind the seat and began covering Jake's windows. "Put a shirt on and get your tools. You are begging to be robbed." He glared at the woman still standing beside the truck. "What are you waiting for? Payment? Get out of here." She flipped him off and went back in the bar. Kyle whirled around and Casi cringed, anticipating the tongue-lashing. He sounded defeated when he handed her his wallet and asked her to go back in and pay the bill. Jake helped him tape the window and pick up pieces of his broken mirror, throwing it in the back of the truck.

They drove in silence to Jake's apartment and he walked toward his unit with his head down. Kyle watched him, then parked the truck and got out. Casi ran behind him, hoping it wouldn't escalate. Jake didn't close the door, aware of the proximity of his brother. He turned with his arms at his side. "Fine, hit me again." Kyle walked past him and grabbed a box, dumping the contents on the floor. He took the bottles from the counter and emptied the fridge of beer. "Now I'm a damn drunk and you're saving me?"

"You're not an alcoholic, but you're drinking way too much to avoid facing your problems. And Lia is one gigantic problem. I take it you haven't made any kind of contact?" Kyle noted Jake's shoulders slump and hugged him tightly. "You and my wife make bad choices when you're under pressure. I'm with you through this, just like you were for me."

"Sorry about the bar. I didn't consider how it might affect her after what happened in LA," Jake whispered.

Kyle smiled at Casi swaying. "She seems ok. Maybe it was good for her to relax for a night. I've been difficult to deal with. Come home with us. I'm sure she will be passed out as soon as she hits the bed. We haven't played video games in a while. Are you up for a challenge?"

13

TRAIL OF TEARS

Casi stared at the total on the register and blinked back tears. She felt her pockets, hoping she had extra money. "Um, can I put some things back?" She realized the logical choice would be the wine as she tried to do the math.

"Honey, can you call Kyle?" Jeannie asked sweetly.

"I walked, and I didn't bring my phone."

Jeannie smiled and slid her own debit card through the machine. "Bring it to me the next time you come in." Casi nodded as she gathered her groceries, cheeks aflame.

The bags were heavier than she anticipated, and she wished she had brought the car as a light rain started. She didn't want to ask for gas money, and her present situation remained overwhelmingly depressing. About a half mile into her sodden journey, a truck pulled in front of her. "Why are you walking in the rain?" Jake scrambled to help her with the bags, which were beginning to tear. She broke down as she told him the saga at the grocery store. "I know exactly how that feels." He grasped her hand and drove back to town.

Jake walked in the store and waited at Jeannie's check stand until she finished with her customer. He handed her the money and smiled. "I guess it runs in the family. Thanks for helping, she's been loopy since Kyle got shot. It's been hard on her."

Jeannie nodded. "I thought she seemed distraught, but I didn't want to say anything. How's he doing?"

"Pretty good. He's back at work, which is great because we've been slammed with orders," Jake reported.

Jeannie squeezed his hand, remembering the mess he had been years ago when he couldn't pay his own bill. "It's wonderful to see you doing so well." He smiled, thankful for his improved financial situation.

When they arrived home, Casi started dinner, trying to avoid Kyle's questions as he sorted through the grocery bags. "Why did you buy organic? It's three times the price. You should take the bags from the mudroom; you're getting charged for things we don't need."

She shrugged and Jake intervened. "Why don't you get her a credit card, so she isn't short of money next time?"

"She needs to try to stay on a budget. It's important for her to learn how much things cost," Kyle stated.

"I'll take you to Costco tomorrow after work. We can get the basics for meals." Jake shoved past him to put away the groceries.

"You should probably pick up wine. You guys go through it pretty fast." Kyle walked away to answer a text.

"Ignore him." Jake refilled her glass.

Casi set the table while the chicken roasted, wondering who Kyle texted incessantly. She knew she couldn't complain but wasn't pleased he had become engrossed in his phone, especially when he still hadn't bothered to add her to their contract.

Jake nudged him. "Maybe when we're at Costco I should add her to our plan so she can get a phone?"

Kyle shook his head. "She doesn't need one right now. I want to see the plan details before we commit to anything."

They sat down to dinner and Casi waited for the critique of her meal, which she realized was not her best effort. Kyle regarded the chicken with interest, poking it with his fork. "Did you cook it with the parts in it?" He peered inside. "Jesus, Casi, it's not even cooked all the way. Don't you know how to check when it's done?" He pushed his plate away and got up to make a peanut butter sandwich, answering his phone when it rang. "Hey, Jack. No, she doesn't have a cell yet. I'm doing much better, thanks." He set his jaw and handed Casi the phone.

"Hi Dad. No, we finished dinner." She glanced at the untouched plates. "I'm fine." Her voice quivered. She nodded to a few more questions, not trusting herself to speak. After a prolonged silence she admitted, "I'm upset because I messed up the chicken and it was expensive." Kyle winced, figuring Jack wouldn't like hearing his daughter in tears over a meal that wasn't stellar. He started cleaning the kitchen, wishing he could shake his bad mood, hating himself for treating her so poorly. She hung up and stared at the screen for a minute. "Who's Lauren?"

He reached for his phone and slid it in his pocket, avoiding his brother's glare. "She's an old friend who is inquiring how I'm doing."

Kyle slammed down the phone and drove to the bank to make the transfer. Instead of heading home, he took the on-ramp toward Seattle. Lauren's face lit up when he walked in the hotel bar and she rushed to give him a hug. "I'm so glad you came."

He shrugged. "I wanted to see you. It's been a long time." He ordered a whiskey, and they sat at the bar to catch up.

She ran a finger over his ring. "So, you're a married man now."

"Yup." He took a sip of his drink. "Things haven't been easy with her transitioning to Blackberry Falls, and your sister has been causing significant problems."

Lauren sighed. "I told her she is crazy to have a baby with your brother. She had her heart set on having a child."

"It's the last thing Jake needed. Hopefully, they'll talk soon, he's still pissed about her tearing up his truck."

"I heard about that; she's gone psycho with this pregnancy."

Kyle put his hand on hers. "I don't want you to misread my having a drink with you. I'll be honest, my marriage is not great, but I'm not looking for an affair."

Lauren smiled. "You were always upfront, and I appreciate that. As much as I would love to get back together, if a friendship is what you're offering, I'm thrilled to be part of your life again."

"That's what I'm offering," he stated.

"You're home late." Jake crossed his arms over his chest.

"I had business to take care of in Seattle." Kyle walked past him to take a shower.

"Business named Lauren?" Jake whispered. "Anna saw you at the bar and told me. What the hell are you doing?"

"Nothing! She's been contacting me since the shooting, I only met with her as a friend. I was clear about that."

Jake narrowed his eyes. "What did she say about Lia?"

"Not much." Kyle hesitated. "Go home after dinner, Casi and I need to talk." Jake glared at him before turning to survey her in the kitchen, happily making dinner. He wanted to protect her from what he suspected Kyle wanted to talk about, but knew he couldn't interfere.

"Don't do it," Jake hissed at Kyle as he left.

Kyle was surprised to see her putting on pajamas when he walked in the bedroom. "Kind of early for bed, isn't it?"

"I have horrible cramps. I'm tired and ready for this day to end." She slid between the blankets.

He nodded, wondering if Jake had alerted her, or if she was perceptive of his moods. He surveyed her rubbing her hand over her stomach and the heat rose inside him. He yanked the sheet aside. "Your scars are not my fault. Would you like to compare?" He lifted his shirt to expose his bullet wound. "I believe I win this round."

Kyle watched her sleeping fitfully, almost waking her twice, wanting it over. The next morning, he directed Jake to go to work without him. "Casi, let's go for a walk." He held the door open.

"Why?" Her eyes welled, and she tugged at her sweatshirt.

"You know why we need to talk, and you keep stalling."

She trudged silently beside him, preparing herself to hear how disappointed he was and how she needed to get it together. He put his hand on her arm and moved her to the side of the trail. He took a deep breath and said, "Casi, I'm done." She took a step back in utter shock, hoping he was referring to the length of the walk. Not their marriage. "I think we would be better apart. I'll take care of you and make sure you're ok, but you need to decide where you want to live and what you will do for a job going forward."

She felt as if she had been punched as she struggled to breathe. "I don't understand. I've done everything you asked, and I do all the cooking and cleaning. I haven't complained about anything." She burst into tears.

"I don't need a maid, I need a partner, and I don't think you can be that." He realized the trail had been a bad idea as people passed by, staring at the sobbing woman.

"What changed? Is this about sex? I'll do whatever you want."

"That's certainly not helping. I won't be in a marriage like Jake where sex is used as a reward. I feel as if you're punishing me for the tubal ligation. I can't take it back, and I'm tired of apologizing." Before he could elaborate, his phone rang, and he barked, "What?", then changed his tone when he heard the voice. "Sorry, Amy, I thought it was Jake. How long has she been there?" He glanced at his watch. "We have to go to work." He pulled Casi's shirt up to wipe her face as she sputtered and cried. "You need to come with me."

They walked in the wood shop and Kyle avoided Jake's glare as he took in Casi's bedraggled appearance. "Can you and Riley go get coffee? Give us an hour and bring back lattes if you don't mind." Kyle handed Amy money.

Casi spotted Mary and her legs buckled. Mary frowned. "Well, you're a mess, aren't you?" She indicated the long table. "We need to talk," adding, "All of us," when she saw the brothers try to sneak away. They could see the fire in her eyes as she looked Casi over. "I've heard all the details about LA. Don't bother lying or making excuses."

"I'm not! Everyone knows everything, I have no secrets, and that's not even good enough," Casi wailed.

Mary cocked her head, unsure of the reference. "And?"

"Obviously, I'm too damaged and nothing will ever fix me. Kyle wants a divorce!" Casi sputtered.

Jake jumped up and kicked the chair. "You didn't even try, Kyle. You give up after a few months because things got rocky? Try being married for sixteen years and having kids, you haven't experienced tough times."

Kyle exhaled. "This is not the woman I married. She's a hysterical sobbing mess, who can't even decipher the lies from the truth."

"Fine! I'll take care of her. She can live with me at the apartment and you can put your perfect life back together without her," Jake yelled.

Mary looked between Jake and Casi. "There isn't any monkey business going on between you two, is there?" Casi smiled at the name and shook her head no.

Kyle regarded her tiny frame, shivering. "I never claimed I wanted a divorce. I said I'm done because I can't live with the constant lying. I believe we can move forward and then I find out something else. It's killing me, Casi, can't you see that? The pain from the bullet was less painful than your deceit."

"I don't have a phone and you'll only let me go online if you're monitoring me. What lies are you talking about?" Her lip trembled.

He took a deep breath. "I'm referring to the photo shoot and the money you made."

"You gave the check back. I made nothing off that editorial."

He noted the confusion on her face. "Tell me about the lingerie shows."

Casi paled and looked at Mary, who nodded. "Those were when I was barely twenty. I modeled lingerie for private parties, that's all."

"You were a hooker," he stated, as Jake raised an eyebrow.

"No! I only modeled. They never touched me!"

"Sonya booked the shows. It was a good source of income for her. Jack found out, and that's when he hired me to step in and manage her career." Mary rubbed Casi's back.

"Dad knew?" She clutched her stomach in despair.

"Yes, and he realized you wouldn't listen to him, but he worried where you would end up if you continued." She turned to Kyle, "Casi never had sex with the men. Her mother supplied the drugs and offered sexual favors of her own."

"Does Dad know about LA?" Casi picked at her nails.

"No. I heard about it from Alix. He is sick about his involvement and I told him to leave town. Your dad is concerned you aren't returning his calls or messages and said you sounded strained on the phone. He asked me to come and check on you." Mary surveyed Kyle.

"What about the photographer? How much did you think he paid to be with you?" Kyle brushed a curtain of hair from Casi's face to see her response.

"I don't even remember going to the loft with him." Casi turned to Jake. "The doctor said I didn't have sex, right?"

"You were assaulted." Jake clenched his jaw. "But no intercourse."

"Apparently you were too drugged out to perform. Your neighbor with the telescope broke in when he saw the man hitting you and dragged him out." Kyle relayed the details. "The photographer paid $1500 but demanded it back after he got out of the hospital."

"$1500? That's one hell of a lay!" Jake whistled. He noted Casi shaking. "But, I'm sure you're worth every penny of it, Monkey."

Casi wiped her face with the back of her hand. "I guess it's good to determine my value."

Kyle's shoulders crumpled, and he knelt and took her hands in his. "You're priceless, Casi. I'd give it all up to make you happy. It seems like the more I do for you, the more crap gets stirred up. Your mom asked for $5000 or she would sell the pictures."

"Don't pay her, Kyle! She's lying." Casi squeezed her eyes closed.

"I already did. I don't want her manipulating you and I don't know how to make her leave you alone." He clung to her with desperation.

Mary reached over and touched Kyle's cheek. "I'll take care of it. She felt cheated because she didn't get paid for the pictures or the photographer."

"I don't care about the money. My concern has only ever been for her safety." Kyle pressed his forehead to Casi's.

"Jake, show me around the building," Mary directed.

Jake waved his hand. "This is it."

Mary grasped his arm and propelled him forward. "I know what you did for her. You're a good man and an excellent friend."

"I don't like being touched." He yanked his arm back.

"Get over it." She kissed him on the cheek.

He rolled his eyes. "I see who Casi got her balls from."

Mary smiled and gave him a squeeze, pointing to a corner stacked with wood. "What's this area used for?"

"Storing wood," he answered bluntly.

"Can you find another place? Casi will need an office of her own and I want it built today," she demanded.

"That would take weeks, if we even chose to do it."

"Today." She patted him on the back and walked to the table. "We're going for pedicures and lunch. Your brother will fill you in on the project I've requested." She cocked her head. "Is that snot all over your shirt? For God sakes, you look like you are in foster care with your raggedy hair and soiled clothing."

Kyle chuckled, "I forgot my handkerchief, and she was a mess."

Mary smiled. "We'll go by your house and get changed. Kyle, you can cook dinner tonight, we have a busy day."

Amy came back carrying a tray of coffee and handed one to Casi as she left, with a sympathetic smile.

Kyle turned to Jake and hissed, "I know about Sonya on the beach in Hawaii."

Jake shrugged. "Good thing I had an STD test, huh?"

Mary admired the house while she petted Dingo and Jezebel. "It is lovely here. I think it's a good place for you."

Casi shrugged. "If he lets me stay."

"Cut him a break, the man almost died for you and how do you repay him? You are dishevelled and burnt out. Who wants to come home to that? Not to mention you've cost him a small fortune. He's put up with a lot and it's time you turn things around."

"He hasn't been easy to live with either. He monitors everything I do and every sip of wine I take." Casi crossed her arms over her chest.

Mary nodded. "Strip down, you need to shower. I'm sure you haven't shaved your legs in months." Casi frowned but didn't deny it. She tried to close the bathroom door and Mary stopped her. "Let's see what you're hiding from your husband. You are a bag of bones. Get on the scale."

"Mary, no!" Casi winced.

"Now!" Mary insisted, shaking her head at the result. "You're at least ten pounds underweight. That's not healthy and you need to start looking polished. You have a new life ahead of you." She caressed Casi's cheek. "You understand Ava and I are old friends. She has a difficult relationship with your mother, but she's only a phone call away if you need help."

Tears littered Casi's face. "She was amazing to me in the hospital, she always knows what to say to make me feel better. The opposite of my mother who crushes me when I'm at my lowest point." She regarded her hands. "I've lost myself and I'm unsure if I can reclaim who I was."

"Perhaps it's time to create a better version?"

After pedicures and lunch, Casi began to feel her old spirit returning. She enjoyed the day, showing Mary around town, thankful the weather was only slightly overcast. They returned home to find Kyle in the kitchen cooking, and Jake setting the table. Kyle poured them a glass of wine as they sat down to dinner.

"You're a wonderful cook," Mary complimented.

"Thanks, I enjoy it for the most part." Kyle stared at his plate.

"Maybe it's something you two could share in the future?" Mary folded her hands in front of her.

He nodded, wondering how much she had heard about his over-controlling behavior. "That would be nice."

"I can cook too and share in the responsibility. Our mother taught us both. We were surprisingly well brought up." Jake narrowed his eyes.

Mary smiled. "I apologize if my foster care comment seemed insensitive. Obviously, after meeting your parents and seeing how they adore you, I assumed you were their birth children." She reached over and took Jake's hand. "I grew up in the system but wasn't lucky enough to be adopted. Once I aged out, I was determined to make a successful life."

"I never knew that!" Casi cocked her head.

"My past didn't define my future; I created my own destiny." Mary grasped her bag and held it in her lap. "I would like a tally of the debt you paid for Casi, and don't hold back, I imagine you keep accurate records."

Kyle realized she meant immediately and retrieved the spreadsheet he created. Mary opened her checkbook and Kyle put a hand over the paper. "No! She's my wife, I'll take care of the debt."

"The car is a generous gift, but she'll pay her own bills, including the money to her mother." Mary wrote in elegant script and handed him the check.

"Now I'll owe you the money instead of Kyle?" Casi slumped. "I'll never be able to repay it."

"It's your money. I've been setting aside a portion of your paychecks for years. You were never responsible enough to handle it, but I want you to be in this marriage by choice, not as an obligation."

Kyle wrapped his arms around Casi. "She wants to stay here with me!" His breath was warm against her neck as he whispered, "Please don't leave. I'm sorry for what I said on the trail. I couldn't have gone through with it."

Casi nestled into the comfort of his embrace. "I won't give up on our marriage. My home is with you."

Mary nodded. "Do you understand why I've pushed you toward getting an education and kept an eye on you all these years?"

"Because you love me?" Casi grinned.

"I do love you," Mary agreed. "I decided you were special years ago, when you were a misguided girl, thinking the world owed you a living. I made it my mission to create an opportunity for when you were finished modeling."

"Why didn't you tell me?"

"You weren't ready. I almost gave up on you when I heard about the photo shoot. I am disgusted you allowed yourself to be dragged down to that level." Mary shook a finger at her.

"I'm sorry. I hate myself for doing it," Casi wailed.

"Self-pity won't get you anywhere. You need to make better choices in the future," Mary cautioned. "My husband is a biochemist..."

"Husband? When did that happen?" Casi's eyes widened.

Mary laughed. "Twenty-five years ago. He's Austrian, and I split my time between there and LA."

"Do you have secret children too?"

"No, that's a conversation for another day. I took you under my wing because I felt a deep connection with you. Anyway, my husband and I developed a skincare line over the years, and we are in the process of bringing it to market."

"Was I your guinea pig?"

"Yes, all those products I gave you were from our line. I needed a live subject to test them on." Mary grinned.

"I like them. I use them all the time. Except the face wash that gave me the terrible rash..."

"Minor fragrance issues. We fixed it. Your intimate knowledge of the product will give you an advantage on marketing. It's time to put your social media skills and education to work."

"You're giving me a job?" Casi gasped.

"A career and a stake in the company. The money remaining from paying your debt, which isn't a lot, will be reserved for your share." Mary opened a travel bag and set a box in front of Casi. "It's not a gift though, you must earn it. You have one month to come up with a marketing plan."

Casi picked up a bottle and smiled. "Macrae Skincare?"

"It's a family name." Mary's smile expanded while her eyes implied there was history she wasn't ready to share.

"Do I get business cards?"

"If you prove you can handle the responsibility. I expect you to rise up to the challenge."

"I will. Do I need to go to LA?" Casi locked eyes with Kyle.

"There will be business trips in the future, including New York, Vancouver, and Toronto." Mary noted Kyle's crushed expression. "Our headquarters will be in Seattle. I'm touring condos tomorrow and will relocate this year. I have no interest in remaining in LA."

14

NAVIGATING

Casi surveyed the bed as Kyle held a out his hand to her. She tugged at her t-shirt, uneasy in his presence. "Where do we stand with our relationship? This morning you wanted me to move out. Do we pretend the last couple of months didn't happen?"

Kyle rubbed his temple. "I wish we could rewind to the morning after the wedding. I would do everything differently."

Casi slid beside him. "I don't blame you for the operation. You chose what was best for me." She cast her eyes to the sheets. "It was foolish to return to LA. I should have stayed here and told you the business fell apart."

Kyle guided her to his arms and stroked her cheek. "I got overwhelmed by everything your mother told me. It would have been better to talk to you and find out the truth."

"The lingerie parties did happen."

"I don't care." Kyle kissed her gently. "I wasn't upset about things you did in the past, only that your mother insinuated you were playing me for money. I questioned whether you really loved me."

"I do! With all my heart." Tears tumbled on the pillowcase.

"Can we put our mistakes behind us and focus on our future?

Mary's offer seems ideal, especially the part where you will work out of Seattle."

"I'm ecstatic and terrified at the same time. I'm entering new territory and you realize how challenged I am with directions."

"I'll help you navigate."

&

Kyle woke up and swatted Jake's hand away. "Why are you poking at me?"

"Get up. I want to go by the coffee shop. Mary suggested I talk to Lia in person, in an area where she couldn't freak out. She said I should be upfront and set a time to talk about next steps." Jake nodded with satisfaction.

"Mary is your personal advisor now?" Kyle threw back the covers.

"Sure, why not? She keeps Casi in line. I figure she's skilled with screw ups. Plus, I like that she was a foster kid." Jake grinned. "Our kind should stick together."

"It is good advice. You might as well deal with it prior to the birth of your child. Plus, we should make an appearance before the tongue-waggers spread rumors of divorce." Kyle shook his head.

Lia glanced up from her register and noted Jake in line, becoming flustered as she gave her customer change. Kyle laced his fingers through Casi's and strolled to Gail's table.

"Getting divorced?" Gail teased.

"We were working some things out, and the trail was a poor choice of venue." Kyle glanced at Casi as she nodded.

"I figured." Gail directed her eyes to Casi. "We haven't seen you around town. I wondered when you'd make an appearance."

"I'm adjusting to living here." Casi scanned the table and smiled at Mary Ann. "A friend of mine is starting a company in Seattle and has offered me a job in marketing. Perhaps you could give me some pointers?"

"That's exciting!" Mary Ann beamed. "I would be happy to get together and share ideas." She nudged Gail, watching her fidget. "Just ask."

Gail sighed. "Is Lia pregnant with Jake's baby?"

"What is she saying about it?" Kyle surveyed the scene at the counter.

"She tried to hide the pregnancy, but it's obvious now. You guys haven't been here in months, so we're assuming he's the father and isn't happy about it." Gail took a sip of her coffee.

Kyle nodded. "That's pretty much it."

"Is he ok? This must be killing him." She eyed Jake with his hands in his pockets as he approached Lia.

"It's not easy. These last few months have been hell and we have been through the wringer," Kyle admitted.

"Show us the bullet wound," Mary Ann asked.

Kyle lifted the edge of his t-shirt and Casi looked away. "It's not a big deal. One more scar for my collection."

Jake ordered lattes and pulled out his wallet. "When is a good time to talk about the baby? What are your expectations for support and how should we proceed?"

Lia fumbled with the money, cheeks ablaze. "Any time after work is fine."

"Come to Kyle's tonight. We'll talk there."

They picked up their order and walked toward the door. Lia rushed to block Casi's exit. "I've been trying to call and message you," she blurted.

"I don't have a phone and I'm not on Facebook right now." Casi directed her gaze to the floor.

"I want to apologize; will you hear me out?" Lia pleaded.

"You can talk to her tonight," Jake suggested.

Kyle turned to her when they got in the truck. "What does she need to apologize for?"

Casi blushed. "I left my Facebook open at her house and she read my private messages to Anna and then freaked out on me."

He chuckled. "Payback's a bitch, huh?"

"Well deserved." She giggled as Jake poked her.

Kyle handed Amy a coffee with a nod as they came in the shop. "Thanks! By the way, there's a computer tech here. He said Mary sent him, so I let him start setting up." Amy pointed to the back area.

He took Casi's hand and led her past the machinery, stopping in front of a newly built room. "The glass is on order, but the shell of your new office is ready. Let us know what finishing touches you want."

"Glass? I thought we were putting in bars; keep the monkey in her cage." Jake shoved his brother.

Kyle recognized the dig at his controlling behavior and shrugged. "Bars would be impractical with the sawdust."

Casi entered the space, shocked to see an L-shaped desk and shelves. Her antique pine desk sat under the window, topped by a plant and flanked by her floral chair. "It's amazing you guys. Thank you."

"We'll keep an eye on the plant." Kyle grinned. "You have a space of your own now. Why don't you get whatever office supplies you might need from Amy while you wait for the technician to finish?"

Casi busied herself arranging things on the shelves until the technician finished with her computer and printer set up. He did a basic walk through, realizing he spoke to a tech savvy woman. She sat at her new computer and scrolled through the programs, setting up a strategy for her marketing proposal, unaware of Kyle watching her from the doorway.

"Leave her alone, she's in her element," Jake scoffed.

"I'm asking if she wants to go to lunch." Kyle fidgeted.

"Bring me back food."

Kyle ordered sandwiches at the deli and turned to Casi. "Can you wait to eat until we get back to the shop? There's an errand I would like to take care of." She nodded, and he grasped her hand, leading her to the store next door.

Casi smiled as she perused the cell phones. "Mary insisted?"

Kyle's cheeks flushed. "I canceled your phone because you needed a break from the crap in LA. And your mother. I understand I was being overly protective by making everyone go through me to speak to you, but it was the only way I could filter out harmful elements." He turned to the sales rep as he approached. "Which one is the most advanced? My wife is exceptional with technology and I don't think a free offer will suffice."

"It's ok." Casi focused on the assortment before her.

"Cost is not an issue. Choose the one that will work best for you in business. If you will be traveling, you'll need advanced features." Kyle indicated the high-end selection. He paid for the purchase and put his arm around her as they walked back to the truck. When he opened the door for her, she slid a hand over his chest as she kissed him. "You don't need to reward me for buying you things." She stepped back angrily, and he corrected himself. "I didn't mean to say it like that. I don't want you to feel obligated to be intimate with me."

"Payment with the only currency I have." Tears sprung to her eyes.

He sighed and helped her in the truck, putting his forehead to hers. "Can we take this one step at a time? I'm desperate for our marriage to work, but I feel like I'm constantly doing or saying the wrong thing."

"How many steps do you think it will take to fix it?"

"Five hundred and twelve," he said without hesitation.

"That will take a long time!"

He kissed her and smiled. "We have forever, right?"

Casi paced the living room while they waited for Lia. "Do you want help with dinner?" She straightened the napkins on the table.

"I've got it." Kyle chuckled. "I'm making chicken."

She smiled at his joke, watching him prepare the venison. "It will be nice to try something different."

Lia arrived, looking nervous. "I'm sorry I handled this so poorly."

Jake nodded, taking her jacket and purse. "I guess you can't drink wine, do you want a soda or something?"

"No thanks. Part of my penance is gestational diabetes. I'm blaming it for my emotional outbursts." Lia shifted her weight.

"Is it serious?" Jake grasped the edge of the counter.

"Not if I'm careful. I monitor my sugar closely and I get tested regularly. I get shaky if I don't eat every few hours." She sighed. "The baby is fine and won't be affected if I'm cautious. It's a boy."

"That part I like. Girls are more difficult." Jake grinned.

"I hoped it would be a girl," she confessed. "I'm having a hard time with this pregnancy, Jake." She burst into tears.

Jake hugged her tightly. "You have to realize what a shock it was. I'm sorry for how I reacted; you threw me for a loop."

She shivered in his arms. "I tried to get an abortion, but they told me I'm too far along."

"Oh, Lia." Casi rushed toward her and took her hand.

Jake helped her get comfortable on the sofa. "When are we expecting this bundle of joy?"

"Late May."

He frowned as he did the math. "It happened in September?"

"I wasn't certain because I had spotting for a few months. I didn't take the test until December." Lia glanced at Casi.

"You planned it?" Jake rubbed his temple.

Lia shrugged. "I wanted to be important in your life, but after your divorce you pulled away. I thought this would bring us together."

"I didn't want more kids." Jake cringed and slumped on the sofa.

Kyle eyed her swollen belly. "He's on his way now. What are the plans for after he is born?"

"I'm still working and can manage expenses on my own. Coffee Junction offers six weeks maternity pay."

Kyle sat in the chair facing them. "We can add him to our health insurance. Are you planning on staying in your place?"

"I might move in with my mom after he's born." Lia winced. "She suggested I give him up for adoption."

Jake clenched his jaw and Kyle reached over to put a hand on his shoulder. "Let's focus on what needs to be done now and wait to consider other options until after the birth. Jake has a two-bedroom place he never stays in. Maybe you could move in there?"

"Sure, let's get married and raise the kid together!" Jake jumped up and stormed to the kitchen to get a beer.

Kyle chuckled as he got up to serve dinner. "That's not what I meant."

"Jake should buy the property across the street and put up a tent. The apartment is big enough for Lia and the baby." Casi grinned.

"Wait, what property is for sale?" Kyle stopped in his tracks with plates in his hands.

"Barry's and Donna's, across the street. They have a double lot. They want a two-story house, but can only build it on the back lot, so they're selling the front piece." Casi flipped her hair back. "Since I've been a homemaker, I've gotten to know the neighbors. It's kind of fun to find out everyone's business."

Kyle set the plates down and walked out the door without a word, and Lia turned to Casi. "I need you to be my friend again. I am sorry for how I acted. I thought you were encouraging Anna to take Jake away. But I never really had him."

"I didn't consider the baby, and I did suggest she should have fun with him. I shouldn't have gotten involved and I'm so sorry for hurting you." Casi squeezed her hand.

"Can we put it behind us? I've felt so lonely these last few months and I miss your friendship." Lia wiped a tear.

"It's been hell for me too, especially being under house arrest." Casi winked at Jake.

Kyle came back carrying paperwork. "Jake, do you want to live across the street? You could afford to buy this property and I can check what the building requirements are, but I had a year to build when I bought this one."

Jake grabbed the flyer from his hand. "Seriously? I will happily live in a tent to be able to own that place. Can I truly afford it?"

"In time." Kyle grinned. "Imagine living so close to me."

Jake went through the motions of their handshake as they locked eyes. "I'll work every weekend to make it a reality."

"We have enough money to cover it. I'll make him a cash offer after I speak to our attorney and check on the building criteria." Kyle bit his cheek and looked at Casi. "We could move the trailer from our hunting property over there but maybe Jake could stay here for a few weeks until everything is finalized if we move Lia to the apartment?"

Casi smiled. "I'm happy to have a house guest who can take over cleaning the bathrooms."

"Deal!" Jake flopped on the sofa. "Home sweet home."

Lia twisted her hands together. "What's the rent for your place?"

"We'll take care of the rent and utilities. Give notice at your apartment and save the money for baby expenses." Kyle put his hand on her stomach. "Let's get this little guy here safely and then we can discuss next steps."

15

HIGHLIGHTS AND HIGH LIFE

"*I* invited our accountant for dinner Saturday night to go over your finances. It would be good for you to meet him." Kyle reclined on the bed as he surveyed Casi taking clothes from the closet, clad only in panties and a bra.

"What was your impression of Anna when you first saw her?" She held up a sheer blouse and cocked her head.

"Why are you asking about her?"

"When you walked up to her booth at the convention, how did she appear to you?"

"Why do I feel like this is a trap? I'm uncomfortable talking about a former lover with you." Kyle raked his fingers through his hair.

"Not from a lover standpoint, your impression of her professionally. Did you place an order because you wanted to sleep with her?"

"I thought she was attractive, but I liked her knowledge of the product and her professional attitude. I placed the order because I felt it would be a good product line for us to use. I asked her out for a drink because of the way she smiled at me after."

"What was she wearing?"

"Do you want me to describe the sex too?" He frowned.

"I already heard about the sex." She waved her hand dismissively. "I want a man's opinion on how she dressed."

"You girls share too much; it's disturbing." His eyes widened. "Have you been quizzing Mary Ann?"

"Attire." She snapped her fingers to force him to focus.

Kyle shrugged. "Maybe a white shirt, sexy enough to show she had a figure, but not sleazy. Slacks, blue or black. Dark, anyway. Heels. Not 'come fuck me' high ones; businesslike." Casi laughed at the description. "I liked how it seemed she put effort into her appearance but didn't overdo it. The pants were great on her, she has a nice ass."

"Hair and makeup."

"You expect me to remember a lot. Did you ask Jake? He saw her recently."

"I did, but he wasn't helpful, because he went there with the expectation of sleeping with her. He also said she had a great ass. I'm searching for a more seasoned opinion."

"Her hair was put up, not librarian-style, but pretty and soft. She has beautiful red hair." He glanced at Casi briefly.

"Back off, I need Dylan." She hit his arm.

"Ouch! I didn't even say anything!"

"Are we making fun of Casi's hair?" Jake chuckled at the doorway.

"We're discussing Anna, and how she presents herself from a professional standpoint." She surveyed herself in a mirror and patted a tuft of hair sticking out at the crown.

"She has a great ass and gorgeous copper hair," Jake replied.

"We've already covered that." She rolled her eyes.

"She holds her own professionally; you certainly wouldn't question her abilities in the company. She has an incredible product knowledge, and she comes across as educated and confident." Jake shrugged.

"Surprisingly helpful information." Casi clapped.

"Why are you tormenting us with these questions?" Jake belched.

"I'll be going to sales meetings and marketing this product, and I need a new look. I don't think beach-girl or nightclub-girl are the right images. I'm considering asking Anna to go shopping in Seattle and help put together outfits." She walked back into the closet.

"Good idea," Kyle agreed, considering Anna had a highly polished image.

As she sorted through her clothes, she heard Jake whisper to Kyle, "Casi has a nicer ass than Anna, but I didn't want her to get conceited. She is also way prettier, with a hot rack."

"Absolutely!" Kyle agreed, making her smile.

"Let's go to the bar," Kyle announced.

"On a Wednesday night?" Casi cocked her head.

"I want to celebrate the offer being accepted on the property." Kyle swung her in his arms.

"That's great news!" Jake grinned. "I can officially move in with you? It makes sense to transition Lia to my place by the end of this month."

"Go get ready." Kyle patted Casi on the backside and waited for her to leave. "I spoke to Lauren, and she said Lia has been extremely depressed."

Jake sighed. "You want me to stay in my place and keep an eye on her?"

"No. I don't think it's advantageous to build up her hopes of being in a relationship with you. Your apartment is closer, and I want to encourage her to spend time with us. Hopefully she will be more stable since she's friends with Casi again." He smiled as Casi twirled in front of them in a short skirt. "There's my sunshine girl!" He took her hand outside the bar and pulled her to the side. "In the spirit of forgiveness and moving forward, I have arranged a surprise for you."

"Inside the bar?" Casi hesitated.

Kyle opened the door and propelled her inside. "Yup."

Casi glanced around the room at the familiar pool tables and patrons. "I don't see anything surprising." A hand slipped under her skirt and pinched her on the behind. She whirled around and saw Dylan, who leaned in for a kiss. "Oh my God!"

"I see what the emergency is, your hair is a disaster! Did you use Kyle's pocketknife to cut your bangs?" Dylan twisted his face in horror as he plucked at strands of uneven hair. She gave Kyle a kiss, going to dance with Dylan, as they laughed and shared the latest news and gossip.

"You realize you've lost her for the evening?" Jake said.

"That's ok, it will give us time to catch up." Kyle ordered two drinks.

Jake slumped on a bar stool. "Or you can lecture me on how screwed up my life is and why I'm a loser."

"Not true." Kyle slid a glass over to him. "I've been hyper-focused on Casi, honestly, since the wedding. I left you to figure out the mess with Lia when we should have dealt with it in the beginning."

Jake ran his thumb over the condensation on his scotch. "You would have suggested she have an abortion if we had caught it early."

"It would have made life easier."

"What about the life of that kid? Doesn't he deserve a chance?"

"You should consider adoption. If Lia is depressed now, how will she be able to take care of a child? There are a lot of wonderful couples who could give him a good home. Look at the opportunity we had."

Jake regarded the ice in his drink. "I'll keep an open mind."

"I hear music, maybe Dylan's doing her hair?" Kyle checked his watch when they arrived home from work. He smiled and halted at the doorway and noted Casi singing to the pop tune while she sat on a stool in a bra and panties. Dylan removed foil from her hair while they shared a joint.

She exhaled the smoke. "Hey, you guys are home!"

"Wash," Dylan instructed. She took a deep puff, walking up to Kyle and kissing him as she exhaled, her lips locked on his. She handed the joint to Dylan, stripped down, and stepped in the shower as Kyle coughed.

"Ok, husband. Let's fix that redneck haircut." Dylan inhaled deeply.

"No thanks, I go to the barber in town." Kyle eyed the joint.

"Yes, that's obvious." Dylan grabbed his hand and led him to the stool. "Don't worry, I do my best work when I'm high. It calms me. Shirt off." He handed Kyle the joint.

Kyle grinned and put it to his lips and inhaled quickly before Jake reached out with a smile. "Let me hold that for you." He leaned against the doorjamb and sighed. "I've missed this."

Kyle stood and brushed off the hair, impressed with Dylan's skill. "I will admit you did a very good job." He ran a hand through his hair and watched it fall perfectly in place.

Dylan perused his physique. "The bullet wound is totally sexy; sends the hot factor off the charts."

"Thanks, that's the look I was going for." Kyle turned to Jake. "Your turn, Brother. You need an updated image."

"No thanks." Jake clenched his fists. "I don't trust you."

Dylan produced pot to lure him to the counter. "I promise I'll make you even more handsome." Jake scoffed, and Dylan shrugged. "Yes, I was unkind in LA because I'm protective of my bestie. I'm aware how amazing you were in helping her out of the gutter recently. Also, I will be the first to admit you are looking totally hot now and I'm curious to see what's hiding beneath that tacky t-shirt." Jake frowned down at his brewery logo shirt. He grinned and pulled it over his head, watching Dylan's lustful expression. "Damn, if Casi gets tired of your brother, she has one hell of a handsome replacement!"

"That's not how it works." Kyle shoved his brother.

Jake surveyed Casi in the shower. "I protect what belongs to Kyle. I would never cause him that kind of heartache."

Casi wrapped herself in a towel. "I'm not his property." She noted the pain in Kyle's eyes. "Although he does own my heart, which I'm fairly certain I can't live without."

"Good answer." Kyle grabbed the joint from Jake and took a hit before handing it to her. "Here you go, party girl." He followed her gaze to Jake standing nude in front of the shower and cocked his head.

Casi giggled. "I see you found your confidence, Jake."

Jake grinned and regarded himself in the mirror. "I discovered it under fifty pounds of fat."

Casi pulled Kyle in her arms as she reclined on the counter. "Don't worry, you're all the man I need."

"Is that so? Maybe you can remind me how well we connect physically later tonight?" He kissed her and checked his watch. "I forgot we are expecting Brian."

Casi's eyes widened. "How much effort will be required on my part?"

Kyle smoothed his hand over her wet hair. "He'll explain everything, and you can sign the papers when you are ready."

"I trust what you have set up." Casi slid off the counter and Dylan began cutting her hair.

Kyle walked to the bedroom and returned with a midnight blue mini dress. "What do you think?"

"I doubt it will fit you, but you're welcome to borrow it." Casi threw her head back and laughed.

He shuddered. "It would be nice to see you in something other than leggings. I miss my free-spirited wife."

"I do too." Casi clasped her hands to her face as she broke down.

Jake grasped Dylan's arm. "Hey, can you help me start dinner?" Dylan nodded and followed him to the kitchen, understanding they needed a private moment.

Kyle knelt before her. "You don't need to wear the dress. It's only a suggestion. You look lovely no matter what you have on."

"I want to feel like myself again." She touched the silky material. "My life imploded after we got married and I'm having trouble adjusting."

"Can you talk to me about how you feel instead of pushing me away?"

"After the wedding, I felt like everything slipped out of my control. The business, the operation, and my career. I lost it all, and I'm not sure who I'm supposed to be now. I'm hurt by Alix's part in it, and how my mother sold me off. When I see your scar, it crushes me to think I almost lost you. I'm embarrassed by my weight, but I hope it makes you less attracted to me because I'm terrified the memories will come back if we're intimate."

"I'm glad the pot made you talkative." Kyle smiled and stroked her cheek. "I survived, and so did you. Let go of horrible stuff and don't let it control you. Let's focus on moving forward and figure out how to balance things better. It's been hard for me too. I hate what your mother did, and I'm disgusted another man thought he could have you. I'm sorry for what happened at the loft and the way I reacted. My anger and moods stem from being incompetent to help, not because my feelings for you wavered. Through it all, I never stopped loving you, and I'll never find you unattractive. I'm not good at sharing my emotions, and it's hard for me to give up control, but I have faith we're meant to be together and we will find our way."

"The only thing I'm sure of is how much I love you."

"Then that's enough. Everything else will fall into place."

"Maybe we should get high more often. It makes it easier to express ourselves." Casi grinned.

"Is that how you felt with Alix?" Kyle winked. "I smelled it in the apartment, and I noted your stash in the drawer. You realize it's legal here?"

"Another plus for Washington!" Casi laughed.

Jake chuckled as he joined them in the bathroom. "I'm right, Brian's gay."

"How do you know?" Kyle raised an eyebrow.

"Come watch him around Dylan, they're flirting."

Kyle greeted Brian, noticing the blush in his cheeks and sideways glances at Dylan, who played to his favor, also instantly enamored. As Kyle finished making dinner, Brian came over and whispered, "Is this a set up?"

He smiled. "No, Dylan is my wife's best friend and hairdresser. We flew him in as a surprise for her. I had already scheduled you to come and do the accounts."

"Did he cut your hair? It looks really good." Kyle blanched, and Brian laughed. "That was a compliment, not a pickup line." He grinned. "My interest lies elsewhere."

Kyle shrugged. "I believe he's single. Go for it."

Jake took out his phone. "I'm calling Anna and inviting her since this is turning into date night."

"Anna's not a date kind of girl," Kyle warned.

"She's been dying to meet Casi, she'll come." He hesitated. "Is it uncomfortable for you since you dated her?"

"I was one of many men she slept with and there were never any feelings. The only woman I care about is my wife." His face lit up as she entered the room, looking stunning in the blue dress. He took her hand and turned to Brian. "This is my wife, Casi."

"It's wonderful to meet you." Brian shook her hand.

"I'm responsible for her hair. She looked like a hobo before I arrived." Dylan fixed her bangs.

"You're very talented." Brian praised.

"I am." Dylan winked.

Thirty minutes later, Anna arrived, and Kyle extended a hand. "Nice to see you again, Casi is excited to meet you."

Anna gave him a kiss with a sultry smile. "If I had known you had such a beautiful home, I would have tried to snag you myself."

"I will be living across the street, so you'll get another chance to live this life." Jake approached with a smile.

Anna leaned in and gave him a kiss. "Sounds like a good deal." She stepped back and regarded Casi. "You are even more gorgeous in person!" Before Casi could respond, Anna planted a kiss on her lips.

"Super-hot!" Jake elbowed Kyle.

"That's as close as we are coming to that threesome." Kyle grinned, and Anna threw her head back and laughed.

Introductions were made, and Brian sat with Casi at the table to go over the accounts. She smiled and tried to focus, and he gave her a knowing wink. "Kyle has set up a retirement savings for you and a joint checking account. He is extremely savvy with money, so you can trust him to have your best interest in mind."

"Where do I sign?" She grasped the pen. "Why is there already money in there?" She noted the balance of twenty-thousand dollars.

"Kyle insisted that was to be put away for your future." He leaned closer. "You got lucky with him. He takes care of his family very well."

Jake escorted Anna down the dock to show her the lake while Dylan designated himself as the bartender, paying special attention to making cocktails for Brian. Kyle set out dinner and everyone gathered around the table, complimenting him on the stuffed pork loin with orzo pasta. Conversation was easy, and it rolled into drinks in the living room. Casi put on music and pulled Dylan up to dance with her. Anna cuddled with Jake on the sofa, amused by the action surrounding them.

"I love your laugh," Jake whispered.

Anna turned to him. "It's easy to laugh around you. I feel at ease, which is unusual for me. I don't normally let my guard down. I adore Casi, and I like how you are caring and protective of her."

He shrugged. "She's a good friend."

"She told me a little about LA and how kind you were to her."

"What else did she tell you about me?"

"Not much, she mentioned your life is complicated but suggested I talk to you about it. She's protective of you as well."

"Did she mention I have another baby on the way?"

"No. I thought you were divorced?" Anna cocked her head.

"I am, but a woman I was involved with thought it would be a great idea to get pregnant without my consent. I already have two kids."

"You understand this thing between us is casual, right? I'm not looking for a boyfriend." Anna put her hand on his.

"I know."

"I'm an independent woman. I came here tonight to meet Casi, but also because I wanted to spend time with you." She gave him a kiss. They watched Kyle clear off the coffee table and give Casi a hand up to dance on top as he smiled at her. "He adores her, doesn't he?" Anna noted.

"He does. Are you alright with that?"

"Your brother and I were never serious, and I love having her as a friend. I've never had a close girlfriend, only sisters. Four still live in Portland and one is near me in the city."

"Why do you stay in hotels if you live in Seattle?"

"My home is for me. I like to keep it private."

"Will you ever invite me there?" Jake's eyes crinkled with amusement.

"I might." Anna held his gaze. "You intrigue me."

"Can you spend the night with me at my apartment?"

"I don't do sleepovers." She set her jaw. "Besides, I think your house guest has a love interest."

Jake rolled his eyes as Dylan grasped Brian's hips in the pretense of teaching him dance moves. "Everyone is lucky in love except me."

"Don't count yourself out just yet." Anna glanced around the room. "Is this seriously a one-bedroom house?"

Jake pointed to a nook by the dining area. "Kyle had it designed with a master only, which he enlarged for Casi. That area was created as part of the open plan with the concept of converting it to another bedroom if needed."

"For when they have children?"

Jake shrugged, unsure if she knew about Casi's procedure. "Or for me when I screw up my life so royally that I need to move in with my brother."

"This new baby is overwhelming you, huh?" Anna snuggled closer.

"It's not what I wanted in my future."

Anna caressed his cheek. "Perhaps we have to accept the cards we are dealt and make the best of it."

"I am an expert at acceptance." He gave her a weak smile. "Would you like a refill on your wine?"

Anna set her glass down. "Actually, I'm in the mood for something a little more stimulating."

"I think there's still half a joint in the bathroom."

"Not tonight." Anna slid her hand over his chest. "Why don't you show me where the laundry room is."

"Why?" Jake cocked his head. "Oh, right this way." He held his hand out.

Anna slid up on the washing machine. "Put all your worries aside and focus on being with me." She ran her hand over his toned abs, snapping the button of his jeans undone.

"I loved watching you dance tonight." Kyle pulled Casi back on the bed beside him. "And I loved watching you laugh."

"It is fun to be a couple and entertain friends."

"We should do that more often." He slipped her panties off. "Now I think we should make love."

"It's been so long; I don't know if I remember how."

He undid his jeans and rolled on top of her. "If memory serves me correctly, you're pretty good at this." He entered her and gasped, reeling in the sensation after so many months.

Casi arched her hips toward him, pulling him closer as she moaned. She felt him tense and started to giggle. "That's all I get after three months?"

He burrowed his face against her neck and laughed. "Sorry, you turned me back into a teenager. Give me a minute to recover so I can redeem myself." He yawned as he flopped beside her.

She wriggled into pajamas. "Rest up. I'm going to get ice cream."

Casi walked to the kitchen and Jake regarded her from the sofa where he reclined with a blanket, watching a movie with Jezebel tucked in his arms. "Pretty speedy."

She giggled. "Yes, it was."

"Bring me ice cream and come talk to me."

She filled a second bowl and brought it to him. He lifted his legs, and she sat, arranging the blanket over them. "Don't fall for Anna. She likes you a lot, but she's not interested in dating."

"You reeled Kyle in, even though he was a confirmed bachelor."

"True, but Anna's more complicated than him."

"Are you insinuating my brother is simple?"

Casi laughed. "He's straightforward. Once I had his heart, he was all mine." She licked the spoon with a grin.

"Do you think she's bothered I have another kid on the way?"

"You told her?"

"I wanted to be honest about my situation."

"I doubt she cares. Her focus is planning for her future, living in a nice place, and she loves working."

"You don't believe she would want to come live in a trailer with me and help raise my bastard child?"

"Probably not. Are you ok if all she wants is sex?"

He shrugged, "Sure, usually my relationships are all drama and no sex, so it is new territory. I think the hardest part is sleeping alone. That's the only part I miss about being married, I liked the activity in the house, people coming and going. At night, when Gail would finally shut up, it was nice to have a body beside me." He took her hand, lacing his fingers through hers as he spoke. "Kyle doesn't remember anything from before we were adopted, but I do. It was lonely. No one brought us food for days. We slept on the floor with a blanket. I recall people passed out, or parting in the house. I'm sure that's what led us to foster care. We were taken to a rundown house in Seattle, with tons of kids screaming and fighting. I carried Kyle around because I was afraid he would get lost."

She leaned against him while he stroked her hair. "Tell me more."

"We were there maybe a year or so. Everyone wanted the sweet, blue-eyed toddler. No one wanted me. I was too old. Too wild and too damaged. The scar on Kyle's chin is from me. I bit him to try to make him ugly, so no one would want him. Guess what he did?"

"Cried?"

"He hugged me, believing it was a game. After that, they locked me away. They told me I was bad and didn't deserve a brother. It was eight days and the longest I had ever been away from him. I howled all night and kicked the walls." He held out his left arm, with eight uneven scars in a row. "I carved one each morning with an old nail, when I saw the sun come up."

"Oh Jake." Casi ran a finger over the scars, stopping at a longer one across his wrist.

"From my teens." He sighed. "The worst day came when Kyle was about to be adopted and I watched through a crack in the door. He cried and searched the room as a woman explained the situation. He screamed and clung to the door, repeating my name. I kicked and clawed at it until my fingers bled. He could hear me and became inconsolable. When they opened the door to make me stop, I ran past them, grabbed Kyle and refused to let him go. They couldn't pry us apart. And then it happened."

"What?" Her eyes widened.

"My dad stated he wanted us both, that it wasn't alright to split up brothers. They argued, and finally the people who ran the home gave in, most likely to get rid of me. We drove to the farm and life began."

"Was it scary to be in a new house?"

"It was different to be in a big quiet home. My room seemed huge, and lonely. They would put me to bed, and I would sneak out and crawl in with Kyle. I figured it was temporary because I was used to being moved around. I made sure to keep an eye on Kyle, getting ready for when new people came to take him." He rolled his eyes. "My mom adored Kyle from the minute they brought him home. She would hold him and rock him, then sigh because she had to deal with me."

"Ah, the dreaded sigh." Casi giggled. "What about your dad?"

"Since I was older, he showed me how to do things, like building and fishing. I loved to help him with the animals." Jake smiled. "Earl's kids were bookworms, so he loved coming over and getting me riled up and my dad encouraged it." He smoothed a strand of hair from her cheek. "My first panic attack happened when I was twelve. I was terrified, and I was convinced I was dying. The doctor explained what it was, and my parents took me back home. My mom stayed with me for hours, rubbing my back and calming me. The contact was soothing, and I felt safe. After that we had a special connection because I finally understood what love was."

&

Casi moaned in her sleep, feeling the warmth and pressure of Kyle's tongue. She raised her hips toward him, running her fingers through his hair as she opened her eyes. "Are you molesting me in my sleep?" He smiled, slowly moving up her stomach, stopping at her belly button. She tried to push him back, uncomfortable with the sharpness of her hipbones as his hand slid over her. He resisted and continued his journey to her breasts, entering her slowly. He sensed her discomfort and knew she held back. He rolled over and pulled her on top, moving her arms as she tried to cover herself. "Casi, stop. I'm not judging how thin you are. Let me make love to you." He surveyed the emotions raging across her face. "It's me touching you, Sweetheart. Erase every other memory." He continued to talk to her lovingly, caressing her body as he thrust until she couldn't resist the orgasm when it took hold. She moaned and threw her head back and he held her hips tightly, not letting her break the connection. "See? We're still good."

"We are. You did better the second time."

"I thought you went to find a replacement last night."

"Never! I just talked with Jake for a bit."

"I heard you guys until I fell asleep."

"I hate how you went through that."

"It was worth it to get the parents we did."

"What do you think about the new baby being adopted?"

"I'm surprised Lia seems detached after wanting a kid so bad. Adoption worked out well for us, so it's not a bad choice."

"I don't think she was prepared for how taxing it would be on her body or that she would be doing it alone. Gail said she loved being a mother. I guess Lia thought it would be the same. Personally, I can't imagine carrying around a soul-sucking life force for nine months and then having to deal with it as a teenager." She shivered.

Kyle chuckled. "Gail was twenty-two and had a husband to take care of all the bills. My mom was always over there helping out too."

"Is that why you never wanted kids?"

"Part of the reason. I saw how hard Jake had to work to keep it all going. When Olivia got sick for the first time, he freaked out. Babies are a lot of work, and now look at the issues he has with her, always some new bullshit."

"Are you happy I'm your only issue?"

"Yes. I can handle you."

"Will you make me breakfast?"

"I've never taken you to Tucker's pancake house, it's awesome."

"I love pancakes!" She bounded out of bed.

"I know you do." He smiled with love for her.

16

COURTSHIP

After picking up supplies at one of their purveyors, Kyle parked on a side street and Jake scanned the familiar area. "What's the real reason we came to Seattle in the middle of the afternoon?"

Kyle pushed him through the door and greeted the tattoo artist. He drew several designs and Kyle chose Casi's name in script with a Florentine design and a heart. He removed his shirt and the assistant prepped his upper left arm with alcohol wipes.

"Maybe I'll get one that says, 'Casi's keeper'." Jake winked.

"Why don't you choose one we can both get as a tribute to our past and where we are now?"

Jake flipped through books. "I like this one, it complements the design we both already have, and what we believe in." He ran a finger over the script; *Dream without fear. Love without limits.*

"I agree. Where do you want it?"

A young woman sporting numerous tattoos looked at them seductively, admiring their well-defined bodies. "I think on your right-side ribs would be cool." She ran a finger over Kyle's scar. "Bullet wound?"

Kyle smiled. "Yes."

"Who's Casey?"

"Casi is my wife."

"Faithful?"

"Completely."

"How about you?" She turned her attention to Jake. "I don't see any women's names on you?"

"I'm not married." He didn't elaborate on the complexity of his relationships.

She smiled and picked up his phone, suggesting a picture of them getting their tattoos. "I added my name in your contacts in case you want to call me sometime. My name's Crystal."

Kyle drove a few more blocks to a mall. When they walked in the lingerie store, Jake grinned. "Doesn't she already own tons of this stuff?"

"I wanted to get something different. Something I chose." Kyle shifted with discomfort.

"Can I help you find something?" a young salesgirl asked, seeing them hovering near the entrance. Kyle blushed as he explained what he wanted for his wife, and the girl smiled. "What size is she?"

"She fluctuates between a four and six."

"She has big boobs." Jake chuckled and pointed to a poster in a stand by a negligee display. "That's her right there." Kyle cringed when he noted the photo of Casi on a bed, legs extended up the headboard behind her. She had a sultry smile as she caressed a ribbon on the outfit. He shuddered, glad she didn't model anymore, and wished he could cover up the image.

"So, she has a body type like this model?"

"That's actually her." Kyle explained. "I wanted something special that I picked out. Sexy but not sleazy."

The salesgirl smiled, seeing his uneasiness, and led him to a section of less risqué lingerie, to his relief. She left him to make his selection, indicating the sizes he needed. A short black lace negligee, with a lightly beaded bra top, caught his eye. Once they discreetly stashed the lingerie in the truck, Kyle detailed the rest of his plan over lunch.

"What prompted this?" Jake asked.

"Since we've been married, it seems like there's been one disaster after another. It is hard for her to give up her career and face where she is financially. I want to show her how great our life can be, and focus on us being together, rather than fighting all the time." Kyle picked at his fries. "When I paid off her debts, it was over twenty thousand dollars. That money made no difference to me; I barely noticed it was gone. When she paid it back, it made me think I've been too focused on saving and making sure I had enough put aside, and I am not really living."

"You have a great life. You can do anything you want."

"Exactly how I planned it, but when is the last time I spent any money? Casi's dad paid for most of the wedding, which was also our honeymoon. She didn't even want a big ring, just a simple band. We live in my house, without a mortgage. I bought her the car because I wanted her to be safe and hoped if she had something that could handle the weather, she would be happier in Washington."

"She is happy, you don't need to bribe her to stay."

"She's here because her life fell apart. I want her to move past it and focus on the future we're building. Mary has so much faith in her to succeed, and I was hard on her for screwing up. It hit me when she tried to make coffee and she flinched because I corrected her for making a mistake."

"Grinding the beans is an important step."

"True." Kyle chuckled. "I realized we barely dated. I fell in love with her so fast and moved to marriage without courtship. She was happy when Dylan was there, and I loved watching her relax and socialize." He smiled. "I've made reservations at a restaurant with a nightclub and booked rooms at a waterfront hotel. I was hoping you could join us with Anna to make it an extra treat for Casi."

Casi smiled when the brothers came home. "We saw your alien baby."

"Does it have two heads?" Jake gave Lia a kiss on the cheek.

"Yup, a little one and a big one." Casi giggled. "At first, I thought it had a giant penis, but the technician said it is the umbilical cord."

Jake chuckled. "He's healthy?" He noted Lia's slumped shoulders as she walked away to set the table.

"He's fine. The doctor says Lia is depressed, but it's normal in some women. It's a hormonal thing," Casi whispered.

"What can I do to make the apartment more comfortable for you?" Jake helped put out the cutlery.

"I'm having a shower next month, so I guess I'll have a bunch of baby stuff." Lia paused and tucked hair behind her ear. "Casi, you're coming right."

"Of course, I'll be there." Casi nodded.

"I didn't want a shower, but my mom's insisting. She says I'll need a lot of things and that I have no concept of the difficulties of raising a child. I'd rather buy them myself because I know everyone is gossiping about my life."

"Isn't it your family who's coming?" Jake asked.

"Yes, and they are the worst. They shake their heads and cluck their tongues. I used to be the poor, unmarried, childless woman. Now I'll be the unmarried, pregnant one."

"People will always talk. I'm sure they've had a few choice words about me." He noted she didn't deny it.

"Why are you shirtless?" Casi shoved Kyle out of her way as he leaned against a cabinet. He grinned and stretched to expose his rib as she reached behind him to the stove. "You got a tattoo!"

"We both did." Jake grinned. "It's our shared experience script."

She frowned. "That doesn't make me feel left out at all, stamping yourself as a tribute to your brother, and not me."

"My wedding band represents my devotion to you," Kyle noted.

"One you can take off." She put the meatloaf on the trivet.

"Would you prefer something more permanent?" He flexed his bicep.

Tears came to her eyes. "I love it!"

"Now everyone will know I belong to you." Kyle gave her a kiss.

Lia watched them and felt a pang of jealousy, aware Jake would never consider getting her name, and regretted the life growing inside her.

&

Casi met Anna at the mall in Seattle, early on Friday. They chatted over coffee while she explained what she needed for meetings with future clients. She wanted to impress Mary and demonstrate how much she valued the opportunity. Anna narrowed it down to a few stores she felt would suit her needs, and they headed out. The first store provided the basic slacks, jackets, and blouses which were professional but not dowdy.

She bought a few skirts at another store, and several pairs of practical shoes, but nothing extravagant. She directed Anna to a shop on a side street she had located on her GPS.

"Please tell me you're not getting a tramp stamp. I won't allow you to ruin your perfect figure!" Anna gasped as they entered the tattoo parlor.

Casi told her about the brother's new tattoos, and the special one Kyle had gotten. "We've been through so much this year; more than I can even share with you because I'm still too fragile. I want to do something permanent as a reminder." She sat with the artist and told him what she wanted to write, deciding on design and script. While he went to make the stencil, she changed out of her top and bra, placing a towel in front of her as she reclined on the chair. She lifted her left arm above her head as he began and winced at the sting while Anna held her hand.

A young assistant smiled when she noted the receipt. "Your husband got your name tattooed on his arm, and he and his brother got matching script."

"That's right." Casi returned her smile.

"I remember them, super-hot! I was disappointed he's married, but his brother said he's single. I gave him my number."

"How old are you?"

"I'm twenty-two. I like older guys because they're more experienced."

Anna and Casi looked at each other and laughed.

The tattoo artist finished and held up a mirror for her approval. She nodded, pleased with how it was tucked beside her breast, discreet in appearance, yet obvious in meaning, *Kyle Jensen owns my heart.*

After getting ready at Anna's condo, they met the brothers at the restaurant. Both severely handsome in dress shirts and ties. "Wow!" Casi hugged Kyle, feeling the smoothness of his freshly shaven skin as she kissed him. "I didn't know you even owned a tie."

"I even tied it all by myself," he mocked.

Anna felt giddy, realizing this was their first real date as they took their seats overlooking the waterfront. Casi smiled at the amount of effort he put into arranging the evening, and made a point of ignoring the waiter's flirting, placing her hand on Kyle's, and letting him order for her. They shared desserts and went to the nightclub on the top floor, brimming with people. The layout was spectacular, with leather seating areas and chrome fixtures. The dance floor had flashing lights surrounded by a large bar. They found an available sofa and ordered drinks. Casi pulled Anna up to dance with her and they joined the crowd for a few songs.

Jake grinned at his brother. "You did a great job planning. She's happy."

Kyle held out a hand as Casi returned and snuggled against him. "I had no idea Seattle had nightclubs! This place is awesome."

"We have the same venues LA has, with a lot more rain," Anna laughed.

Several hours later, Kyle put his arm around Casi, kissing her passionately, growing with intensity. "You're getting me very excited. You had better stop or I'll need to ravage you in the car before we drive home." She took a sip of her drink.

He slid his hand up her thigh. "I have another surprise for you." He nodded to Jake and grasped her hand and strolled from the lounge to a hotel a few blocks away.

"I don't have clothes for tomorrow." Casi cringed as she mentally assessed what she needed for the night.

"I packed you a bag." He read her pained expression. "It will prove how well I know you." He handed her the key card. "Mrs. Jensen. For tonight, anyway."

"I'm not objecting to the title." Casi kissed him and took the key.

Jake hesitated, and Anna laughed. "You don't know my last name?"

"I have no idea," he admitted. Kyle tried to remember when they had registered, straining to recall what had been written on the purchase orders, but couldn't come up with it. The desk clerk had rolled his eyes and simply written 'Anna', as the brothers chuckled.

Casi stopped to survey the view of the waterfront, pulling Anna with her. "Damn, isn't it fantastic!"

"And to think we won't be looking at it." Anna giggled. "Thank God I knew about the hotel or I would have been a disaster if I expected Jake to know what to pack."

Kyle stood in the lobby watching them and breathed a sigh of relief that the evening had turned out better than he had planned. He turned to Jake and paled, unsure what to do at that moment.

"Kyle?" Lauren rushed toward him, dressed in chef attire.

"I didn't know you worked at this hotel." Kyle gave her an awkward hug and glanced at Casi, still engrossed in conversation with Anna.

"I started here about a year ago. I'm in charge of the catering department." She eyed Jake as he fumbled with his phone.

"I would imagine they do a lot of events at a hotel like this." Kyle checked his watch, inventing an appropriate exit.

"Are you here for business?" Lauren scanned their clothing.

"We're doing a night in Seattle for fun." He rubbed his temple and turned to make the inevitable introductions, noting Anna staring at her phone.

Lauren's eyes watered as Casi walked toward them, oblivious to the pain she caused. "Is that your wife?"

"Yes." He raised an eyebrow when they made a sudden detour.

"I guess they need to use the bathroom," Jake suggested.

Lauren cast her gaze to him. "You are on a date with the redhead? You aren't bothered your child will be born in two months?"

"It bothers me a lot, but it has nothing to do with me being on a date."

Lauren pouted and regarded her watch. "I guess I'll see you around." She gave Kyle a hug.

"Sure, I'll give you a call. It was good seeing you."

"Why are you encouraging her?" Jake punched him when she left.

"I like her as a friend." Kyle rubbed his arm.

"Then tell your wife about her!"

"You will explain the 911 text when we get to the room," Anna informed Jake as they approached the elevator.

Casi walked in the expansive room, taking in the view and the amenities. "Amazing!" She walked to the bed and smiled when she saw a pink box wrapped with ribbon.

Kyle smiled as she opened the gift. "I look forward to seeing it on." He undressed and reclined on the bed while he waited. "Wow!"

She stood at the doorway in the negligee with the stretch lace clinging to her curves, wrapping her in the pattern and revealing a glimpse of her perfect figure. She turned slowly, so he could get the full effect.

"It looks incredible. Can I have a private lingerie show?"

"Kyle! Why are you ridiculing me?" She clasped her hands to her face.

"I'm not being hurtful. We're together forever, and from now on, I'm the only one who will ever get to see you like this. I love you Casi."

She exhaled and walked across the room, taking her time to pose. "That's the extent of a private booking." She glanced away.

"What about the husband show?"

"He gets a lot more." She lifted the hem of the negligee as she moved toward him. She stopped at the bed and leaned forward, slipping the straps off her shoulders to reveal her breasts. He slid his hand up her thigh, caressing her as she knelt on the bed beside him. She straddled him and gasped with pleasure. Her breathing quickened as the orgasm took hold, and she moaned for more. He arched his hips as he released, and she screamed in ecstasy. She pressed her forehead on his and caught her breath, gently kissing him as she sat up. "I have a surprise for you." He watched with curiosity as she removed the negligee and turned to show him the writing beside her breast. "What do you think?"

He ran a finger over the script and his eyes watered. "I love it! Thank you for declaring it for eternity."

Jake and Anna walked in their room, and she slipped her dress off. "Let's hear about the emergency."

He contemplated the best way to explain. "It wasn't so much of an emergency as an attempt to make the night perfect."

"Does it involve the mousy woman in chef clothes?"

"She's Kyle's ex-girlfriend, Lauren, and he never mentioned her to Casi."

"Who cares?"

"Kyle does. She was devastated when they broke up and hysterical when she found out he got married. She's still not over him and he's made the fatal mistake of trying to be friends."

"You've piqued my curiosity." She reclined on the bed.

"You can't tell Casi."

"Oh hell no! I refuse to stand by and let him cheat on her. I consider her my best friend."

"He's not cheating. It didn't seem important to mention her but after he got shot, she called to see how he was doing, and they started talking. Casi was in a bad place emotionally, and it would have been insane to tell her about an ex-girlfriend."

Anna grinned. "She's the brunette I saw him with at the bar!"

"Yes. They met to catch up."

"Why not introduce them tonight?"

"Kyle has been through hell with Casi and it meant a lot to him to take her out. When I saw Lauren, I was concerned it would cause drama and ruin the night. Plus, there's one other thing…"

"You slept with her too?" Anna rolled her eyes.

"Yuck, no." Jake shivered. "But, the woman who's pregnant with my kid, is her sister, and of course she'll blab about you."

"You're such a hillbilly!" She playfully smacked his arm.

He grinned and pushed her back on the bed. "You are jealous everyone wants a baby with me. Just wait, he'll be adorable with my blue eyes."

She stroked the side of his face, fighting her growing feelings for him. "I think we need to end this, Jake."

"I can't. I'm falling in love with you." He gazed at her.

"Jake, no!" She pushed him back and rolled on top of him. "This is a mistake." She held his gaze and admitted to herself they were making love for the first time.

She snuggled in his arms and he whispered, "I'm aware you don't do sleepovers, my little Gingersnap, but this is my room and I'm not leaving."

"Maybe I could make an exception?" She put her head on his chest and listened to the rhythm of his heart, knowing he had captured her own.

❧

"How did I do?" Kyle surveyed her reaction to the bag he packed for Casi.

She smiled as she held up several matching sets of bras and panties. "A little excessive on the lingerie, but you rocked it on the outfit!" She waved a hand over the sweater and jeans perfectly matched with brown suede boots. "I love how you even remembered my toiletries and makeup."

"Full points for knowing your routine?" He grinned. "This

morning I will take you for a breakfast of salmon eggs Benedict before getting crumpets and coffee while walking around Pike Place Market."

"You are a perfect planner." She sighed and knelt in front of him as he sat on the bed. "Listen to me, without interruption, and hold off judgement. If you want us to move forward, we have to be able to discuss things openly." He held his breath and nodded. "I must talk to Alix and forgive him."

"He has too much control over you." Kyle's eyes flashed with anger.

"That's why it's essential to allow him to apologize, otherwise he'll continue to manipulate my emotions. You don't understand his addiction and how it affects him. He feared he could easily slip, so he was ultra disciplined with himself and of me."

"Do you love him?"

"I never did. I let him dominate my life because I was lost. He always made good choices, but when he started to spiral down, he attempted to take me with him. When he realized what was happening, he called you." Tears slid down her cheeks and she put a finger to his lips. "I must dictate what happens in my life and make my own choices."

"What are you saying?" Kyle grabbed her hand. "Are you leaving?"

"No! I need to see Alix and my mom. I want to release this hate. I keep analyzing why they did it." She gasped for air. "And I must do it by myself."

Kyle hugged her tightly. "I don't want you to go to LA."

"I'll need to go, eventually. It's one of the places in my territory for the marketing campaign." She wiped a tear. "I'm not ready to face my past yet, but Alix has been messaging me and it's making me anxious to keep it from you."

Kyle squeezed his eyes shut, considering he was in a similar position with Lauren. "Actually..."

Casi shook her head. "I'm not asking for permission. I just needed you to hear me out before I text him." Kyle cringed at the lost opportunity to bring up Lauren as she grabbed her phone and texted with remarkable speed and efficiency. She turned the screen to him before she sent it. "I'm doing ok and moving on with my life. I'll meet you at some point, but not in BBF. If I come to LA, I'll call you. For now, work on getting better and understand I've already forgiven you. I'm not hiding anything from Kyle anymore. My marriage is my priority and I have a new career to focus on."

"What's BBF?"

"Blackberry Falls, silly."

"That's hilarious!" He pulled her on his lap and gave her a kiss.

"Want to see my new career attire?" Casi surveyed the brothers on the sofa while Lia tried to get comfortable in the recliner. "I'll do a fashion show."

She came out in each outfit, explaining how it complemented her professional image, bringing their attention to her shoes and accessories and explaining how she would wear her hair. Kyle smiled as she posed, thrilled to note her enthusiasm. Lia complimented her extensively and Jake became bored as she highlighted her color choices. "It's brown." He yawned after she described a blouse as caramel.

"Says the guy who wears jeans and t-shirts every day." She waved his comment away with a swoop of her hand. The last outfit featured a navy knee-length skirt with deep slits on the thighs. She paired it with a low, draped blouse and navy kitten heels. She came out with a twirl, showing them how the skirt fluttered when she walked, or twirled. "Apparently, I'm supposed to wear pantyhose. I thought I'd feel like an old lady, but look!" She flipped her skirt up to reveal a lacy garter that clipped to the stockings with satin bows.

"Sexy!" Kyle choked on his beer, while Lia giggled.

"Jesus, Casi! Now I'll have that image stuck in my head!" Jake complained.

"I hope you're not planning on doing that at your presentation?" Kyle wiped the front of his t-shirt.

"That's how she will snag the clients." Jake patted her on the backside.

"I would suspect it is mostly women in the industry," Kyle asserted.

"You would be surprised how many men are representatives for the stores I'll be working with." Casi shrugged.

"Then the skirt stays down." Kyle insisted.

17

OLD ENOUGH

Jake grinned as he texted Crystal, intrigued by her interest in him. She gave him an address in South Park where she had a shared apartment. He realized he was making a mistake but could feel Lia becoming more dependent on him as the pregnancy advanced, constantly questioning his frequent trips to Seattle. He expected Lauren told her about Anna, and even though he explained early on about their relationship status, she pushed for more. Lia joined them most nights for dinner since they relocated her to his apartment, and he felt claustrophobic. His feelings for Anna confused him, and he tried not to act desperate and push her away. Crystal seemed like a good distraction, especially when she sent him a nude picture.

Jake parked in front of her apartment and knocked on the door. She kissed him hello and took his hand, leading him to her room decorated with scarves and red lights. He understood he should turn around, but when another girl smiled invitingly from the bed, he tuned everything else out. He assumed Crystal was in her early twenties, but this girl appeared even younger. They both had a multitude of tattoos and piercings and were obviously high. He took the joint and inhaled deeply. "How old are you?"

"Old enough." The girl smiled and undid his jeans.

Crystal kissed his neck and assisted him in removing his t-shirt while the other girl proved her oral experience, making him moan. Jake let them take the lead, passing the joint between them as he found pleasure in their young bodies, eventually falling asleep in a tangle of limbs. He awoke sometime later with a throbbing headache, desperately wanting to leave. He found his clothes and phone, but could not locate his watch, wallet, and keys. He wondered if it was a setup, the girls distracting him as their roommate ripped him off. He called Kyle, not elaborating on the circumstances. He glanced at the sleeping girls with their phones clutched to their chests and cringed at the possibility of a record of his reckless behavior. "Can you bring Casi when you come?"

Kyle was making dinner with Casi and Lia when Jake called. The silence and low voice on the other end indicated his brother's involvement in something beyond his capabilities to solve. Kyle cleared his throat. "Casi, Jake has a flat tire and I need you to come with me to pick him up."

"Why? I have no clue how to change a tire." Casi cocked her head.

"We need to take your car."

"Can't you take it without me in it?"

"I'll need to drive Jake's truck back." He shot her a look to indicate that was the end of the discussion. "Lia, we'll be back in a bit. Maybe have a snack if you can't wait until dinner to eat."

Casi waited until they entered the freeway to request the truth. "Is he drunk again?"

"I'm not sure what he got himself into. He asked me to bring you, which I can't figure out." Kyle found a parking spot on the poorly lit street.

"Do you think he came to buy drugs?" Casi scanned the area with people huddled in doorways and a drunken man urinating on the sidewalk.

Jake met them at the door of the apartment, looking nervous. Kyle held Casi in front of him protectively. "What the hell did you do? I'm not comfortable bringing Casi to this kind of place."

"Are you high?" Casi watched him fidget.

"I'm not requesting an interrogation. I need your help with something." Jake led them up the stairs. He indicated the girls on the bed and then told them about his missing belongings.

"Why did you force me to come? Did you need to brag about your orgy with skanks?" Casi winced at the scene containing a condom wrapper, joint, and a bottle of tequila.

"There may be pictures I need you to erase; you're good at violating people's phones." Jake shoved her forward.

She rolled her eyes as she perused the girls. "I see you took Crystal up on her offer?"

"I didn't know about the other girl until I got here."

Casi slid Crystal's phone from her hand gently and scrolled through her photos, making gagging sounds as she saw the pictorial of sex. "I deleted your texts and phone number as well as the photos."

"Good," Jake and Kyle said at the same time.

She knelt and moved the curtain of hair shrouding the other girl's face. "How old is this girl?" Her eyes widened.

Jake blushed. "I asked, and she said old enough."

"Seriously? If you must ask, I'd say she's probably off limits." Kyle punched him on the shoulder.

Casi deleted the pictures, turning the phone to figure out the logistics of a difficult angle. "Stop that! Erase them!" Jake scolded.

"My eyes will never be the same after seeing that!" She shivered and rifled through a handbag.

"Is my stuff in there?" Jake wrung his hands.

"No, but her driver's license is." She held the ID up to his face. "She's 17!"

"Fuck!" Kyle turned to avoid looking at the nude girl.

Casi poked Jake on the chest. "She's the same age as your daughter, Pervert!"

"I want this filed in that special place where we put Casi's bad decisions; never to be spoken of again," Jake demanded.

"Fair enough." Casi giggled. "Kyle's the one who has to keep cleaning up after us. Who do you love more, me or Jake?"

"I love you differently, and you're both screw ups." Kyle sighed.

"If we were drowning, and you could only save one of us, who would it be?" She proposed the age-old question.

"Neither of you. It's time you both learn how to swim." Kyle grinned. "Let's get the hell out of here before these girls wake up and cause a scene."

Casi scanned the room. "Did you use a condom?"

"Of course, I did!"

"You're not exactly the poster child for birth control," Kyle stated.

"How many?" She grasped the wrapper with two fingers as if it were contaminated.

"I'm thirty-eight, how many do you think?" Jake grabbed it from her and shoved it in his pocket.

They heard the wail of sirens in the street and Casi pointed to the stairs. "Get him out of here. I want to check something."

"I'm not leaving you here," Kyle said.

"Wait for me by the car, I'll be right there." They leaned against the truck and Kyle hoped he hadn't made a fatal decision by leaving her behind. A few minutes later, she bounded out of the house with a smile. She held up the keys. "Sticky-fingered roommate."

"Follow me, ok?" Kyle opened her car door. "I'll take our drugged-out child." They drove in silence until Jake sat forward suddenly, announcing he was about to throw up. Kyle pulled over as he bolted from the truck. Casi parked behind them, reading Kyle's text. "He had to puke."

"Why? Did he just realize seventeen isn't legal?" Casi added a giggling emoji and Kyle responded with a hysterically laughing gif.

Casi sipped her coffee, watching Jake lightly snoring as he sprawled on the sofa. He woke and smiled at her, his blue eyes reading her thoughts as he reached for her mug. "Kyle said I should let you sleep and then take you to work. I planned to give you another ten minutes before I started poking you." She handed him his wallet and watch. "Was the threesome what you thought it would be?"

"Too many demands on me. I have trouble trying to satisfy one woman."

"It never appealed to me. I prefer all the attention," she mused.

"Where did you get my stuff?"

"The roommate, a computer geek, swiped them. I saw him hovering outside the room and flirted with him after you guys left," she reported.

"Do you think he'll cause trouble?"

"He was illegally downloading from the internet and I captured screen shots. There is no proof you were there, and he doesn't know the other girl. Crystal is his roommate. I let him keep your money."

"Thanks." He gave her a kiss and handed her the mug as he walked to the bathroom to take a shower.

Lia smiled at Casi, sitting at the vanity in her bra and panties, doing her makeup. Jake stepped out of the shower and wrapped a towel around his waist. "Good morning." He nodded as she handed him a latte.

"Kyle said Casi would drop you off on her way to work. I wanted to catch you before you left," Lia said.

"What did he really say?" Jake sipped the coffee.

"That she would bring your drunk ass to work when you awoke from your coma," Lia giggled.

"That sounds more like him," Jake surmised.

Casi sorted through her clothing, deciding what to wear as Jake reclined on the bed and critiqued the outfit choices, agreeing when she finally settled on her spice brown pants and caramel blouse.

"Very sophisticated," Kyle said from the doorway. He shoved Jake over and sat beside him.

"You didn't trust me to drop him off?" Casi frowned.

"I forgot about your meeting in Seattle. I wanted to see you before you left. Are you nervous?" Kyle reached for her hand.

"I feel prepared but it's crucial I impress Mary. I have a lot to make up for." She fluffed her hair in the mirror. "Up or down?"

"Down." Kyle nodded. "The new cut is professional."

"Thank you." Casi beamed.

"I'll walk you out." Kyle slapped his brother on the side. "Get dressed and be in the truck in three minutes, you've wasted enough time."

Jake dressed for work. "What did you want to talk about?"

Lia sighed. "We should make a decision about the adoption. They are pressuring me to commit, but you need to sign. Do you want to meet some couples who are interested?"

"I realize people are excited at the prospect of a baby and I should jump at the chance to make him someone else's responsibility. I won't sign yet."

"I can't wait to not be pregnant anymore. I hate being tired and my fingers are like pin cushions from the stupid blood tests," Lia cried.

Jake gave her a kiss. "He's not fully baked yet. Give him a few more months. Tell the agency we refuse to commit until he's born. This child deserves our full consideration, not a hasty decision."

They came out to see Casi leaning against her car as Kyle kissed her. He checked her gas gauge and tires and then wished her well. "You're wearing my shirt." Kyle frowned at Jake.

They drove to the shop without talking. When Kyle parked, he sat for a minute before reaching for the door handle. Jake put his hand on his arm. "Let's discuss it now. I'm already late and I can't work knowing you're pissed off at me."

Kyle turned to face his brother. "You put Casi in danger. She shouldn't have been in that sketchy neighborhood. We brought her to Washington to be safer than she was in LA." His nostrils flared. "I understand you're in a difficult spot, but I've seen you implode too many times not to recognize the signs. Is the next step me holding your hand while they pump your stomach at the hospital, or should I be more concerned about a suicide attempt?"

Jake covered his face. "I'm not that out of control!"

Kyle rubbed his shoulder. "Get your shit together. Tell me what I need to do to help you and I'll drop everything to make it happen." Jake nodded with tears in his eyes. "It would kill me if any harm came to you. You know that, right? You've always supported me and I'm your best friend."

"I know." Jake leaned in and hugged him.

"It seems like you're going out of your way to create more issues for yourself instead of dealing with the shit in front of you. You need to talk to Olivia. She's been texting Casi constantly, and she won't tell me what it's about, but I'm getting the feeling it's not good."

Casi arrived at Mary's condo twenty minutes early. She parked and checked her makeup in the mirror, determined to prove she was taking the job seriously; no more immature model girl.

"Look who's here early." Mary smiled and scanned her appearance. "I see you had a visit from Dylan?"

"Kyle flew him in to fix me."

"Your attire is polished and professional."

"Thank you." Casi exhaled and made a mental note to thank Anna for the invaluable advice.

Mary directed her to a table where she had coffee and pastries set out. "I'll give you the tour after you show me what you've come up with."

Casi opened her portfolio case and removed mock-ups. She created a power point presentation but felt the ad copy looked better on the poster board. She leaned the colorful pictures against the bar. "First, I did a market review. There are a multitude of skincare lines targeting older women, fostering the fear of growing old, and a million reasons why aging is negative. You always taught me to respect myself and be proud of my body and face. My idea is to target a younger clientele and get them to understand the benefits of starting early with proper skincare, promoting a healthy image, and a loyal customer base." She took a breath and tried to read Mary's reaction. "What makes us different than the other lines? The ingredients are natural, plant based, and no fillers. No testing on animals, and ethical business standards. Those are major selling points. We are not pitching an unrealistic dream or the fountain of youth. We encourage a healthy regime with quality ingredients at a reasonable price point." Casi set up several more posters, detailing the core values they would promote and advertise. She opened her laptop and initiated the power point, explaining her research and facts, backing up her statements. She outlined a solid marketing campaign, building name recognition with a loyal customer base; no flash in the pan, glitz, or over-sexualizing. She shared her personal experience, purposely wearing light makeup to highlight glowing skin and a healthy complexion. "I'm thirty-one and have used the line for thirteen years. After trying every major product during my career as a model, I can confidently state Macrae Skincare Line outshines them all."

"The Washington climate is certainly beneficial to your skin, which is a definite asset when you are meeting clients." Mary slid a small white box across the table.

Casi lifted the lid to discover business cards embossed with the company logo and a title of Marketing and Promotions Executive. She wiped tears from her cheeks. "Thank you."

"Why are you crying, Sweet Girl?"

"You had the cards printed already. You believed in me even after I failed you so many times."

"I never stopped believing in your potential; I needed you to have faith in your own abilities." Mary patted her hand. "You can't cry on a sales call, even if they hate your presentation, which is brilliant by the way."

Casi giggled, predicting she would be nervous to approach the store executives, but she adored the product and figured she had essentially been in sales for almost half her life.

Mary showed her around the condo, beautifully decorated with a view of Puget Sound. "I used Roberts on the cards because I wasn't sure if you had taken Jensen. We can change it in the future."

"I still haven't decided. Does that make me a bad wife? I have been through tremendous changes in a few months and it is the last of the old me that I am holding on to."

Jake regarded his sullen daughter across the dinner table. "Olivia is this about the baby? I can't change what's happened and you're old enough to accept that."

"It's not like we ever see you anymore, so what does it matter?" Olivia snarled.

"Obviously, I suck as a father, but why are you giving Mom a hard time? She's always been here for you."

"I have no privacy here, and she's always in my business!"

Gail rolled her eyes. "You do whatever you want. You got two tattoos without permission, and I have lost count of your piercings. Every week your hair is a different color. I have no idea who your friends are or where you are half the time."

Olivia stared them down. "I'm going to have a baby of my own and I'll do things on my own terms."

"Awesome, when you have children you can raise them however you want." Jake sighed. "But you are our child and you must follow the rules."

"I'm already pregnant. Unlike you, I actually want mine."

Jake lashed back at the challenge. "You had better be kidding!"

"I'm not, and there's nothing you can do about it." Olivia crossed her arms over her chest with defiance.

"You're getting an abortion!" Jake pounded the table.

"It's my body. I'm choosing to have this baby!"

Jake hurled his plate across the room, leaving a pattern of pot roast slowly dripping down the wall toward the shattered china on the floor. "Is this an attempt to get more attention?"

"You only care about your stupid brother!" Olivia accused.

"I gave up everything to raise you. An abortion would have been a hell of a lot easier!" Jake exploded.

"Jake, stop," Gail pleaded.

"Go ahead, Olivia. See how awesome your life turns out. You think the rules are unfair? Try taking care of a child on minimum wage. Who is the loser who knocked you up? What does he say about it?"

"He loves me and we're getting married!" Olivia cried.

"Perfect, you can be someone else's problem!" Jake bellowed.

"You never wanted me anyway," she sobbed.

Gail put her hand on Jake's, hoping he would not tell her the truth. He rubbed his temple, staying silent as he tried to calm the rage building inside, and Olivia stormed out of the room. "Do you want me to call Kyle?" Gail asked as the shaking began, and Jake struggled to catch his breath.

Reid contemplated his dinner, disturbed by the turn of events. "Do you think our family will go to hell?"

"Don't worry, Reid," Jake managed. "We are already there."

Kyle arrived twenty minutes later, almost hitting Olivia's car as she peeled out of the driveway. He noted Gail wiping the wall as Reid picked up shards of dinnerware. He sat beside his brother, rhythmically rubbing his back, and Gail filled him in on the drama. Jake turned to him. "I've got a baby on the way who I don't want, and a grandkid coming from a child I also never wanted. I can't do this, Kyle. The walls are caving in on me and I can't breathe."

"No one wanted us either, but things worked out in the end. You took care of Olivia, but now she has to be accountable for her choices and accept the consequences of her actions."

"I'll never be free," Jake choked.

"What would you do if you were?"

"Travel maybe. See somewhere beyond this coast. Anything other than take care of kids all my life."

"The trailer will be in place by June. We'll fix it up and you'll have your own space; a kid-free zone," Kyle asserted.

"Can I still come over to your house?"

"Of course, I would be lost without you."

18

SMALL-TOWN MEN

*C*asi hung her dove gray skirt and glanced at clothes crowding her side of the closet. She did a quick inventory of designers and considered options as she changed to leggings. She stood in front of the mirror and contemplated her appearance. Her weight had increased, and she felt more like herself. She pulled on her running shoes and headed for the trail, easily hiking the first four miles. She stopped at the ridge and regarded the lake, glimmering in the cool spring mid-afternoon light. She inhaled deeply and considered her new life. She was pleased with the changes she made, forging a new path with a brighter future.

It helped that Mary understood the complexities of changing her last name, perhaps reading into the deeper meaning behind it. She sighed; aware the surname represented the last connection to her family. As much as her mother claimed to hate Jack, she had never dropped his name. It was a tie to her past that Sonya couldn't release and one of the few things she and her mother had in common. She twisted her wedding band; thankful Kyle had not pushed her to change it. She smiled as she descended the trail, planning his birthday dinner and excited at the perfect opportunity to show his family how focused she was on their relationship. She feared she had disappointed Peter especially and was anxious to prove Kyle hadn't been misguided to marry her.

§.

Kyle and Jake were watching the outdoor channel when she came home. Casi poured a glass of water and sat on the coffee table in front of them to get their attention. "I sorted through my clothes and realized I own a lot of expensive designer things I'll never wear again."

"Move your head, you're blocking the TV," Jake said.

"I might set up an account on eBay and sell them."

Kyle smiled, reading her devastated expression. "It's a good idea. You could probably get decent money."

She nodded. "I could help out with expenses around here."

"There aren't any bills you need to pay. It is unexpected income, so use it for whatever you want. Maybe new clothes for your job?" Kyle suggested.

"I'll sell you a kid," Jake offered. "You can take the new one who's a blank slate, or the old pregnant one. Your choice."

"I like Kyle's idea better."

"I wonder if I could sell them on eBay?" Jake pondered.

"Her boyfriend works at the refinery. Maybe he should start selling stuff to support his kid," Casi stated.

"Did you meet him?" Jake asked.

"No, but I get the feeling he's not happy about the baby..."

"Tell me what you know!"

Casi winced. "Olivia was in tears because he wouldn't return her calls and refused to commit to a relationship. I did a little research online." She filtered the information to honor her promise to Olivia. "He's twenty-two and already has a couple of kids."

Jake shook his head. "Why would she want a child with trash like that? Is it to get back at me and show me what a bad father I am? Or, is it jealousy about Lia being pregnant?"

She took a moment, as Kyle turned down the TV, interested to hear the answer. "She feels like Lia broke up your marriage. She claims the pregnancy was an accident, but I think she's lost. She's not getting along with Gail and has no interest in college."

"She's going to college, even if she has to strap the baby on her back to attend classes," Jake declared.

Casi smiled. "She's only six weeks along and she's been having cramping. It's possible she might miscarry."

"God, let's hope so!" Jake exclaimed.

"Jake, you can't tell her that. Take her to lunch and try to hear her out. Let her share how she feels."

"Can I take her to the bar instead?"

Casi smiled and turned to Lia as she entered. "Kyle's birthday is next week. I want everyone to come for dinner."

"Don't go to any trouble, just order out. You're busy with the thing for Mary." Kyle shrugged.

"I'll grill steaks," Jake said. "You can make a salad."

"No! I'm making the whole damn dinner and you're both going to like it!" She shifted to the computer to get recipe ideas. After an hour of generic meals, she typed in 'what do small town men like to eat?' Images of steaks, pork chops, and ribs came up, making her laugh.

"What's so funny?" Kyle raised an eyebrow.

"Dylan sent me a joke on Facebook" She shut down the images and erased the history.

Casi surveyed the restaurant and watched Ava interacting with customers. From a bystander's view, her stepmother was beautiful and outgoing as she joked good-naturedly with a table of locals. She assessed there was more to the woman than met the eye, sensing a fierce loyalty and determination beneath the surface. Ava turned and her face lit up when she spotted Casi, igniting a familiar tug at her heart for the person her mother had trained her to hate. Casi smiled and fell into the warmth of her embrace, comforted by the love in her tone. "Sweetie, Mary said you were outstanding in your presentation. I'm so proud of you for seizing this opportunity."

"Thank you. I'm excited about working in a new field, although it's incredibly intimidating."

"You'll do great. Your ability to adapt and your in-depth technical skills will propel you in the right direction." Ava smiled at her and took out a piece of paper from her apron pocket. "One of my prep cooks claims this is his family's secret recipe for ribs. I translated it to English, so hopefully the steps make sense."

"I appreciate you getting it for me. I want to impress everyone with my cooking skills." Casi scanned the room. "Is Dad here?"

"He's across the border today, sourcing ingredients for the brewery. Did you need to speak with him?"

"No." Casi shrugged. "I wanted him to see how well I'm doing. I realize it was hard for him when everything happened."

"It was difficult for him to stand back and let you go through it alone." She smoothed her hand over Casi's hair and gazed at her. "I insisted we had to let you and Kyle deal with things in your own way."

"But you sent Mary." Casi grinned.

Ava blushed. "She has always had a plan for you. I suggested the time may be right to put it into action."

"It must be nice having her live closer to you."

Ava exhaled. "Yes and knowing you're safe is paramount."

Casi hugged her tightly. "Thanks for giving me another chance."

"I'll never give up on you."

Casi prepped the ribs with the dry rub and took them to Lia's apartment the day before the party to keep it a secret. She used Ray Dawson's recipe for potato salad, following his advice to sprinkle vinegar immediately after draining the Yukon gold potatoes. She planned a fruit and cheese platter with selections from a shop in Seattle she had found by accident after getting lost one day. Jake took Kyle fishing, and she told them to be home by five at the latest, understanding it took him only minutes to shower and the guests would arrive at six. She re-read her directions and placed the ribs in the oven to cook while she made the sauce for basting. She opted for the whiskey cake, guessing it would be a hit with the salted caramel glaze.

She smiled when the brothers arrived home. "Looks festive." Kyle noted the elaborately decorated table and fruit and cheese platter looking like something from a magazine. He scanned the clean kitchen void of anything suggesting dinner had been prepared. "Did you want salmon tonight?" He held up several large fish on a string.

"No thanks, I have something else planned." Casi smiled at their confused expressions as they went to clean and package the fish.

As predicted, it took Kyle twenty minutes to get ready, and she directed him to the sofa while Jake showered. She handed him a drink in a copper cup. "Lynchburg mule, whiskey instead of gin. I got the recipe from Joe, the bartender."

Kyle took a sip, "Awesome!"

She lifted her skirt and sat across his lap, giving him a kiss. "I don't want you to think I am too busy cooking to kiss you on your birthday."

Jake put an ice cube down her shirt. "Guests are here." He grinned and directed her attention to the door.

Casi shivered and extracted the cube. "Welcome everyone. Help yourselves to an appetizer while I fix drinks." She smiled at Lia. "Cranberry spritzer with a twist of lime?"

Georgia nodded to Lia, keeping her real feelings hidden. "How is the pregnancy going, Dear?" Lia shrugged and filled her in on the details of the baby, lamenting how it was taking a toll on her physically. "It's nice you're having a boy. I loved raising mine."

"I wanted a daughter," Lia sighed.

"Maybe Olivia will have a girl and you can trade." Peter prodded Jake.

"Did she call you?" Jake slumped in his chair.

"Olivia's pregnant?" Lia's eyes widened.

"Of course, it makes me the perfect small-town man; a father and grandfather at the same time." Jake swirled the ice in his drink.

"Dinner time." Casi waved everyone to the table as she set a large green salad bowl beside a bottle of wine.

Kyle eyed the potato salad generously garnished with bacon. "This looks delicious."

"Help yourself. Jake, I need assistance, please." Casi grasped his arm.

"It's late to start the barbecue. You should have told me to do it when I got home." He opened the fridge and frowned at the absence of steaks.

"Put these on the table." Casi smiled and opened the oven.

"Holy cow!" Jake grinned at the large platter.

"Cabernet chipotle ribs. A secret family recipe." She gave Ava a wink. They dug in, exclaiming they had never eaten such delicious or tender ribs. Even Jake admitted they were superior to his. "I made dessert too." She noted, watching bone piles increase.

Kyle looked up mid-bite. "Did you make that cake?"

"Yes, I did. We will have it with coffee in the living room." She insisted Jake could help her clear the dishes while Kyle told everyone about his day of fishing and the upcoming elk trip Jake was planning.

Jake surveyed the tidy kitchen as he put the last dish in the dishwasher. "You sure made this easy. I'm impressed."

Casi smiled with satisfaction at the compliment and carried the cake to the living room. "Happy thirty-sixth birthday!" She bent forward to let Kyle blow out the candles. "Make a wish."

"I already got my wish when I met you." He gave her a kiss.

"I believe the universe gave us all a gift when you came into our lives." Peter patted Casi on the back as she cut the cake.

Georgia nodded and squeezed Ava's hand. "We have been blessed with this union in so many ways."

As they prepared to leave, Georgia hugged Jake and whispered, "Maybe you could stay at Lia's tonight and give them time alone?"

Jake scanned Kyle, cuddling with Casi as they bid everyone goodbye and agreed they deserved to have the house to themselves. "Sure, I can relocate." He smiled and texted Anna instead. When he received a response with an address, he put a piece of cake on a paper plate and gave Casi a kiss. "Great job on dinner. See you in the morning."

"Where are you going?" She observed Lia had already left.

"Seattle." He grinned and showed her the text.

"That's her home address!" Casi's mouth dropped.

Jake arrived at Anna's, impressed with the high-rise apartment building on the waterfront. She opened the door with a smile, wearing a negligee, prepared for his arrival and a night of lovemaking.

"I brought you cake. Casi baked it." He gave her a kiss. "Nice place."

"I don't eat sweets." Anna directed him to put it on the counter.

Jake opened drawers in search of a fork. "You can take a bite." He held a forkful for her, ensuring it had enough glaze.

Her eyes widened. "Wow, that's good. Casi made it?"

"Yup, one of her few talents. She made excellent ribs, too! In fact, the whole dinner, including the drinks, was amazing. Which is why I figured it might be a good idea to visit you so Kyle can reward her properly." He surveyed the elegant living room with chic style. "You invited me to your home. Does this mean you like me?"

"I wasn't in the mood to meet at a hotel."

Jake grabbed her in his arms and carried her to the bedroom. "Liar." He tossed her on the bed and pulled off his shirt, smiling as he undressed and joined her. She brought him toward her for a lingering kiss, moaning as he continued down her neck toward her breasts. She gazed into his deep blue eyes and drowned in the love they held for her. She wanted to look away and break the contact, feeling too close to him, but kissed him passionately instead. She released her true feelings as she writhed under him in ecstasy and relished the climax. When he rolled to the side, she threw back the covers and walked out of the room and he frowned as he watched her leave. She returned, carrying the cake, and rejoined him in bed with a smile. She pushed him away when he tried to take a bite. "I'm not sharing." She giggled and put the empty plate on the nightstand.

"I love you, Anna." Jake caressed a wisp of her copper hair.

Her tears fell, dampening the pillow. "I love you, too," she wept. He smoothed the blanket, not asking if he could spend the night as she snuggled into his arms.

Casi smiled at Kyle. "I'll take a quick shower and give you the rest of your birthday present." Her eyes clouded. "I'm sorry I don't have money yet to buy you a real gift."

"You can't buy me anything that is better than spending time with you. I appreciate the effort you put into this evening. It was the ultimate experience." He kissed her. "Hurry up in the shower." He chuckled as he got in bed, knowing it would be awhile. Casi shaved her legs and layered on lotion and powder, mixing the scents to a heady delight. She entered the bedroom wearing a sexy negligee and smiled when she discovered Kyle was asleep, deciding to join him in slumber instead.

Casi awoke the next morning to Kyle kissing her stomach, making his way down to part her thighs. She moaned her approval, arching to meet his warm tongue as his hand caressed her breast. She ran her fingers through his hair, encouraging him to continue, still sleepy and relaxed, but excited by the intimacy. He entered her slowly, taking his time to enjoy the union of their bodies and bring her to a sensuous orgasm. When he climaxed, she felt him shudder against her, holding her tightly as the feeling overtook him. He put his head in the crook of her neck, catching his breath, as their slick hot bodies melded together. He smiled. "I got morning after my birthday sex. Sorry, I was out last night as soon as my head hit the pillow."

"I thought about waking you, but I realized how tired I was."

"Are you guys still sleeping?" Jake frowned at them tangled in the blankets. "You had all night, now get up and make coffee."

"Go take a shower." Kyle chuckled. "We'll stop at Coffee Junction."

Jake showered and wrapped himself in a towel and started shaving.

"That's my razor. Yours is the blue one." Kyle smacked his arm.

"That one is dull." Jake shrugged.

"I used it to shave my legs," Casi confessed. "How was Anna's last night?"

"She enjoyed the cake. She never eats sweets but made an exception." Jake grinned. "I told her I loved her."

"What did she say?" Casi's face blanched.

"She said she loves me, too. She even gave me a toothbrush to leave at her place." Jake leaned against the wall with a smile.

Casi strolled to the bedroom and grabbed her phone, texting as she went to the closet. "Anna, why didn't you tell him? Did you change your mind?"

Jake swooped behind her, suspicious of her sudden exit, and grabbed the phone, reading the message. "Tell me what?" Casi fidgeted with a silk blouse in her hands. "Stop covering for people. Put me first for once!" He looked down when her phone buzzed with a response. "Ugh, couldn't do it. I have feelings for Jake, but the wedding is still on." Tears sprung to his eyes. "That would have been nice to know."

Kyle pushed beside his brother and read through the messages. "Jesus, Casi. Why didn't you say something?"

"I didn't understand you were falling in love!" Casi cried. "I thought she was a distraction from all the crap in your life." Jake threw her phone, cracking the screen when it hit the floor. She picked it up, letting tears pool on the broken glass. "I didn't deserve that! And neither did my phone!"

He shoved her out of his way. "Don't worry, I'm sure the responsible brother has insurance."

❧

Casi glanced up when Anna walked in the building and texted Amy to take Riley out for coffee. Jake cranked the music and Anna ignored the yellow line, shouting to make him listen. "I should have told you last night, but now you need to hear me out and stop acting like a teenage boy." He glared at her and snapped the stereo off, crossing his arms over his chest. "You knew from the beginning what this relationship was. I think it shocked us both when we developed feelings for each other."

"Feelings?" Jake narrowed his eyes.

"When we fell in love." Anna straightened her shoulders. "I'm still getting married, next month, to a man I don't love."

"Why?" Jake demanded.

"Because I'm a grownup, not a little girl who has the luxury of being in love. I carefully planned my life to achieve certain goals. I am thirty-six years old and have an opportunity to marry someone who will provide me with an affluent life. I'm sorry if that sounds cold, but it has always been my plan."

"How can you marry someone else if you love me?" Jake pouted.

"I don't love your life." She realized she needed to spell it out. "You're divorced with two kids, and another on the way with a random woman. You sleep on your brother's couch, and as far as I can see, you are content to live that life. How do you see me fitting in?"

Jake set his jaw. "I forgot to tell you; my teen daughter is pregnant."

Anna stepped toward him. "You live your life reacting to things as they happen. I am sure you are a good father and you work hard, but I do not want to be a part of this small-town, chaotic world you are juggling. There is no room for me here. The fact that you blamed Casi for any of this tells me you are not in control of your environment. You let Kyle take care of things, picking up the pieces and telling you what to do. You're too dependent on him." She shrugged and whispered, "He even sent you to me to improve your bedroom skills." She nodded to Casi and left abruptly.

They stood in silence, not sure what to say. Finally, Jake flipped the stereo back on and grabbed his bandsaw. "I guess it's good to hear what a loser I am. I'm sure you girls had a good laugh over that."

"I wish you hadn't let him get hurt. You should have told him Anna planned to marry someone else." Kyle shuddered and walked to the workbench. Casi hit the emergency power shut-off switch, and the room fell into an eerie silence. "What?" Kyle stared at the inoperable jigsaw.

"Jake, Anna and I never speak about you negatively. I would be the last person to call you a loser." Casi wagged a finger at him.

"Whatever, it doesn't matter." Jake waved her away.

"It matters to me! I love you and would never stand by and enjoy watching you get hurt." She burst into tears.

Jake hugged her tightly. "I love you too, Monkey Moonshine. I'm sorry I blamed you. My heart disconnected from my brain."

Kyle cocked his head as he observed them. "I'm on the fence about whether I'm more surprised to witness two emotionally guarded people declare their love for each other or Casi's uncanny electronic dominance."

19

LIARS

"You look pretty. Where are you off to?" Jake smiled as Casi walked in the living room wearing a pink floral dress.

She slipped on high-heeled sandals. "Lia's baby shower. I think she invited Gail and Mary Ann, which is good since I won't know anyone else."

Jake grimaced. "Kyle should be back soon. He went to pick up the permits for the property. Can you wait?"

"I'm already late. Tell him I'll be home for dinner, and make sure it's good, baby shower food always sucks." She waved goodbye.

"It might not suck today." He cringed, suspecting Lauren most likely catered the event.

Casi wished she was on time but had been distracted finishing a report for her meeting the next day. She entered the home and located Lia, giving her a hug. "Sorry I'm late."

"It's fine. Everyone is still eating, help yourself." Lia pointed to a table laden with colorful dishes and turned back to listen to advice from her aunt.

Casi filled a plate and poured a glass of punch. She spotted Gail and Mary Ann and pulled a chair to sit with them, confused when an elderly woman clipped a clothespin to her dress. "I'm glad you guys are here. I wasn't sure if you would show up."

"To my ex-husband's lover's baby shower?" Gail clasped her chest.

Mary Ann took Gail's hand, understanding the joke masked a deep regret. "She invited the whole town. I believe her mom wants to punish her for getting pregnant. We came to show our support for Lia."

Casi nodded. "You always take the high road, Mary Ann."

She smiled. "The view is better up there."

Gail tensed. "Casi, did Kyle ever tell you about someone named Lauren?"

"Not that I remember. Why?" She glanced up to see a tall, athletic woman approach abruptly.

"This is Lia's sister, Lauren," Gail made the introduction.

"Hello." Casi smiled brightly, noting only a slight resemblance between the sisters. Lauren waited to see if the name would register before turning away in disgust. "She's not very friendly."

"Are you aware Kyle dated her?" Mary Ann placed a hand on hers.

Casi bit her lip. "I recall him saying something about her being an old friend when I noticed her name on text messages. He didn't elaborate."

"You crossed your legs!" A woman happily retrieved the clothespin from Casi's skirt.

Casi shrugged, never being successful at shower games. "I bet if more women crossed their legs, there would be fewer baby showers." She shivered when she received a stern look from Lia's mother, Fran.

"Are you Kyle Jensen's wife?" an aunt asked.

"Yes, I am." She pretended not to be offended at being reduced to a title.

She felt a symphony of eyes on her as the woman continued, "We were very surprised to hear he got married. He convinced everyone he was a sworn bachelor with no interest in marriage."

Fran quipped, "I guess he had a change of heart after all."

"When are you starting your family?" a woman inquired.

"Um, we're not," Casi said. "We don't want kids."

"Don't want to ruin your figure?"

"We're not interested in being parents," Casi sighed.

"Let's focus on Lia since it's her shower." Gail motioned to a stack of presents in an attempt to redirect the conversation.

"You're not bothered it's your ex-husband's baby?"

"Jake and I are friends. I'm happy for Lia, and I'm sure the baby will be darling." Gail gripped Mary Ann's hand tighter.

"Can we leave and hit happy hour instead?" Casi whispered.

"Unfortunately, you're about to hear something your husband should have told you." Mary Ann noted the fire in Lauren's eyes as she stormed toward them.

"Have I done something to offend you?" Casi asked.

"Are you incredibly stupid?" Lauren barked as chairs swiveled to watch the drama play out.

"Lauren, don't!" Lia yelped, being shushed by her mother.

"I saw you in Seattle, at my hotel with that redheaded whore," Lauren declared.

"Anna?" Casi cocked her head.

"Obviously, Kyle didn't want me to meet you. He regrets marrying you and he admitted it's a disaster. He got swept up with how pretty you are and now he's trapped because he moved you here and you don't possess any job skills," Lauren snapped.

"I don't know where you're getting your faulty information from. I have a job and can take care of myself." Casi willed the blush in her cheeks to subside as she processed the accusations.

"I get my facts straight from Kyle, we talk all the time. We've been friends for over a dozen years, and we were practically engaged before he got cold feet." Lauren's eyes filled with tears. "We were on a break when he met you. Your presence in his life is temporary."

Casi glanced around the room and saw all eyes on her, waiting to read her reaction. "I guess you weren't important enough to mention."

"I think it's more likely people feel sorry for you since you fell apart in LA. I hear your mother is a real piece of work. Maybe that's why you struggle with reality."

"Really?" Casi gasped.

"You claim you don't want kids, but the truth is you are incapable of getting pregnant because Kyle ensured you would be sterile. He thinks you would make a terrible mother; too self-absorbed and narcissistic, I believe were the words he used." Lauren set her jaw. "You don't belong here."

Rather than fulfilling the expectation of a catfight, Casi set her glass down. "I'm not sure why you felt this was an appropriate place to blindside me with your bullshit, but today should be about your sister. I care about Lia, so I will leave and let her continue her baby shower without the soap opera you are desperate to create. I'll be sure to tell my husband to set the record straight for you." She made a swift exit, fighting back the tears until she was safely in her car.

Casi drove by Kyle and Jake, marking the water and power lines for the property. She walked in the house, grabbed a beer, and kicked off her shoes. She stomped down the dock and sat on the edge, dipping her feet in the icy water. She didn't bother wiping the tears, wanting to release the pain in her chest. She fought her gut reaction to jump in her car and drive away from the devastation and forced herself to remain home, focus on her presentation, and tune out the gnawing feeling of betrayal.

Kyle sighed when he came in the house, dirty and tired. He took salmon from the freezer and put it in the sink with water. "I guess she didn't feel like starting dinner."

"Are you a fucking moron?" Jake asked.

Kyle glanced out the window at Casi sitting on the dock. "She got home two hours ago; you don't think she could defrost something? She knew we were busy with the trailer."

Jake cocked his head. "Today was Lia's baby shower. How do you think it went with her meeting Lauren? Did you prepare her for that? I hope in your numerous texts to Lauren, you instructed her to be pleasant."

Kyle's eyes widened. "Crap, I totally forgot."

"All your ex-girlfriends seem to love Casi, so I bet they hit if off."

Kyle walked down the dock and sat beside her, watching her stare at the lake. "I take it you met Lauren today?"

"Yup, she's awesome. I can see why you want to keep her as a close friend. Would confidante be a better word? She was aware of the most intimate details on our marriage. It would be nice if you shared your true feelings with me instead of hearing about your real motivation for ensuring my infertility from a stranger. Even my mother was not off limits for your little gossip fest. It was a perfect conversation at a baby shower full of people I don't know." Tears streamed down her face.

"I'm sorry…"

"Unless the next words out of your mouth are about you admitting you are a fucking liar, I don't want to hear it!"

"I didn't lie!"

"You did, Kyle! Do not try your bullshit answer of forgetting to tell me. You don't forget someone you almost married, or that you had lunch with last week!"

"Are you going to listen or just yell at me?" He clenched his jaw.

"I don't want to hear it. You've had two years to tell me." She jumped to her feet. "I'll see Alix whenever the hell I want to without your permission." She stormed in the house and before Jake could speak, she yelled, "Don't ever accuse me of not telling you things. You're a fucking liar!"

Jake looked at Kyle. "I guess she's not making dinner."

Kyle walked in the bedroom and watched her change, putting his arm out to stop her as she came toward the door. "Let me know when you're ready to listen. I promise there's nothing going on. We're only friends." She nodded, and he let her walk by, realizing she had a legitimate right to be pissed. He inhaled sharply and texted Lauren. "I understand I failed to handle introductions properly and didn't comprehend the magnitude of a first meeting between you and Casi. I misunderstood the boundaries of our friendship and didn't suspect you would twist my words to lash out at my wife and tear her apart with half-truths and bitterness. It's probably best if we suspend further communication since you're unable to handle our current status." He switched his phone off, not wanting to read a reply.

20

SEX WITH THE EX

Jake received a text from Gail, asking if he could come to her house. She was having trouble dealing with Olivia, who had become rebellious and moody since the pregnancy announcement. She returned home with another tattoo, which Gail felt he would be better at handling.

"She took off with her boyfriend." Gail shrugged when Jake arrived.

"Have you met him?" Jake questioned.

"Unfortunately, there's not much to him."

"Is Reid still at school?" Jake checked his watch.

"For another hour. Would you mind fixing the master bathroom door while you are here? It won't shut properly and it's the only place I can ever be alone." Jake smiled, realizing she was on the front-line with the kids. She sat on the bed and watched him adjust the hinges before taking a plane to the edge of the door. "Did Casi talk to Kyle about Lauren?"

"More like yelled. She's pissed he didn't tell her and angry with me for being an accomplice. She says she's not ready to talk about it."

"I understand her reaction. Lauren put her on the spot. Mary Ann

169

and I didn't mention it because we thought it should come from Kyle."

"He definitely dropped the ball," he agreed. "Try it now." He showed her how much easier the door closed. She came over, uninterested in the repair as she leaned in to kiss him. "What are you doing?" He stepped back.

"Haven't you wondered what it would be like to sleep with me now that we're not married?"

"You're crazy." Jake bent to pack his tools.

"You're not with Lia and don't get to Seattle often. Are you sure you don't want to have sex...for old time's sake?" She removed her shirt.

"I don't trust you."

"Think of it as proving to me how stupid I was to divorce you. Show me what I'm missing." She slipped off her tennis skirt.

"Like revenge sex?" He grinned.

"Exactly." She caressed his chest. "You look like you did in college and it is turning me on."

"You used to be pretty wild back then." Jake pushed her on the bed.

"Can we put all the crap behind us and relive our past?"

"I didn't come prepared for this." He searched his pockets in vain.

"You rarely did." She giggled and reached in the drawer of her nightstand to retrieve a condom. "They're left over from my boyfriend after you."

He had heard from the kids her romance fizzled, not surprised at the time. He made love to her gently, building in intensity as he felt her relax under him. He didn't want her to go through the motions like she used to. "Stay with me," he whispered when she closed her eyes.

A tear slid down her cheek. "It hurts." When he pulled away, she rubbed his back and wrapped her legs around him. "Not physically. The memories of our last few years are painful."

"Let them go. We can't change anything except our future." He kissed her softly. She held on to him as the orgasm began, letting the sensation erase her feelings of regret.

Gail curled in his arms when he rolled to the side. "You got a new tattoo."

"Kyle and I both got it."

"I like it."

"The tattoo or the sex?"

"Both, but the sex was awesome," she giggled.

"Not like when we were married, huh?"

"Not at all! Don't tell me you learned all that with Lia?"

Jake smiled. "No."

"The girl from Seattle!" Gail recalled Lia fuming about her. "I guess you keep upgrading."

He took her chin in his hand. "Lia was never an upgrade from you. I waited until our marriage crumbled before I ever considered stepping out, and I'm not proud I did."

"I wish I'd never had an affair either. You deserved better."

He clasped her hand. "How do we handle our pregnant daughter? We're way too young to be grandparents."

"I guess we need to be supportive? My mother was horrible to me, even though I was twenty-two. It drove a wedge between us, and I think that's where a lot of my unhappiness stemmed from."

"I'm pissed Lia is pregnant. I thought I was done with raising kids. She is considering adoption. I should agree, but I can't do it yet." He hesitated. "Did you know we were adopted?"

"I suspected. Your mom always fretted when you would shut down, and she felt like she failed you." Her eyes glittered with laughter. "I'll gladly take the new baby! I adore them when they're little. I bet he'll be darling, and Reid was so easy. Lia wanted a daughter, so she can deal with Olivia. I feel it's a fair trade."

Jake smiled and smoothed her hair back. "You're a wonderful mother. I regret not appreciating it when our children were younger. You made it seem effortless, and my involvement was unnecessary." He exhaled and rubbed his temple. "I don't know how I'll feel when this one is born."

"Wait to sign. Make sure you don't have regrets. I promise to help if you need me." She kissed him tenderly. "I wish we had gotten along this well when we were married."

"Perhaps we've matured enough to be friends without the bitterness and disappointment of being in a relationship."

"Do you think we could have sex again?"

"Now?" His eyes widened.

"No! In the future. I would like it if this is something we could still share."

"It's a definite possibility." He glanced around the bedroom. "Do you like living here? It's a lot smaller than our old house and not in the area you enjoyed living in."

She snuggled in his embrace. "The expenses were too big for the return. Your brother convinced me I would be happier if I downsized to this townhouse, and he was correct. I like it now. It's closer to town and the schools. Kyle was also right about getting rid of the housekeeper and gardener, but don't tell him. I despise my mundane office job, but I feel settled here, and other than our daughter's issues, my life is good."

Jake smiled. "My brother is pretty frugal, but he has a good handle on finances. It's best to listen to him."

A knock and a jiggling of the handle caught their attention as Reid asked, "Mom? What are you doing? Why is the door locked?"

They bolted out of bed, scrambling for their clothes. "Just a second, Dad is fixing something." She opened the door and Reid surveyed Jake, adjusting the hinges. Gail noticed the condom wrapper and slipped it in his back pocket before Reid could see it.

Olivia walked in, hearing their voices. "Why is Dad here?"

"I came to talk to you," Jake said.

"I don't need your advice," Olivia whined.

"I would be the last person to give you advice. I'm more interested in listening to you," Jake said.

Olivia observed the unmade bed and the flush on her mother's cheeks. "You guys had sex, didn't you? That's so gross!"

"It's not gross. How do you think you guys were created?" Jake teased as Olivia looked repulsed and stormed out. Reid regarded his parents, unsure what to make of this information, wondering if he should share it with his prayer group. Jake put a hand on his shoulder. "Would you like to go fishing this weekend? I haven't spent a lot of time with you lately."

Reid's face lit up at the unprecedented attention. "I can go either day."

"Then let's make a weekend out of it. We can camp out at my new property." He turned to Gail. "I'll pick him up after school on Friday?"

"That would be fine." Gail smiled at the grin on Reid's face.

Jake gathered his tools and went down the hall to Olivia's room. He knocked on the door, not waiting for her to answer before he opened it. "Tell me how you feel about your pregnancy, so I can be supportive."

"How do you feel about your kid on the way," she challenged.

"I'm scared to death and I'm angry. I didn't anticipate doing this all over again. When your mom was pregnant with you, it was unexpected. We got married because it was the responsible thing to do. I worked two jobs to support you guys and had zero social life. Your mother excelled at raising you and we gladly welcomed Reid to give you a sibling." He sat beside her on the bed. "It's always been about you, Olivia. I realize you think I'm a failure as a father, but I made you my priority."

She nodded as a tear slid down her face. "Now you're replacing me with a new child."

"You're irreplaceable. This new baby is also a surprise. I guess I learned nothing about birth control since college. I'm sure I'll disappoint him, too." He rubbed his temple. "We're considering giving him up for adoption, but I'm struggling with the reality of that." He squeezed her hand. "I'm not ready to be a grandfather. I can't even handle being a father."

Olivia hugged him. "Why can't you talk to me like this all the time? I want to be close to you, but I feel like I don't know you at all."

"I guess you don't. Can we talk about the tattoos? You don't seem to have a plan; you look like a leopard with random spots."

Her eyes widened. "Dad, that's mean!"

He pulled off his shirt and pointed to his cascade of the symbols of the Pacific Northwest. "This is where I come from and who I am. Each tattoo represents something about my life."

She studied the intricate design, noticing most of it for the first time. "It's beautiful. Like real artwork."

"This script is from a personal experience in my teens." He pointed to his ribs. "Kyle and I both got this last month."

"What about the snake?"

"It's because I'm a badass." Jake grinned. He put his t-shirt on. "I can cover them because they are for me, not a statement for anyone else."

"What should I do now?" She frowned at her forearm.

"Don't get more. Wait until you are dedicated to having a design which reflects what you stand for." He eyed the tacky rose with a butterfly. "I would consider having it removed. It's generic and a poor choice of placement."

Olivia nodded. "Casi said I should stop punishing you."

"Sometimes, she's pretty smart." He put an arm around her shoulders. "I do love you, but I don't know how to show it."

"Casi said you demonstrate it by taking care of me and making sure I have everything I need. She said she didn't appreciate her dad either and is thankful he didn't give up on her for being an ungrateful brat."

"I guess you two have a lot in common." Jake kissed her on the forehead. "What are we doing about your pregnancy?"

"Ricky won't text me back."

"Is that your boyfriend?"

"Yes. He said he needs time to figure out what he wants to do, and I should leave him alone. My friend said he already has two other kids with a girl in Olympia."

"He doesn't sound like a good guy."

"I'm scared to be alone. I've been having a lot of cramps, but I'm afraid to go to the doctor," she whispered.

"What if I took you? That's one thing I do well."

"Casi said that, too."

"See? I have references."

She smiled. "I'll make an appointment and text you?"

"I'll answer promptly. I am the man you can always depend on."

"Hey, Dad?" she said as he got up. "I think you'll be great with the new kid. You made all your mistakes on us."

Jake chuckled. "That's a good way to interpret it."

Jake stopped for coffee on his way back to the wood shop. He placed his order, nodding to Lia at the espresso machine. As he reached for his wallet, he heard giggles from the line behind. He glanced back and saw the condom wrapper on the floor, unaware Gail shoved it in his pocket. He paid and reached down and picked it up, tossing it in the trash, ignoring the whispers. He waited for his coffee, engrossed in a text, not wanting to make conversation.

"Texting Anna?" Lia asked. "She won't let you discard it at her place or is that your way of reminding me you're a free agent?"

He turned the phone to her. "Casi. I knew she would find it funny. Since she was blindsided by your bitch sister, I like to keep her informed."

Lia read Casi's reply. "Lol, that's hilarious. Bring me a coffee." She started another latte. "That is your brother's fault. He's the one leading a double life. Lauren didn't appreciate his angry message. She deserved better."

Jake returned to the wood shop and saw Kyle sitting at his desk with his hands clasped behind his head. "I had sex with Gail." He stepped back when he noticed Casi's head below the desk. "In the office?"

Kyle chuckled and Casi rolled her eyes as she gathered index cards from the floor. "You pervert. I am trying to share my marketing presentation with Kyle and the notes slipped out of my hand. What do you mean, you slept with Gail? Like intentionally?" Casi sat back on her heels as Jake handed her a coffee. "No way, trickster. I don't want your spit in drink. Give me the other one." She pointed to the cup with her name and a heart. He exchanged it and cautiously took a sip, continuing when it tasted like a regular vanilla latte.

"Why don't I get coffee?" Kyle frowned.

"Apparently, you're leading a double life." Jake shrugged. "Maybe your girlfriend is bringing you one? Unless she's still pissed about the nasty message you sent her because she attacked your wife."

Kyle flipped him off and Casi smiled. "We've put his secret life on the back burner until I'm in the mood to talk about it, which isn't now because I need to present to my first client."

"If I were you, I'd keep it on the back burner. Lauren is boring as hell which is probably why he forgot about her," Jake declared.

21

THE MAN FROM SEATTLE

By the beginning of May, Casi became increasingly busy with the skincare line and meetings with Mary to give updates and adhere to the strict timelines. Her confidence increased as she became more familiar with the products and realized how her skills applied to the job. Mary told her it was because she had been training her for ten years, but she had been too self-absorbed to notice. Traveling to Seattle several times a week, Casi realized she missed the pace of city life, the diversity of the people, and the surrounding action. She enjoyed living in Blackberry Falls, in their beautiful lake house, and being with Kyle, but worried she might be too complacent.

Casi arranged a meeting with an executive from a large department store who showed an interest in carrying the line. When Grant put his hand on hers in response to a question, she became aware of her desire to be noticed. Everything revolved around the baby on the way, Jake's property, and Olivia's troubled pregnancy. Jake had taken Olivia to the clinic and held her hand while the doctor performed a D&C, informing them the baby hadn't formed properly and her body attempted to shed the damaged cells. Olivia had been devastated, and Jake was relieved. It created a new bond between them, and he made sure to spend as much time as he could to foster it. Casi didn't want to admit her jealousy over being eliminated as the go-between.

She couldn't remember the last time she had been intimate with Kyle. Jake was always present, needing something from them, or bringing Reid to spend the weekends. In fact, he had become so integrated in their lives she didn't even bother separating their laundry when she put it away and assumed there would be three to five people for dinner. Kyle would pull her toward him in bed, but they were both so tired at the end of the day, they felt like they were going through the motions.

To make matters worse, Kyle's renewed friendship with Lauren tested her patience. Casi declined to read the apology from her, considering it to be an excuse to regain Kyle's trust. He seemed relieved to discuss their shared passions, moving on from the conflict and blind to Lauren's feelings for him. Casi tried to take more interest in cooking, but became easily bored when Kyle would divulge the reason why one oil was superior to another. Ultimately, she wanted to eat dinner and not receive a history lesson on where the food came from. She encouraged him to share that part of himself with Lauren, figuring it was a safe topic they had in common. She hadn't taken him up on his offer to talk about his prior relationship, due to lack of curiosity and inability to discuss it without getting angry. She had also not pursued her threat to contact Alix, still unable to revisit the trauma.

Grant Bishop from Stanwick's department stores sent her an email wanting to meet for lunch to finalize the details of the product line. He suggested a sidewalk cafe to get away from the offices and discuss when they would launch in the eleven stores. Mary was thrilled about the monumental contract, impressed with the suggested premium product placement. Casi was excited but concerned because she found him attractive and the constant attention became addictive. She mentioned her husband several times, ensuring Grant knew she wasn't looking for anything else. He was also married, which she hoped deterred him. She monitored her speech with Kyle, hearing how often she talked about Grant, the excitement in her voice, and a slight flush at the mention of his name.

Casi parked in a garage a few blocks from the cafe and checked her hair, longer now and styled in a sexy cascade of waves around her face. She chose the blouse for Grant, making sure to highlight her lace bra, seductively peeking through. She wore the navy skirt with the kick pleats and tried not to think of the garter and stockings beneath, reminding herself this would not go beyond flirting.

Kyle and Jake drove to Seattle to finalize the paperwork for the transportation of the trailer which would be moved to the property in the next month. They had been able to connect to the city sewage system and although it had taken additional paperwork and money, it would be the better choice long term. They filed the last of the certificates and decided to get lunch before heading back.

"Are you even listening to me?" Kyle asked, exasperated his brother was distracted, a common occurrence these days.

"I'm busy watching your wife flirt with some guy in a suit."

Kyle redirected his attention. Casi sat at an outdoor table across from a handsome man, leaning toward her, while she threw her head back and laughed. "It's probably that client she keeps talking about." She crossed her legs, and the garter was revealed, which didn't escape the eyes of the man. She leaned forward, and they could see the lace of her bra from across the street. She played with her hair, giving him a coy smile. "You know how she flirts. She's probably working the guy to get a better product placement."

"Does she always drink at business meetings?" Jake observed the waiter replace their empty cocktail glasses with fresh ones.

Kyle watched her play with the straw, batting her eyelashes. The man put his hand on top of hers with a suggestive smile, and he wanted to cross the street and punch him.

"Are you waiting until he bends her over the table before you react?" Jake kicked his brother's leg under the table.

Kyle clenched his jaw. "I'm not going to act like the jealous husband and ruin a business deal for her. I'll talk to her when she gets home." He averted his eyes and pushed his burger away, having lost his appetite. He cringed when the man pulled out her chair and put his hand on the small of her back while he checked out her backside when she smoothed her skirt. He led her to his Jaguar and opened the door, and she slid in with a smile.

§

Casi came home late, having gone by Mary's condo to give her new figures and update her on the deal. Grant had taken her back to her car and helped transfer product information, pamphlets and samples she brought for him. When she closed her trunk, he kissed her without warning, putting his hand on her waist and leaning into her. She responded, letting herself get caught up in the moment. She came to her senses within minutes and put a hand on his chest and pushed him back. "Let's keep this strictly business, ok?"

"For now." He gave her a wink.

Casi needed this deal to work and could not screw it up with an affair, she reasoned. It shocked her that the fact she was married was an afterthought and the guilt consumed her.

"How was work today?" Jake asked.

Distracted by her phone as she answered an email, Casi shrugged. "What? Oh, fine, busy."

"I made halibut." Kyle grabbed plates from the cupboard.

"I'm not hungry. I had a big lunch." She untucked her shirt, which Kyle noticed was buttoned up more than it had been at the café.

"I'll bet you did." Jake narrowed his eyes as she walked to the bedroom to change. "Maybe a little sausage?"

She showered and yawned as she informed them she was going to bed because she needed to be in Seattle early for a meeting. Kyle stayed up, seething about the situation, playing a video game with Jake. Finally, he slipped in bed, staring at her as she slept. He ran his hand over her hip, caressing her smooth skin as he made his way to her breast. She pushed him away. "I'm too sleepy."

He put his hand on her shoulder and pulled her toward him. "Why don't you tell me about your lunch?"

"Why do you care what I ate? I'm too tired to talk about food."

"I don't care about the meal. I'm interested in who you were with."

She peered at him. "A client. I told you about him. He owns the eleven stores I'm launching the line in."

"And it is standard business practice to drink at lunch and flirt? Is that where it ended or was there more after you drove off in his Jaguar?"

Casi threw back the sheets and yanked on a t-shirt and underwear. "Are you following me around now?" She stomped to the kitchen, unwilling to continue the discussion.

"It didn't look innocent to me," Jake interjected from the sofa.

"Why are you always here? It's continually about your needs, your baby, and your problems. Stay out of my business!" Casi yelled.

"Maybe if you weren't sneaking around on my brother, I wouldn't care about what you do."

Kyle grasped her elbow and directed her back to the bedroom. He closed the door and leaned her against the wall, putting his hands on either side of her shoulders. "Please tell me what happened. I'm sorry you are feeling left out, but there's more than us in the universe right now."

She took a deep breath, understanding he would be able to tell if she lied, and part of her wanted him to know. "He's a client. I flirted with him and had a few drinks," she paused. "He kissed me when he took me to my car after lunch. I let him and then told him we should keep it professional from now on." She looked him in the eyes with defiance.

He surprised her with his reaction, shoving the contents of the dresser to the floor, then pushing the piece against the wall in a horrific crash. "When will you stop?"

Jake responded to the commotion and witnessed Casi in tears, pleading, "I only kissed him!"

"I had sex with your mom in Hawaii. She was on the beach doing drugs and I figured I might as well take her up on her advances. I see who you inherited your nice tits from. And I guess your promiscuous nature." Jake flipped her off and stormed back to the living room.

Kyle stepped over the clutter on the floor and went back to bed. She wept, noticing he hadn't reacted to Jake's comment. "Did you already know about Hawaii?"

"Everyone knows, even your dad."

She stood in disbelief, shaking from the revelation. She wanted to grab her car keys and drive to LA and confront her mother, but she knew the morning meeting was too important to miss. She slid back in bed, not sure where else to go.

Awakened by Kyle's firm hand fondling her breast, Casi was surprised by his roughness and lack of intimacy as he moved on top of her, entering her without making eye contact. He made no attempt to excite her or bring her to orgasm, filling his needs only. She felt foreign in her body, confused by what was happening. When he climaxed, he rolled off and sat on the edge of the bed. "Kyle, talk to me." She reached for his hand.

"If you're going to let other men touch you, I guess I might as well enjoy myself too. There has to be some incentive to being married to you." He stomped to the bathroom.

She grasped the blankets to her chest, feeling violated. She cried silently as he showered and turned away when he came back to the bedroom. He fixed the dresser, picking up the items from the floor, not caring how they ended up as he put them back. Jake came in and went to shower as Kyle got dressed. Neither of them addressed her or reacted to her tear-streaked face.

"Let's stop off for coffee, I'm not in the mood to make any," Kyle stated as they left the bedroom. He hesitated at the door and sighed. Jake nodded and headed to the truck as he returned to the bedroom. He sat on the edge of the bed and grasped her hand. "Give me time to absorb this." He touched her cheek gently. "I'm sorry about what I said. My anger took over."

Kyle and Jake barely acknowledged Casi throughout the week, acting like she didn't exist. They made dinner, which she picked at while she read emails on her phone. They sat on the sofa drinking a beer or scotch, watching sports or playing video games. At one point, she became enraged at their juvenile behavior and grabbed Jake's controller, navigating through the level with ease, revealing her excellence in a game they never asked her to play. They stared at her wide-eyed as she blew away their opponent. "You guys suck." She threw the controller at them and stormed away.

The standoff went on for over a week. Casi spent time with Lia after work, helping her prepare for the baby. She enjoyed decorating his room and arranging the tiny outfits, starting to feel excited for the creature who would make an appearance in the next month. Lia was exhausted from the pregnancy and enjoyed the attention she received from Casi, feeling she was the one person she could share her doubts about motherhood with. "I'm sorry I didn't give you a heads-up about Lauren," Lia said, as she watched Casi fold baby clothes.

"Kyle should have told me. I'm sure it was awkward for your sister to meet me as well."

"She was madly in love with him and it devastated her when they broke up. I didn't think about it when I invited you to the shower. I'm sorry for how she treated you."

Casi nodded. "Can you tell me about their relationship? I'm not trusting Kyle to be honest."

Lia filled her in on the years of friendship, which had led to a romantic relationship. She told her about Lauren's career and general demeanor, ending with the fact their relationship as sisters hadn't been close since their brother had gone to jail several years prior. Casi listened intently, relishing the intimate peek into Kyle's past.

"Jake slept with my mom in Hawaii," she blurted. She surprised herself when she started crying uncontrollably, feeling more betrayed by Jake than her mother.

"I knew he was acting weird!" Lia rubbed her belly as the baby moved. "I made a mistake getting pregnant. I thought it would make me feel like I had a purpose in life, but I've been overwhelmed the whole time. I'm not finding any joy in setting up this room, and I only had the shower because my mom insisted. She says I must take responsibility for my actions and acknowledge I made a horrible choice. Then I can give him away without regret, to a family who can properly care for him."

"Wait until he's born. You might change your mind."

"I can't do it, Casi! I hate this thing inside me!"

෴

Casi glanced at her phone when it buzzed as she drove back from Seattle. She frowned at the urgent priority setting. "Come home now. Please!" She tried not to panic and stayed within the speed limit for the remaining few miles. She parked in the driveway minutes later. "What's going on?" She rushed in the house.

"Get changed, quickly." Kyle surveyed her skirt and heels with a silky blouse. "Lia's in labor and it's not going well. Jake is freaking out." It was three weeks early, and she knew Lia was terrified about the delivery. She put on jeans and a t-shirt, pulling on tennis shoes as she climbed in the truck.

They arrived at the hospital to discover Jake frantically pacing the waiting room. He raced over to fill them in and Casi stopped short when she saw Lauren. "She needed an emergency C-section," she informed Kyle.

"She'll be ok." Kyle put his arm around her as Fran came to his side seeking comfort.

"She's hysterical. None of us could be in there," Fran sobbed as Kyle rubbed her back. "Sign the papers! She needs this nightmare to be over!"

"I'm glad I rushed home to witness this," Casi muttered under her breath. She found a vending machine and got coffee, drinking the bitter liquid while she hung in the background.

They sat in the waiting room for an eternity before the doctor finally came out. Jake and Fran jumped up, firing questions. He took a step back and silenced them with a look. "We performed a caesarean, and everything went well. She's resting now. The baby is fine. He's slightly underweight and we will monitor his lungs to make sure he's healthy enough to go home in a few days."

"I'd like to see my daughter," Fran demanded.

"She asked me not to send anyone in," he said. "Except Casi?"

Casi stepped forward, handing her coffee to Kyle as she introduced herself to the doctor. She followed him down a long corridor to Lia's room. "How are you doing?"

"It was so horrible!" Lia wailed, gasping as she turned. The nurse adjusted the large bandage and Casi sucked in her breath in an attempt not to vomit.

"Jesus! They sliced you right open, huh?" She cringed, and the nurse gave her a scolding look before administering more pain medicine.

"Casi." Lia grabbed her hand. "Make Jake sign the papers. I don't want this child."

"Can I see him first? I want to check him out in real life compared to his alien photos." Casi smiled and squeezed her hand.

"Can you show her the baby?" Lia asked the nurse, figuring she had been the only one to show interest throughout the pregnancy.

The nurse led her to the nursery and directed her to wash her hands, then gave her a gown. Casi tried to explain she only wanted to look and had no intention of holding the wrinkled blob. She glanced at a large window at the far end and realized everyone had gathered to get a glimpse of the infant. The nurse picked up the tiny bundle and placed him in her arms before she could protest, helping her adjust her grasp to support him. She gazed at his little face as bright blue eyes tried to focus and his tongue darted out like a lizard.

"Crap, don't make me love you!" she whispered, wanting to hand him back, but hugged him tighter instead.

"You can take him over to the window," the nurse suggested.

"I don't want to drop him." Casi doubted anyone would want him if she damaged him.

"He'll be fine." The nurse smiled, familiar with new parents.

She walked carefully, wishing he would stop looking at her. She hadn't expected to feel anything, assuming she would be annoyed by cries and stench. He smelled slightly medicinal, but also sweet, and the weight of him in her arms penetrated her heart, making it swell with love for him.

"Am I allowed to kiss him?" Casi asked, wanting to feel his soft skin against her lips before she said goodbye.

"Yes, you can."

Casi kissed him gently on the cheek, and he turned his mouth, making her giggle as his gums made contact. She tuned out everyone except Jake as she moved the blanket from his face. She wondered what they were thinking. Kyle probably calculated the bills and care associated with him; glad he would find a new home. She knew Jake was hesitant to sign, most likely considering his own past. She wondered if any of them could love him at first sight or were they caught up in the enormity of the responsibility that came with this tiny life. She glanced at Lauren, who had her eyes locked on Kyle, and she turned away, not wanting to witness the intimacy between them.

"Do you want to feed him?" the nurse asked. She helped Casi settle in a rocking chair and showed her how to hold the bottle. He sucked madly at the nipple and she smiled, watching the concentration on his face as she stroked his cheek with her finger.

"I'm glad you didn't come out of me," she whispered, imagining the pain Lia experienced. "I love you with all my heart and I can't let them give you away, even if I must raise you myself."

Jake nudged Kyle. "I can't do it. It's not right."

Kyle nodded. "We'll keep him. He's our responsibility."

"I think Casi is already attached and it would be like taking a puppy back to the pound," Jake surmised. Kyle watched her rocking the baby, assessing she had fallen in love.

Casi handed the baby back once he fell asleep. She wanted to talk to Lia and convince her to keep him, but they wouldn't let her in the room, wanting Lia to stay asleep. She walked to the waiting area, glad Fran and Lauren had left. Jake looked at her intently and she searched for the right words, made so much harder after their argument. "I'm not signing the papers," he finally said. "You might need to help me raise him, but I can't give him away to strangers."

She nodded, fighting tears. "I'll help you."

She walked to the truck with Kyle and stared at her hands while he drove. Without warning, he pulled over and sighed, running a hand through his hair. "I can't do this anymore. The guilt is killing me…"

She lunged forward and put her hand over his mouth, unwilling to hear the next words. She knew he wanted to confess his love for Lauren and how he made a mistake marrying her instead. She wasn't ready to give up on their relationship and feared she would never see the baby again. "Don't say it, Kyle. I can't hear it. I'm not strong enough, and today was harder on me than you could understand."

He moved her hand. "Casi, we need to talk about this. We are not alright in our marriage."

"Please take me home. If you have any love at all left for me, you'll give me a few more days," she pleaded.

He frowned, bewildered by her statement. He knew he was correct. She hated him for signing for her procedure, and holding the baby had made it all clear.

After five days, Lia was discharged, and the child still didn't have a name. They referred to him as the baby and tried to help Lia find interest in naming him. She seemed indifferent to the whole process and angry Jake hadn't signed the papers for adoption. He told her he would take sole custody, still hoping she would grow to love the baby in time. The hospital informed him they had ten days to declare a name. Lia refused to breastfeed, and Jake enlisted Gail's help in choosing a formula. Jake stayed at the apartment most nights, barely sleeping as he tended to the constantly crying child. As promised, Casi took care of him when she wasn't in Seattle and he was easily soothed, gazing at her as she danced around and sang to him. She could quiet him with a touch, and Jake began to rely on her assistance. Lia grew to resent the child who continually demanded attention. It bothered her Jake turned to Gail and wondered at the nature of their relationship. She knew her lack of mothering instinct disgusted him, but she also wanted to punish him for insisting they keep the child. She was thankful Casi had taken to the baby and was amused by how enamored he was of her. Her mother chastised her for letting another woman tend to her child, but Lia was glad she had Casi to lean on.

The brothers returned from work to witness Casi holding the baby with one arm, drinking a beer, and dancing. Kyle was astonished by her patience, figuring she normally didn't have a long attention span for tiny objects.

"Thank God she's here for him," Jake whispered, noting Lia sleeping in a chair, sorry she wasn't bonding with the baby.

"You wanted him. Give him a name." Kyle peered at the baby cuddled against Casi's breast.

"Hey, you guys are home." Casi smiled as she twirled.

Kyle gazed at her, still hurt about her kissing the man in Seattle and confused by her outburst on the drive home from the hospital. They hadn't spoken about it, and he had barely seen her all week. He involved himself in work and she immersed herself in the baby.

Casi handed Jake the child while she went to prepare a bottle. Lia woke and watched him cradle their infant son in his muscular arms, smiling and talking to him. She wished she felt something other than jealousy for the child getting all his attention. The baby cried, wailing and turning red. Kyle shook his head, irritated he couldn't watch TV. Casi came back with the bottle and Jake attempted to hand him to Lia.

"He doesn't like me; he only cries when I try to hold him."

"You need to bond with him," Jake pleaded.

"Face it. I'm a bad mother," Lia wailed.

"Come here, Billy Bob, my little chicken nugget." Casi cuddled him and he immediately stopped crying.

"That's not his name!" Jake gasped as Kyle laughed.

"It is until you come up with a better one." Casi giggled.

Casi sat beside Kyle on the sofa, cross-legged, pulling a pillow on her lap for the baby while he sucked at the bottle hungrily. She tipped her beer back, mirroring him. Kyle wished he wasn't still upset because he admired her dedication and commitment but couldn't bring himself to tell her.

Jake slipped his phone back in his pocket. "Mom says we should go there this weekend and decide on a name."

"I like Billy Bob. It's catchy," Casi teased.

"We must turn in the paperwork on Monday. It'll be helpful to take him to Elmvale so Mom can help us."

"I have a meeting in Seattle on Friday, I can't go." Casi felt Kyle's glare.

"The kid only wants you. Come after," Jake stated.

22

HEARTBREAK

Casi finished her meeting and arrived in Elmvale by six, feeling ill at ease due to the unresolved issues. Georgia settled Lia in the guest room, unclear about the status of their relationship. They ate dinner while the baby cried and Casi leapt from the table when the meal concluded to soothe him. She heard Kyle announce he was going out while she sat rocking the child. Georgia gave her a sympathetic smile and eyed the t-shirt with spit-up on the shoulder. "Why don't you change into something a little more...sexy."

Casi tugged on low-rise black jeans, with a V-neck white t-shirt, and bolted down the stairs in minutes. Peter waited for her by the front door, keys in hand. "Why did Kyle leave?" She wrung her hands as they drove.

"I don't know, but Georgia said to take you to find him." He patted her knee. "What's going on with you kids?"

"I'm not sure." She stared out the window.

He put his hand on hers and drove to town, finding Kyle's truck where he assumed it would be, at the bar. "End the games. Be direct and let him know if he's being an ass."

Casi walked in the bar and spotted Kyle drinking and laughing with a pretty, raven-haired woman, who had her hand on his arm while she listened intently. Casi ordered a whiskey and watched him interact. They seemed familiar with each other, faces close, as she shared a story and he smiled at her. Casi wondered if Kyle had felt like that watching her with the man from Seattle. It hurt to think she betrayed him and questioned if he was tired of her angst and ready to move on with someone more stable. Kyle leaned against the bar, comfortable with the attention he received from the woman. "Can I get a shot of tequila?" Casi raised a finger in the direction of the bartender. She downed the bitter liquid and sauntered up to Kyle, kissing him passionately.

Kyle pulled back and turned to the woman. "Nicole, this is my wife, Casi." He glared at her, not impressed with her jealous behaviour. "How did you get here?"

"Your dad dropped me off." She directed her gaze to her feet.

"Wait here," Kyle scoffed as he turned and left.

The woman smiled. "I dated Kyle in high school. I'm Nicole." She extended her hand.

"Sorry about breaking in." Casi blushed.

"I've been married for twelve years; I understand the ups and downs."

Kyle narrowed his eyes at the Buick parked a few spaces down. He knew his father wouldn't leave Casi at a bar without ensuring she was safe. He leaned on the edge of the open window. "How did you know I was here?"

"This is always where you run to," Peter answered.

"Why did you bring her? I came here to be alone."

"She's your wife, you can't run away from her when things get tough." Peter grinned. "Your mother told me to."

"Maybe if she started acting more like a wife, I wouldn't feel the need to get away from her."

"Are you a good husband? It seems like you might be more concerned about your brother than your wife. I also hear Lauren's back in the picture?" Peter started the car, making it clear he was stuck with Casi whether he liked it or not.

Kyle walked back inside and surveyed Casi laughing with Nicole over drinks. He ordered a whiskey and joined them. After a few hours, Nicole sighed and checked her watch. "I told the babysitter I would be home by midnight." She hugged Kyle. "Now that I am back in town, we will have to catch up."

"I would like that." He smiled and watched her leave, suddenly uncomfortable with the thought of being alone with Casi. "Are you ready?" He left bills on the bar and directed her toward the door with a firm hand on her shoulder as they wove through the crowd. He clenched his jaw as he drove, not revealing what the dialogue was in his mind. He glanced at her as he took a turnoff for a dirt road, winding his way up a steep grade until they were perched above the river with the town twinkling below. "This is the ridge. It used to be our teenage hang out." He pulled off his shirt and gave her a half-smile. "If you want to act like you're in high school, why don't you show me what you've got?" He leaned against the door as he undid his belt and unzipped his jeans.

"Fine." She removed her shirt and scooted closer.

"Keep going." He slipped the strap of her bra off.

She complied and kissed his neck, slowly working her way down his well-defined chest as she loosened his jeans. She understood he mocked her, but she knew she could drive him crazy and make him need her again. He responded to her touch and his breathing quickened, one hand gently caressing her hair as he smiled at her with pure pleasure.

A sudden bright light accompanied a rap on the glass. "Roll down your window, please," the gruff voice requested. Casi lunged for her shirt and clasped it to her chest, keeping her back to the window. Kyle stuffed his shirt over his lap, blinking into the blinding beam of light.

"Well, Kyle Jensen, I haven't seen you out here since high school. What brings you this way tonight?" the officer asked, amused at what he had seen.

"Hello, Officer Raymond. I was showing my wife the ridge."

"Wife? I'm sure there are better places to take her than here. You should head home. There's a storm coming, and you don't want to get stuck on a dirt road." He surveyed Casi, who still had her back to him. "Everything ok?"

"Fine," she snapped.

"Have a good evening." He grinned as they quickly redressed, and Kyle backed the truck out.

Casi raced through the pouring rain, slipping on the porch steps, but refusing Kyle's attempt to help when she tumbled to her knees. The baby wailed as Lia walked him on the upper landing and Casi bolted up the stairs, colliding with Jake on his way downstairs to get a bottle. "Where are you going in such a hurry?" he asked.

"She's embarrassed because we got caught at the ridge by Officer Raymond." Kyle winked.

Casi burst into tears and shoved Jake from her path, not anticipating his solid stance. She ricocheted from the step, grabbing wildly for support while he scrambled to rescue her without success. Kyle rushed to catch her before she landed in a heap on the floor. She collapsed in his arms, undone with distress.

"What's going on?" Georgia hurried to the hallway in response to the commotion.

Kyle smoothed Casi's hair and kissed her forehead. "She tripped." He sighed and gathered her in his arms. "We need time alone. Can someone else please deal with this crying kid?" He pushed past his brother and carried her to the bathroom, securing the door. "You're soaking wet. Let's take a shower and unwind for a moment."

They stripped down and stepped in the steaming water, and Kyle wrapped his arms around her. "I'm sorry about Grant," she whispered.

"I hate that you kissed another man, but I realize it may have been a reaction to a deficit in our marriage." He put his palm to her cheek to force her to look at him. "We need to talk about things. Don't shut me out."

"I can't bear to hear what you might say."

"I love you and I would be lost without you. I could spend years apologizing for the procedure to no avail because you continue to punish me for my mistake. I have acted like a sullen teenager and given you zero credit for stepping up, but…"

"I can do better. Please don't leave me," she choked.

"What are you talking about? I would never leave you!" His eyes widened with bewilderment.

"You love Lauren and I'm a burden you feel obligated to." She wiped her eyes. "My heart is breaking."

"Are you crazy? I don't have any feelings for her other than friendship. I never did. That was one of the primary issues in our relationship." He bit his bottom lip. "I over-shared because I was lost when things fell apart in LA, but she lied about what I said. I didn't consider the ramifications when I vented because I have an easy rapport with her. And Jake was consumed with his own issues."

"I don't like you talking about me or my mom."

"I told her we were having problems, but I never said anything negative about you personally. I may have bitched about your mom." He raised an eyebrow. "Do you complain about me to Anna?"

Casi nodded. "Can you find someone other than Lauren?"

"How about if I come to you instead? That's what I should have done in the beginning." He pressed his forehead to hers. "Please be honest. How much do you hate me for eliminating your ability to be a mother? I see the way you are with this child and it kills me that I didn't consider you might change your mind." His eyes watered. "You keep evolving faster than I can adapt. I understand why you wanted to be with a successful businessman now that you have transitioned into a professional career woman."

She slipped her fingers around his wrists. "It shocked me to fall in love with that baby, but I don't want my own. He's a special gift and I'm excited about watching him grow. That's more than enough for me. I completely comprehend the work and bullshit that goes into raising a child, and I prefer to be on the sidelines." She kissed him. "I don't want Grant. I was flattered by the advance because I'm used to having you to myself and I was jealous of all the people vying for your attention. It was immature and selfish, and I'm mortified I acted that way."

Kyle gazed in her eyes. "I've been dealing with some past issues that were dredged up with this joyous birth and previous relation-ships. I haven't been at my best." He caressed her breast. "I haven't been a good partner. Can I make it up to you?"

A smiled curled from the corners of her mouth. "You owe me an orgasm. It hurt when you treated me like a cheap lay last week."

"That's harsh." He cringed. "And valid. I'm sorry for being a jerk." His eyes crinkled with amusement. "It actually punished me more because I wanted to make love to you but I behaved like a frat boy out of spite. Sex with you is usually a blissful escape."

"Then show me how you can do it properly." She wrapped her leg around his waist as he slipped his hand between her legs, making her moan.

§

Early the next morning, the baby started up again. Kyle tucked a pillow to cover Casi's ears, hoping she wouldn't hear him. Georgia put on a robe and sighed, watching Lia sobbing with the child in her arms. "Give him to me. Try to get some rest." She rocked the baby and signaled to Jake to follow her to the living room. "What are you going to do?" she whispered, glancing up the stairwell to ensure they were alone. "She isn't bonding with him."

Jake ran his hand through his hair and exhaled while he prepared a bottle. "I didn't want this." He eyed the hysterical child.

"I know, Sweetie, but he's here." Georgia rubbed his back and winced as the baby arched and howled.

Casi appeared and transferred him to her chest, immediately silencing him. "It's okay, Billy Bob. Auntie is here." The baby's lip trembled, and he locked his watery eyes on hers.

"You have a magical way with him." Georgia smiled at her.

Jake handed her the bottle. "Sorry we woke you. I realize I've been unfairly relying on you to care for him."

"I promised I would." Casi settled on the sofa.

Jake sat beside her and put an arm around her shoulders. "I'm sorry about the way I treated you." He peeked at his mother. "And that thing in Hawaii."

Georgia clucked her tongue. "You had to take Sonya up on her advances?"

Jake blanched. "Casi told you?"

Georgia shivered. "Sonya did. That is a new low, Jake Jensen."

Casi laughed. "Ha, that is a proper punishment for you to be chastised by your mother." She threw her head back. "You are literally a mother fucker."

Jake's face contorted with disgust as the women laughed. Kyle yawned and slid between Casi and the arm of the sofa. Georgia smiled. "We have other chairs."

"I like it here." Kyle grinned and inspected the baby. "When he's not crying, he's actually really cute."

Georgia nodded. "I believe he will resemble his father, which of course is similar to his uncle."

"Lucky kid." Kyle poked him in the belly.

"Austin." Casi beamed. "That's a perfect name! I saw it on a book in Kyle's bedroom and it seems fitting."

"That was my brother." Peter strolled in the living room and handed Casi a cup of coffee. "I agree, it's a good name for a Jensen."

Jake smiled. "Unless Lia disagrees, I'm happy with it."

Casi gave him a high-five. "Excellent, now go make me pancakes."

23

SWEETHEARTS AND SECRETS

Kyle leaned against the doorjamb with a smile. "Want to go to a party?"

Casi glanced up from feeding the baby. "At the skatepark with teenagers?"

Kyle chuckled. "No, grownups this time. Nicole decided to throw a get-together at her house to announce her homecoming."

Casi grinned and transferred Austin to Jake's lap. "Your turn." She raced up the stairs and changed to a denim mini-skirt with a colorful halter-style top and her best cleavage enhancing bra. She put on pink strappy sandals that made her legs appear even longer. She fluffed her hair and applied light makeup with pink lipstick.

"Thanks for abandoning me. I'm going to play Candy Crush by myself while you're gone," Jake threatened.

"Good luck. I'm sure you'll still be on the same level when I get back." Casi smiled when she noted the defeat written across his face and gave him a kiss. "I'll play with you tomorrow. It's more fun together."

Jake looked at Georgia when they left. "Just like old times. I'm stuck at home taking care of babies while Kyle has a social life. I never appreciated how much Gail did." His voice broke. "Maybe it was because she actually loved her children."

Peter patted him on the shoulder. "How about a game of chess? You can probably still beat me with a one-arm handicap."

They drove through town, up a winding road to a large house above the river. "Wow, this is a gorgeous place," Casi exclaimed.

Kyle nodded, familiar with the area, but surprised at the size of the house. "This used to be a trailer park. It was dismantled a few years back, and they built a subdivision. Nicole moved to Japan after college and they bought this place a few months ago when they returned. Nicole is a teacher and her husband does something with computers."

They walked in the party, blasting Kyle's style of music. He enthusiastically greeted friends he hadn't socialized with in years. Nicole invited most of their high school friends, wanting to reconnect, and they readily accepted a chance to relive their youthful past. She gave Kyle a kiss, long and lingering. She hugged Casi and introduced her husband, Gary, a computer geek with glasses, who had a weak handshake.

They drank and played ping pong, which turned into beer pong and talked about high school. "Anyone up for a video game tournament?" Gary pushed his glasses up the bridge of his nose and he noted key elements of the game designed by his company. A few guys volunteered, placing their twenty-dollar wager in the pot.

"I'll play." Casi smiled and people chuckled as she sat on the sofa, crossing her long bare legs.

Kyle extracted a bill from his wallet and whispered, "Are you sure? I bet these guys are amazingly good."

"It'll be fun to try." Casi giggled and took a controller, scanning the buttons and features. She held her own in the first level, learning the secrets and the intricate layers of challenges. A crowd gathered as they entered the second round and Casi moved up a position, pacing herself as she concentrated on the goal. On the final level, she obliterated her opponents so completely Gary stared at her, mouth open, confused by the beautiful woman and her gaming skills.

She smiled as she put down her controller, picked up her winnings, and received a congratulatory kiss from Kyle. "You never cease to amaze me."

"Joey and I used to scam people at arcades back in the day. No one believes a pretty girl can outplay them." Casi gave him a wink.

The party moved outside when the rain stopped. People lounged around the pool, partially drunk, happy to leave their adult lives behind and pretend they were teenagers again. Casi returned from the bathroom to hear a group of women trying to convince Kyle to join them for a swim.

"Oh, come on, you were never shy in high school," they teased.

Nicole reclined in the hot tub with a couple of other women, and a few men brave enough to strip down eighteen years later. The group continued to coerce Kyle until he finally removed his shirt to cheers and whistles. Casi smiled as she watched him undress, not ashamed of his well-defined body, which would rival any high school athlete. Nicole watched him with great interest, probably remembering the boy she used to date and impressed with the man he had become. "New tattoo?"

"Two, actually." He showed her Casi's name on his arm.

Nicole continued her appraisal as he stepped in the water. "What's the new scar from?" She eyed the round imprint with a spider leg pattern.

"Bullet wound." He shrugged.

"Are you serious?" Her mouth dropped.

"I got shot in LA. Just a random act."

Nicole sighed. "You are an honest to God superman!"

Kyle nodded sadly as he settled beside her. "I've survived a few tragedies." He gazed at Casi. "Come join us."

Casi surveyed the inebriated group relaxing in the warm bubbles and flung her top to the side as she shimmied out of her skirt. All eyes turned to the exquisite woman in a pink lace bra and panties in disbelief. She smiled and shed the last of her clothing as Kyle gave her a hand over the edge. Gary designated himself the bartender, ensuring Casi had a drink as he blinked and blushed, making Nicole giggle at his awkward behavior. She pulled Casi toward her and waved him away. "Go play with your electronics, Gary. I want to get to know Kyle Jensen's wife."

Casi smiled and chatted about her life, only mentioning the highlights of LA before launching into a conversation on her current career. Nicole grasped her hand with surprising force. "I'm so happy Kyle found you. He's an amazing guy, and the boating accident really shattered him. He deserves all the happiness in the world." Her eyes shifted to where Kyle sat with his arm around a woman who was wiping a tear as she leaned against him. "That's Amber, Kyle's high school sweetheart." She nudged Casi. "She broke his heart in the eleventh grade. I dated him after that, but he was always guarded with his emotions."

Casi scanned the woman objectively; brassy blonde and attractive, but the years had not been kind. A hardness enveloped her like someone who had seen a tough road and had made a lot of bad choices. Kyle regarded her with sadness, mixed with a tenderness she tried to decipher. "What did she do to hurt him?"

"Jake, of course." Nicole winked. Casi's eyes widened and Nicole nodded. "Kyle dated Amber for about a year and they were each other's first loves. He caught her with Jake in the barn and almost killed him!"

"That's terrible!"

"It gets worse." She paused for dramatic effect. "Amber got pregnant! And she didn't know which brother might be the father!"

Casi surveyed Kyle with an arm around Amber as she tearfully recounted a story from her life. She felt jealous of this woman, but also enraged she had hurt Kyle. "Is there a Jensen kid running around town?"

"Abortion. Jake took her. Kyle wouldn't have anything to do with her after that. He barely spoke to his brother for almost a year."

"That's so sad. She looks like she's had a hard life."

"She has four kids with different dads. She waitresses at the diner. She never left town and high school was her heyday. After all that stuff went down, she got a little wild but then burned out when everyone went off in different directions."

"Why did you invite her?" Casi asked.

"She heard about the party and wanted to see Kyle. I figured you wouldn't mind, he's obviously madly in love with you." Nicole sighed. "After the boating accident, we all scattered to the winds of change and loss. Now that I'm back in town I would like to reconnect with old friends."

Kyle cringed when they got out of the truck and they could hear a symphony of wailing from the front porch. "I guess you will be back on baby duty."

Casi grasped his arm. "How about if I get him to go to sleep and then we can sneak away to our bedroom?" Jake threw the door open and hoisted the child in her arms. She noted Austin's blotchy cheeks and a hoarse cry. "Has he been upset since we left?"

"Pretty much. I hope your party was worth it." Jake yawned.

"It was fun." Casi smiled.

"Amber was there." Kyle locked eyes with his brother.

"Oh, really?" Jake glanced at Casi and blanched. "You told her!"

Kyle frowned when he observed the sly smile on Casi's face. "No, did Nicole tell you something about Amber?"

Casi patted Austin's back as she held him against her shoulder. "Let's go up to Jake's room and you can fill in the details while I put your child to sleep. Also, I would like free rein to snoop through your stuff."

"Where do you get off having bargaining power?" Jake questioned.

Casi cocked her head. "This silence is quite nice, isn't it?"

"Fine, search all you want. I doubt I have anything incriminating, plus you probably weaseled the juicy details from your new girl-friend," he said as they ascended the stairs.

Peter smiled when they reached the landing. "Thank God you're home. We didn't think anyone would be sleeping tonight."

Casi glanced at Lia curled up in the guest room bed. "Did she ever come downstairs or hold the baby? What does she think of the name?"

"She ate dinner but went back to bed." Jake shrugged. "She says she doesn't care what we name him."

"Then his name is Austin." Casi kissed the baby on the cheek. She made a sharp right as she entered Jake's room and scanned a bookshelf. "Get comfortable, I'm very thorough."

Jake reclined on his bed while Kyle took a seat beside him. "So, what did Nicole say?"

"Amber and Kyle were madly in love until you came and stole her." Casi grinned at her condensed version.

Kyle frowned. "You were alone with her for about five minutes."

Casi shrugged. "People feel comfortable around me and like to share things. Normally, I'm excellent at secrets, but this one is already out of the bag so you might as well fill in the details." She found condoms and read the expiration date, throwing them at Jake. "Maybe that's the problem." She opened a book from one of his college classes and a piece of binder paper fluttered out. She picked it up as Jake bolted from the bed, unclear what it contained. She pulled back, not letting him take it from her as she read the letter aloud. Amber begged him to run away with her and raise the baby and confessed how much she loved him. She had drawn a heart and put their initials inside it. "Did you love her?"

"No, I didn't even like her that much." Jake fidgeted.

Casi surveyed his shattered appearance. "Have you ever been in love before Anna?"

"You are off topic." Jake threw a pillow at her. He watched her twirling with Austin and sighed in resignation of her persistence. "When I was seventeen, I loved a girl named Janie. She broke my heart."

Casi peered behind trophies and trinkets on the shelf, smiling at a worn teddy bear with a missing eye. She ran a finger over books, taking a mental inventory. "Was that part of your motivation for breaking up Amber and Kyle? You wanted him to experience the pain of being crushed?"

Kyle whipped his head around to stare down Jake. "Was that why?"

Jake narrowed his eyes. "Not intentionally. It was jealousy over the time they spent together, and he rarely wanted to visit me at college." He shrugged. "Amber initiated it. I was flattered by the attention and let it play out. I misjudged how much Kyle cared for her and how he would end up hating me. He ditched the idea of college and planned an elaborate trip to Europe with Grady to avoid me." He rubbed at a scar on his inner elbow until Kyle grasped his hand to stop the action.

"I didn't hate you." Kyle squeezed his hand. "I was angry and hurt. Going to Europe was a fantasy trip, and not because..." He glanced at Casi.

She grinned. "I know about Amber's abortion."

"Do you just smile sweetly, and everyone divulges secrets?" Jake asked.

"Pretty much." She caressed Austin's cheek, and he smiled and relaxed into a deep sleep.

Jake's face clouded. "I took her to the clinic and waited in the car like a coward. I drove her home and told her I was done with her." He pressed himself against the headboard. "I lost a year with my brother, and almost permanently when he had the accident. Karma punished me twice."

"I woke up in the hospital and the first thing I saw was Jake's face and the fight we had dissolved into thin air." Kyle exhaled. "I found out he donated blood and told them to take it all."

"I didn't want to be alive if he died." Jake gripped one of Austin's fingers between his own. "I can't handle my life without him, and he doesn't admit what a burden that is, but he even turned down a scholarship to play baseball to attend college with me instead."

Kyle chuckled. "You have that backward. I turned it down because I was good, but not exceptional. I wouldn't have made it at pro ball, and it seemed like a waste of time to focus on something that was never my dream. The accident shattered my life. I suddenly had phys-ical limitations, and I lost my confidence and had terrible night-mares. I didn't want to be alone, and I realized we were better together. I depended on you just as much as you needed me. My life is richer with you. Even if I'd gone to Europe, I would have come back, and we still would have had the business."

24
───────

AUSTIN

"It will be good for you, Lia." Casi secured Austin in the stroller.

"It's at least three miles. Why can't we drive?" Lia complained.

"Your doctor said you can reverse diabetes if you lose the weight you gained during your pregnancy. I'll help you."

"This pregnancy was such a mistake. Not only do I need to lose more weight, but I've got stupid diabetes," Lia whined.

"You can change both of those things and now we have sweet little Austin, who's awesome most of the time."

Lia touched his face. "He is cute. I'm glad he got Jake's eyes. I'm feeling a bit more attached to him. Thanks for helping. I couldn't handle it by myself."

"I promised you wouldn't be alone. Austin is part of our clan." Casi grasped Lia's hand as she pushed the stroller down the hill. "We made it," she announced as the coffee shop came into view.

"Maybe it's lame, but I like working here." Lia sighed.

"It's good to keep busy and feel like you have a purpose. What are the primary things you enjoy about this job?"

"I like being in the middle of the action and people feeling useful. Lauren says I'm ridiculous, but my dream has always been to own a coffee shop. A small one, not part of a corporation like this. I would feature a variety of coffees and teas and make the baked goods from scratch." Her eyes lit up as she listed the features her shop would have. "This job appears basic but there is a lot that goes into running a place such as ordering and inventory."

"That's an awesome goal. Why does she think it's dumb?"

"Her dream is to own a restaurant and maybe a small hotel. She says I don't have any skills and I let people tell me what to do. I believe her bitterness comes from jealousy about me having a baby."

"Because she wants one, or because he's a Jensen?"

Lia smiled. "Both. She wanted a baby with Kyle."

Casi stopped outside the coffee shop. "Was Kyle always firm about not wanting kids, or is that only with me?"

"He never wanted children," Lia assured her. "Lauren was convinced he would change his mind if she got pregnant."

Casi raised an eyebrow. "Did she try?"

Lia shrugged and avoided the answer. "Of course, now she can see how the Jensen brothers won't be tricked into marriage."

Casi opened the door and Lia hesitated when she saw Gail and Mary Ann at a table, then smiled and brought the stroller over. Gail peered inside and fought back tears as the blue-eyed baby gazed up at her. "He's so adorable!"

"You can hold him." Lia turned toward the action at the coffee bar. "I need to talk to my manager. He's been asking when I'm coming back to work. I'll get our coffees, Casi."

Gail picked up Austin and held him tightly. She smiled at Casi. "I hear you've been amazing with him."

Casi shrugged. "He's ok." Gail smiled at her and they broke into laughter. "Truthfully? I'm totally smitten. I love this kid."

"Does it make you want one?" Mary Ann asked.

"Nope. I'm happy with this little nugget," Casi concluded.

Gail hugged him. "I see why. I could hold him all day."

"How are the men with him?" Mary Ann asked.

"Kyle's not interested, but Jake's awesome. It's sweet to see him holding this tiny tidbit and taking care of him. He's excellent with diapers!"

"I taught him that," Gail giggled. "The smell never bothered him. He's remarkably patient with babies. I wish Olivia knew how much he did for her; walking endlessly throughout the night or dealing with disgusting diapers."

"Borrow Austin and let her see how much work is involved in taking care of a baby," Casi suggested.

Gail gazed at the child. "That's a good plan."

Lia came back with two cups. "I can get on the schedule next week." She bit her lip and frowned at the baby in Gail's arms. "I'm bored at home and I hate not having money. Jake takes care of most of the expenses, but it sucks to be dependent. I'll have to figure out if I can afford daycare."

"What shifts are available? I can take him on Tuesdays and Thursdays. We can all watch him on weekends," Casi offered.

"I'm happy to babysit on Fridays." Gail beamed. "I only work Monday through Thursday."

"You would be willing to watch him?" Lia raised an eyebrow.

"Sure. I would prefer that to answering phones and filing. My job skills are more suited for taking care of babies." Gail kissed his cheek.

"Do you guys think I'm a terrible mother for not wanting to spend all day with my child?" Lia tugged at her sleeve.

"There's nothing wrong with wanting to work. Everyone has their own way of parenting. I stayed home, but I had a husband with a good job and an amazing mother-in-law to help me do everything around the house. I dedicated myself to raising those kids and look how my daughter turned out? A rebel without a cause." Gail threw her head back and laughed.

"Wait, where are you going?" Kyle grasped Casi's arm.

"I have a meeting in Seattle."

"But what about him?" Kyle pointed to Austin in the bassinet.

"You can watch him for a few hours. It's not like it's hard, he just lays there and drools. Jake will be back from the college visit with Olivia at four, and Lia's off work around then. You can pretend you're a mom and cook dinner and clean the house while the baby sleeps." Casi giggled. "Have you seen his teeny tiny bits? So funny."

Kyle chuckled. "I'm sure he's normal for a baby." He kissed her goodbye and frowned at Austin with distrust as the infant cooed. "I don't want to be a parent." He breathed a sigh of relief as Austin's eyes fluttered closed, and he sat back to watch the game on TV. The first hour went well, and he began to think babysitting wasn't too difficult. Getting up to make a sandwich, he noted the blanket move and peered inside the bassinet. "Stay asleep," he whispered. When the crying began, he rocked the cradle, hoping the movement would be calming. He checked the troubleshooting guide Casi left and considered his options. "Are you hungry?" He followed the directions on the can of formula, put off by the smell. "Jeez, how can you eat this stuff?" He secured the bottle in Austin's mouth. The baby took most of the formula, then continued to cry. Kyle cringed and moved the blanket aside, assuming the time had come to change his first diaper. "I hate everything about this," he declared, picking up the infant and holding him at arm's length to avoid contact. He carried him to the bathroom and located the diapers, reading through his cheat sheet. He smiled at Casi's color-coded depiction, knowing she wouldn't ever change a diaper. "Stay." He placed his palm on Austin's chest to adhere him to the towel on the counter. He removed the soiled diaper, wishing he brought a bag for disposal. Austin continued to cry, arching his back with his lip quivering. "I don't like this either." Kyle cringed and used six baby wipes to remove any trace of poop. He ran the faucet and considered his best option, deciding to slide a hand under to support him by his belly, holding his backside under the running water. "Sorry kid, but I'm supposed to make sure you're clean or you'll get a rash." He held him up for inspection.

He set Austin back on the towel and reached for the new diaper, shaking his head when he started to pee. He held the cloth over him, avoiding getting sprayed. "Why did you do that? I cleaned you perfectly and now we need to start over." He washed him again, quickly wrapping him. "Ok, no more until your dad gets home. I'm your uncle. I'm not required to do this. When you're older, I'll take you fishing and hunting, but this changing stuff is bullshit." Austin cried through the securing of the diaper and Kyle checked three times to make sure it wasn't too tight, finally feeling confident it would stay in place. He searched the bathroom and wondered where they kept clean baby clothes. He gave up and retrieved one of his t-shirts, pulling it over Austin's head and tying the hem in a knot. "Good enough."

He put the baby back in his bassinet and the crying intensified. "What do you want? I've fed and changed you." He rubbed his temple in dismay. Dingo cocked his head and looked at the crying baby and then back at Kyle. "Dogs are easier." Kyle reached for the baby and cradled him against his chest. "Are you happy now?" He eyed the remote control for the TV on the coffee table and clasped Austin securely as he grabbed it, pleased with his smooth acquisition. He switched to a documentary on the migration of whales, giving Austin a running commentary. He cooed and watched Kyle with interest, making him smile. "Ok, maybe you aren't so bad."

Two hours later, Jake arrived home to see Kyle asleep with Austin cuddled on his chest. Casi came in behind him, smiling at the scene. Kyle yawned. "It's past four."

"You seem content," Jake said.

"This kid is a lot of work." Kyle patted him on the back.

"Did you make dinner?" Casi teased.

"It was all I could do to feed and change him. He cries if I don't hold him. I think he's spoiled from all the attention you give him." Kyle smiled.

Casi scooted beside him on the sofa, smiling at the clothing choice. "Babies are needy. That's why it takes four of us to raise him."

25

PUZZLED

Casi checked her phone for messages after leaving the meeting, not paying attention as she walked to her car. "It's nice to see you care about calls from some people." She looked up to see her mother standing beside her car. "I guess Dad got tired of me calling him to find out how you were. He told me you worked in Seattle."

"How did you find me?" Casi sighed.

Sonya snapped, "I talked to that twit at your husband's business, and apparently, she has your schedule."

"You shouldn't have come; I don't want to see you."

"Casi grow up! You want to blame me for your bad choices? Fine, but I never forced you to do anything."

"You lied to me!"

"I told you about the photo shoot and you came willingly. You chose to return the check after your husband freaked out. You were better off without him, have you realized that yet?"

"I'm much better with him. My life is amazing, and I don't want anything to do with you or that chaos in LA."

"You're a salesgirl now?" Sonya eyed her attire.

"I do marketing and promotions for Mary's skincare line."

"What a lucky girl, your other mother created a company for you, and even moved to Seattle to be nearby. Maybe I should move here, it's picturesque." Sonya waved a hand around.

"I don't want you here. Stay in LA and live your own life."

"Would I be intruding? You've already got your precious daddy and step-mommy to worship you."

"Why did you come?" Casi inhaled sharply.

"I wanted to see you! You can't write me off and pretend your life is perfect. I know about your past."

"The whole world knows thanks to you! Kyle doesn't care. He loves me and we're making our marriage work."

"Marriage shouldn't be work. You're fooling yourself to think you are happy in that tiny town." Sonya charged toward her.

"I am happy!" Casi clenched her fists and squeezed her eyes shut.

"Prove it. Tell me what is so delightful in this meaningless life."

"I'll get a drink with you here since you came all this way, but then you can turn around and go back to LA."

"You can show me your home on your terms, or I will go by myself and talk to your friends and discover all the details of your new world." Casi glanced at her phone, but Sonya read her mind. "No need to tell Kyle. We will make it a surprise."

"Will you leave after I give you a tour?"

"Of course. I only came to ensure you are alright."

"Bullshit." Casi clicked the locks open on her car.

Sonya slid in and admired the leather interior. "I see you earned yourself a nice ride. I'm proud of you."

"I didn't earn it. Kyle bought it for me because he wanted me to be safe in the Washington weather."

Sonya rolled her eyes. "By the way, how's Jake?"

"I heard about Hawaii; you can stop playing games."

"I wonder if he's improved since then, maybe I need to give him another lesson." Sonya inspected her heavy makeup in the mirror.

"He's not interested. He has a new baby now with Lia."

"She trapped him into marrying her?"

"They're not married."

"Then he's available."

"Not for you. He's my family, leave him alone."

"Oh? Are you doing both brothers now? What fun. Kyle seems a little uptight, but maybe he'd be more relaxed in a threesome," Sonya pondered.

"Stop it!" Casi screamed, almost missing her exit.

❧

Jake looked up from the router and winced, nudging Kyle as they came through the door. "Sonya," Kyle greeted her dryly.

"Oh Darling, don't be so stiff." Sonya kissed him. Jake backed behind a band saw to avoid contact.

Casi explained Sonya's visit, mentioning it would be temporary. "Too bad we have a one-bedroom house," Kyle said.

"I'm sure you own a couch." Sonya smoothed a hand over his chest.

"I sleep on it," Jake said.

"That could be cozy." Sonya gave him a wink.

"She's only staying for dinner," Casi declared.

"You're not making me feel welcome," Sonya pouted.

"Why do you think I never gave you my new phone number? I blocked you on Facebook, can't you take a hint?" Casi scowled.

"I think we should have a conversation in private." Sonya pinched her hand and directed her to the side.

"She doesn't hide anything from me. Say whatever you want," Kyle said.

Sonya glared at him. "You've made it your mission to turn her against me. We were perfectly happy before you came along. You have a desperate need to control her and lock her away from the world."

"She has a career and makes her own money. I don't tell her what to do, and she can come and go as she pleases." Kyle leaned against the workbench. "It is her choice not to be around you."

Casi nodded. "Would you like to see my office before you leave?"

Sonya blinked at the cozy space. "Well, I guess you seem content in this bourgeois life."

"I love working here. I get my own area and I travel to Seattle several times a week. I finally have a purpose," Casi beamed.

"Being my daughter wasn't enough?"

"That's not a job, Mom. I'm still your daughter, but I needed a career, and this fulfills me."

"Then let me be a part of it. You would never have made it as far as you did in modeling without me," Sonya asserted.

"You got me a lot of exposure and made me stand up for myself. But that chapter is over now, and I've chosen to start fresh. If you want to be involved in my life, you need to be separate from me. I can't take care of you and I'm not going to let you destroy what I have with Kyle."

"You leave people when they're at their lowest, Casi. You did it to your best friend, Katie, and now you did it to me." Sonya's nostrils flared.

"That's not fair! Why is it on me to take care of everyone?"

"I need help and you're only concerned about yourself."

"Are you going to rehab?"

"I don't need it. I'm not an addict, I like to have fun. Let me stay with you for a few weeks. It will be like old times; we'll have a blast together." Sonya grabbed her around the waist and shook her hips.

"There's no room. Why can't you stay with Dad?"

"Ava makes me uncomfortable. It's difficult for me to see her with Dad, the only man I ever loved." Sonya clasped her chest.

"You can stay in the trailer across the street from our house," Kyle said from the doorway. "It would be a good place for you to figure your life out." Casi grinned, knowing it would be Sonya's worst nightmare.

Sonya surveyed the old trailer with distaste. "This is a hovel. Why can't Jake stay here, and I'll sleep on the sofa?"

Kyle shrugged. "This is your choice. You can shower at the house, but this is where you'll sleep."

"I'll clean it and get new sheets. It's nice and quiet here, it will be good for you." Casi nudged Kyle as they walked back across the street. "She won't stay there. Before we know it, she'll be creeping into our space."

"I'm going to start locking the door," Kyle declared.

The first week went as expected with Sonya finding additional reasons to come over other than showering or having meals with them. After three weeks, Kyle locked the door when they weren't home, not feeling comfortable with her entering as she pleased. On a whim, he came home from work early, figuring Casi was in Seattle and Sonya had become increasingly restless with being left alone. He realized they must have left the patio door unlocked, hearing music as he approached the house. He surveyed the kitchen, cluttered with dishes, and what appeared to be an attempt to do laundry. He walked toward the bedroom, following the sound.

"Can I help you find something?" Kyle observed Sonya waltz out of their closet in a robe, clothes in hand.

"I'm borrowing a t-shirt from Casi. That's not a crime, is it? I know how you like to dominate her. Do I need permission?" Sonya pouted.

He ignored the criticism. "Actually, it would be nice if you asked her before you borrowed anything."

Sonya disrobed, standing seductively. "Is it ok if I use her shampoo, or did you want to call and check with her?"

Jake came in and laughed when he saw her in the nude. "Kyle is not as dumb as I am, Sonya. Don't even bother trying to seduce him."

She shrugged. "Did you want to join me, Jake?"

"No thanks, I don't repeat my mistakes." He turned and walked out.

"We need to get rid of her." Kyle joined him in the kitchen.

"I agree, but where do we dump the body?"

Kyle chuckled. "Maybe Jack will take her?"

"Doubtful. He's aware she's here and hasn't extended an invitation."

"True, but there has to be an end in sight. I thought the trailer would scare her off after a few days."

"She's like a cockroach, she adapts to her environment."

"You need to move to the trailer. Casi and I haven't been alone in weeks, and I'm tired of feeling claustrophobic."

"You've been spending a lot of time with Lauren."

"Only because I can't handle being here with Sonya! I don't want Casi to feel bad because she actually seems to enjoy having her around."

Jake shook his head. "I think she feels responsible for her and worries she'll do herself in if she's left alone. She also wants to prove how well she's doing in her career. Your little sunshine girl has confidence issues when it comes to her mother. A cloud washes over her and she shuts down."

"I realize that. Between Sonya and your kid, I never get a minute alone with my wife. It's been weeks since we've made love."

"Not my fault; you have a whole bedroom to yourself. Austin imprinted on her from birth. I can't help it if they bonded."

"Maybe Sonya could move to the apartment and take care of him?"

"She calls him the leech and tells Casi to stop holding him so much or he'll become gay. So, I'm not good with that idea." Jake frowned.

Casi asked Jake to entertain Sonya for the evening, suggesting he take her to the bar. He agreed, wanting to ease Kyle's tension. She spent the day cooking a nice meal and cleaning the house, wanting everything to be perfect to surprise Kyle when he came home.

She ignored Sonya's attempts to derail her evening, yanking the flimsy apron from her hands. "Please stay out of my way."

"How sweet, you're surprising your husband with a home cooked meal and wearing nothing but an apron?" Sonya chided.

Casi smoothed the transparent chiffon apron. "We want time alone, Mom. Go out with Jake and have fun at the bar."

"I guess you're worried about his girlfriend, Lauren. You can't cook like her, but I'm sure you compensate for that in the bedroom."

"I'm not concerned about their friendship."

Sonya shrugged. "Dad and Ava were friends before they betrayed me. Have you talked to Alix?"

"I'm not ready. It's not the kind of conversation I want to have over the phone. I booked a meeting in LA next week and I might contact him then."

"Kyle said that's ok?"

"I don't need permission from him."

"Enjoy your fantasy. Don't be disappointed when he doesn't respond the way you hoped; husbands never do."

Kyle received a call from a jeweler in Seattle. "Mr. Jensen? I had an odd inquiry from a pawn shop who recognized our jeweler's mark," he said, hesitating for a moment. "You had a jade pendant designed and when you bought the engagement ring, I assumed it was for the same woman?"

"Yes, I also purchased the diamond constellation for my wife last Christmas. Is there a problem?"

"Not to interfere, but we could have given you or, um, well, your wife, a much better price for those pieces if you had brought them here. Is there a reason you didn't want to do business with us?"

"I didn't sell anything!" Kyle fumed, deducing who did. "Where's the pawn shop?" The jeweler gave him the address, and he turned the truck toward Seattle, convinced this was the last straw with Sonya. He knew Casi would be devastated to find out her necklaces had been taken, and he wondered what other items might be missing.

"You understand this isn't a date, right?" Jake reiterated. "I'm taking you to the bar to let Casi and Kyle enjoy some time alone."

"I'll still put out at the end of the evening," Sonya purred.

"How many times do I have to turn you down?"

"I'm curious to see what you learned from that woman in Seattle. I suspect she's quite the tiger."

"How did you hear about her?"

"Casi introduced me to her. She's lovely. What a rock of an engagement ring she has. Does it bother you she chose money over a small-town lover?" Sonya blinked innocently and caught a glimpse of Kyle's truck coming down the hill as they walked to the car. "Oh Jake, there's something Casi wanted from you before we left."

"Can't it wait?"

"No, she said it was urgent."

Jake figured he would get a lecture about not sleeping with Sonya as he entered the house. "What did you want?" He froze when she turned around in her see-through apron, wearing only lace panties. "Is this a joke?"

"It's not for you. Why are you here?" Casi snapped.

"Your mom told me to come over." He averted his eyes.

"Can't I have one evening alone with my husband?" She glared at the clock. "He's not with Lauren, is he?"

"He said he needed to do something in Seattle."

"Like her?" Casi's eyes filled with tears and Jake embraced her.

"Are you fucking kidding me?" Kyle growled.

Sonya entered, pleased with the scene. "Sorry, Casi, I tried to warn you he was home. I guess I wasn't fast enough. I hope you had time to fulfill the fantasy Jake requested."

"Shut up, Sonya," Jake said in disgust.

Kyle's knee made immediate contact with Jake's groin, sending him to the floor in excruciating pain. "I'm tired of this bullshit! You can all play your games without me." He stormed out of the house.

"Kyle!" Casi yelled, hesitant to run in her scandalous attire. She watched him peel out of the driveway and turned to her mother. "You ruin everything! Why can't you let us be happy?"

Sonya shrugged, "This is so much more fun."

Jake leaned against the counter, trying to ease the pain in his groin. "Sonya, you have five minutes to get your shit together. We're done with your lunatic ass."

"Aren't we going to the bar?" She batted her eyelashes.

"Four minutes." He scowled as Casi ran to the bedroom in tears.

After a silent drive, Jake pulled in Jack's driveway and yanked Sonya from the truck. "Come on crazy-pants, I'm returning you to the mother-ship." They waited on the doorstep and he fought off her advances, unwinding her and re-zipping his jeans. "Knock it off!"

Jack answered the door, obviously having been awakened. "Why are you here?" he yawned.

"Our life is like a jigsaw puzzle with everyone having their special place," Jake explained. "This oddball piece doesn't fit. She's caused enough havoc. It's time for someone else to babysit."

"No, Jack," Ava snapped as she stormed toward them. "She needs to find somewhere else to go. This is our home."

Jake backed up toward the truck. "Sorry, no take backs. This is the end of the line as far as I'm concerned."

Jack wrung his hands as Sonya pushed past him into the house. "What a charming home. Jamie would love the way you decorated. It's so cheerful. What a lovely place to raise a child with a beautiful garden to play in."

Tears sprung to Ava's eyes, and she glared at Jack. "Take her to the airport now or you can sleep on the couch. I'm tired of dealing with this insanity!" She slammed the bedroom door.

Jack sighed, not surprised Sonya landed on his doorstep, knowing he should have anticipated what to do with her. He glanced at his watch and opened a door in the hall. "I doubt there are flights at this hour and I'm not heartless enough to dump you at the airport for the night. You can sleep in the guest room, but you will leave tomorrow. We've had a long day at the restaurant and neither of us are in the mood." Jack sighed and gathered blankets, realizing Ava's threat was real.

§

Jake called Anna as he left Bellingham. "Are you up for a night of romance? I can be at your place in under an hour."

Anna sighed and glanced at Casi, covering the phone with her hand. "What time's your flight?"

Casi grinned. "Soon. I need to get going, anyway."

"You have one hour to get here or I'm going to bed. I leave for Italy in the morning. Remember, I'm getting married?" Anna instructed.

Jake chuckled. "I'll give you the perfect wedding present."

Casi hugged Anna goodbye, wishing her well on her trip as she left for the airport. Jake arrived in fifty-nine minutes, panting slightly from running up the stairs. "I made it."

"I should turn you away on the principal of almost being a wife."

"You have no principals." Jake pulled her toward him and slipped her negligee down to fondle her breast. "Will you still let me come here after you return from your honeymoon?"

"I'm selling the condo."

"We could meet at hotels like old times."

"This is the final time. After the ceremony, I must be true to my husband." Anna grasped his hand and directed him to the bed.

"You don't love him." Jake undressed.

"True. This is a business arrangement for me. He owns a shipping company and it will put me right where I want to be, married and wealthy."

"Run away with me instead. We can be poor and happy." She giggled as he pushed her back on the bed. "I love you, Anna, isn't that enough?"

"Stop talking. Make love to me and we can pretend tonight will never end." She wrapped her legs around his waist.

Jake complied, taking his time to bring her to orgasm. After he climaxed, he stroked the side of her face. "Please don't marry him."

"We need to live our lives separately for now," Anna reiterated.

"Do you want to see a picture of my son?" He reached for his phone and opened the album.

"He's gorgeous just like his dad." She smiled. "Casi adores him."

"She's a great mom." He grinned. "Lia is struggling with post-partum depression. Now that she's back at work, we hope she'll feel better."

"I'm sure it's not the ideal situation for her."

"I could give you a cute baby."

"How would I explain that to my husband?"

"Tell him you're in love with another man."

"I'm leaving for the airport in eight hours. Do you want another go at it before I'm married off?" She straddled him.

"Why not? It's my birthday."

"Really?"

"Everyone forgot because they were too worked up about Sonya. My parents called me, but Casi was preoccupied with planning a romantic evening, which failed. Kyle got pissed off and kicked me in the balls. How's that for a birthday present?"

"Poor Jake." She slid down and kissed his stomach. "Do you need CPR?"

"I might." He groaned as she ran her tongue over him.

Two hours later, they sprawled beside each other, exhausted and satisfied. Jake kissed her tenderly. "How long do I need to wait until I can be with you again?"

"I'll be gone a month, but I'm serious about being faithful when I get back," Anna said.

"Shouldn't that have started as soon as you were engaged?"

"Not according to the pre-nup." She winked.

"You do fine. Why do you need a rich husband?"

"It's not about the money." She ran a finger over his bottom lip. "I'm tired of people asking why I'm not married or why I don't have kids. Society expects certain things from a woman, no matter how successful she is. This will pacify my parents and move me up the ladder in society. I'll be the envy of all my sisters, having the richest husband." She fought back tears.

"I thought one of your sisters is a lesbian?"

"She is, but she's in a relationship with a lawyer. My parents don't talk about it. They tell people all their girls are married, except poor Anna. She's too head strong and independent," she quoted.

"I like how bossy you are."

She slapped him playfully. "Nice translation. By the way, speaking of controlling...tell Kyle, Casi left for LA tonight."

"Why? Her meeting is not until Monday?"

"She is upset about Kyle and her mother. She didn't feel like sitting around the house waiting for him to come home and explain what happened. She figured she would head to LA early and work on her presentation instead," Anna said.

"I wish she had told him." Jake sighed.

"Does he realize how hard she's worked? She's excellent at marketing, and her presentations are amazing. I don't think he gives her enough credit for what she's accomplished," Anna stated.

Kyle sat on a barstool beside Mary Ann and nudged her with a smile. "Do you come here often?"

She laughed. "Where's Casi?"

He rolled his eyes. "Her mother has been in town all month. I've had enough of the Roberts women."

"Isn't one of them a Jensen now?" Gail asked.

"Nope, that's too old fashioned. She'd rather keep her name, so she and her lunatic mother have something in common." Kyle ordered a round of drinks and told them about the perils of mother in-laws, making them giggle with his colorful names for Sonya. As the liquor flowed, they joked and kidded each other, sharing intimate secrets.

"I can't believe Lia isn't more into that darling baby," Gail confessed. "He's like a tiny Jake, with a better attitude."

Kyle smiled. "Casi loves that kid. He's glued to her the minute she walks in the door."

"Jealous?" Mary Ann asked.

"Honestly, I am a little. Between her friendship with Jake, and devotion to the baby, not to mention countless hours of counseling Lia and girl talk with Anna, I'm last on the list. Once her mother entered the picture, there was no time left for me. Tonight, I came home from rescuing jewelry her mom pawned, to see her in the kitchen wearing lace panties with heels and a sheer apron, wrapped in Jake's arms."

"Did you forget today is Jake's birthday? We thought we'd see him here, not a disgruntled brother," Gail said.

Kyle rubbed his temple. "I did forget. Do you think that was Casi's present for him? Her mom said something to that effect."

"It was for you, Moron!" Mary Ann giggled. "She told us Dylan gave her the apron as a wedding present and how she wanted to surprise you one night. I'm sure what you saw was innocent."

"Why do these things always backfire? I married the hottest woman on the planet, but we're never alone," Kyle lamented.

"You've been spending a lot of time with Lauren," Gail said. "Maybe Casi feels left out too. We met her mother, she criticized Casi constantly. I imagine that's hard for her because she is so upbeat normally."

Kyle nodded. "Her mother is a definite issue. Lauren and I are only friends. There is nothing wrong with me hanging out with her."

"Maybe you should limit your friends to people you didn't date in the past." Gail rolled her eyes. "I guess that would eliminate most of the women in Washington."

As the evening wore on, Kyle lost count of the drinks he had, swaying slightly as they headed out the door. "You're not driving, Kyle." Mary Ann grabbed his arm.

"Are you inviting me home?" He winked at her.

"I'll drive you to your house," Mary Ann confirmed, unlocking the door for him and bidding Gail goodnight.

"I can't take another minute of Sonya, especially when I'm drunk.

I'll probably snap and say something and get everyone pissed off, and we are already on thin ice." Kyle slumped in the seat.

"You can sleep on my couch," Mary Ann said.

"Thank you."

When they arrived at her house, she arranged a blanket and pillow on the sofa. "Do you want to text Casi and tell her where you are?"

"Nope, I need to sleep off this alcohol." He turned and kissed her.

"Kyle, what are you doing?" She pushed him back.

"It was a friendly kiss. I'm not trying to take it farther."

Jack slept fitfully on the sofa, not sure how to proceed once morning came. He moaned to the sensation in his groin. He ran his hand through her hair, waking when he realized it wasn't Ava. "Sonya, stop!"

"Don't tell me you don't like it." She lowered her head.

Jack willed his body to stop responding as he gripped her arm to tug her off. He glanced down the hall and noticed the bedroom door remained closed, praying Ava didn't wake up. "Stop, this is wrong."

"That is one thing we always did right." She straddled him and locked his arms in place with her knees with surprising force. "I'm only taking back what has always been mine."

"Listen to me, I'm telling you no!"

"That's not what your body is saying. Remember how good we were together? We were always able to make each other climax within minutes?" He winced as she rocked her hips against him, and the intense pleasure overcame him. She laughed triumphantly. "You never could resist me." He shoved her off in disgust and rolled over, yanking the blanket up, feeling hollow and dirty.

Jack woke the next morning to the smell of coffee. He walked to the kitchen and watched Ava as she stood facing the counter. She shook her head, and he could see her sobbing. "I'm sorry." He slumped at the table and put his head in his hands.

"You are disgustingly weak!" She slammed coffee down in front of him. "I'm not doing it again. Get out of my house."

He understood her anger stemmed from knowing what had transpired during the night and hoped she had been perceptive rather than a witness to the event. "I was asleep! She used me to try to break us."

"At what point did you wake up?"

Jack cringed. "When I realized it wasn't you."

Tears rolled down her cheeks. "Did you even try to stop her? Why are you always the victim?" She glared at him and narrowed her eyes. "Go take a shower, you smell like her."

Jack nodded, finishing his coffee in one gulp. "This is what she wants. Don't let her destroy us. Everything good in my life is because of you. You get to choose the outcome and I'll leave if you want me to." Tears filled his eyes as she pushed him away. "Please give me another chance."

Ava poured herself another cup, turning as Sonya sauntered in. "I want you out of my house today." She placed coffee in front of her and handed her the sugar bowl.

"What does Jack want?" Sonya spooned sugar in her cup.

"This is my home! I bought it before we married. We built the restaurant together and sacrificed to make it work. You don't get to come here and take whatever the hell you want to prove how you can manipulate him."

"You took what you wanted when I was married to him."

"You treated him like garbage and preyed on his emotional scars. I never interfered before, even when I should have with Casi. I let you tear that girl to shreds and manipulate her because you are her mother and always made sure I knew my limited role in her life. We have all created new lives for ourselves, and there's no place for you. I'm sorry things haven't worked out well and I've been patient through the years with your drug use and money woes, but it ends today. We'll pay for your flight to LA or Vancouver, or wherever the hell you want to go, but we are done with you."

Sonya nodded, realizing she was serious. She had only seen her that angry once before and knew she was not a woman who would back down. "I'll check flights for LA." She added more sugar to her cup.

"I'll book it for you." Ava grabbed her laptop. "Perhaps it's time to go to rehab and start taking control of your life."

Kyle opened his eyes and surveyed the room, trying to remember where he was. He heard Mary Ann laugh and recalled the night before. "Want some aspirin?" she asked.

"Yes, please." He rubbed his eyes. "Sorry about kissing you last night."

"I didn't mind." Mary Ann smiled.

"Can I take you to breakfast? I'm starving and I'm not quite ready to face the shit storm at home." Kyle stretched and yawned as he checked his watch.

Mary Ann drove to Tucker's pancake house. Her phone buzzed for the fourth time and Kyle chuckled. "Gail?"

Mary Ann smiled. "I'm sure she wants to hear what happened."

"We're only having breakfast." He hoped rumors didn't start when people noticed his truck in the bar parking lot overnight. "Have you been here before?"

"No, but Casi said I should check it out. She's crazy for pancakes, huh?"

Kyle smiled, suspecting the real reason Casi wanted Mary Ann to come to the restaurant. They found a booth to the side and ordered. The waitress refilled their coffee, and the owner came to talk to Kyle, being a long-time friend. "Tucker, this is my friend, Mary Ann."

Mary Ann grasped the hand of the husky owner with sandy hair and green eyes and smiled, catching on to Casi's insistence to go for breakfast. Kyle mentioned Mary Ann's spices and jams company, and Tucker grinned. "Can I have your number so I can call you? I would love to hear more about your products."

She smiled as he returned to the kitchen. "Is this why you brought me?"

Kyle grinned. "What do you think?"

"Did I detect an accent?"

"Russian. He was an Olympic weightlifter, and he came to Seattle a few years ago, with his two daughters, Sacha and Siena, after his wife died. I met him through an outreach program we donate to. He wanted to open this place, and we helped with the fundraiser."

"He's handsome. How old are his daughters?"

"Pretty young, maybe six and eight? They help in the back on weekends." He pointed to girls giggling and peeling potatoes while their father cooked on the grill. "Did I redeem myself?"

"For dumping me for Casi, or kissing me?"

"Ouch," Kyle laughed. "I meant for last night."

"Yes, and Casi has been a good friend, so I'm glad she lives here now. Whatever you did to screw it up with her, fix it!"

❧

"Where were you last night?" Jake stormed toward Kyle in the driveway.

"I got drunk and spent the night at Mary Ann's," he admitted.

"Stupid idot!"

"I slept on her couch. We went out for breakfast and I introduced her to Tucker. Where's Casi? Is she with her mom?"

"She's in LA, and I took Sonya to Jack's last night."

"Why's Casi in LA?"

"Sometimes I wonder if your brain is broken. The sexy 1950s housewife getup was for you, but who knows where you were? Sonya lied to get me to come over and Casi was in tears because her mother convinced her you were hooking up with Lauren. Casi took off early for her business trip because she was hysterical after you left."

"I wasn't with Lauren! I attempted to get jewelry back that Sonya pawned. I didn't realize I had a deadline to be home."

"You forgot my birthday."

"Gail told me. I'm sorry. You should have reminded me."

"When? After you yelled at Casi, or before I dealt with her mother like you should have done weeks ago?"

"Can we celebrate this week? I already made reservations for a fishing trip for next month." Kyle exhaled. "I have to fix this mess."

"We'll celebrate when Casi comes back. She can make me a cake because she also forgot, and she owes me a kiss. Seeing her in skimpy lingerie isn't going to cut it if it isn't intended for me in the first place," Jake asserted.

26

LOVE LETTER

Casi sent the text and placed her phone on a table by the window as she scanned the generic hotel room. The magnitude of her career accomplishments struck her while she hung her business wardrobe neatly in the closet. Although she had been excellent at modeling, she was controlled by the puppeteers in the industry. She preferred being confident with her appearance, but astonishing people when she did her presentations and they grasped she had a brain.

Her phone buzzed, and she sighed as she picked it up, having already anticipated the call. "Hi, Mom."

"Your father threw me out. Can you believe that? Dropped me off at the airport without any regard for my welfare," Sonya claimed.

"What did you do to piss them off?"

"It's that bitch, Ava! Threatened by the love between us."

"How did you express that love?" Casi winced. Sonya cackled and relayed the nighttime escapades with too many details while Casi considered throwing up. "Mom! I don't want to hear about you assaulting my father, and why would you do that to Ava?"

"He was willing. Ava deserved it. You know they were having an affair for years while we were married."

"You were rarely sober during your marriage. Why are you surprised he found someone else?"

"Your father's not the saint you think he is. He had numerous affairs. Ava was the most persistent."

Casi rolled her eyes, tired of hearing how terrible her father was, yet convinced her mother still loved him. "Then you should punish him and not have sex with him anymore."

"I enjoy watching him trying to protest. He always gives in and that's when I know he still loves me," Sonya concluded.

"Love? I think it's more likely he can't resist your sexual prowess. You've had a lot of practice."

"Be thankful I've been so open about my skills; you've learned a lot from me. It will come in handy when you need to keep your own man."

"You're convinced that's what Kyle sees in me, aren't you? I'm a great lay."

"Well, I hope you are. It's a woman's most valuable asset. Your friend, Anna, seems to grasp that. She's a lot like me."

"Anna's nothing like you," Casi laughed. "Ok, maybe in her sexuality, but she's also smart and excellent at business."

"I'm not bright?"

Casi giggled, not realizing the comparison. "You must be smarter about your choices. You may be able to win over most men with the promise of sex, but you need to figure out how to keep one."

"That's harsh!"

"How do you expect to get by in the world?"

"When are you coming to LA?" Sonya ignored the question, which she had no answer for.

"I'm already here. I came a day early because you made my life hell and I needed to regroup before my meetings."

"Perfect, take me to the bar and we can find my next husband."

Casi exhaled, wanting to stay in the hotel and watch movies. "Where are you staying?"

"Did Casi text you back to say she's ok?" Kyle paced the room.

"I told you she did. She's at the hotel preparing for her meetings. She had three today and then another tomorrow. That should give you time to work on your apology," Jake replied. Kyle sighed, re-measuring the piece of wood for the third time. Several minutes later, Jake walked over and slapped him. "I've never hit a woman before, but I can't handle the whining! Get on a fucking plane and go to her. You can be there before she gets done."

Kyle rubbed his cheek, surprised by the slap. "What if she doesn't want to see me?"

"Grow some balls! Stop blaming her for things her mother did. She's your wife, try being a husband."

"Great advice from someone who's divorced."

"I'm a slow learner. Plus, I never loved my wife. I wanted it to be over, which is why I did nothing to save my marriage," Jake asserted.

Casi opened the door to her hotel room and set down her laptop, purse, and product samples, as she directed the young man inside. "You can put the boxes over there." She froze when she spotted Kyle sitting at the table by the window with a bottle of whiskey and two glasses.

"Should I have gotten a third glass?" Kyle asked, coldly.

Casi squared her shoulders. "Eric, this is my husband, Kyle. I guess he came to surprise me. If I had known, I would have asked him to carry the boxes from the car and saved you the trouble." She handed him a tip.

"No problem, I'm happy to help," he said as he left.

"He's young." Kyle sipped his drink.

"He works for the hotel. I met him yesterday when I picked up the supplies for my presentations. Why are you here?"

"To see you." He filled another glass and handed it to her.

"I'm only here another day. Why didn't you wait until I got home to tell me how our marriage isn't working? Or did you need to spy on me and confirm your suspicions of me cheating?"

"I felt like being with you. Alone." He followed her glance to her cell phone and moved it to the dresser. "Can we spend the night together? We don't even need to talk."

"Ok." She melted in his embrace.

"I noticed a pizza place across the street. I can get dinner and we can watch TV or maybe rent a movie?"

"That sounds perfect." She waited until he left, watching from the window as he crossed the street before she sent the text.

Kyle entered the hotel, balancing the pizza, as a man held the door. "Thanks." He almost dropped the box when their eyes met. "Why are you here?" Alix had been preoccupied with texting and hadn't noticed the man he held the door for was the same one he was being warned about. "We might as well get this over with."

Alix knocked at the door. "I said not to come." Casi felt faint when she noted Kyle behind him.

Kyle pushed Alix in the room and set the pizza down. "I'll get drinks while you catch up." He left the door ajar.

"I didn't see the text in time," Alix whispered.

Kyle returned with three cokes and opened the pizza box. "I hope it's not awkward with me here. Casi's been clear about her friendship with you and my lack of choice in that. I can wait downstairs if you like."

"It's fine." Casi snapped open the soda and slid it to Alix.

"I don't drink soda, Babe, you know that," he said.

"You inject poison in your veins. You can drink a damn coke!"

"Fair enough." Alix quietly took a sip. "I want to apologize. I knew the shoot was beneath you, but I needed the money and your mom pushed me to convince you to do it."

Casi's eyes watered as she turned to Kyle. "I asked him to come here because I want to put it behind me. I told you I needed closure."

Kyle took her hand and nodded. "I understand." He held her hand while Alix recounted the events leading up to the shoot. He had known the company was failing for weeks before telling her, hoping it would recover. He heard about the editorial from a promoter wanting girls who were new to modeling.

"No agent would sign a model after that kind of shoot." Casi cringed, considering the naïve women trying to make it in the industry.

Alix sighed. "There are so many chicks streaming into LA attempting to become a star. These guys prey on the ones desperate enough for the money. You were rare, Casi. Most girls go home after a year or two when they realize the business is a lot of smoke and mirrors. Fame doesn't really exist."

"I made good money," Casi challenged.

"Some days," Alix countered. "Mostly because you had Mary managing your career. I don't think you understood how much it costs to get by in life."

"I did pretty well."

Alix leaned forward and took her hand. "Babe, you would get a check for a few thousand bucks and think you were living the life. You never paid rent or had to maintain a house. Your main expenditures were shoes and handbags. Your life was an illusion. I paid all our living expenses, and you partied for free at clubs."

Casi blushed, embarrassed to be called out on her altered reality. "You punished me by setting up the shoot?"

"No, Babe, I love you! I was delusional as well. People were paying ridiculous amounts of money for my paintings and everyone picked up the tab. I thought I was a fucking rock star. After you left, I started to see the hypocrisy of it. It's not real. No one wanted my art; they wanted the image of owning a piece of me." He sipped at the soda with distaste and pushed it away. "When I needed money, all of a sudden everyone became too busy to get back to me. My installations dried up and I had nothing saved. I had been living on a dream and a promise for a long time, and when the drought came, no one wanted anything to do with me."

"How much did you get for the shoot?" Casi asked.

"I got $2500, but it wasn't about the money." Alix cringed.

"Why then?"

Alix rubbed his temple. "I slipped. I started with cocaine because I needed the edge. You know how they always have it at the clubs."

Casi could feel Kyle's eyes on her, asking the question. "It was always around, but I didn't do it. I only smoked pot, occasionally, and drank. A lot."

"Coke isn't my thing either," Alix confirmed. "I needed the boost, but it became too intense and I started to feel overwhelmed."

Casi sighed. "You went back to heroin?"

"I had to escape. Someone had it at the club. I didn't want to do it, but after the business collapsed, I couldn't resist. The cycle started all over again. I needed the drugs and a way to pay for them. My street cred carried me for a while, but then they wanted real money. I sold all my paintings and then I had nothing. Drugs alter my head space and I can't paint under the influence. I was ruined," Alix confessed.

"How was my mom involved?" Casi asked.

Alix cast his eyes to his hands. "I bumped into her at a club after her husband ditched her and she was spinning out of control. She was pissed you left her. She said we needed to show you where you belonged."

"Where I belonged?"

"She said Kyle would leave you if you did the shoot. She felt you abandoned her for a safe life where no one would expect anything from you. She wanted you to marry some Hollywood big wig so she could tag along. The photographer was supposed to make the introduction, but he wanted to sample the product first."

Casi raced to the bathroom and threw up, not realizing the scope of what had been going on. Kyle came in and wet a cloth, tenderly wiping her face. "Are you ok? I'm sure you weren't anticipating that."

She nodded, staggering back to sit across from Alix. "Did you have sex with my mother?"

Alix hesitated. "I was lonely after you left, Babe. We were only supposed to be on a break. I never expected you to get married. The club girls weren't cutting it. They acted like novices. I needed passion like you had, and your mom provided it."

"I'm flattered and repulsed at the same time," Casi choked.

"That's when she started telling me about her plan. She said she let you get married so you could get the fantasy out of your head. She was happy when you told her things weren't going well, but she worried you might get pregnant to try to save your marriage, so it thrilled her when you had that procedure."

"You knew about that?" she asked tearfully.

"She told me Kyle arranged to get you fixed so you couldn't blind-side him with a pregnancy and have a claim to his small-town fortune," Alix repeated.

"That's not what happened!" Kyle pounded the table with his fist.

"She said it was a blessing in disguise. She met the Hollywood guy at a party in Beverly Hills and showed him a bunch of pictures of you."

"Why didn't she marry him?" Casi asked.

"She slept with him, but he wanted a younger version. He's a big-time director, Casi. He desired a trophy wife and you fit the bill."

"Well, I'm sorry I missed out on that opportunity," she spat. "I guess the photographer told him I wasn't worth the money."

Alix chuckled. "Your pervert neighbor messed that guy up! I guess he was spying on you as usual and saw the dude hitting you. He ran over and beat the shit out of him and left him in the alley. The guy was in the hospital for two weeks and then demanded his money back from your mom. I had already taken off to Africa to get my head straight."

"Did she pay him back?" Casi asked.

"She already spent it on drugs. She took it out in trade."

"Sex?"

"Probably, but she also recruited young hopefuls to pose for him. It's like shooting fish in a barrel when you troll Instagram for models. They'll do anything to be famous." He grasped her hand. "You wanted to hold on to the mirage. You were afraid to step away from the spotlight. You knew what you were doing."

"You think I wanted to pose for that magazine? To have that kind of life? What would be next? Porn?" Casi cried.

"You hoped your career would go up in flames. You wanted it to be over but couldn't walk away from the promise of the next big job. You took the drugs your mom gave you because you couldn't face the reality of what you needed to do." Alix sighed.

Casi clasped her hands to her face and Kyle put an arm around her shoulders. "You were trying to flush your career, but I believe you had a different motivation."

"Money?" Casi sobbed.

"Love. You wanted LA to be over because you knew where you really belonged, and who you belonged with." Kyle kissed her cheek.

"That's what scared your mom the most. She was afraid you found the love of your life." Alix stood and kissed her. "I've got to bounce. I'm meeting a possible client for an installation of my street series. It's time for me to reclaim my name." He smiled and put a slice of pizza on a napkin.

"Thanks for coming. It's good to have an honest conversation." Casi hugged him. "I'm not sure where we go from here."

"Can we try being friends? I care about you," Alix said.

"Friendship would be good." After he left, Casi grabbed the bottle of whiskey and poured a generous shot in a glass before topping it with coke. "I guess my secrets are out of the bag."

"I'm still here. You haven't scared me off yet." Kyle unbuttoned her shirt. "For the record, I didn't leave you after the shoot. I was disappointed, but I won't walk away because I don't agree with your choices."

"It was a terrible decision."

"The shoot or my commitment to our marriage?"

She smiled. "Me doing the editorial. You've proven your loyalty and I'm a lucky woman."

"You are severely sexy in that attire. I haven't mentioned it in the past because I didn't want you to believe I was undermining your position as a professional." He slid a hand under her skirt to caress her thigh.

"We could role play." Casi grinned. "Do you want to be the boss or the subordinate?"

"Can I be the boss this time?" His eyes crinkled with amusement.

Casi laughed and slid off her panties while he watched. "This isn't some fantasy you have about Amy, is it?"

Kyle gasped. "My receptionist? I only fantasize about you."

"Just checking. What's my job?"

Kyle brought her laptop over. "You can be my secretary and I'll dictate a letter. Your computer skills are a definite turn on."

Casi sat in a chair and he stood behind her. "What would you like me to type, Mr. Jensen?"

"I would like to write a letter to my wife."

She added her email address. "What's the subject?"

"Hope." She wrote in the subject line and moved the cursor to the body of the message, awaiting his dictation. "Dear, Ms. Roberts."

"Actually," Casi interrupted. "Your wife wanted to tell you she had her name legally changed to Jensen."

"She did? When?" Kyle caressed her shoulder.

"A few weeks ago. She needed to let go of her old name; it didn't suit her anymore. She wanted to surprise you on Saturday and show you the new business cards." She slid one across the table. "But the night was ruined."

Kyle kissed the top of her head, running his hand down to her breast. "Dear, Ms. Jensen," he started.

"Your wife would also like to inform you she prefers to be a Mrs. She's proud to be your wife and isn't hiding her relationship status. It's even on Facebook now."

"Is it? Well, then I guess it's official," he laughed. "Dear Mrs. Jensen. Your husband is deeply sorry for being an ass. You are the most important person in his life, and his poor behavior reflects his insecurities rather than a deficit on your part. He has allowed too many people to interfere in the relationship and promises to do better in the future."

Her fingers flew across the keyboard as a tear fell. "Your wife has sent a reply," she announced, typing as she spoke. "Mrs. Jensen readily accepts your apology. There are so many things she's also sorry for and hopes you can forgive her. She loves you with all her heart and is sickened she wasted so much time focusing on the wrong things. She asks you to be patient and help her find her way in the world because she knows she can make it if you are by her side."

Kyle smiled. "I've forgiven her for every misstep already. My heart is smarter than my brain most of the time. We have forever to figure out what the hell we are doing. Not only will I stay by her side, but I'll carry her when she's unable to walk on her own. Everything I have is hers, and all I need in return is her love."

Tears streamed down her face. "Your wife has given you her heart forever. Her love is undying and even though she acts like a child at times, she has never questioned her feelings for you. When she kissed that stupid man, it had nothing to do with desire. She liked how he only saw her as a professional woman who had a career and knew nothing of the useless girl she had been. She regrets the kiss because it hurt her husband and made him question her feelings and not trust her anymore."

"Tell my wife I was hurt because she let a man see a side of her I was too blind to recognize. I was caught up in my own feelings when I should have noticed the beautiful and strong woman she blossomed into. Going forward, I'll give myself to her without reservation and trust her intentions to always be true." He kissed her neck and reached to run his hand over her leg, making her moan as he brushed his fingers between her thighs. "Mr. Jensen needs to confess he accidentally kissed Mary Ann the other night when he went to her house and realizes it is as bad as kissing the man in Seattle."

Casi frowned over her shoulder. "Mrs. Jensen is curious who initiated the kiss, and if it went any further. She's also questioning what the hell you were doing at a former lover's house."

"Your dumb husband kissed the unwilling participant. He was drunk and angry with his mother-in-law. He didn't like seeing his brother look at his wife, who was amazingly gorgeous in her skimpy get-up. He's selfish and wants to keep her all to himself."

"Your wife admits alcohol can lead to stupid circumstances and gives him a pass since she trusts Mary Ann. The scandalous attire was only intended for him. The brother was never meant to see it. Her relationship with him is limited to hugging and the occasional kiss." She giggled. "Her body is only for her husband to ravish."

"Fair enough. Please tell Mrs. Jensen I want to ravish her at this moment. She has me on fire with her scent of oranges and silky-smooth skin, and I can't wait any longer." She sent the email to both addresses and closed the laptop as she stood before him. He touched a strand of her hair, let loose from the pins, and moved the blouse aside to expose her breasts. "You're so beautiful." He slid the skirt to the top of her thighs, kissing her stomach as he caressed her.

Casi brought her mouth to his, kissing him tenderly. She straddled his lap and raised up on her knees to hover above him momentarily, and he groaned when she lowered, pulsing against him rhythmically. "Mrs. Jensen, you're about to make me climax."

"I'm about to join you, Mr. Jensen," she breathed, rolling her head back as the sensation started. They held on for a moment, sharing the union of their bodies as the orgasms took hold. She rested her head on his shoulder. "I'm happy you came." She giggled. "I mean to LA. It's nice to have you here, and it was better to have you witness what Alix said."

"I'm glad you were not alone to hear that. Plus, it's inebriating to be intimate with you after such a long dry spell."

"What do you love about me aside from sex?"

"I fell in love with you before we were intimate. I loved your vulnerability and optimism. You're sweet and caring, quirky, goofy, and free-spirited. I adore your sense of humor, and random intelligence, mixed with moments of blissful ignorance. I feel safe to show you the authentic me and share my secrets with you. My life is so much better with you in it because I feel alive and happy when I'm around you. You've made me into a man who loves you fiercely, and a boy who is silly and love-struck. I'm excited to wake up and see your pretty face. When we fall asleep, the feeling of you in my arms makes my life complete. You are everything I've ever wanted, and sex is icing on the cake."

"You've given it a lot of thought." Casi's eyes widened.

"I'm telling you what is written in my heart. We were destined to be together." Kyle kissed her. "Do you want candy? I saw a vending machine in the hall."

"Tonight keeps getting better!" She giggled and slid off his lap. "I'll find a movie." She ate a slice of pizza and put the rest in the mini fridge, figuring they could eat it for breakfast. She undressed and got in bed, scrolling through the movies on demand. She laughed when he came back with an armful of candy, tossing it on the bed in a heap before he undressed and joined her.

"I am not sure what you are in the mood for." Kyle sorted through the pile and selected a Snickers bar.

"My dad had sex with my mom," Casi blurted.

"Willingly?"

"Apparently, he was asleep when it started. She said he couldn't resist her after he woke up."

"Does Ava know?"

"Probably. My mom likes the families of her victims to be aware. It makes her feel powerful." She tore open a wrapper and bit into the candy.

"I'm surprised your dad gave in. He adores Ava, and she's super-hot."

"Ava is incredible, but my mom is like heroin. Once you've had it, it's hard to resist. She made it her mission to prove she can steal him back. It's been one of my issues with my dad over the years." She sighed. "Ava left him because of it right before I moved to LA. She started a new life and bought the house they live in."

"But she took him back?"

"Eventually," she mumbled. "He fell apart and began acting like a lunatic and drinking too much. He got fired for being drunk at work and showed up at our house ranting we cost him the woman he loved. He had a gun and threatened to kill himself."

"Wow, he did lose it!"

"Ava gave him another chance, and he moved to Bellingham to be with her. As far as I've heard he hasn't stepped out of line again."

Kyle brushed a hair from her cheek. "Can I ask why you resent Ava? She adores you but you seem hesitant around her like you don't trust her."

"My memories are vague from my childhood. I remember her working at my dad's restaurant and she seemed cool. She was always nice to me, but my mom hated her. She insisted they were having an affair and my dad would leave us for her."

"Ok, and then he did," Kyle concluded.

"Basically. I'm pretty sure the affair started when I was about twelve and he left when I was fourteen. Our home life sucked, but I hated her for stealing my dad. It's stupid now because she makes him happy and he is a much better person with her than he was with my mom."

"You felt left out?"

"Abandoned. I'm trying to let it go and rebuild a relationship with her. Obviously, she has better judgment than my mom."

"I believe she genuinely loves you. Let her in."

"I hope my mom didn't destroy them." She wiped a tear away. "I don't like coming from people who are flawed."

"It doesn't make you weak. Our relationship is different, we'll never give in to temptation."

"There's something in their past no one will share with me. My mom uses it as a weapon to crush Ava, and then she swoops in and seduces my dad."

"You know too much about your parents sex life," Kyle shivered.

"I'm sure your parents get it on."

"I'm sure they do, but I don't need the details." Kyle covered her mouth with his hand. "I'm going to tell you something you'll find hysterical, and completely not understand as being a low point in my life."

"Awesome." Casi clapped.

"When I told you Lauren and I were always mostly friends, I meant it. Our sex life was dull. She kept pushing for marriage, and I resisted on many levels, but especially because we were not well-suited in bed."

"I like where this conversation is going."

"I figured. Anyway, one night I came home a little drunk. I forgot she planned to cook dinner at my house, and she was pissed. She started nagging me about marriage and I finally had enough," he cringed. "I told her to get on her knees and show me she had what it took to be my wife." Casi rolled on the bed with laughter. "It wasn't funny. It was awkward and horrifyingly bad."

"She was inept at giving a blow job?"

"She felt I wanted to humiliate her, which wasn't the case. I needed something more than the vanilla sex we'd been having. I tried to demonstrate what I wanted; more spontaneity and excitement, but she translated it as kinky." He stroked Casi's cheek. "You and I are on the same page. We have fun and enjoy being together. I wrote it off as a failed attempt to spice things up, but she took it as a marriage proposal. She informed our friends I had committed to her and then told my mother how I treated her."

"Why did she think you'd want to marry her if she wasn't into the same things you were?"

"She was desperate to be married and said she loved me. I told her I didn't love her, but she thought I had cold feet. We went to Elmvale over Christmas and my mother made my father talk to me about the expectations of a husband."

"This keeps getting better," Casi giggled.

"Things went downhill from there. We were in the barn with Jake, building the rabbit hutch. My dad started talking about sex, obviously having been coached. He inferred my mother was a goddess in the bedroom and they had a healthy sex life, which I'm sure isn't what she assumed he would share."

"Go Georgia!"

"His intent was to explain how marriage is a partnership and both people should have similar feelings. Secretly, I think he skewed the message because he never liked Lauren. My mom came up to my bedroom to make sure I understood my behavior had been inappropriate. I freaked out and yelled at her because she made me sound like a pervert. I suggested if she wanted to be involved in my sex life, she should show Lauren how to give a proper blow job since I had heard she excelled at it."

"Oh no!" Casi gasped.

"She slapped me across the face and started crying. I took off to the bar. She gave my dad an earful, and he showed up with Jake. He said I ensured he wasn't getting laid for a long time and I should carefully consider if I wanted to marry a woman who made me so miserable."

"Is that why you didn't marry Lauren?"

"I almost did propose, Casi. On Valentine's Day. I let her believe I would, but I couldn't go through with it because I didn't love her." He winced. "I had the ring in my pocket, but I choked when I considered spending the rest of my life with her."

"Did your parents think you wanted to marry me because of sex?"

"They saw a gorgeous woman with a knockout figure and assumed I was caught up in the fantasy. They knew I was adamant about not getting married, but witnessed me head-over-heels in love with you. When my dad talked to you, he was trying to get a sense of where you stood. He told me later you had an incredible heart, and I had obviously found my soul mate."

Casi smiled. "I'm glad you waited for the right woman. Are you capable of feeling love now?"

"I'm incapable of living without the woman who stole my heart and showed me what real love is." Kyle shoved the candy off the bed and rolled on top of her. "She's perfect for me in every way."

ABANDONED

"What time is your meeting?" Kyle whispered.

"Ten. I should be done around noon." Casi yawned and glanced at the clock. "What are you going to do while I'm there?"

"I am thinking of taking your mom to coffee and see what I can do to help her get her shit together. What do you think?"

"You've already helped her a lot, but she's devious. She'll tell you she needs money, but then blow it on drugs."

"I assumed that. You said she was staying with a friend? How long do you think that will last?"

"A friend means her dealer. He'll get tired of her in a week. She usually convinces someone to let her stay in their pool house or spare bedroom, and then she irritates them, and they unceremoniously ask her to leave."

"The loft still hasn't sold. What if we take if off the market for now and let her live there?" Kyle stroked her cheek.

"Why do you want to help her?"

"Because I know you will, and I would prefer it to be a choice we make together. I can't have her in our home and it's not good for your dad, or fair to Ava, if she is around. I'm paying the mortgage on the loft anyway, and it's still an asset we can sell down the road."

Tears welled in her eyes. "This is when I feel married. It's amazing to have a partner to help me with the hard things in life."

"It's easier to make decisions together." Kyle caressed her stomach and grinned. "By the way, I introduced Mary Ann to Tucker."

"Did she like him?"

"You'll need to get the details, you're better at that. He asked for her number and she happily gave it to him."

"I'll bet she liked his sexy Russian accent!" Casi giggled.

Kyle parked and carried the boxes to the conference room for Casi. "I'll be back at noon to pick you up?" He smiled and gave her a quick kiss. He watched her set up her computer, noting how her demeanor changed, becoming efficient and driven. He realized he hadn't given her credit for how hard she worked to achieve her goals or understood what her job entailed. As the clients filed in and greeted her, he hung back and observed them interacting. He understood what she meant about Grant. These people saw an attractive woman who was professional and prepared. They were unaware of her past and how she looked in lingerie. They focused on her presentation, asking questions which she readily answered. He slipped out, leaving her in her element, glad he witnessed how far she had come.

Kyle phoned Jack, planning to relay his plan for Sonya. Ava answered in a cold tone, informing him Jack was at the restaurant. "Can you give him a message for me? I'm in LA with Casi and we need to make some decisions about Sonya." Kyle winced as she broke down in tears. "I heard what happened and I'm truly sorry. Please don't blame Casi. She's upset about it too." He could hear she was trying to find her voice and gave her a moment to compose herself.

She finally answered, "It's not Casi's fault and Jack and I will get through it. I'm glad you are with her in LA, she deserves to be a priority. She's had to handle her mother's drama for too long. Whatever you decide, you can count on us to help. There are a lot of tragic things from the past I'm trying to deal with, and I can't handle Sonya's antics anymore." He relayed his idea, and she agreed it would suit everyone's agenda. "It's best if she can stay in LA. It wasn't only what happened with Jack, but having her in my home felt like a violation."

"The loft will be ideal. She can come and go as she pleases, and we don't need to be personally involved. I need Casi to be able to focus on her career and not have the hindrance of her mother. Our marriage has been hard enough already," Kyle sighed.

"I know that feeling all too well," Ava mused.

Kyle chuckled. "If you choose to have revenge sex, Jake would gladly participate. He thinks you're gorgeous."

Ava giggled. "Wouldn't that be a hoot!"

They chatted for a few more minutes and he was relieved to hear her laugh and return to her familiar jovial mood. After he hung up, he called Sonya and asked her to meet him for coffee.

"Why are you in LA? Can't she go on a business trip alone?" Sonya snipped.

"I'm here because I want to support her as she ties up loose ends. Alix was last night, and now we have you."

"You make me sound like a burden on my daughter!"

"You are. You add nothing to her life, except chaos. She's a young woman who has a new career and marriage to focus on."

"You have no problem inconveniencing her with a screaming baby. It's not even hers, and she acts like its mother," Sonya accused.

"His name is Austin, and she loves him. We are all committed to raising him together as a family."

"So, I'm an outsider?"

"You are Casi's mother and she wants you to be taken care of. Meet me for coffee and hear what I have to say."

Kyle waited at Coffee Bean, not surprised when Sonya arrived thirty minutes late. "I had to walk, I don't have a car," she complained.

"It's two blocks." Kyle regarded her with disgust. "Is this how you envisioned your life?" He watched her fidget across the table from him.

"Poor and desperate? My husband abandoned me, and I had to raise a daughter on my own."

"That was over sixteen years ago, and your daughter has been supporting herself since she was eighteen."

"I did everything for her. She was never alone. I may have had unconventional ways, but I took care of her." Sonya narrowed her eyes.

"You use people and seem to find joy in destroying them."

She glared at him. "I still love Jack. Ava stole him from me. She shouldn't be surprised I need him. Your brother was purely for fun. I never forced Casi to do anything she didn't want to do."

"And Alix? You know he is an addict. Why would you drag him down with you?" Kyle challenged.

Sonya regarded him for a long time as she swirled her coffee, realizing he wasn't buying her lies any longer. "What's the offer? Rehab? I won't go, I don't like rules."

"Rehab would be a waste of money. You do whatever you want, and that's fine because it's your life. I won't allow you to hurt Casi anymore, so you need to stay in LA."

"I knew you would distance us. I warned her you would control her!"

"I don't control her, and you won't either. I'm offering you the loft to stay for up to a year. We have one requirement; you only see Casi if she comes to LA. We don't want you in Washington. The loft is for you to sleep, not turn into a drug haven. I suggest you attend NA meetings. Alix is willing to escort you. Other than that, you can do as you please," Kyle stated.

"Who's we?" Sonya inspected her nails with disinterest.

"Casi, Jack, Ava, and me. This is best for everyone."

"Your grand offer is to let me stay in my daughter's loft?"

"I pay the mortgage. We'll sell it next spring and any profits will go to Casi. This is an opportunity for you to get your life together. Don't read anything more into it." Kyle leaned in and whispered, "You want to get high and sleep with lowlifes? That's your choice. From now on you can be accountable for your own decisions."

"What about the utilities?"

"Jack will take care of those and he will send grocery certificates. We are all trying to help you."

"And my phone?"

"Your problem."

"Give me the key." She held her hand out.

"I need to get it from the real estate office. I'm picking up Casi at noon from her meeting and we will fetch you after lunch. We'll stop by Target and buy things you might need to get settled."

"I'm not invited to lunch?"

"No, you're not. We'll text you when we are on our way." Kyle threw away his cup and put two quarters on the table. "In case you want a refill."

Sonya stared after him, shocked by his indifference. She glanced around the coffee shop, suddenly afraid and alone. She scrolled through the numbers in her cell phone, realizing she didn't have any friends.

"I expected your call. I hope you were smart enough to take Kyle's offer. God knows you usually make the wrong decision," Ava said.

"I want to talk to Jack," Sonya sniffed.

"He's at the restaurant. We had a problem in the brewery he needed to deal with." Ava paused. "You didn't break us, Sonya, even though you tried."

"He was my husband first."

"True, and you have a daughter together. I accept you will always be in his life, but on my terms. I don't need you dredging up painful things from the past or seducing him. We agreed to put those events to rest and you can't keep threatening to turn on us. I honored my pact even when you betrayed me. if you haven't realized it yet, you always come out the loser in the end."

"Everyone has abandoned me!"

"I realize you are used to having Casi close by, but she has a wonderful and fulfilling life. Perhaps it's time to move home and start over."

"I won't go back to my family in that piss-ant town, and I don't know anyone in Vancouver anymore." Sonya swiped tears away.

"Maybe that's a good thing."

"Let me move to Bellingham. I can work in the restaurant with you like we used to. I promise I won't tempt Jack."

"No." Ava sucked in her breath. "Some days, I'm barely holding on as it is. Jack, the bungalow, and the restaurant are mine and you can't be a part of them. It took me too long to rebuild my life and I don't have the strength to start over again."

"But I don't have anything."

"Stay at the loft and go to the NA meetings. When you're stronger, maybe you'll see things differently."

28

———

WORTH

Kyle met Casi after her meeting and took her to lunch at a bistro. He held her hand and smiled as she happily ate her crispy fish tacos. "What?" She wiped salsa from her chin.

"I'm admiring your business attire. You've found your niche. At first, you were like an Anna clone, but you've come into your own," Kyle concluded.

Casi smiled. "I feel like myself now. It was weird to wear suits and sensible heels, but I think I can pull it off."

"You definitely excel at it. People are probably wondering what you're doing with a lowly, jeans wearing workman."

She leaned forward and kissed him. "I'm proud of who my husband is. We're a perfect fit and you are delicious in your jeans."

Kyle relayed her mother's response, leaving out his harsh words. They texted Sonya and drove to a nearby Target, filling a cart with basic household items and enough food to get by for a few weeks. Kyle insisted on paying, wanting her to feel indebted to him, rather than expecting it from Casi. He parked on the street and unloaded the bags.

"I'm not coming." Casi glared at her former window and crossed her arms over her chest. "I'm fine with keeping it, but I won't go in there again."

"Don't be ridiculous! You need to help me get settled," Sonya demanded.

Kyle cringed as he regarded the building, imagining the impact on Casi. He wrapped her in his arms and whispered, "I'm sorry I brought you here. I should have come alone. Are you alright in the car or do you want to drive up the street and get coffee?"

"I will be fine waiting in the car." She gave him a kiss and opened the Facebook app on her phone while she hummed to herself.

"I won't be long." Kyle directed Sonya toward the door. He put the bags on the counter in the kitchen and handed her the key. "Alix will be by later to take you to a meeting."

Sonya scanned the empty loft containing only a mattress and box spring. "Can't you at least help me make the bed?"

Kyle glared at the mattress and a chill ran down his spine. "I can't be here, Sonya. The worst day of my life happened in this room."

"This isn't where you were shot."

"It's where I found Casi unconscious and realized she'd been betrayed and used by the people who should love and protect her." Kyle slammed the door as he left. He discovered the car empty and panicked, checking up and down the sidewalk as his heart threatened to leap from his chest. He was about to call the police when he noticed Casi strolling across the street. "Where were you?" He rushed to her side and pulled her in his arms.

Casi smiled up at a window across from her loft. "I realized there was someone I never took the time to thank."

Kyle exhaled. "I'm glad he was there for you."

"I considered what you said at the restaurant about how I looked professional. I wanted him to see I was worth saving."

"Oh, Sweetheart!"

"I told him I moved to Washington with my husband and my life was amazing. It was the first time I saw his face."

"What was he like?"

"Kind of creepy," she giggled. "But sweet, too. He has a speech impediment, and I suspect that might be behind him being a recluse. I told him I would be forever thankful for his intervention."

"Did you tell him your mother was moving in the loft?"

"I did, but I didn't tell her about him. I figure he'll enjoy spying on her, kind of a visual thank you gift." Casi grinned.

"Seems like a fair deal."

Jake strolled down the dock and jumped in the lake. He swam to where Kyle lounged in an inner tube with Casi on top of him, their limbs intertwined.

"What's up, Lovebirds?" Jake splashed them.

"We just got home. The lake beckoned, and we couldn't resist taking a swim." Casi dipped her toes in the water.

"I bet you need to relax after you left me at work while you played around in LA for days. Did Kyle tell you about the cake?" Jake dribbled water on Casi's warm skin.

"Yes. I'm sorry I forgot your birthday." Casi leaned forward and gave him a kiss. "I'll make any cake you want."

Jake gripped the side of the inner tube, distracted by the water beading. "The chocolate one is fine."

"What's wrong?" She stroked the side of his face.

"Anna's getting married today, to her rich husband."

"It's only temporary." Casi squeezed his hand. "It won't last. She feels like she needs to do this, but she does love you."

"She thinks I can't take care of her."

"Anna can take care of herself. She's doing it for her family and to be accepted in society. She seems strong, but appearances are important to her. There are different pressures for women in this world."

"Did you marry Kyle for the sake of appearances?" Jake poked her ribs.

"I married Kyle because I love him, and he has an amazing brother. I don't give a flying fig what society thinks of my choices," Casi laughed.

Kyle picked up the steaks he ordered from the butcher, pleased the weather cooperated to celebrate Jake's birthday, belatedly. Jake admitted he wasn't bothered they forgot him, and ultimately, he had gotten birthday sex from Anna. Kyle insisted they would have a barbecue and celebrate properly with their parents, Jack and Ava. Casi had a tearful discussion with Ava about her mother's interference and refused to broach the subject with her father, adamant his misstep wasn't her issue to judge. Jake appointed himself the bartender, happily mixing drinks as they gathered on the back porch on the warm afternoon.

Lia juggled Austin, trying to soothe him as he screeched and arched his back. "Where's Casi?" Her eyes watered as she struggled with the child.

"She's finishing the caramel glaze," Kyle reported.

"Forget the cake, we need her to hold the kid." Jake took Austin in his arms and tried to rock him, but the crying intensified.

Casi stepped out to the porch, licking the frosting from her fingers. She slid one sticky finger in Austin's mouth as she rocked him, calming him immediately. "Casi, he's too young for sugar," Georgia laughed.

"I think the whiskey calms him." Casi shrugged.

"Whatever works." Jake shivered.

Ava regarded Casi with the baby, twirling on the porch in her floral cotton dress. "She's incredible with him." She smiled sadly, and Jack took her hand and gave it a squeeze.

Casi settled between them. "Do you want to hold him? He is your grandkid by proxy since I won't be having any."

"We've decided to raise him as a collective. We each do our part, and share in the joys of parenting," Jake announced.

"I carried him for nine months." Lia shuddered.

"Casi holds him and buys him ridiculous clothes. I do diapers and Kyle gets to help pay for college," Jake outlined.

"If he's as smart as your first two, that won't be a concern." Kyle chuckled.

"Reid will go to college. If Olivia gets through her senior year, I'll consider it a win." Jake shrugged.

Casi transferred Austin to Ava's arms. "He's sweet when he's not crying."

Peter grinned. "I prefer how ours came to us past this finicky bit. It was like getting puppies from the pound. We got the wild one and his scrawny brother. Kyle looked like a plucked chicken." He slapped his knee. "But they were both housebroken, so I've never changed a diaper in my life."

"I'm sure you wouldn't have done it, anyway." Georgia rolled her eyes.

"I've done it once, and that was enough for me." Kyle frowned at Jake's broken demeanor and cringed when he noted Lia glaring at him. He scanned the guests on the porch and shrugged. "Jake and I were adopted. And for the next question, we are biological brothers, and these are our real parents. Nothing existed before them, and we don't normally discuss it because it's not relevant."

Lia regarded Austin and turned to Jake. "Is that why you refused to sign?"

Jake exhaled. "I created him. He's ours to raise."

Ava reached over and grasped Jake's hand. "Love makes a family, not biology." She glanced at Jack and flushed.

"What she means is I cut off contact with my family because we had a difference of opinion of how I should live my life and who I chose to live it with." He laced his fingers through Ava's.

Casi frowned. "Is that why I don't know anything about them? What about Mom? She never speaks about her family. Is she an only child too?"

"I've never met them." He eyed Ava. "I believe they live somewhere far up north. Anyway, we are happier with the relationships we formed later in life." He smiled at Georgia. "And the wonderful friends we have made."

Casi smoothed a finger over Austin's cheek when he fussed. "All you people are my family and I can't imagine it being any better."

29

BABY-MAKER

"When will this kid do something more interesting?" Casi prodded Austin with her toe as he cooed on the area rug beneath her.

"Tired of your toy?" Jake stepped over him to sit on the sofa.

"He just flops there and stares at me."

"Kyle does also, and you don't find him dull." Jake tickled her. "He's only three months old. Give him a few more months to start crawling and then it will be tons of fun to make sure he doesn't end up in the lake. Don't you have twelve more outfits to try on him?"

"This is already his fifth one. He started to squirm too much, and it wasn't exciting anymore." Casi giggled as Austin tried to put her toe in his mouth and then mimicked her laugh.

"That's gross." Jake shoved her foot away from the baby.

Dingo ran inside and jumped over Austin with practiced ease, while Kyle almost trampled him, coming to an abrupt stop. "Why is he on the floor?"

"Casi got bored with him," Jake said.

"We can't return him now, you'll need to figure out a way to make him more entertaining. What about the clothes you keep buying him? That was fun for you yesterday," Kyle suggested.

"It's only amusing when he wears them the first time, then it becomes repetitive." Casi twirled sections of her hair.

"You guys expect a lot from an infant." Jake relocated Austin to Casi's lap.

Austin bounced and cooed, trying to get her attention. "Can I give him ice cream?"

"I told you not until at least six months," Jake reiterated.

"Why do people have kids?" Casi jiggled him on her thigh. "They are boring as shit."

"This one wasn't on purpose. You had a vote, and you wanted to keep him." Jake chuckled as Austin's face contorted and he filled his diaper.

"Disgusting, take him back!" Casi quickly handed him to Jake.

Jake helped Lia bathe Austin and put him in his crib. He smoothed his hair tenderly, smiling as the infant drifted to sleep. "Are you starting to like him more?" Lia asked as she watched him.

"I always liked him for who he was, but I'm over resenting him for breaking into my life. It's not so bad having him here." Jake shrugged.

"When he's sleeping or taking his bottle, he's so peaceful. It's the crying that makes me feel like I'm losing my mind." Lia shivered and Jake put his arm around her, slowly taking a detour to her breast. "What are you doing?" She frowned and pushed his hand away.

"He didn't get here by chance, Lia. We used to enjoy being with each other." Jake unbuttoned her shirt with a sly grin.

"That was almost a year ago, and since then you've found a lot of new women to entertain you."

"Only two."

"I guess math isn't your best subject." She walked to the living room and flopped on the sofa.

"What does it matter?" Jake sat beside her and put her feet on his lap.

Lia shrugged. "Lauren said Anna is gorgeous and there's no way you would ever want to be with me again."

"Anna is stunning, and she's married now. But you're beautiful too, Lia. Don't listen to Lauren. She's jealous of you and says hateful things."

"When did Anna get married?" Lia cocked her head.

"I'm not with her anymore, none of that matters." Jake slid on top of her as he kissed her neck. "Do you have condoms?"

"No. I haven't been with anyone since you." Lia gazed into his deep blue eyes. "Will you stay the night with me?"

"Yes, and you can sleep while I tend to our child." He smiled. "Let me check the truck. I'm not sure what the time frame is on pregnancy after giving birth, but let's not risk it."

"He's crawling!" Casi clapped when Austin rocked on his belly, madly moving his arms and legs.

Jake chuckled at her excitement; aware the baby wasn't at that stage yet. He nudged Kyle, observing Casi crouch, giving an unexpected view into her shirt as she encouraged Austin. "She's baiting him with her breasts."

"It would make me crawl to her." Kyle grinned.

Lia returned from the bathroom after throwing up and reclined on the sofa. "Morning sickness?" Casi giggled.

"No more kids!" Lia pressed her palm to her forehead. "I've been sick off and on for a few days. I'm sure it's something going around. I come in contact with a lot of people at the coffee shop."

"You shouldn't be around Austin if you have the flu. We don't need a sick baby," Jake cautioned. He shoved Casi. "Plus, I've used a condom every time so don't curse us with your voodoo."

Kyle sat in an armchair, surveying Lia, then raised an eyebrow at Jake. "When was the last time you bought condoms?"

"Why are you so interested in my sex life?" Jake took a swig of beer.

"I'm curious. I assume the box from Costco is gone by now, and I don't recall you buying more." Kyle nudged his brother with his boot.

"I'm skilled at buying them at the store. I am the one who taught you." Jake held up a middle finger.

"You didn't use the ones from the cup on the dryer, did you?" Casi jumped up to check. "Where's my twenty dollars?" She shook the empty container.

"It was money from my jeans," Jake claimed.

"Once it's in the laundry, it's mine." Casi put a hand on her hip.

"You didn't wash condoms, did you?" Jake cringed.

Casi's eyes widened. "I found a bunch of junk in the dryer and I put it in the cup. Your mom said she taught you to clean out your pockets after she found a lizard and a used condom in the same week when you were teenagers."

"The lizard was mine. I caught it at the river and wanted to build it a habitat, but I forgot about it after I got home." Kyle smiled.

"Wasn't it already in a habitat at the river?" Casi giggled.

"Mine was going to be epic, with several levels and a tree house," Kyle explained. "It survived the laundry basket, and I moved on to another project. I'm sure the condom belonged to Jake."

Jake chuckled. "Yup, Lisa Evaristo! Her dad was pounding on the door and I had to make a fast getaway through her bedroom window. I ran home and forgot to toss it."

"I found a bird in the dryer three months ago," Casi said.

Kyle chuckled. "It was a quail from my hunting jacket. You didn't put it in your treasure bin, did you?"

"No. I chucked it!" Casi shuddered.

"Then why didn't you toss condoms that went through the wash?" Kyle threw his head back and laughed. "That's like leaving candy out for a kid."

"I put them there as a prompt to discover the story behind them." She raised an eyebrow. "Give me back my twenty dollars."

"Use the money to buy a pregnancy test." Kyle grinned.

"Not helpful!" Jake hissed.

"Jake, the baby-maker. When will you learn?" Kyle slapped his brother on the back. "I hope you only impregnated Lia with your faulty birth control rampage." Lia burst into tears and he cringed at his insensitive joke.

Jake jumped to his feet and grabbed his wallet. "Go get a test. If it's positive I'm holding you both responsible!"

Casi smiled at the twenty-dollar bill. "You cursed yourself when you stole my money. The lesson here is to stay out of my belongings."

Kyle chuckled. "I think there may be another lesson in this."

They returned an hour later with two kits and a bag of chips. Casi went to the bathroom with Lia to keep her company. Jake knocked on the door a minute later, barely waiting for Lia to zip her pants before he entered. "Well?"

"It's not ready yet, you need to wait five minutes." Lia washed her hands.

Kyle peered in. "What's the verdict?" He smiled at Casi eating chips while she sat on the counter swinging her legs and singing. He leaned against her and reached in the bag. "What are we looking for?"

"A plus sign. Haven't you ever done it before?" Casi asked.

Kyle turned to look her in the eye. "I've always used a condom or if I was in a relationship, we discussed alternate birth control."

"What would you have done if I had been pregnant?" Casi rested her chin on his shoulder with a sigh.

He kissed her cheek. "I would have been disappointed if you were trying to use it as leverage for marriage." He gazed at her. "You already had me hooked from our first kiss. Although I don't want children, I would adapt if that's what you wanted. Why did you get plain chips? They taste stale."

"That's all they had and no dip. It was a crappy store." Casi licked the salt off and shrugged.

"Can we trust these?" Jake spun around.

"That's why we got two." Casi yawned.

"What world do you live in where that logic makes sense?" Kyle checked the expiration dates on the boxes.

Jake eyed the tests, waiting for the fuzzy line to develop as Lia cried in her hands. "No!" He grabbed the stick from the counter and held it in front of Casi's face. "This is your fault. You knowingly left damaged condoms around, fully aware I'm the only one in this house who uses them."

"That argument won't hold up in court." Casi rolled her eyes. "I think it's just baby season. Anna is pregnant too." The color drained from Jake's face and she poked him. "It is her husband's child. She was on the pill when she was with you and this kid was done by in-vitro. She wanted to make sure it took. She's not crazy about having sex with him. This will seal the deal for her future and give him an heir. It was on her list of things to do before she turned forty."

Jake put his hands on his knees and sucked in air as he tried to process the information. Lia shoved him to get his attention. "I'm having an abortion. I won't do this a second time!"

"Absolutely not!" Jake belted.

"I gave in on Austin because I planned the pregnancy, but this one is an accident. I can barely handle one. There is no way I'll have a second unwanted child."

Jake got down on one knee and took her hand. "We'll get married. That's what you wanted, right? I understand it's been hard on you, but we will be a family now and raise both kids together."

"No, Jake!" Lia wrenched her hand away.

"Casi, please help him," Kyle whispered. "An abortion will send him over the edge. You know about Amber and how that affected him."

Casi slid from the counter and put an arm around Lia's shoulders. "Marriage is a good idea, Lia. You guys are basically together, and you already have Austin. You can move in with Jake and you'll be right across the street from us. We'll help you. His proposal sucked. But in the end, you will be married and have the life you envisioned."

Lia winced. "My family will think I'm insane. They gave me such a bad time over Austin."

"This is our family, Lia. We do things our own way," Casi said.

Jake dusted off his knee. "Make an appointment and find out the due date. I'll go with you if you want. I promise to be more involved this time. We'll get married next month before you are even showing. No one will be aware we fucked up."

"Let's go out to dinner in Seattle." Kyle squeezed Lia's hand. "We'll buy a ring and make it official. You can tell your sister a romantic version of how this went down. There is no need to tell them the actual details."

Casi suggested Vegas for a convenient and cost-effective venue, and everyone agreed. They planned three nights, returning home on the fourth day. Lia's mother volunteered to take care of Austin, not wanting to attend what she deemed a sham of a wedding. No one revealed the truth about the pregnancy, only that Lia and Jake decided to move in together and felt it would be best for Austin.

Lia invited her sister, who said she would see if she could get the days off and would get back to her. Lauren called their mother immediately to commiserate. "What do you think of Lia marrying Jake?"

"I think it's one more mistake she's making with that man. It should have been you and Kyle," Fran said. "Typical that she's doing it in Vegas, as common as a baby out of wedlock."

"I still don't understand why Kyle didn't want me," Lauren cried.

"Men think with their penises. He met a pretty woman and convinced himself it was love. I'm sure she makes him feel like a king in the bedroom, but it won't last. Kyle made a foolish mistake, but he's an intelligent man. Eventually, he'll want substance over fluff. Be patient, he'll come around."

"I wish he never met her. We would have worked through things and been planning our own wedding. I've seen him with Lia's baby. He would want one with me."

"There's still time. It's better he's getting it out of his system now. I learned the hard way what happens when you get married young and a man hasn't sown his wild oats. She can't have children, so their marriage isn't substantial and can be easily erased."

"Do you think I should go to the wedding? I hate witnessing Kyle with that stupid bitch. It tears my heart out."

"Be there for your sister and show Kyle how level-headed you are. He'll be attracted to that in the long run. Take a friend and have a good time. I'm sure there are exhibits which will interest you, and encourage Kyle to join you," Fran plotted.

"Georgia will be there. He will see how close I am with her still. You're right, I need to be patient and believe this is a temporary setback. It might even make our future relationship stronger."

"You'll win in the end. Smart women always do."

Jake entered the coffee shop and sat beside Gail. She looked at him with tears in her eyes. "Is it true?"

He nodded and whispered, "She's pregnant. I don't want her to get an abortion and Austin needs us to be a family."

"I hate that it hurts so much." Gail squeezed his hand.

"I don't have a choice. I need you to understand and help me explain it to the kids. I called Olivia, but she hung up on me."

"I'll talk to her. Are you getting married in Vegas? I always wanted to go there; it seems like fun."

"I wish things didn't turn out this way." Jake surveyed Lia showing her co-workers the engagement ring.

"You're doing the right thing. She has wanted to be married for a long time, and men walk all over her. She deserves to be your wife, and it will be better for your children."

"You'll always be my first wife." Jake gave her a kiss.

"I'm glad I was." She smiled at him. "Our friendship is what I value the most now. Perhaps this is how it was meant to be."

Jake answered his cell phone and waited for the caller's anger to dispel. "Mom forced me to call you. She says I am required to hear you out since you're always patient with me, which is a joke because you rarely take an interest and you're hardly a role model," Olivia scolded.

"I'm an example of what not to do. Look at how screwed up my life is and do the opposite. I'm a victim of bad decisions and faulty condoms."

Olivia giggled. "Were Reid and I not enough for you?"

"You are way more than enough. Austin came into this world under false pretenses, and now I'm adding another one to my collection of mistakes. I hope this doesn't inspire you to get pregnant again."

"Just the opposite. Mom demanded I hold Austin while he cried for an hour. Then I had to change his diaper. I never want kids."

"When did Mom take care of Austin?" Jake asked.

"She takes him on Fridays when Lia works. It's her favorite day of the week. She's crazy for him and kisses him constantly."

"She's excellent with babies. I guess it's a good way for you to get to know your brother."

"He is my brother, huh? That's weird."

"Things certainly got complicated. I'm headed to Vegas next week to marry Lia. What do you think of that?"

"I think you should take me so I can hang out with Casi while you drown your sorrows at the bar."

"It will be nice when you can come and drink with me. I think we'll relate to each other better as you get older."

"I drink now."

"I'm sure you do, but I meant legally. Can you finish high school before you formally become a party girl?"

"How about I finish school and you stop having kids?"

"After this new one? It's already in the oven. Oh, and not that you hang out with the coffee crowd, but we are keeping this child a secret for now."

"Mom told me. Why don't you get fixed?"

"I'm not sure if they can fix all that's wrong with me, but it's not a bad idea." Jake smiled as he entered the café after the call ended. He noted Anna sitting at a corner table by the window. "You didn't want to meet at a hotel?"

Anna smiled. "I asked Casi to tell you I'm pregnant. Our affair has officially come to an end."

"Sex won't hurt the baby."

"I know, but it seems tawdry. I gave in after I got back from Italy, but I need to move forward as a married woman. What did you want to tell me?"

"Lia's pregnant, again." Jake clenched his jaw.

Anna cocked her head. "I thought she wasn't enthralled with the first one. Why would she want to do it again?"

"This one was an accident. We're getting married next week in Vegas. I have to do it to convince her to keep it." He smoothed the tablecloth.

"We will have children close to the same age."

"We could arrange play dates." He smiled while his eyes welled.

She sighed and ran her finger over his hand. "At some point, you'll need to give up on us, Jake. It wasn't meant to be."

He touched her ring, estimating he couldn't have bought her something so expensive. "Love is never enough, huh?"

"Kyle and Casi are rare. Most people do what they need to do to get by and enjoy a decent life."

"Like marrying a guy who can buy you a Mercedes?"

She shrugged. "What were my other options? Maybe things would be different if we had fallen in love after your divorce, but two more kids and a girlfriend with expectations of your devotion to her? I don't want to be a part of that." He redirected his eyes to the plant on the windowsill, devastated by her words. "Marry Lia. It will tidy up your mess. After all these babies are born, we'll get together and laugh about our choices."

Jake nodded. "When I came to your house on my birthday, you said I didn't need a condom. Were you already pregnant?"

"I had the in-vitro procedure the week before. I wanted to be with you, with nothing between us. I've never taken that risk before with anyone." She turned her head, and he could see she was trying not to cry. "My husband wanted a child, and I knew it might not happen right away. The thought of him attempting to impregnate me endlessly was horrible. I needed the memory of being with you."

Jake held her hand discretely behind the breadbasket. "I wish we could run away and forget this stupid life we're living."

"We both have people who need us to do the right thing." Anna ran a hand over her stomach.

30

VEGAS

"Why can't they fly to Vegas without us?" Casi stomped her foot in annoyance of Kyle's insistence for her to hurry so they would be on time to meet Lauren.

"It's easier to go together so we can take the shuttle to the hotel."

Casi rolled her eyes, having been to Vegas numerous times and never finding it difficult to get a shuttle or an Uber. She knew his schedules were important to him, and she suggested the hotel but let him plan the itinerary. Lauren had been upset she wasn't included in the wedding preparation. Kyle tried to make it up to her with endless calls, going over the details and including culinary exhibits he knew she would enjoy. He was happy she was bringing a friend, only wishing it was a boyfriend instead of a woman she worked with.

"You are cutting it close." Lauren pursed her lips when they arrived at the gate.

"It's Vegas, not an international flight." Casi sipped her coffee and made it obvious that was the delay in meeting them on time.

"Reel her in," Jake whispered to Kyle.

Lauren introduced Kyle to Sandra, and she smiled at him admiringly. He shook her hand and turned. "This is my wife, Casi."

"Darn," Sandra teased. "I hoped you were single."

271

"Sorry." Kyle smiled and avoided Lauren's glare.

Jake checked his ticket as they boarded and nudged his brother. "Who booked these seats?"

"Lauren did." Kyle shrugged. He hesitated when he realized the issue as Lauren took the seat in the middle, between him and Casi.

"Big surprise." Casi put in earbuds and cranked her music.

"I thought we could finalize plans and make use of the time." Lauren smiled and took out a floral notebook with a matching pen.

Jake attempted to change with Lia, but she insisted she needed the aisle in case she had to use the bathroom. He slipped behind Casi, pulling her earbuds out. "Switch with me."

"Why?" Casi asked.

"I don't like being in the middle," he pleaded.

Kyle read the panic in his brother's face and put his hand on his arm. "I'll change with you."

"No! We need to go over the itinerary." Lauren glared at Jake. "You must sit in your assigned seat in case of emergency."

Casi rolled her eyes. "If the plane goes down, we'll all be cremated, and it won't matter what seat we're in. They can get our DNA from the little bits strewn about in the wreckage." She smiled at the alarm on Kyle's face due to her graphic depiction. "Take the window, Jake, and Kyle can go in the middle so he can finish over-planning unnecessary details." She raised an eyebrow at Lauren. "Move to the aisle. We are holding up this plane." Lauren noted passengers mumbling and quickly complied.

"Thank you," Jake whispered.

"I'll always have your back." Casi gave Jake's hand a squeeze as she relocated beside Lia.

Casi dressed for the evening in a shimmering ruby mini dress, plunging almost to her navel. She paired it with a rhinestone criss-cross bra, peeking through the material. She accented the outfit with rhinestone stilettos, completing the look. Her hair was full and sexy, complementing her sultry image with dark eye makeup, revisiting her club-girl image. She hadn't told anyone how excited she was to be in Vegas, suggesting it as a convenient place to get married as a ploy to get out on the town again. Her new life was comfortable and fulfilling, but she missed the rush of the big city life and crush of people at the nightclubs.

"Holy shit!" Jake halted when they met in the lobby.

"What? We're in Vegas, no one will even notice me." Casi shrugged.

"Highly unlikely." Kyle smiled at the response she received as they walked to the Bellagio hotel to try the buffet. After dinner, Casi suggested a strip club for the men but was met with protest from the women. They agreed on a burlesque show, shocked when they realized what that entailed, as Casi giggled and called them hicks.

Kyle slipped an arm around her waist. "I hope someone thought to bring lingerie to entertain her husband Vegas-style."

"You will have to wait and see." Casi gave him a wink.

They strolled the strip, dancing and drinking, fitting in with the party crowd. Kyle directed them to a country western bar, escorting Casi to the dance floor, falling in step with the line of dancers.

"Hillbilly." Jake shuddered in protest.

"You listened to country music when I first met you," Casi said.

"Yup, I only play it when Jake's not around," Kyle admitted.

"We should go line dancing and you can teach me. Do you think there are clubs in Seattle?" Casi twirled back to their seats.

"I believe there are a few." Kyle sighed at the tears in Lauren's eyes, recalling the bars they frequented.

"Let's try this one." Casi pulled Kyle toward a venue with neon lights and music vibrating across the strip. She spun out to the floor. Not lacking for partners, both male and female. A handsome man embraced her and planted a kiss on her cheek. Her eyes lit up. "How did you know where to meet us?"

"I have informants." He chuckled.

"She's making out with an old guy on the dance floor and Kyle doesn't care?" Lauren whispered to her sister.

"That's her dad. They came for our wedding." Lia giggled. "That's her step-mom. Isn't she gorgeous?"

Peter and Georgia greeted them as Ava took a seat beside Jake and he put his arm around her. "I'll keep you company while your husband is occupied with that floozy."

"You're almost a married man yourself." Ava smiled at Lia.

"Ready to peruse alternate places? I think I've gone deaf." Jack greeted them and lead the way through the casino. "Any gamblers in the crowd?"

"Only with birth control." Kyle chuckled and shoved his brother. "I play cards, but I know the girls are excited to be out on the town tonight."

While half the group searched for a bathroom, the brothers, Casi, and Jack waited by a fountain on the main boulevard. Ava laughed when she returned to discover the quartet sharing a joint. "I guess you can find anything in Vegas."

"Kyle smokes pot now?" Lauren's eyes widened with shock.

"He always did." Georgia smiled at Peter's eager expression. "Yes, you can join them."

Sandra grinned and rushed forward. "When in Rome."

Lauren narrowed her eyes. "I think Casi is a bad influence."

"Peter used to smoke pot with the boys in high school. They would sneak out to the barn and think I couldn't figure it out when they came back laughing and hungry."

Ava smiled. "Jack and I partied back in the day." She glanced at Lauren. "It's quite prevalent in the restaurant business."

"Some of us rise above." Lauren jutted her chin forward.

Casi strolled to a theater for a male revue. She removed a credit card from her bra and handed it to the ticket taker while Kyle raised an eyebrow. "What else did you stash in there?"

The bouncer surveyed Casi. "She gets in for free."

Casi handed the women tickets and insisted everyone would attend. "This is Lia's bachelorette party!"

"I've never seen male strippers." Georgia clasped a hand to her mouth.

"What are we supposed to do?" Jake whined.

"Go to a show! You are in Vegas!" Casi gave Kyle a sultry kiss and smacked him on the backside. "Enjoy your evening."

"I don't think it's appropriate for married men to attend a strip club." Lauren glared after the men who were laughing and high fiving. "Lia you should put your foot down. You have been too liberal with Jake already."

Georgia laughed, "Lauren, you're too conservative! There is nothing wrong with them having a gander at pretty women."

Ava whispered to Georgia, "Jack can look at any woman who is not Sonya. She is the only one I don't trust."

The show was entertaining as the dancers worked the crowd, finding interest in Casi, and pulling her on stage for a private dance. She insisted Lia join her and ensured she received most of the attention.

Lauren winced when a dancer slid on her sister's lap and she turned to Sandra. "This is disgusting. Do you want to leave?"

Sandra whistled and waved bills in the air. "Are you kidding? This is awesome! Your friend Casi is so much fun!"

Georgia nudged Ava. "Do you think I should be worried? Jake just ended a sixteen-year marriage. What is the rush to get married since Austin is already here?"

Ava leaned closer. "Have you noticed Lia hasn't had a drink?"

"Oh hell, she's probably pregnant, and he's trying to do the right thing after the bad time he got with the last one," Georgia sighed. "When will that boy learn to use birth control?"

"That would be my guess. Lia doesn't seem excited about the wedding unless that's because her sister is a stick in the mud."

"Kyle dated Lauren for quite a few years. She was devastated when he declined to marry her and then within a year, he fell madly in love with Casi."

"Oh, that explains the evil eye." Ava bit her lip. "I hope you feel he made the right choice."

"Absolutely! Lauren is a lovely woman, but Kyle and Casi are a perfect couple. I adore her, especially how she ignites a fire within

Kyle." Georgia smiled. "He was on autopilot for years after his accident and only focused on his business goals. Not only has he brought out the best in her, but he's allowed himself to feel again."

When they reached their hotel room, Casi directed Kyle to bring an armchair to the center of the floor. He complied, smiling when he noticed the mirrored closet doors. She told him to undress while she changed. He fidgeted in the chair, unsure where to look, feeling exposed. He watched her strut toward him and relaxed into the fantasy. He admired the bustier with the lace-up front barely containing her breasts. The stockings and high heels were over the top sexy, accented by a tiny lace thong, which he swiftly removed. The view in the mirror and the sensation of satin and lace against his bare skin made him crazy with desire. "Do you want to get wild?" she asked.

"Absolutely!"

"Show me how I turn you on." He smiled and moved his hand to stroke himself while she twisted around him, maximizing the exposure of the outfit and the reflection in the mirrors, taunting him. She kissed him, letting him touch her for a moment before she slipped away, prolonging the temptation. She bent and brought her mouth to his, then traveled down his stomach.

"This is an incredibly sexy outfit," Kyle breathed, alternating between the view in the mirror and watching her. She stood, letting him undo the ribbon on the bustier with his teeth. He took his time, teasing her with his tongue. He turned her toward the mirror, caressing her as she smiled back at him. "You might want to get on top soon." She sat on his lap facing the mirrors and rested her head on his shoulder, kissing him passionately. He held on for as long as he could, watching her have an orgasm, as she writhed on top of him. He shuddered and joined her, pulling her tightly against him to share the sensation. "You turn me on like no other woman ever has." He carried her to the bed and slipped off her shoes, tossing them over his shoulder before removing her stockings. The clothing littered the room, and he collapsed beside her. "I guess we should try to sleep." He yawned and glanced at the clock.

Casi stroked his cheek. "You haven't been sleeping well. What's on your mind when you're tossing and turning?"

Kyle looked sheepish. "I'm worried about Jake and his latest mistake. It's not only the financial impact, but I can see how it is undermining his confidence." He kissed her. "Thanks for changing seats on the plane. Small issues like that overwhelm him."

"He needed to be beside you."

"His anxiety is worse in public places when his environment is rocky. Committing to Lia and realizing what the future brings with another pregnancy and her depression is an assault on his stability."

Casi rubbed his back. "Turn over. Let me be the protector tonight and watch over you while you sleep. I'm your partner to help with Jake and you can trust me to keep you both safe." He relaxed under her touch and drifted to sleep as she wrapped herself around him.

Jake brought Lia to him when they entered their room, kissing her passionately. She pushed him away. "I don't want to be compared to those women at the strip club."

"There's no reason to get upset about the club, it was no big deal."

Lia wiped a tear. "I'm not sure if it's the pregnancy that seems to put me in a bad mood or the constant belittling I get from my family. I'm angry and unhappy, and you know that's not like me."

"Your pleasant demeanor is what attracted me to you in the beginning. Maybe you should stop texting your mom; she has too much influence over you. If you are feeling pressured, we can forget about the ceremony and call this a vacation."

"We have to go through with it! I already had one child out of wedlock, and I'm not having a second. You proposed to me; I didn't ask you to marry me!" She burst into tears.

"I was sincere about the proposal, but I won't go back to a hateful relationship for the next sixteen years."

"Lauren and my mom keep telling me I'm making a mistake and reminding me how men never take me seriously. I want to be married. I'm tired of being the woman who works at the coffee shop who no one ever wanted to commit to."

"You are the mother of my children and I'm happy to commit to us being a family," Jake assured her.

"Haven't you heard I'm the woman men call when they are trolling for a good time and their wives are out of town?" she repeated the rumor.

"I'm the guy who is unpredictable and troubled, whose brother has to take care of him. Why do we care what people say?"

"I need to make our relationship official even if it turns out to be temporary."

Jake smiled. "At least we are going into it with realistic expectations."

"Dim the lights and I'll be back in a few minutes." Lia withdrew a satin negligee from her suitcase. "I did intend for this getaway to be romantic."

Jake squeezed her hand. "Tune it all out. It's just you and me, together."

31

———

BITTERSWEET

*J*ake pounded on the door until Kyle finally appeared, yawning and rubbing his eyes, wrapped in a bedsheet. "Jeez, how long were you planning on sleeping?" Jake pushed past him into the room.

"What time is it?" Kyle barely noticed the group of four entering his room as he blinked at the clock. "I was completely out. I haven't had such a solid sleep in months."

Jake held up a stocking. "Did she wear you out?"

Kyle grinned and surveyed the room strewn with lingerie as his eyes rested on Casi stretched out on the bed in a peaceful slumber. "No, but I had an angel watching over me as I slept."

"Get in the shower, we are meeting our parents downstairs in ten minutes." Jake yanked the curtains open and allowed the sun to fill the room. He cocked his head when he noted the chair in front of the mirror. "Kinky."

Kyle caressed Casi's back. "Time to wake up."

"Why?" She burrowed deeper in the blankets.

"Turn the water on cold and throw her in." Jake shrugged.

Kyle smiled and knelt beside the bed. "We are going out for breakfast to get pancakes."

Casi threw back the blanket and charged to the bathroom without noticing she had an audience. Kyle chuckled and cast his sheet aside, turning to follow her.

Sandra craned her neck to get a peek while Lauren crossed her arms over her chest and fought back tears when she noted Casi's name emblazoned on the arm of the man she loved. "They can meet us in the lobby!" She slammed the door as she left.

Lia hesitated at the doorway and Jake nodded. "Go with your sister. I'll make sure they stay on task."

"I can stay and help you. Maybe Kyle needs me to pat him dry with a big fluffy towel." Sandra grinned.

Jake chuckled. "How are you and Lauren friends?"

Sandra glanced at the closed door. "We've worked together for a while. She's an amazing chef and I suspect she will open her own place one day." She shrugged, realizing she was skirting the question. "We don't normally socialize together. I've never been to Vegas, and it seemed like a fun way to spend my days off."

Casi stumbled to her suitcase and selected low-rise jeans and a crocheted halter top, which exposed her mid-drift. Jake rushed them out the door, not letting her find earrings. "It's their fault," he announced when they entered the lobby ten minutes late.

"Casi, you look like you're half asleep." Georgia giggled and brushed the hair from her face.

"I need coffee," Casi moaned.

Jack smiled. "I'll ask the concierge where a good place is."

"I know where to go." Casi perked up and marched toward the boulevard. She stepped out, ignoring the line waiting for taxi's and signaled a shuttle who made an illegal U-turn to skid to the curb in front of her. She indicated for her group to get in quickly before anyone could make a fuss about her hijacking the ride. She gave the driver the address, and they drove along the strip to another casino several miles away. It was older, but Casi claimed they had the best breakfast around.

"It must be good." Jake eyed the line stretching around the corner.

"I've heard about this place. It's supposed to be awesome, but we'll never get in," Lauren said.

Casi greeted the hostess with a kiss and a whisper. The woman smiled and led the group to a long table. "Did you have a reservation?" Kyle asked.

"We do now." Casi winked.

"Thank God you have a beautiful daughter," Peter whispered to Jack, who nodded, noting she seemed to be able to bypass lines.

A waiter poured Casi a steaming cup of coffee, not noticing there were nine other people at the table in need of caffeine. She perused the menu, oblivious to the attention. "Do you guys want to go to the pool later?" She yawned and sipped her coffee.

"Whatever you think would be fun." Lia tugged at her shirt sleeve.

"I haven't had waffles since I was in LA," Casi mused. "Hey Jake, remember when..." She was abruptly grabbed by the arm and yanked from her seat by Ava.

"Show me where the bathroom is." Ava directed her to a small hallway and exhaled. "Today is Lia's day to be special."

"I'm not doing anything to ruin it. I'm trying to be helpful!" Casi's cheeks burned, and she felt like she was a teenager again.

"You don't realize how much attention you get constantly."

"Why is that my fault?" Tears sprung to her eyes.

Ava stroked her arm affectionately. "Each time Lia sees Dad hug you, or Kyle gazes at you with so much love in his eyes, she looks like she's about to cry. Jake tends to your every need, and Peter and Georgia dote on you too. I'm not asking you to change, but for today, can we make it about Lia? Tomorrow is your day."

"You know about tomorrow?"

"It might be the most important day of Dad's life, but let's not forget who put the care packages together for you." Ava winked. Casi nodded, fighting back tears. Ava grasped her chin and spoke softly, "Sweetie, I adore you. We had our rough patch, but we've put that behind us. I'm not chastising you; I'm pointing out what I see because you are a loving and generous person. I understand you have gone out of your way to help Lia and be a great friend. My concern is she has a lot of family pressures and maybe we should let her shine today."

"That's fair." Casi sighed. "I was trying to tune Lauren out and I may have been more self-involved than I should be."

"I heard about Lauren and Kyle," Ava whispered. "She has been unpleasant to you and I'm proud of you for rising above that."

"I'm a work in progress."

"What are you wearing to the wedding?" Ava eyed her outfit choice.

Casi winced. "I might need to buy a new dress."

Ava laughed. "If it's anything close to what you had on last night, that would be a good idea." She gave her a kiss on the cheek.

They walked to the table and took their seats, picking up their menus like nothing happened. "Did you get in trouble for being a brat?" Jake teased.

"We were talking over plans for dinner tonight," Casi said.

"I thought Kyle and I were making the reservations," Lauren snapped.

Kyle put his arm around Casi's shoulders, seeing her eyes water. "If Casi knows a good place, we should go there. She's more familiar with this town." He whispered in her ear, "Is everything ok with Ava?"

Casi nodded and gave him a meek smile. Kyle glared down the table, not happy she had become despondent. She put her hand to the side of his face. "I'm fine. I was complaining it was drafty in here, and Ava said I should have thought to bring a jacket."

"I didn't hear you." Kyle quickly removed his denim shirt and wrapped it around her.

"Thank you, I feel much better." Casi buttoned it to her collarbone.

"There goes our excellent service," Jake teased, catching a look from Ava. He glanced at Lia, fumbling with her menu, trying to ascertain what everyone would get. "Do you want me to order for you? I'm having waffles, bacon, and eggs. I think it's wise to start with a hearty breakfast." He put an arm around her shoulders and watched her look to Casi for advice.

Casi gave her a bright smile. "I'll have the same thing, but maybe with pancakes instead."

❧

"Are we going to the pool?" Jake asked when they returned to the hotel.

"Let's not. There are so many drunk people, they're probably peeing in it." Casi noted the relief on Lia's face. "Why don't we walk around and see what else is going on?" After several hours of exhibits and a magic show, Casi anxiously checked the time on her phone, hoping she could sneak away and buy a dress. "I think I will head back and take a nap, so I'm refreshed for tonight's main event."

"It's not like you are the one getting married," Jake said. "I can't believe you would abandon your friend on her wedding day."

"I'm not, it's just..." Casi tried.

Ava smiled. "Jake, you will need to entertain yourself. Casi is making reservations at the spa as a treat for Lia."

"Yes," Casi agreed. "Is everyone in?"

"A spa sounds wonderful! We don't have anything like that in Blackberry Falls. I imagine the ones here are really fancy." Lia's face lit up.

"I thought it would be a fun thing to do together." Casi smiled at Ava.

"I don't like people touching me." Lauren shivered.

Jake whispered to Kyle, "Don't we know it, Ice Princess." Kyle pretended to cough, trying not to laugh at the comment.

Lauren frowned in his direction. "We can get tickets for the culinary exhibition at the Paris hotel while they do the spa."

Kyle watched Casi hanging up from making reservations and whispered, "Why do you look troubled? What's really going on?"

Casi bit her bottom lip. "Ava pointed out I should wear something a little more conservative for the wedding."

"You don't own anything demure. Is that what the tears were about?"

"I wasn't crying," she mumbled. "I'm trying to be a good friend to Lia. It's a new role for me to not have center stage."

"You're a great friend. Go to the spa and have a good time. Use our debit card." Kyle caressed her back.

"No, I would like to pay for this." She smiled. "For the first time in my life, I have disposable income."

"Look at you!" Kyle gazed at her.

"Kyle, do you want to go to the exhibit?" Lauren repeated.

"No thanks, I have an errand to run." Kyle met Casi's questioning look. "I'll see you back at the hotel. You can trust me to take care of this."

"Cool, the women are gone. Are we going to another strip club?" Jake observed everyone splinter to varied locations.

"Nope, dress shopping." Kyle grinned.

"What is that code for?" Jake raised an eyebrow.

"No code. I'm being a good husband and helping my wife find a less risqué dress for your wedding."

"Why? I don't care what she wears." Jake shrugged.

"It may have been pointed out that she should shine a little less today." Kyle narrowed his eyes at Jack.

Jack laughed. "I'm sure Ava has Casi's best interest at heart."

"Well, have fun." Jake headed toward a casino.

"You have an equally vested interest if you want a happy wife tonight in your room. We know how Lia's moods crash in an instant lately."

Jake rolled his eyes. "Can we make it quick and do some gambling after?"

"Sure, I could play a few games of cards. Dad, do you and Jack want to come and show me how to shop for a woman?"

"I'll tag along just to watch you try," Peter laughed.

They walked through several stores, finally finding one with suitable clothing. The saleswoman asked if they needed help, noticing the four men wandering aimlessly. "We need a dress for a girl with a killer figure, who wants to appear less hot," Jake stated.

"Less hot?" she repeated.

"She would like to let the bride be the center of attention at the wedding tonight," Kyle offered, being more precise.

"Ah, I see," she said, understanding the dilemma. She asked her age and size, bringing over several options. They agreed on a tea length, sleeveless dress in a floral print. It came up to the collar bone in front with a keyhole cut-out in back. The skirt was an A-line that would flow over her curves, belted at the waist. Kyle gladly paid the two hundred dollars even though he assumed it would be worn once.

Casi smiled as she watched Lia giggle excitedly when the receptionist confirmed they had appointments for the full treatment of pedicures, manicures, and facials. "I've never been anywhere so classy," Lia exclaimed. "Sometimes I treat myself to a pedicure at that place in town, but I haven't been able to afford it since I cut back my hours."

Ava glanced at the price chart and whispered to Casi, "I'll help pay. I didn't realize how expensive it is, I suggested it off the top of my head."

Casi smiled. "I knew how much it would be when I booked it. I want to pay for everyone. You and Georgia have done so much for me, and now I can truly afford to be generous." She caught a glimmer of sadness in Ava's eyes. "I'm not being arrogant."

Ava squeezed her hand. "I know, Sweetie. I'm so proud of the woman you have become. You have a wonderful relationship, but you're independent and strong too. That's everything I hoped for when you were a little girl."

"Why do I feel you won't tell me things about the past?"

Ava nodded to the attendant who indicated for them to come to their rooms. "There's no point revisiting things from long ago. It's better to focus on our lives now."

Casi raced in the hotel room, panting from running up the stairs. "Makeup and hair and I'm good to go."

"Take your time." Kyle greeted her with a kiss. "What do you think?" He waved a hand to a dress hanging from the curtain rod. Her eyes welled, and he cringed and checked his watch. "You don't like it?"

"It's perfect!" Casi smoothed her palm over the material.

"Good, because it took four men to pick it out, and it cost two hundred dollars!"

"That's not cheap, but I could probably wear it again for a business function. I'll pay you back when we get home."

"From your secret stash of cash that you keep in a shoe box?"

"You discovered my treasure box?"

"By mistake. I was measuring to make another rack for your growing collection of shoes. I knocked it over, but I put it back in without really looking at it," he confessed.

"It's not that secret." She giggled. "I was impressed by your stack of bills in the safe and I wanted to start my own."

"Can I get you a small safe that only you have the combination to? I don't think it's wise to have that much money in the closet."

"It is only twelve hundred dollars, or I guess a thousand now." She regarded the dress. "It would be better if we both had the combination, in case of emergencies."

"An emergency like you forgot the combination?" Kyle grinned. "I don't want you to pay me back. I'm up a couple hundred from playing Blackjack. Also, I like the idea of keeping my hot wife under cover for business."

Casi turned toward the bathroom and hesitated. "Do you think I make everything about sex?"

"Can I have more information before I say the wrong thing and end up sleeping alone?" Kyle cringed. "I was kidding about keeping you covered. That wasn't a reference to kissing that guy."

"I understood the joke and I'm not offended." She grasped his hands. "At the spa, Lia was talking about how she always wanted a traditional wedding and was disappointed she was getting married in

Vegas. She said Lauren's been chastising her for making poor choices and claims I am a bad influence because all I am interested in is sex." She sighed. "Lauren pointed out that my only talent is wearing skimpy clothing and how I manipulate you with lingerie and kinky sex."

Kyle smiled. "Lingerie isn't kinky. It's sexy and I love it. I think it's awesome we are married and are incredibly attracted to each other. She has no idea of the crap we've been through, and how intimacy brings us closer."

"Are you sorry we got married in Hawaii and that I wasn't more involved in the wedding planning?"

"Not at all," he paused. "Between us, ok?"

"I'm good with secrets."

"I know you are. Lauren has been saving money since she was sixteen, to put toward a wedding. Her dad wasn't in the picture and she had a fantasy of an elaborate ceremony and honeymoon in Italy. Aside from buying her condo, that was her major savings account. When we started talking about marriage, she pressured me to put money aside. I thought it was a ridiculous expense, but I did it anyway. When you and I got married, it barely cost me anything, and I loved the vacation in Hawaii and our simple ceremony. I felt it was the perfect way to start our future together." He took her hand. "I used the money from my wedding savings account to buy you the car instead. It made me feel good to see it go toward something so much more practical."

"I prefer the car to a fancy affair. Thank you for taking such good care of me. I wish I had reacted better when you gave it to me." She wiped a tear. "I was overwhelmed."

He brushed her tears away with his thumb. "You were in a different place then. I know you love the car and I'm relieved you're in a safer vehicle." He blushed. "Part of it was selfish. I wanted you in Washington and assumed if you had a car fit for the weather it would make an easier transition."

She leaned in and kissed him. "You were right to want me with you. It's where I belong, and I discovered who I was meant to be."

"We are both evolving, and I honestly feel closer to you each day. I was never in love with the idea of marriage, but when I met you, I couldn't wait to commit my entire life to being with you." Kyle sighed. "I'm sorry Lia didn't get her perfect wedding, but Vegas is what Jake can afford with having a baby, and another on the way. Building his house is his main priority. He's made a lot of sacrifices through the years to raise his family, and he doesn't need the pressure of an expensive event. Lia got to come to Hawaii, she can consider that a honeymoon. Now go get ready so we can attend this sham of a union and come back and have sex!"

She pulled up her hair in front, arranging a cascade of soft curls. She slipped on the dress, noting it fit perfectly. She spun in front of Kyle and he nodded. "You look sweet and innocent." She threw her head back and laughed as she lifted the skirt to expose her lacy panties. "I like the secret sultry touch!"

They walked in the lobby hand in hand. Jack smiled and kissed her cheek. "You look lovely, Darling."

Ava clasped a hand over her heart. "Perfect."

The ceremony was quick and simple, exchanging vows and rings. Lauren stood at her sister's side and smiled at Kyle as she fought back tears. She had imagined her own wedding for as long as she could remember, carefully planning every detail and compiling ideas in a scrapbook. She knew Lia was settling for Jake, wanting to be a married woman, but she realized she was jealous her sister would take the Jensen name instead of her. She let herself imagine for a moment her dream of marrying Kyle was actually happening.

Ava slid her hand on top of Casi's sensing it was hard for her to witness Kyle at the altar with Lauren. Casi squeezed her hand back, needing the support and appreciating Ava's intuition. "You don't think Kyle will ever leave me, do you?" she whispered, watching him smile at Lauren.

"Not intentionally, but don't let your guard down. Ex's who are still in love with your husband can be a problem. Men are incredibly stupid at times." Ava clenched her jaw.

After the ceremony, they went to a restaurant Casi suggested. It had an expansive rooftop lounge overlooking the strip, and everyone was pleased with the fabulous meal. Jake took out his credit card and picked up the bill, frowning at the total. "Use the business account," Kyle whispered.

"It's not that. It doesn't add up; I think they forgot to put on half the entrees and alcohol." Jake turned the folder to his brother.

Casi smiled and introduced a handsome man who approached the table. "This is Pablo. He's a friend of Dylan's and that's how I got the recommendation for his restaurant."

"Oh, Darling, I'm your friend too." Pablo kissed her cheek. "We'll always have Aspen." He feigned heartache and held his palm to his forehead.

Kyle smiled and shook his hand. "The food was excellent. Thank you for taking care of us."

"My pleasure. I was told you are an accomplished cook and would appreciate a fine meal," Pablo said.

"Lauren and Sandra are chefs." Kyle noted disappointment cross Casi's face. "But this is certainly one of the best meals I've ever had. I'm glad we had the opportunity to dine here."

They moved to the lounge and Casi whispered for Jake to dance with Lia, asking the DJ to put on a romantic song. She let them have their moment, declining to dance with her father or Kyle as she relaxed on the bench seat and sipped her cocktail.

Casi excused herself for the bathroom and Jack walked to the DJ, putting a tip in the glass as he requested a song for midnight. Casi pushed through the door as a gust of wind caught her skirt, sending it billowing around her before she could catch it. Her lacy panties were displayed to the entire lounge, welcomed by leers from the male patrons and a round of laughter from her own group. "Poor Casi, she tried so hard to be demure," Ava giggled while Kyle chuckled and rushed to help her control the material.

At midnight, Jack smiled and held out his hand to escort Casi to the center of the lounge. He held her tightly and whispered in her ear as they danced. Ava strolled to the edge of the terrace with a glass of champagne, gazing at the lights below. Kyle caught Jake's eye, wondering if he should go to comfort her when he noticed her wiping tears. Jack smiled and delivered Casi to Kyle's side before joining Ava at the railing. He put an arm around her shoulders, and she put her head in the crook of her neck and cried softly while he rubbed her back.

Casi frowned at Kyle. "More secrets, I guess."

32

———

THE WEIGHT OF WORDS

Casi arranged for everyone to meet in the lobby the next morning, indicating they should have eaten and to dress comfortably. They took a shuttle to a small airport, and she giggled at their confused expressions. "We're doing a helicopter tour over the Grand Canyon!" She insisted it was already booked and paid for. She split them into groups, suggesting she and Kyle go with Ava and Jack, including Sandra as their fifth person. Secretly, she wanted the experience with Kyle without Lauren in the mix. Jake said it was a bad idea to split up brothers in case one of them went down to a fiery death and the other would be traumatized for life.

"Come on, we all need to do this." Jack put an arm around Casi. "It's her special day, and this is what she picked."

"Why does she get to be special today?" Jake asked.

Kyle paled. "It's your birthday!" He wrung his hands. "I was focused on our first anniversary! I have everything planned and organized. This wedding threw me off! I knew something was amiss. I kept having nightmares about forgetting an important thing. I swear I checked the calendar." He glared at his phone and scrolled through highlighted dates. "Why didn't anyone remind me?"

"You're forgetting everyone's birthday this year," Jake teased.

291

"I was sworn to secrecy." Jack grinned.

Kyle rubbed his temple. "Last year you were in LA for your birthday and told me not to worry about it because you hung out with Dylan. It was the week before our wedding." He frowned at Jake. "Why did you pick October to get married?"

Jake shrugged. "Casi planned it."

Casi looped an arm around Kyle's waist. "I wanted to celebrate with everyone, and their ceremony was a great way to make it special." She squeezed Jake's hand. "This tour was an opportunity to do something out of the ordinary."

Jake exhaled and gave her a kiss. "Thank you, Monkey. This is not something I would have thought to do for myself and it is certainly exciting to step away from family life for a few hours."

"That was thoughtful." Kyle pulled Casi in his arms. "You've spent a lot of money being a good friend."

Casi shrugged. "I'll have to leave that snakeskin Coach purse on the shelf at the boutique." She noted the look in his eyes. "No, I don't want it as a gift for my birthday. Spending time with you doing fun things is enough of a present."

"I should at least pay for Lauren and Sandra."

Casi giggled. "To be truthful, I got a discount because I booked two full helicopters. Don't mention it though, I want Lauren to think I'm generous."

Kyle winked and drew his thumb and forefinger over his lips. "Your secret is safe with me." He hugged her tighter. "I would like to reiterate that I have been planning something significant to celebrate our anniversary."

"I blame Lauren for distracting you."

"I will be a coward and let her take the heat for my ignorance."

She directed them to the counter. "I guessed everybody's weight, but they'll do the final check now."

"No!" Lia backed toward the door.

Jake smiled and took her hand. "Only the lady behind the counter can see it. They must ensure the helicopter is balanced." She winced and handed him her purse as she stepped on the tile.

"You need to hold whatever you'll be taking on board," the agent said.

"I'll keep her purse with me on the helicopter if necessary." Jake cocked his head. "How much do I weigh?"

The agent raised an eyebrow. "198 pounds with the purse."

Jake chuckled, "What was my sister-in-law's guess?"

Casi giggled when the agent said, "312 pounds."

"Brat." Jake poked her in the ribs.

"What did you guess my weight as?" Kyle asked.

"185 pounds." Casi grinned, and the agent nodded.

Kyle smiled. "Same as in college."

They each took their turn, laughing when Georgia handed Peter her purse, then attempted to stand on one foot. "Mom, you do realize you'll weigh the same, right?" Kyle explained.

"Shush. This is how I weigh myself." She held her breath and balanced.

Peter got on the scale and mimicked Georgia's stance, making everyone laugh. "You look like a flamingo," Jake teased.

Lauren glared at Casi, thankful the weigh-in was private, but wondering what the guess had been. They laughed when Casi went to the bathroom, the only one to go after she had been weighed.

"Hey, when's Lauren's birthday?" Jake asked Kyle.

"April 10th, why?" Kyle flipped him off. "Smart ass."

Jack put an arm around his shoulders. "Kyle, when Casi was a little girl, her mother made her birthdays miserable, always building it up into some grand occasion, then dropping the ball at the last minute. Sonya would leave her at the venue to go get high and forget her or come back an intoxicated mess. Casi created a diversion to distract us each year and take the focus off the celebration. I caught on after a few years and started a game where she could pick an outrageous activity and I couldn't decline. When I left, she refused to celebrate anymore and made it the worst day of the year. Those were usually the times I had to pick her up from someone's floor where she passed out. What had been a special day for us, became me watching her throw up, or worse, be so out of it, I had to carry her to bed and let her sleep it off. When she moved to LA, I would wait for the phone call to find out if she was alive the next day. I've seen the pictures of her at the clubs, dancing like she didn't care, but I knew how much she was hurting. I've never stopped feeling guilty about leaving her. I thought she was old enough for me to make a new life, but I realized too late how vulnerable she really was." His eyes watered. "When she told me about this excursion, I didn't tell you because it was one promise I could keep to my daughter. She may seem high maintenance, but underneath she's still that abandoned little girl."

When the helicopters became airborne, Casi took Kyle's hand and smiled, excited to share the experience with him. The celebration tour landed in the canyon for a champagne picnic, and even Lia took a sip. Jake walked over and grasped Casi's hand as the guide explained the history and geology of the canyon, and Kyle listened intently.

Jake led her to a rock formation and smiled. "It was a rough year for you, Monkey, but I predict better things are in store. Thanks for being an incredible friend and forcing me to love you. I couldn't have made it through the shit storm without you and I appreciate you allowing me to express myself without judgement or criticism."

Casi smiled. "We were both wrong about each other in the beginning. Kyle obviously is the smart one who knows us better than we know ourselves."

"Without a doubt." Jake smiled and gave her a kiss.

Kyle did a double-take when Casi stepped out of the bathroom in a sultry snakeskin-print dress held together at the sides by a crisscross of golden chains. The top was a form-fitting bra, which enhanced her cleavage to the maximum. "Do you have anything on under there?"

"Of course!" She lifted the skirt to reveal sheer bands of full coverage panties. "You don't like the dress? I can change."

"It's amazing, don't change a thing. I may not be able to keep my hands off you." He scanned the phenomenal dress, which couldn't fit better, draped enough to be suggestive and open enough to be ultra sexy.

"Then don't." She winked.

"Holy shit! Are you kidding me?" Jake's jaw dropped, and he walked around Casi to take in the entire view.

Casi walked ahead, long legs maximized by the short skirt, and Ava whispered to Georgia, "Can you imagine having such a great figure you could wear a dress like that?"

"If I had a body like hers, I would definitely wear that outfit. Youth is fleeting. Good for her for enjoying it," Georgia praised.

Peter whispered to Kyle, "Bravo for marrying such a fox. That woman is a showstopper."

They went out for sushi, laughing when Casi made the waiter spill their cocktails as she adjusted her dress to sit. When they left, Jake tried to lift the hem to see if she was wearing anything underneath. "What is your obsession with my underwear?" she scolded. They got in the elevator, and she hiked her skirt up. "Is everyone happy? I'm wearing underwear, ok?"

"Good lord." Jack turned away. "Why are there mirrors everywhere?"

"Very nice, Dear." Georgia smoothed her dress back in place.

Casi chose a dance club with the anticipation the non-dancers would enjoy the plush sofas lining the walls while they had cocktails. She blended in the crowd and Dylan appeared at her side. She squealed with delight and Jake nudged Kyle. "How sweet, Dylan remembered her birthday."

Kyle elbowed him, hoping what he had arranged for later would make up for his oversight. Brian joined them, shaking hands with the brothers as they made room for him on the sofa. "Congratulations on the wedding." Brian smiled at Lia.

"How did you hear we got married?" Lia looked at Jake.

"From Dylan. He wanted to surprise Casi for her birthday. I guess she usually spends it with him, so he suggested we fly here for a few days."

"How do you know Dylan?" Lia asked.

"Um, I met him at Kyle's," Brian started.

"Jesus, Lia, they are a couple," Jake finally said.

"Oh, ok." Lia nudged Lauren and whispered, "Brian's gay?"

Lauren turned her head and mumbled, "I guess."

Dylan greeted them, squeezing between Jake and Brian. "Doesn't Casi look delicious?"

"Very," they agreed.

"Seriously?" Kyle narrowed his eyes as he witnessed Alejandro leading Casi in a sensuous dance. "Did you invite him?"

"Not me. That's a complete co-inky-dink!" Dylan joked.

"That fellow is quite a dancer," Peter observed. "Does Casi know him?"

"Oh, she knows him very well." Jake chuckled. "That's Alejandro. They used to date."

"Oh, that's the soccer player," Georgia exclaimed.

At the conclusion of the song, Alejandro leaned in for a kiss. Casi pulled back, knocking herself off balance on her stilettos. In one smooth movement, Alejandro slipped his arm under her, preventing a fall, but finalizing the kiss. She put a hand to his chest and pushed him back as Kyle jumped to his feet. "Alejandro, you remember my husband Kyle?"

"Did you just get married?" Alejandro cocked his head.

"It's been almost a year." Casi bit her bottom lip.

"You didn't mention that when we had coffee a few months ago."

Casi paled and scanned Kyle's glare. "Last December. I had a lot of things on my mind. It was an oversight."

Kyle's expression softened. "Now you are aware, perhaps you should find another dance partner. This one belongs to me." He inhaled sharply as the words pierced the conversation.

Casi looped her arm through his and smiled. "Yes, that is correct."

Alejandro sighed. "It was nice seeing you."

"Enjoy the rest of your weekend." Casi turned to Kyle and gave him a kiss. "I need to use the restroom. Do you trust me to go alone?"

Kyle cringed. "That macho bit was for his benefit. You know I'm not normally the jealous type."

"I don't mind belonging to you. It's a nice feeling to be protected."

Jake shoved Kyle when he returned to the sofa. "You should have just punched him."

Kyle shook his head. "I don't blame him for trying."

"Here comes trouble," Dylan said, assessing a brewing situation as Casi was intercepted on her way back from the bathroom.

A group of girls circled her, forming a sullen wall. "Look who's in Vegas," one girl said in a mock friendly tone.

"We heard you crashed and burned. Are you here with Alix?"

"I'm with my husband and family." Casi squared her shoulders and indicated the group behind them. "Feel free to hook up with Alix, he's all yours. Not that you needed my permission in the past."

"Oh, precious, you're with your family in Vegas. Trying to prove you've still got what it takes? That makes you kinda....old?"

Casi took a step forward, outwardly surveying their outfits as a challenge, maximizing her assets in the skimpy dress. "I got bored with all the lame parties and wanna-be's posting their ridiculous photos on Instagram, thinking that makes them real models." She shamed them with her glare. "I don't need to prove myself to pathetic posers in last year's designer knockoffs, too ordinary to go anywhere except in a crew of B-list club-crawlers. I'm done with LA. I moved on to a real life and I'm ecstatic skanks like you aren't part of it." She put a hand on her hip, staring them down as they skulked away, embarrassed and defeated.

"I wanted her to hit one of them," Jake lamented.

"That was better than a punch," Kyle said. Proud she stood up for herself and glad she wore a dress that made the other girls look like pre-teens playing dress up.

Casi stood with her back to the group, regaining her composure and attempting not to cry. She moved toward the bar in the pretense of getting a drink. Ava got up and walked beside her, wrapping an arm around her waist and ordering two glasses of whiskey. "You look amazing in this dress."

"Thanks. I wore it for Kyle," Casi mumbled.

"He's certainly enjoying it." Ava patted her on the hip. "I realize those girls brought back what happened. You did crash and burn, Honey, but you fought your way back up and you're stronger and better than ever. At least you know you can overcome anything. So many people are barely living because they are afraid of making mistakes. You're a wonderful daughter and wife, and above all, you're a strong woman who can stand on her own two feet, in stilettos, I might add. No one can crush you unless you let them. Don't give into the rants of jealous women, you are miles ahead of them in every way."

Casi leaned into her embrace. "Thanks for being one of my role models."

"I fought to get to where I am as well. Strength comes from overcoming challenges and soaring above," Ava assured her.

Casi sat beside Kyle and he put his arm around her, taking a sip from her drink. "Did you want to stay here or try another place?" he asked.

"We're staying here," Dylan insisted before she could answer.

Jake checked his phone as it vibrated, distracted by the caller. He glanced at Lia, then walked toward the bathroom. After ten minutes, Lia sniffed back tears and Lauren glared at Kyle. "What's he doing?"

Kyle stormed in the bathroom and grabbed the phone. "Hi Anna, were you calling to congratulate Jake on his marriage?"

Anna replied with her deep husky laugh, "Oh, Kyle, you're hilarious. You are always taking care of your big brother. Tell Casi I said happy birthday. She wasn't answering her phone."

"If you saw the dress she was wearing, you would understand. I'll be happy to tell our family you called. I'm sure that would make his new wife ecstatic. How's your husband, anyway? I hear you're pregnant, congrats."

"Why are you hanging out in the bathroom?" Casi boldly walked in, not caring that several men were at the urinals.

Kyle smiled. "Anna called to wish you a happy birthday."

"That was sweet." Casi squeezed Jake's hand. "Enough of the pity party, get back out there and dance with me."

"Hey, get out of the men's bathroom lady," a man hissed, staggering to the urinal.

Casi rolled her eyes. "I can see why you're shy." She led Jake to the dance floor, delaying the inevitable fight from the anger etched on Lia's face.

"Everything ok?" Georgia asked.

"Yep. Jake was helping me with something I planned for later," Kyle said.

Casi chose a hip-hop song, which Jake acted out, singing the rap portion, making her laugh. Before she could leave the floor, a Latino man took her by the hand, leading her in a sultry dance.

"Casi is a good dancer, isn't she?" Dylan said. "With a little practice, I'm sure she could master the samba."

"Yes." Kyle raised an eyebrow when a beautiful woman held out her hand to him, guiding him to the floor.

"What's going on?" Jake asked, observing the woman running her hand over Kyle's hip, encouraging him to follow her lead.

"That's Enrique and Maria, they're dance instructors. I bought Casi and Kyle dance lessons for her birthday!" Dylan clapped with glee. "All the girls get Enrique and the boys get Maria. Now get up there!" He gave Lauren the once over. "Unless you would prefer to dance with Maria?"

Georgia and Ava giggled as Enrique coached them with his sexy accent, wrapping himself around them to demonstrate the steps. Jake grinned as Maria ran her hand over his hip, pulling him closer to demonstrate the move. After an hour of lessons, they traded partners, feeling accomplished with their newfound skills. "This is so much fun," Kyle whispered to Casi. Jake danced with Sandra, since Lia refused to join, while Enrique and Maria gave instructions, pleased with their enthusiasm.

The group returned, laughing and worn out, thanking Dylan for the fabulous gift. "It was a wonderful thing to do for Casi; you've been a great friend to her," Kyle said.

"The only thing she ever had with Alejandro was dancing and sex. You already excel at one of those things," Dylan said with a wink.

"You'll discover I'm a loyal friend, and I'm including you in my sacred circle." He patted Kyle's thigh. "We have one more tradition to uphold before Brian and I head out to see some scandalous shows."

"No, not this year." Casi pulled away.

"Yes, Darling. This is our tenth anniversary; we must do it!"

"How did you guys meet?" Lia asked.

A wave of sadness crossed Casi's face. "At a shoot for an editorial. Dylan was doing hair, and I was in a bad place." She blushed and glanced at Jack.

Dylan put an arm around her and finished the story. "I was sharing a hovel of an apartment with a clown, a bartender, and a male stripper. We were missing a hot model. Casi fit the bill, and she moved in with me straight away, and stayed for a year. It was heaven."

Casi smiled, thankful for his rendition. "Ok, let's do it."

They led the group to a lounge advertising karaoke and Jake handed his phone to Kyle. "Make it go to the video setting. This will be epic!"

Dylan put her name on the list as Casi glanced around the packed room. "I don't think I'm drunk enough for this." The group squeezed in, cringing as she took the stage, wondering how painful it would be to watch. Lauren leaned into Kyle, taking the opportunity to make physical contact under the pretense of trying to see better. The music began and Casi took a deep breath. She started softly, then smiled at Dylan and belted out the pop tune, shocking them with her incredible voice.

Jake turned off his phone. "Damn it, she doesn't suck."

"She's awesome!" Kyle's eyes widened as he admired her svelte figure in the racy dress highlighted by the bright lights of the stage.

Ava's lips curled into a satisfied smile. "Our little girl has grown up."

Jack nodded. "Yes, she has." He smiled at her with love. "She has a gift like someone else I know. Perhaps nurture supersedes biology after all."

&

Kyle kissed Casi in the elevator, ignoring protests from his brother. "This is our floor lovebirds." Jake held the door.

"Not anymore." Kyle pushed the button with a smile.

"Wait, what if I need something?" Jake said.

"Call the front desk." Kyle chuckled.

"Jake, leave them alone." Georgia whispered, "You have your own wife to spend the night with now."

Jake stood frozen in the hallway, feeling panic start to rise in his chest. Lia rushed ahead and slammed the door, not waiting for him to follow. Peter walked back and put a hand on his shoulder. "He's in the same hotel. Do you want me to go for a walk with you?"

Jake sighed. "I should deal with Lia. I'm fine."

"We head home tomorrow. Come to our room if you need me, it won't disturb us," Peter said.

"Maybe you'll be having your own romantic evening," Jake joked. "I wouldn't want to interrupt."

"It wouldn't be the first time," Peter laughed,

Jake took a deep breath and opened the door, anticipating the glare he received. "What did I do now? Did I give too much attention to Casi or Kyle? Or maybe the pretty girl who taught us to dance even though you refused to participate?" He emptied his pockets on the dresser.

Lia grabbed his phone and tried to activate it, holding it out to him when she realized there was a password. "Unlock it!"

"Why? Did you need to make a call and you wore down your battery texting your mom?" He recalled his lengthy conversation with Anna.

"What was so important you had to be alone for thirty minutes? It wasn't about our son because I checked," she fumed.

"You forget I have two other children."

"Prove me wrong and unlock the phone!"

"Why are we fighting every five seconds?"

"Show me who it was or get the hell out!" She threw the phone at him.

Jake retrieved it from the carpet and grabbed his key card before slamming the door. Halfway down the hallway, he collided with Jack as he stepped from his room with an ice bucket. "Are you going to get ice too?" Jack joked.

"Yup, with scotch over it," Jake replied. Jack handed the bucket to Ava and followed him to the elevator. "I don't need a babysitter."

"How about a friend?"

Jake nodded and pushed the button for the first floor. They walked to the bar and ordered drinks. "I left my wallet on the dresser. I assume Lia is pawing through it." Jake slumped in his seat.

Jack paid for the drinks. "It's good you brought a friend." They sipped scotch, feigning interest in whatever sports station was playing.

Jake sighed. "I thought I was doing the right thing, but somehow ended up the asshole once again. We fight constantly and I'm unclear what to do to make her happy."

"Pregnancy can be rough on a woman's hormones." Jack grinned.

He nodded, watching the ice melt in the scotch. "Faulty condoms this time. I'm blaming Casi for washing them without my knowledge." He settled back in his seat. "The worst part is, Lia is normally a happy person. It's not even postpartum depression. I am failing her, and my inadequacies bring out the worst in her. At least my ex was satisfied raising children, even if our marriage was a disaster."

Jack sipped his scotch. "I tried every which way to please Sonya, but she was never content." He directed his gaze to Jake. "She despised being a mother. She was jealous of the attention Casi got from me, even if it was making her dinner or helping with homework." He swirled the ice in his glass. "I began the affair with Ava as an escape from my home life. She's an incredibly strong woman, and it was invigorating to be around her." His eyes clouded. "I've cheated on her twice, both times with Sonya. It's not from desire, but an inability to turn away from my darkest demons. Sonya knows how to coax them out of me, and I certainly don't deserve Ava's forgiveness."

"I guess she really loves you."

"Ava and I work because we survived tragedy together and understand each other's deepest fears and regrets."

"Lia and I don't have much in common."

"Except your children." Jack put his hand on his shoulder. "When you realize your marriage is doing more harm than good, it's time to leave. I stayed too long. I wanted my own restaurant, but my family demands were too high to afford it. My wife nagged constantly, and I adored my daughter, but she challenged me to my core. One night I came home and sat in my car looking at a house I didn't want to go in and had no idea how to make the next mortgage payment. I could hear Sonya and Casi screaming at each other, and I turned the car back on and went to Ava's place instead. That was when the affair started. Casi was twelve. I wanted to end my marriage since Casi was three because my life was unbearable. I planned to take her with me, but the plan imploded. I knew I couldn't leave without her, so I stayed married, figuring I could wait it out until she went to college. By fourteen, Casi had gotten out of control, already wild and rebellious. She knew we were lost in our own worlds and took advantage. She came at me one night, furious because I wouldn't let her go to a party. Sonya was screaming and making threats. I snapped, and I belted Casi so hard I knocked her down and bloodied her lip. I had never hit her before; never hit any woman. She looked at me from the floor, hurt and betrayed. I hated who I had become, and I didn't recognize myself. The worst part was when I came to say goodbye, she cried and wrapped her arms around me, begging me to stay. I couldn't trust myself, and I wouldn't let her believe it was acceptable for any man to hit her. I struggled to get my shit together after that, overindulging her and trying to buy her affection. When things fell apart with Ava, I hit rock bottom. Casi became the adult, trying to put me back together. No daughter should see her father like that, and it distorted our relationship. I walk on eggshells around her. She hides things about her life, and I pretend she had a perfect childhood. But she'll always know I hit her and abandoned her. Two things I can never take back."

"At least you only had one child to disappoint."

Jack grinned and clinked his glass to Jake's. "I had a vasectomy when I realized one was all I could handle."

33

FOREVER

yle led Casi to their new room with a panoramic view of the strip. The hotel expertly fulfilled his upgrade request, moving their belongings while they were at the club. Chocolate dipped strawberries, champagne, and a selection of bubble bath were set out around the whirlpool tub.

"Wow, Kyle, this is fantastic!" Casi exclaimed.

"I'm sorry I forgot your birthday. I promise to do better next year. At least I can make tonight memorable." Kyle smiled and handed her a glass of champagne.

Casi sat on the edge of the tub, smelling the assortment of bath salts. "I've had difficult birthdays in the past. I purposely made you focus on Jake's wedding so we could have fun and you wouldn't feel pressured to buy me a present." She smiled at him. "You've given me so much already."

"I may not always show it, but you are the most important person in my life." Kyle watched her slip off her dress. "You are an incredibly beautiful woman, and those girls at the club can't hold a candle to you. I was shocked how well you did at karaoke. With your looks and talent, I'm surprised you never considered a career in that field." He gave her a hand to enter the tub.

"I mimic other people. I don't possess the talent it takes to be a performer. Modeling was difficult enough, and I was only judged on my looks. Honestly, the only opinion I care about is yours."

Kyle moved a small metal table to the side and placed the strawberries and champagne on it. He undressed as Casi watched him and sipped champagne. He sat across from her and handed her a strawberry. She ran her toes over his chest, smiling as the bubbles popped against his skin. "Can you tell me why you seemed upset when you talked about meeting Dylan for the first time?" Kyle smoothed a hand up her calf.

Casi handed him her glass to refill. "When I came to LA, I was the typical girl with stars in my eyes. I left Joey and my best friends to become a model. I did those stupid lingerie shows to make enough money to pay the rent, but it was never enough!" She burst into tears.

"You don't need to tell me." Kyle pulled her in his arms.

She wiped her eyes. "I want this to stay between us."

"I promised I would never share intimate details."

"Joey and Dawn were getting married and asked me to be in the wedding. Five years had gone by and it was a natural progression because we were all close friends." She sipped her champagne. "I was embarrassed to go because LA was a disaster, and my mom kept finding degrading ways for me to make money. I promised my friend, Katie, I would get a place and she could come live with me. I finally saved up enough and I told her to pack her bags. Everything was happening. Katie was excited because she had been in a bad situation for a while and couldn't wait to leave. My mom discovered my stash of money and used it, but promised the landlord I would take it out in trade..."

Kyle nodded, recalling Sonya referring to something of that nature. "It didn't make you a whore, Sweetheart."

"I felt like one! I was drugged out of my mind and didn't stop drinking the whole weekend I went back for the wedding. I slept with Joey the night before and then worked my way through the bridal party."

Kyle chuckled. "How big was the wedding?"

"Three groomsmen," she clarified. "They had been after me all through high school and I figured I might as well give in; I wasn't worth anything anymore. I bailed on my friend and never talked to her again. Joey must have called my dad out of concern because he showed up to take me to the airport. He desperately tried to get me to move to Bellingham, but I couldn't even look him in the eye. When I got back to LA, I showed up to the editorial drunk, and that's when I met Dylan. He helped me through the shoot, and I told him about my life. He insisted I move in with him. Mary gave me a strict warning and took over my accounts. She knew my mom couldn't be trusted anymore. I'm sure the suggestion came from Ava because they're old friends and I suspect she has secretly looked out for me over the years." Casi downed the rest of her glass. "So, that's who you married!"

Kyle kissed her tenderly, letting the passion build, and enjoying the taste of strawberries on her lips. He caressed her body, savoring the silkiness of the bubbles on her smooth skin. "I told you my first year of college was difficult. What I didn't mention is how I pushed past the pain I was struggling with. I partied so much on the weekends, I barely remembered what happened. I would get high and pick up random girls, never asking their names. I didn't care where we had sex, but my preference was quick and dirty, and send them on their way. Jake looked out for me; always made sure I had condoms and got me home safely after. There were numerous times I puked on him." He grinned. "I got better at balancing the partying with classes and managed to get through my first year. I honestly can't tell you how many women I've slept with. That's who your husband is." Kyle laughed at her expression. "My confession turned you on, didn't it?"

"It did. I think one of our role plays should be me as the slutty college girl seducing Kyle, the man-whore."

"We can definitely add that to the list, Tonight I have something special for you." He lifted her to the back ledge of the tub and kissed his way down her neck toward her breasts, lingering as he stroked a hand up her thigh. She reclined and surveyed the lights of the strip and the full moon piercing the night sky. Kyle slowly moved from her belly button. He increased the pressure, surprising her with his intensity and knowledge of her body. The orgasm started with a vibration building up from her spine. A spasm rippled through her entire body and her breathing quickened as she moaned for more, experiencing a kaleidoscope of colors bursting in her mind. The sensation seemed to last for hours, coming in waves so intense she tried to catch her breath before the next one hit; blinding her with the magnitude and breadth. When it finally subsided, she lifted her head to see him watching her with a satisfied grin on his face.

"What the hell was that?" Casi panted.

"Your g-spot," Kyle confirmed.

"I thought it was a myth. Where did you learn that?"

"I Googled it."

"You're hilarious! Jesus, did you do that on your phone today?"

"While we were waiting for the helicopter. You stated you wanted a special experience as a gift. I felt this was suitable."

She hugged him. "Was there a video?"

"A diagram. I improvised a lot," he said proudly.

"You did well; that was sensational!"

"Want to move this party to the bedroom?"

"I might need a little recovery time. I feel like I'm made of Jell-O!" Casi rinsed the bubbles off before stepping to the tile. The overflow of water made the floor too slick to stand, and she tumbled forward onto the table, sending the platter and the ice bucket flying across the room with a crash. Kyle laughed at first, thinking she merely slipped but rushed to her side when he saw the bright red splatter. "Ouch! That was more clumsy than sexy. Where's the blood coming from?" She scanned her hands for damage.

"Your chin." Kyle lifted her face to discover the source. "Oh, that needs stitches." He winced at the long gash. He inspected the table and noted the culprit; a sharp piece of engraved metal filigree, broken around the edge and speckled with rust. "When was your last tetanus shot?"

"You're making it a big deal. I only need a bandaid." She regained her balance and strolled to the mirror, shocked to see her chest emblazoned with blood. "I look like a chick from a horror movie!"

He held a towel firmly to her chin as he called the front desk to find out where the nearest clinic was and ordered a taxi. "I'm sorry, Casi, but you need stitches." He tried his best to clean her up, helping her dress in jeans and a top, not caring that none of it matched as he bent and laced her tennis shoes. He got a new towel, wanting to minimize the scene as they walked through the lobby. He dressed and hoped they could make it to the car unnoticed. Most hotel guests barely glanced at them, being drunk at this hour. He put his arm around her, keeping pressure on the cut as they rushed through the lobby.

"What are you doing?" Jake cut them off at the exit.

"Just out for a walk," Kyle joked.

"Why does Casi look ragged?" Jake scanned her half-wet hair and disheveled outfit.

Jack noticed the blood dripping along her neck and his eyes went wide. "What happened?"

"She slipped getting out of the tub and hit her face on a table. She needs a few stitches," Kyle reported.

"Can I come? I want to watch her get sewn back together." Jake peered under the towel and clucked his tongue. "That's a good one."

"It seems like you're in excellent hands." Jack kissed Casi on the top of her head. "Let me know how it goes."

Jake shook his hand. "Thanks for being a friend tonight."

"Why aren't you with your wife?" Kyle asked.

"She threw me out. This marriage might be short-lived." On the way to the clinic, Jake told them about his fight with Lia.

"It was rude of you to take a call from Anna at the club in front of Lia." Casi wagged a finger at him.

"Quiet. You're not supposed to talk. It will make it hurt worse when they patch you up," Jake teased.

The doctor removed the towel from her chin, clucking his tongue that it was still bleeding profusely. "Stitches are necessary because of the location and length," he decided.

"I think she should get a tetanus shot," Kyle said.

"I don't need one." Casi pushed Kyle's hand away. "I had one before when I was a kid after a rusty slide incident. I'm set."

"I'm afraid not. They are actually due every ten years." The doctor shrugged. "Let me numb you while we discuss it."

Kyle held her chin firmly, nodding to Jake. Casi screamed as the doctor injected the needle in her chin, feeling the burning sensation across her face. Jake swiftly unbuttoned her shirt and gripped her shoulder while the doctor gave her the tetanus shot. "You fucking liars!" she swore.

"Should we tape her mouth closed to make it easier to stitch her up?" Jake rubbed her back and smoothed the shirt in place.

The doctor laughed. "You have a wild one on your hands."

"I hate you guys," Casi sobbed.

Kyle kissed her forehead. "Tetanus is a serious condition. The pain of the shot is nothing compared to what could happen. It's my job to keep you safe." He grasped her jaw as the stitching began.

"Almost over, Monkey Moonshine," Jake assured her, wiping her tears and giving her hand a squeeze.

The doctor finished and dabbed on antibiotic cream, covering the wound with a large bandage. He asked her to keep it dry for a few days and gave them extra supplies to take home. He explained there would be bruising, and her jaw may be sore after the numbing agent wore off.

When they got back to the hotel and entered the elevator, Casi gasped at her reflection in the mirror, taking in the mismatched outfit, wild hair, and mascara stained cheeks. The bandage made the cut appear worse, and she shook her head as the brothers tried to stifle their laughter. "If this isn't the ultimate walk of shame!" She crossed her arms over her chest. They got back to their room to discover it had been cleaned with no trace of the incident. They laughed, wondering what the maid must have thought happened in the blood-filled bathroom. "You've gotta love Vegas!"

Jake entered his room and sat on the edge of the bed, waking Lia gently. She looked at him with bleary eyes, "What's going on?"

"It was Anna on the phone. She called to see how the wedding went. She's married now, and pregnant. I can't take this constant fighting. I gave you a chance to walk away, and you said you wanted to be married. I'll be divorced for a second time before I live a life I hate again. Please figure out what you want before you force me to make a decision on my own."

"Why is there blood on your shirt?"

"Casi face-planted out of their bathtub and I went with them to get her face repaired."

"Is she ok?" She followed him as he turned on the shower.

"Twelve stitches and a tetanus shot. She'll be fine." He stepped in the shower and lathered his hair.

Lia took off her nightgown and joined him. "I'm unclear if I want to stay married to you forever. Can we wait until this baby is born before we make any decisions? I'm afraid to be alone."

"Let's bring this child into our family and worry about the long-term situation after that." He kissed her tenderly.

Casi had a painful sleep as the numbing wore off and the pillow irritated the wound. She woke the next morning to find a bruise radiating up from the bandage. She applied eyeliner and mascara; glad they were heading home after breakfast. Kyle took her hand as they entered the restaurant, joining their group at a table. Georgia was the first to notice. "Casi! What happened?"

"I slipped when I got out of the tub," Casi mumbled.

"Tell us about the part that had you so wobbly you couldn't stand on your own two feet." Jake poked her with a fork.

Casi shook her head as laughter erupted and she focused on the menu. She was hungry, but it was painful to even drink coffee, spilling it when she put her lips to the rim. Kyle watched her struggle, then got up and left the restaurant, telling Jake to order for him. He returned twenty minutes later carrying a large Starbucks cup with a straw and placed it in front of her. She tried to smile, wincing when the stitches burned. She took his hand instead, sipping the vanilla latte and letting the warm liquid ease the pain.

When they returned to their room, Casi packed her suitcase and turned to Kyle. "One more week until our first wedding anniversary. Can you believe it?"

"It's been a hell of a year."

"How many times did you want to end it?"

Kyle sat on the bed and took her hand. "Just once. After the shit happened in LA. I felt overwhelmed and hated how our life became complicated. You had changed so much, I thought I'd lost you already. I felt completely alone and miserable."

Casi slid on his lap. "I'm sure you questioned why you married me. I was a disaster."

"It was more that I wondered why you married me. You didn't want my name or my life. If all you wanted was sex, we could have stayed dating. I was desperately in love with you and it scared me to see my life spinning out of control with yours," he confessed.

"Why didn't you call it quits?"

"I couldn't. The thought of being without you was worse than living in the chaos. When I told you on the trail I was done, it wasn't true. I wanted you to react and fight for our marriage. You were like a zombie, floating through each day. When Mary came, I was frantic you might leave me." He pressed his cheek to hers. "When did you consider it the end?"

"After Christmas. I hated fighting and feeling like you had taken over my life. I knew my career was over, but I didn't want to face it because I wasn't sure how to transition. There was a vast emptiness, and I couldn't picture myself settling down in Blackberry Falls."

"Why did you stay?"

"I loved you and I knew I had to push past my fear and trust everything would work out in the end. I always ran from things when they were uncomfortable in the past, but my heart ached at the thought of not being with you. Our life is amazing now, and I love you more than ever. I'm in it for the long haul."

"I would do it all over again if it meant being here with you today." Kyle gave her a kiss. "My love for you has only grown stronger, too. We're going to make it last forever and a day."

Always and Forever

CABERNET CHIPOTLE RIBS

Serves 6

1 rack baby back ribs (3 pounds)

2 tablespoons olive oil

1 tablespoon chipotle chilies in adobo, minced

1 teaspoon salt

1 teaspoon granulated garlic

1 teaspoon celery seed

1 teaspoon smoked paprika

1 tablespoon brown sugar

½ teaspoon dried oregano

½ teaspoon dried sage

1 tablespoon salted butter

½ cup onions, diced

2 cloves garlic, minced

1 jalapeno, minced

1 cup Cabernet

½ cup cherry preserves

4 tablespoons lime juice

1. Rub the ribs with the olive oil and minced chilies in adobo. Mix the dry spices and sprinkle generously over the ribs.

2. Let the ribs sit overnight in the fridge or at least four hours. Bring to room temperature 1 hour before cooking.

3. Preheat a grill to medium or an oven to 300-degrees. Wrap the ribs in foil and place on the grill or in the oven on a sheet pan.

4. Cook for two hours covered, then uncover and place directly on grill or sheet pan.

5. In a medium saucepan, heat the butter. Add onions, garlic, and jalapeño and sauté 6 minutes. Add the Cabernet, preserves, and lime juice. Bring to a boil.

6. Baste the ribs with the Cabernet mixture and cook another 30 minutes, basting every 10 minutes.

7. Cut the ribs apart and transfer to a platter. Pour remaining sauce over the ribs to finish.

THE CATWALK SERIES CONTINUES WITH
TRUST

Death, deception, and demons from the past plague the idyllic union of Casi and Kyle.

Casi continues to polish her professional image and hone her business skills while focusing on the opportunities ahead. Determined to prove her worth beyond sizzling in a swimsuit, she leaves the superficial chaos of modeling behind. Unfortunately, money can't buy happiness for her mother, Sonya, who refuses to abandon her tumultuous lifestyle and settle into the picture-perfect world Casi created.

Kyle reveals dark secrets from his youth he hoped would stay buried. Seeking forgiveness, he trusts his unfailing love for Casi to overcome the painful memories. He adjusts to the whirlwind pace of their new routine, pushing aside jealousy and insecurities to become the ideal husband, brother, and son. Jake continues to battle challenges and troubled relationships, but still fiercely protects his bond with his brother and supports Casi emotionally.

When Casi is blindsided by a tragedy, she is left reeling from the grief it causes as deception is unveiled. She realizes the secrets her family protected may only be the beginning of revelations from her childhood. She questions the validity of her relationships and must learn to trust again. She embarks on a journey of self-discovery, needing to move beyond the anguish of delusion that torments her.

Standing on the precipice of a brilliant future and the illusion of the past, can Casi step forward or will the haunting lies swallow her back into a realm that is familiar?

The third novel in the Catwalk Series continues an epic journey of love, intrigue, and triumph, revealing deeper stories within the captivating saga.

Trust Without Limits and Love Beyond Loss

Canadian-born author, Suzy Quenneville-Orpin, has always had a vivid imagination and a keen desire to write. Suzy views the world through her own narrative, weaving in the fascinating challenges, triumphs, and lifestyles of the people she meets. An unapologetic daydreamer, Suzy's early experiences in Toronto ad Woodland Beach, Ontario provided the perfect upbringing to fuel her creativity and discover the wonder of the roads less traveled. A move to the west coast brought new opportunities and an appreciation for the Pacific Northwest.

Follow Suzy to discover more about the Catwalk Series.
 www.facebook.com/sqorpin
 www.twitter.com/authorsqorpin
 www.instagram.com/sqorpin
 sqorpin@yahoo.com
 www.amazon.com/author/sqorpin